Kitti Homme

About the Author

Born in Bozeman, Russell Rowland is a fourth-generation Montanan. He served in the Navy, and has worked as a teacher, ranch hand, surveyor, lounge singer, and fortune-cookie writer. He lives in San Francisco.

in
open
spaces

in
open
spaces

RUSSELL ROWLAND

 Perennial

An Imprint of HarperCollinsPublishers

IN OPEN SPACES. Copyright © 2002 by Russell Rowland. All rights reserved. Printed in the United States of America. No part of this book may be used or reproduced in any manner whatsoever without written permission except in the case of brief quotations embodied in critical articles and reviews. For information address HarperCollins Publishers Inc., 10 East 53rd Street, New York, NY 10022.

HarperCollins books may be purchased for educational, business, or sales promotional use. For information please write: Special Markets Department, HarperCollins Publishers Inc., 10 East 53rd Street, New York, NY 10022.

FIRST EDITION

Designed by Jamie Kerner-Scott

Library of Congress Cataloging-in-Publication Data
Rowland, Russell.
   In open spaces: a novel / Russell Rowland.
      p. cm
   ISBN 0-06-008434-0
      1. Montana—Fiction. I. Title.

   PS3618.O88 I6 2002
   813'.6—dc21   2001051354

02 03 04 05 06 ❖/RRD 10 9 8 7 6 5 4 3 2 1

To my parents
and
In loving memory of my grandfather Frank Arbuckle

in
open
spaces

Prologue

I read somewhere, years ago, that "montana" is Spanish for mountain, or mountainous. As a native of eastern Montana, I'd venture to guess that Mr. Ashley, the man who suggested this name for our fair state, never traveled east of Billings. Because if he had, he wouldn't have seen anything resembling a mountain.

What Mr. Ashley would have seen instead is a fraternal twin to its other half, a rolling expanse of land that shares little or nothing with its western sibling besides the same birth date. While western Montana rises up like the front end of a head-on collision with Idaho, our half lies quietly dramatic, its treeless knolls and dry gullies twisting and rippling for miles in every direction.

Carter County, my county, forms the far southeastern corner, sprawling like an old wool blanket spread carelessly across the ground, complete with ridges, wrinkles, hollows, and an occasional hole. The closest thing Carter County can claim to a mountain is the buttes—a series of sandstone flattops that look like the beginnings of mountains, as though some ambitious fellow came along and started building a mountain ridge, but didn't have the energy to finish it. The Finger

Buttes cross the county at an angle, south to northwest, like giant stones laid out to keep the wind from blowing the blanket away.

But back to Mr. Ashley. I understand his mistake. He had obvious reasons. For one thing, Montana is a damn fine name—a noble-sounding name that rings especially full and rich when spoken by a man with a deep voice and a steady character. Someone calm and patient enough to linger on the n's so that the word hums slightly, bringing a smile to your face in the same way that a nice song would. And it's impossible to deny that the mountains cluttering western Montana are magnificent. Maybe the only creation that can crowd into the perfection of a blue sky and improve on it.

But despite all that, I prefer the prairie. Mainly because I've lived my whole life here, of course. But there's more to it than that. When I finally had a chance to see the Rocky Mountains, they affected me in a way I didn't expect. I was still a young man—twenty-three, to be exact. My older brother Jack and I drove to Bozeman in the spring of 1925 to buy some oak flooring for the big house my folks were building. On that clear spring day, we rounded the curve into the Bozeman Pass, and I'd never seen anything so beautiful. There the mountains sat, blue-purple and surprising, like two black eyes.

Up until then, I had not seen any ground higher than the Black Hills of South Dakota. My glances at the sky were brief, just long enough to figure out what kind of weather we could expect. So my neck wasn't used to holding my head at the angle required to view these towers of rock. Jack and I stared for fifteen minutes, rotating, squinting into the bright sun, shading our eyes. We paid the price later, too, with necks so stiff we had to sleep without pillows. But it was well worth it.

We decided to get closer, so we drove until the two-rut road ended, gawking, saying little. Then we climbed from the flatbed and stared a while longer.

"Let's climb the damn thing," I said.

Jack, in a rare moment of skepticism, peered up at the rising slope of pine, his eyes small and dark. It looked as if we could reach out and brush our hands across the tops of the trees. "I don't know, Blake. I think it's a little further than it looks."

"Ah, come on. Let's climb it."

Jack gave in, but he proved to be right. Just as our necks weren't used to bending backward, our legs weren't prepared for ground that pushed back. We didn't make it far before we had to rest our cramping calves. I could barely breathe. I began to feel a little stifled up there. I panted hard as we kneaded our aching muscles. "I don't know if there's a special shoe for this type of thing, but if there is, I bet that it doesn't look anything like a cowboy boot," I said.

Jack laughed, and although his smile quickly faded, he seemed more relaxed than he had in years. Something about being up in the middle of those trees seemed to affect him in a different way than it did me. And for a brief moment, I thought about asking him about all the things I'd always wanted to know. About the army, and the years he had disappeared, and about his wife Rita. I wanted to know about his intentions for the ranch. Now that he was the oldest, he was the natural heir, but because he'd spent so much time away, I had more time invested, and I wanted to know whether he planned to take over when Dad and Mom couldn't take care of the place anymore. I even felt like I had a case for taking over the ranch myself, but we had never discussed the possibility. Just as we had never discussed any of this with our father. For that tiny moment, that conversation seemed possible. But I hesitated, and that was all the time it took for those small dark eyes to narrow, and for his thin lips to purse. He sighed, and looked away, and I could feel him drift. And I knew it was too late.

I turned my attention to the view from where we sat. We could see nothing but trees except far in the distance, where rolling farmland stretched out in patches of green and brown. It was beautiful in a different way from our own ranch—the colors were darker, and the landscape had more abrupt angles.

"I wonder what land is worth out here," Jack said.

I shrugged. This question had not even occurred to me. "Probably a hell of a lot more than out where we are, huh?" I said.

Jack chuckled. "Oh yeah," he said.

It wasn't much longer before he suggested we head on in to Bozeman.

In town, we argued about where to stay. Jack thought we ought to treat ourselves to a room in the Grand Hotel, the most expensive place in town.

"We can't spend that kind of money," I said. "Mom would kill us."

Jack frowned. "What're you going to do, squeal? How's she gonna know? Come on, let's live it up for once. How many chances like this are we ever going to get?"

I was too intimidated to put up a fight, knowing Jack would get surly if I did. But I could hardly look at my parents for the next two weeks, especially when Jack told them a bold-faced lie about how much money we spent.

That night in Bozeman, as I lay in that fancy hotel room, something about the day gnawed at me—something besides the ache in my muscles, or the argument with Jack, or the money. I tossed through a couple of sleepless hours before I figured out what it was. It finally struck me when I imagined being back home, standing at the top of a divide, looking at the circle of open space, the miles and miles of grass around me.

I realized that the mountains just don't give you much. You hike a ways, and the trees are thick as hair around you, so you walk a few painful yards further. And maybe you find a small clearing, and can see a little further. Even at the top, you might be able to see forever, but everything is miles away.

That's what bothered me about it, and still does. I realized that the lack of breath I experienced halfway up that mountain was not just the result of the climb. I felt closed in, smothered, up there with so little space around me. I didn't like not being able to see what was coming, or where we'd been. And I know that if I lived in mountain country, I could never love the land around me like I do my own. That night, I figured out why people like me fall in love with the prairie, even as brutal and unforgiving as it can be. Because when the earth spreads itself out in front of you, completely vulnerable, completely naked, you simply can't help yourself.

Book I

fire

1

fall 1916

The windows of the old Model T rattled as the mail truck bounced along the winding gravel road from Belle Fourche, South Dakota, to Albion, Montana. It was well past midnight, and I tried to sleep, but my head bonked against the window each time I dozed, until it felt as if I'd grown a corner on my forehead. There was also the matter of Annie Ketchal, the driver, who loved to talk. When I saw that Annie was the driver that night, I cringed, because I knew I wouldn't get much sleep. Because of her job, she knew everyone, and not only did she know them, but she had a gift for finding out more about them than anyone else knew. At the age of fourteen, I usually found the information she passed on interesting, and sometimes even shocking, but on this night I simply wasn't interested in lives outside of my own.

"Sorry about your brother Blake," she said after a few miles.

"Thanks, Mrs. Ketchal," I answered, feeling my jaw tighten, my lower teeth settling against the upper.

My heart seemed to press against my chest, as if a strong hand had a firm grip on it, squeezing it tightly, telling it, "Don't beat . . . don't you dare beat." And I knew as sure as anything that this pain would never go away. I thought I would feel this bad for the rest of my life. My fourteen years hadn't taught me that you feel this kind of pain sometimes, and that although it may never completely disappear, it does fade. And if anyone had tried to explain that to me then, I would have silently told them to shut up and leave me alone, to let me get a little sleep. Just as I now silently wished that Annie Ketchal, as friendly as she was, would be quiet and let me and my struggling heart be.

I had been standing at the blackboard doing a math problem when the telegram arrived. I was an eighth-grader, just beginning my second year at the Belle Fourche School, fifty miles from the ranch. I boarded with an older couple during the week and caught the mail truck home most weekends to help with the harvest, or haying, or feeding the stock.

Brother George drowned in river.

read the telegram. My mother's words, as always, would never pass for poetry, but it told me everything I needed to know.

I gave the telegram to my teacher, and standing there as she read it, my mind reviewed all of the immediate concerns of a fourteen-year-old boy. First, I knew that I would be going home immediately. And I knew that there was a good chance that I wouldn't be coming back. I thought about the dollar a day I could earn if I stayed home, and wondered what I might be able to save up for. And I felt a certain sense of relief about not coming back, because in the year and change that I'd been in Belle Fourche, I had never adjusted to life in town. I didn't like the pace. I spent most of my time in the classroom wishing I was sitting on a horse in the middle of a broad pasture. I couldn't keep my mind on the books in front of me, especially when the sun was shining. And although I did well in school, I never felt the same satisfaction from getting a test with a big blue A on it as I did from stepping back and admiring a stack of hay I'd just pitched, or pulling the forelegs of a calf, watching it slosh to the ground and shake its moist head, ears flopping. At my core, I relished the thought of going home.

What I did not think about in the moment was that my life would completely change with this news. I thought about George and his baseball, and how he could scoop a ground ball and whip it to first base with such fluid grace that it seemed as if he caught the ball in the middle of his throwing motion. But I guess I wasn't ready to think about the fact that I would never see him again.

So when the teacher asked me if I was okay, I nodded without hesitation, and it was true at that particular moment.

"All right," she said. "You go on ahead then."

So I walked to the boarders' house, told them the news, packed my bag, and caught the mail truck home. But after several hours in the truck, the reality started to penetrate. I remembered a day the previous winter—an early morning when we were out feeding the stock. It was colder than hell that morning, and George, Jack, Dad, and I were doing whatever we could think of to keep warm, pounding our gloved hands together, running in place, working our jaws to keep the skin on our faces from freezing. George was talking, as he often did. He was talking about cattle, and sheep.

"People talk about how stupid animals are," George said, stomping his boots against the ground. "But just look at this. Every morning, we get up and come out here to feed these bastards, who aren't at all cold. We come out here and risk our lives to wait on these animals, and they're the stupid ones? I think we're the stupid ones. Not only that, but we paid money for these sons of bitches. We paid money for the privilege of waiting on these goddam animals."

He kept along in the same vein, a half grin on his face the whole time, and the rest of us were laughing so hard, we felt warmer than we had all morning. Even Jack, who usually had little tolerance for George's monologues, was laughing. It was one of those simple moments where the presence of one person made life better for all of us for a time.

"So many youngsters dying," Annie Ketchal said. "What was he, nineteen?"

"Yes, ma'am, nineteen in July," I said, taking a deep breath. Besides wishing that Annie Ketchal would let me sleep, I was annoyed that she was breaking the custom of our people, which was not to pursue a potentially unpleasant line of questioning. She knew better, but as I noticed in my previous rides with her, Annie didn't think much about what she said. I suppose that with such a lonely job, having an audience was more important to her than etiquette.

"So many," she repeated. "I lost a nephew last year, and another three years ago." She shook her head. "Smallpox, the first one was, and the other just had a bad cold. That was all it took." She snapped her fingers, indicating how quickly it happened. "This country is rough on the children," she said. "The women and the children." She continued shaking her head. "'Course the men don't fare much better, but you'd expect to lose a few of them, as hard as they work just to break through this ground."

I nodded, not knowing what to say—actually, knowing that it didn't matter what I said, or whether I spoke at all.

"What was he like?" Annie asked. "I started driving after he quit school. So I never really knew him."

Besides being offended by the indelicacy of the question, by having to explore something I didn't want to think about, I was also fourteen and answered accordingly, shrugging. "I dunno. He liked baseball."

But the question echoed in me. I thought of it often over the years, when others died. In terms of George as well as the rest. And it seemed that the answers changed as I grew older. If I were to answer the question now, I would say that George was solid—even-tempered, unusually even-tempered for such a young man. That despite taking his work seriously, he was also extremely capable of enjoying life. He never seemed to be overwhelmed by the more overwhelming aspects of our existence.

I guess my manner told Annie that I didn't want to pursue this line of questioning, as she did not press for more details.

"You're not planning to stay and work, are you, Blake?" she asked.

I swallowed hard, thinking to myself that this was none of her business, but not wanting to be rude. "Don't know. They're probably going to need me."

"Oh, Jesus," she muttered. "I'm sorry, Blake, but I just think that's a shame, you being as bright as you are and all. I'm sorry. I shouldn't say that."

That would be the most accurate statement you've made all night, I thought to myself.

In the best of conditions, the fifty-mile drive along the winding gravel road from Belle Fourche to our ranch took about three hours. But Annie had to drop a mail sack at each box along the way, an average of every couple of miles. So we traveled all night. And Annie didn't miss a beat, sawing away hour after hour with her stories, most of which I'd already heard, about the people on each ranch we passed. There was Tex Edwards, whose first wife, the heir to one of the bigger local ranches, mysteriously drowned in a puddle four inches deep. And Lonnie Roberts and his wife Ruth, both of whom Annie claimed to be consistently unfaithful. And finally, there was Art Walters, whose wife Rose had been one of the many locals who fell victim to the "loneliness." Someone found her wandering along the road one day with her baby son in her arms. Rose, who moved out from Ohio to teach school, had been muttering to herself about bathtubs when they found her. Bathtubs and maple trees. They sent Rose back to Ohio, and no one had heard a word since.

I pointed my eyes straight ahead, at the road, answering questions when asked, but mostly letting my mind drift. I thought about George, and about how my parents would take the loss. Dad would take it more personally, like a punishment from God. He would work even harder, trying to gain favor, trying to get more land to prepare for the inevitability of more tragedy. And he would spout invectives, throwing blame in blind directions—at the government, and the weather, and the "goddam banks." Mom would turn it more inward, saying things like "We should have . . ." or "Maybe if we'd . . ."

While Dad worried about what we should do, Mom would plan what we would do. And we would follow her plan. It was a system that worked well for them, as Dad worked harder than any man I knew, and Mom was a skilled organizer.

I thought about the fact that I was the second oldest now, behind Jack. How they would need to rely on me. I knew that none of them would be moping around, thinking about George, and that they would have no tolerance for anyone else doing that either. Because it would affect a person's usefulness.

"You tired, Blake?" Annie asked just a couple of miles from our ranch.

Well, my head was rolling around like a BB in a washtub, so the answer seemed pretty obvious. But I nodded and leaned against my satchel, which sat on the seat between us. It was late fall, a cool night, and lightning had just begun flashing orange off the bottom of a dark cloud cover. The clouds were so thick that my beloved prairie was hidden by darkness, as if a black curtain had been pulled down over my window. But when the lightning flashed, the landscape lit up as if it was late afternoon, if only for a brief moment.

Annie pulled off the road to a solitary mailbox perched on a twisted fence post. We were at Glassers', our closest neighbors to the south. Cold air blew through the cab as Annie hopped out and plucked Glassers' canvas mail sack from the truck bed. A clap of thunder rumbled across the horizon. I looked up at the sky, hoping to see lightning. But the flash had already come and gone.

* * *

I woke up, my head pounding the window one last time, when Annie wrenched the wheel and turned into our drive, passing under the suspended chunk of driftwood that announced the "Arbuckle Ranch," followed by our brand, Rɷ (an R and a buckle).

"Here we are," Annie declared.

I bent stiffly at the waist, retrieving my felt cowboy hat from the floor, where it had fallen on one of the collisions between head and window. I tugged my hat onto my head.

"You tell your folks I'm real sorry about George," Annie said.

I don't remember being so happy to put some distance between myself and another person, but I minded my manners, remembering that her intentions were good. "I sure will. Thanks, Mrs. Ketchal." I pulled my satchel from the cab. "Thanks a bunch for the ride."

I lugged my bag toward the house. The truck sputtered and clattered behind me, and the cold air bit my face.

"Hey, Blake!" The truck had stopped, and Annie's head poked from the window. I groaned, wondering what else she could possibly have to tell me. But her hand popped out, a gray bag dangling from her fingers. I dropped my satchel, trotted back to the truck, and grabbed our mail sack. And I thanked her again.

Our sheepdog Nate, a pesky black-and-white Border collie with skewed ears, hopped in front of and between and beside my legs, nearly tripping me as I dragged my satchel toward the house. It wasn't until I stepped up onto the stoop that it occurred to me that the house was going to feel different. I stopped, standing in front of the door, preparing myself for the fact that George would not be in the tiny bedroom we shared with our other two brothers. I wondered where his body was, and decided it was likely laid out in the barn, that they probably had a coffin built by now.

I swallowed, took a deep breath, pushed Nate to one side with my boot, and wobbled on rubber legs through the squeaky door. I set the mail on the table, and crept through the sleeping household, past my parents' door, which was open a crack. I saw the outline of their prone figures, and heard their whispered breath.

I smelled the memory of kerosene and the wood stove as I continued past the girls' room, then to my own, where Jack and our youngest brother Bob were asleep. I squinted toward Jack, who was sixteen. He lay on his back, mouth wide open. Bob was curled up like a baby. I set my satchel on the floor.

Two beds stood empty, and I stopped in front of George's. I thought of never seeing his spry figure sprawled across the narrow mattress. I sank onto his bed, where I felt a lump under my leg. Under the mattress, I found George's baseball wedged in a hollow there. I also found some papers, but I stuffed them back where they were, feeling as if I had crossed onto sacred ground. But I kept the ball, cradling it in my palm, and I crossed the room and fell onto my own bed, still fully clothed, and finally, thankfully, slept.

"Blake, wake up. Wake up, son."

I lifted my head, with difficulty, and saw that the bedroom window was still pitch-black. "What?"

My mother Catherine leaned over me, and I could barely see her face, round and dull white as a full moon behind a cloud. Her light red hair sparkled like stars around her face. She was dressed.

"What?" I asked. "It's not morning yet, is it?"

"There's a fire in the buttes over at Glassers'." Mom spoke as she always did in such situations, with a gentle urgency that made it clear you needed to hurry but didn't inspire a sense of panic.

I lay staring blankly, my brain stunned by lack of sleep. I felt as if I had just drifted off seconds ago. George's baseball slept on the blanket next to me.

"Are you all right?" Mom asked, touching my arm.

I nodded. "I think so" was what entered my mind, but I never got around to voicing it.

"Come on, son." Mom left the room, and I heard her walk outside.

I lifted myself to a sitting position, shook my head, and reached for my hat, which lay open-faced on the floor. Jack's and Bob's beds were empty. I stood, groggy, and staggered outside. Mom and Bob sat in the wagon. My dad, George Sr., was hooking the team up to the yoke. The cold air reached in and held my lungs motionless for a moment, and I had to force a deep breath before I could even move. Although it was still dark, the sky had that just-before-dawn glow.

I stumbled over to the well, where Jack waited with two fifty-gallon barrels. Dad pulled the wagon over, and after loading the barrels into the back, we dumped bucket after bucket into them, filling them until they spilled over. Then Jack and I crawled into the bed, laying out between the barrels. He yawned, rubbing his small, dark eyes. His nose hooked down over his tight mouth. I studied my older brother for a sign of how he might be taking George's death. Although Jack and George had personalities that couldn't be more different, they were probably closer than any of the rest of the brothers.

Dad flipped the reins, and the team surged forward.

"Are the girls home?" I asked.

"Yeah," Mom answered.

I worried about the two little ones, who were only four and eight, being home alone. But I didn't figure it would make much difference if I said anything.

In our country, there is a quietness, a silence that surrounds you and fills you up, beating inside like blood until it becomes a part of you. The prairie is quiet even during the day, except for the sounds of work—the snort of horses, the clang of a plow's blade against rock, and the rhythm of hooves pounding the ground. But these sounds drift off into the air, finding nothing to contain them. No echoes.

It's quieter still at night, when you can sit for hours at a stretch and hear nothing except the crickets, or the occasional cluck of a chicken. At night, the darkness seems to add to the silence, making it heavier, somehow more imposing. It is a silence that can be too much for some, especially people who aren't fond of their own company. And it seems that living in such silence makes you think twice before speaking, or laughing, or crying. Because when sounds are that scarce, they carry more weight.

So like most people I know, we Arbuckles don't say much, especially in times of tragedy, when no one knows what to say anyway. When something leaves us wondering, we mostly sit and stare off across the prairie, as if somebody might come along and explain a few things. This stoic silence does not come naturally to some people. In those early homestead days, it led to frequent cases of the loneliness, or suicide. And although most of us talked about these afflictions as if they only happened to newcomers, we all knew better. We all lived with a constant awareness of how vulnerable we were. All of us. It didn't take a genius to notice that some of the sturdiest have been broken down by the pervasive weight of unpredictable weather, and uncooperative livestock, and more than anything, the silent wondering about all these by-products of life on the prairie.

There was only one person in our family who did not possess this stoic nature, and it was George Jr. George took on the silence from a completely different angle, challenging it by doing all he could to fill it up. He talked all the time, but not in a nervous, chattering way. He talked slowly, softly, in a rhythmic, expressive stream, almost like a song. He would pause, chuckle, shake his head, then start again—telling stories, discussing the articles he'd read in the latest newspaper, or plucking a random topic from the air and sorting through the various thoughts he had, moving easily from one side of a debate to the other. I always found the running monologue soothing, and entertaining. But it sometimes got on people's nerves, especially Jack, who would often tell George to shut up, and give us a little peace. To which George usually responded with a smile and a shake of his head. Then, after honoring Jack's request for a minute or two, he would start in again. He couldn't help himself.

Although I didn't see it then, I assume now that there was something of a nervous energy behind this habit. And I wonder whether the silence did get to George, and that he just hid it better than others. From what I learned later, I eventually had to question how he felt about living out here.

That morning, the quiet was magnified by his absence. With my brother less than twenty-four hours gone, the river seemed louder than usual. It wasn't, of course. I just noticed it more. I noticed how beautiful and soothing the gentle rush of water sounded, and I was struck by the deception of that sound. I wondered where George had gone down.

I was always amazed when anyone drowned in the Little Missouri River, which was only twenty-five or thirty feet across, not even big enough to rate a name of its own. It just didn't seem possible that someone, especially an adult, could not find a way to crawl out once they fell in. But every couple of years, some unfortunate soul would plunge into its muddy flow and not emerge until their lungs filled with water.

After about twenty minutes, we could see the soft glow of a blaze along the row of buttes. It was near dawn, and the darkness had just begun to fade along the horizon, as if the fire was leaking into the sky.

I was surprised how wide awake I was, and I wondered how long I'd slept. I wrapped myself tightly in my wool coat, pushing my stiff hands deep into my pockets. Down in the corner of one pocket, I felt a lump. I pulled out a piece of chalk, and realized I must have stuck it there without thinking after I read the telegram. Finally, we reached the base of the buttes, where Dad reined in the team and we hopped from

the wagon. Dad, Jack, and I unloaded the barrels, then lugged them up
the steep incline, a forty-foot climb. It took us nearly half an hour to
carry our awkward cargo one at a time to the top.

"I'm tired, Mom," I heard Bob say behind us.

"Quiet, son. We're all tired."

The buttes cross Carter County like the spine of a bull, sprouting more
trees than the flatlands. Spruce and pine stand in rows along the table-
like tops like sentries in a watchtower. The fire burned among the dry
grass and leaves along the floor, inching its way up an occasional tree.
The yellow-orange-red blanket spread slowly but steadily, and it
smelled too much like a campfire to feel very dangerous. But from the
way people were shouting and racing around, it was clear that the fire
posed a real threat, that it could spread further, down into the meadows below, where the grass was dry enough that it would ignite like
paper. After the soothing quiet of the prairie on our way to these
buttes, the shift to this shouting, rushing activity was a bit startling.

But once we positioned our barrels, I found myself inspired by the
spirit of battle. Months of sitting in a classroom had me restless, and I
was excited about being back at work again. I grabbed a burlap bag
from the pile, dunked it into a barrel, and ran toward the flames.

"Over here, Blake," someone yelled. "Upwind. You'll get smoke on
that side."

I rounded the outer edge, beating the ground with the wet burlap,
stomping the embers when the flame was gone. My folks and my
brothers worked around me, waving their sacks, which sizzled against
the fire.

The blaze covered nearly three acres, and about twenty of us surrounded it, with a few shouting directions, pointing, and arguing strategy. It was invigorating to be doing something with my muscles again.
I fought hard, thinking I'd be able to maintain the same pace until it

was over. The ache in my chest was gone, and in my youthful view of the world, I was convinced that it had disappeared for good, just as I was sure a few hours earlier that it would never go away.

I batted down flames until my gunnysack was dry and useless, then I rushed back and dunked it again—back and forth, back and forth, probably ten or twelve times before my back started to clench. And I felt the heat through my leather soles. Blisters tickled the bottoms of my feet. Soon my body struggled to keep up with my enthusiasm. And then I couldn't.

As the adults fought to keep the flames under control, I sat with a guilty conscience and watched for a few minutes. The fire showed a maddening persistence as the crew beat it down, only to have it flare up again. But a routine had evolved, and the team moved from battle to post with the efficient pattern of an ant colony, one column going one way, one column the other.

Art Walters found a tree with a jagged black streak running from its tip to its roots.

"Looks like this is where she started," he announced, pointing. "Lightning, I'd say."

He got no arguments. For one thing, his discovery was obvious. But also, we all knew Art well enough to see that his real objective was not finding the source but taking a little break. We knew what to expect, and Art delivered. He took some more time to talk about the tree, then he studied it again, came up with a few more theories, and talked about those. Everybody ignored him, and Art took on a meditative expression, as if the job required someone with that quality.

I always found Art baffling. For one thing, nobody in the county ever questioned his devotion to work, or his dependability. There were few people among us who were more willing and eager to help out someone in need than Art Walters. But it seemed that he was so uncomfortable with the notion of resting, so driven, that he couldn't feel guilty about it alone. He had to make sure everybody noticed.

"This tree wasn't already like this, was it, Gary?" he asked Gary Glasser. Gary didn't answer, but Art didn't even notice.

"I wonder if this tree was already like this," he muttered.

I finally got up, gave my gunnysack a good soaking, and rejoined the fight. But it became hard to breathe. The hot air seemed to gather at my lips—thick, like cotton, thick enough to be bitten, and chewed. The sack slipped from my stiff, dry fingers. The heat slowed others, and many of us stood panting, pulling hard, labored breaths, our sacks hanging limp. Some leaned against trees, hands on their thighs.

A wind came up, and the fire began to creep east, pushing the tired, diminished circle away from its core. Weary eyes grew bigger as the finger of flame spread toward Glassers' grazing land. We ran clumsily in that direction.

And as the fear of losing the battle increased, we all found strength that moments before seemed impossible. Our bodies rose and fell, like wheat bending in the wind. The flames receded, then progressed, receded, progressed. Our effort was punctuated verbally, with groans and shouting, as we did all we could to drown out our screaming muscles. Finally, after a couple of hours, we had tightened the circle to a manageable size.

Little had been said all morning. The danger had focused all of our energy. Other than instructions, talk was not productive. A few people mentioned George, just enough to convey their condolences. Even if we hadn't been fighting a fire, they would not have asked too many questions. But as the danger passed, I found myself wanting more. I found myself wondering whether people missed George, whether they felt his absence as much as I did.

In our country, most of the work is done alone, in solitary, wide-open expanses of dirt. And although there is a certain pleasure that you get from this kind of work, the opportunity to accomplish something with a group is a welcome break from this routine. When there was little left but smoldering black grass, and a tiny flame here and there, the jokes started flying, and smiles spread beneath the soot that coated everyone's faces.

"Hey, how come you're not serving breakfast here, Gary?" Art complained. "We come out here and work our tails off and there's nothing to eat?"

Gary, who was as serious as any man I've known, even made a stiff attempt at a joke. "Tell you what, I'll let you all be my friends for another year."

I staggered amid the collective sense of proud accomplishment, feet dragging, to one of the barrels. I held on to opposite sides of the rim and lowered myself headfirst. Water surrounded my boiling skull, then moved up my shoulders and chest. It felt as though the heat eased up from my feet, through my legs, my torso, and then poured from the top of my head into the barrel. I held my breath and stayed under for as long as my lungs would allow. The water's soothing cool began to seep back up through me just as the heat had departed. But as I started to pull myself out, someone grabbed my legs and jerked me with such force that my chin caught the barrel's rim. I shouted as I fell to the ground, and I rolled over and jumped to my feet, ready to take a swing at the practical joker. But instead I stood facing my mother, who reached up and took a firm hold of my raised fist.

"Don't fool around with water at a time like this." Her eyes were wide and scared, and her head quivered a little, her frizzy red hair shuddering.

I frowned, not sure what she meant by "a time like this," but then I realized, and nodded. And Mom squeezed my upper arm, conveying her forgiveness, and returned to the fire. I lay on my back and leaned my head against the barrel's rough planks. I wiped my chin and studied the streak of blood across my palm. But I was too tired to care about a little blood, wondering whether I'd ever be able to stand. I didn't want to fall asleep in front of the whole community. So I raised myself up to my elbows, shook the water from my hair, and struggled to my feet. I propped myself against the barrel, supporting my tired legs with my tired arms. Water trickled into my clothes, which felt good.

I turned, checking the fire. Five people stamped the last of the flames, kicking the ground to kill any stray embers. My folks were among them. Mom looked as if she could do the whole thing again, then chop down a tree for good measure. She was built, it seemed, for the life of perpetual labor. Thick, with broad shoulders. Most of her children, myself included, inherited her squat, solid torso, and her bowed legs. George Jr. and Jack were the only ones built more like Dad—lithe, sinewy bodies that were strong in their own right but much less durable.

So Dad trudged forward, matching Mom's resolve. But his stride was not as steady. Most of the crew stretched out on damp burlap, quietly resting. Wisps of smoke drifted along the ground, like fog, its smell saturating our clothes and hair.

I finally tried walking, tilting from one side to another, like a baby, tottering slowly down the slope. My legs held me from memory, my arms dangling at my side. I fell once, rolling headfirst back onto my feet in a fluid motion that felt unremarkable, even practiced, as if that was how one goes down a hill. I crawled into the wagon bed, rolling my burlap bag into a pillow.

But to my surprise, I could not fall asleep. I was so tired my eyelids twitched. Images raced around behind my lids like moths in a jar, bumping together and circling each other. I clenched my eyes tight, trying to stop the flickering pictures, but it did no good.

I remembered George's last birthday, just months before. Katie, the eight-year-old, had just learned about surprise birthday parties, and she insisted on throwing one for George. The only problem was that she didn't quite grasp the surprise aspect of a surprise party. So she did all the planning, folding little paper hats out of pages from a Sears catalogue, inviting everyone we happened to see, regardless of whether George was around or not. We all watched with amusement while she pursued this plan, and none of us was more amused than the guest of honor. George smiled, his blue eyes twinkling, while Katie made a chocolate birthday cake the evening before, and arranged all the chairs in the house.

On George's birthday, which was a Saturday, it became clear that Katie still expected to surprise George. She pulled me aside and instructed me to ask George to go down to the river and plant some willow fishing poles. So we did, catching a few nice frogs and baiting some hooks, then burying the poles as deeply as we could in the mud. We chuckled every time we thought about what would happen when we got home.

"If I ever find another girl that puts this much effort into my birthday, I'll marry her on the spot," George said.

A half hour later, we rode back to the house, where there were several vehicles parked out front. And when we walked in the door, and the lights were off, and when everyone jumped out, yelling "Surprise," George clutched a hand to his heart. His mouth dropped open, and he fell straight back, landing flat on the hardwood floor. Katie squealed, and my brother had made one eight-year-old girl very, very happy.

I was just about to give up trying to sleep and get up to see where everyone was. But thankfully, the rest of the family came along. I heard the thump of barrels being loaded, feeling guilty about not giving them a hand, and I wondered whether someone had helped Dad and Jack carry the barrels. This question was answered when I heard Gary Glasser's voice.

"Thanks for coming, all of you," he said. "Especially at a time like this."

"Well, we know you'd do the same," Mom said.

"It's appreciated anyway," Gary answered. "You know we'll be at the service. You'll let us know when it is, right?"

"Of course." Mom's dismissive tone surprised me. She wasn't generally so short with people unless she was upset. And I could tell that Gary felt it, too, as he said another quick thanks, then I heard the crunch of his boots against the ground.

"Now what sense is there in not telling him there's not going to be a service, Mother?" Dad asked softly.

"He'll find out soon enough," she said.

I opened my eyes and twisted toward the front. "No service?"

An awkward silence followed, and I was confused.

"There's no service . . ." Dad hesitated, his head tipping from side to side.

"We haven't found the body," Mom finished.

I frowned, looking from one parent to the other. I pictured George floating in the water somewhere, or hung up along the shore. I pushed the thought from my mind. And then I wondered how they knew for sure that he'd drowned. My voice was high, thin, when I spoke again. "Can't we have a service anyway?"

"No," Mom answered emphatically. "We will not have a service without a body."

"Easy, Mother," Dad said.

"Well, now he knows."

"It's all right," I said. Although my mother's blunt manner sometimes put people off, and was often misinterpreted, I found it comforting somehow to know exactly where I stood with her, even at that age.

Dad set the team in motion, and we moved forward in silence as the facts settled into my mind. But there wasn't enough. I wanted to know more.

"Where did he go down?" I asked.

Mom and Dad glanced at Jack, who was staring off across the

prairie. Then they exchanged a silent look. Dad spoke. "They had a real gully washer up in the Little Missouri Buttes a few days ago, so the river was high. . . ."

Mom turned sideways on the bench. "George and Jack were moving some cattle, and George went to water his horse. He was gone for a while, so Jack went to check on him, and he found George's horse along the bank. We found his hat later, downstream. . . ." Mom paused, raising her chin, sucking air in through her nose.

I looked at Jack. His felt cowboy hat was pulled down just an inch above his small eyes, which were still aimed directly out, across the prairie, away from us.

I didn't understand Jack—never have, never will. He seemed to be the unhappiest person I ever met. And the reasons for this unhappiness, just like the reasons for most of his actions, were a complete mystery to us all. Because he rarely spoke. And he had an air about him that gave you the strong message that he had no desire to speak. So I sat looking at him, and wanting to ask him things, wanting to find out whether he knew more about what happened. But he was so far away, I knew any question would go unanswered.

The wagon lurched, dipping through a gully. Dad yelled at the team. "Come on, Pint. Ed."

"He could still be alive," Bob said.

A long silence followed, and I felt a small sense of panic at the thought, of how frightening it would be to see someone you thought was dead suddenly walk into the house. Yet it did seem possible.

"You never know," Dad muttered, voicing my thoughts.

"I don't see much use thinking like that," Mom said. "We've all suffered enough. No sense having him die twice."

At first, I felt myself obey this suggestion, surrendering to years of conditioning. After all, logically, it was best to assume George was dead, and be surprised if we were wrong. But a voice somewhere inside me protested loudly, not wanting to give up hope.

I pulled myself to one elbow, and looked around to see how much further we had to go. I groaned when I saw the tiny house in the distance. I turned back, looking in the direction we'd come, at the buttes. There was still a faint hint of smoke drifting just above the tabletops. And the sun, moving higher into the sky, floated in the smoke like a giant orange balloon.

"Tired, Blake?" Dad asked.

"Mm-hm."

"When did you get in? I didn't hear a thing."

"Don't know. Way after midnight."

"It was five," Mom answered. "You only slept about a half hour before Annie came back and told us about the fire."

I groaned again. And laid back into the jerking, rolling motion of the wagon.

But any thoughts of rushing into the house and falling into bed died the minute the wagon came to a halt. Mom had to cook breakfast. Bob went to feed and water the team, and Dad and Jack had to get the horses ready for their day in the fields. Which left the milking to me.

If not for the swishing tail of our old milk cow, and the mewing of our mousers rubbing against my legs, I'm sure they would have found me sound asleep against that old cow's ribs. As it was, I milked her dry, although the udders kept slipping from my weary fingers. And as I milked, I thought about the day, about how much work I'd done in the hours since I'd returned home, and how if I hadn't been there to do the small things I did, someone else would have had to take the time to do them. Time they didn't have. And I knew that they needed me. That the ranch was my master now. My teacher. It was time to stay.

I carried two full buckets into the house, where I was so hungry that I gladly delayed sleep for another half hour when I smelled bacon, eggs, and fried potatoes. I realized that I hadn't eaten dinner the night before. I devoured my first helping, then filled my plate again.

"Hi, Blake." My sister Katie greeted me as she came from her room and sat up to the table. She rubbed her eyes, which were red. Her cheeks were moist.

"You okay?" I asked her.

She nodded. "I'm fine. I was a little scared when I woke up, because I didn't know where anybody was. Muriel was the only one here."

I tousled her curly head. "You're okay now, though?"

Again she nodded, but she was clearly putting on a brave face. I imagined that Mom had told her to stop her crying, that we had enough to think about without someone crying. I could see she was still scared.

"Are you going to work on your garden today?" I asked her.

This made her face light up. Katie was the worst gardener in the county, but to her credit, she was the only one who didn't realize it. She was fiercely proud of her tiny formation of drooping, dried plants, and she tended them—digging, weeding, and dumping buckets of water over them—with a devotion we all admired with some degree of amusement.

"I'm gonna see if there's any potatoes today," she announced.

"Great," I said, shoveling food. "Maybe we can go out to the little house later this afternoon."

Katie's eyes grew. "Really?" she asked.

I nodded.

Katie bounced in her chair.

A few years before, Katie and I had been rummaging through the old deserted shed behind the original homestead house that Dad had built in 1898. Katie suggested that we pretend that the little structure was our own house, and that we were pioneers. It had become her favorite game. She used whatever knickknacks she could find to set up a tiny household, with a table, and two old tin plates. She adopted Mom's personality, instructing me to do the same chores she heard Mom give our father. I took an old hammer and pounded on the walls, pretending to put up pictures, and do repairs. We pretended to paint, and Katie set up an old orange crate, using it as a fake stove. As I got older, I had lost interest in the game. But any time Katie needed cheering up, I knew what would do it.

We all ate with ferocious, focused energy, as we usually did after a hard day of work. One chair, next to Dad, stood empty.

"When are you going to go back to school, Blake?" Katie asked.

I cleared my throat. "Well, I don't think I'm going back," I said.

All heads rose, and my mom's hand fell, her fork clanging against her plate. "What?" she asked.

I finished chewing a mouthful of food, and swallowed. "I'm not going back. I'm going to stay."

Although I could see the confusion in my mother's face, she looked down at her plate, took a deep breath, and resumed eating.

"He's right, Mother. We're going to need him now," Dad said.

"Yes," she said. "Yes. Of course." She took a bite of eggs and chewed, but her dream of having one child finish high school had been dashed one more time. George had never even considered the possibility, leaving school when he was twelve. And although Jack would have liked to stay in school because it was easier than working, by the time he was fifteen, they needed the extra back. He was barely passing anyway.

"I don't want to go to Belle Fourche, either," Katie announced. "I want to stay here, too."

"Well, you've got a few years to think about that, honey," Dad said.

"I don't have to think about it," Katie said. "I already know."

"I bet you'll think twice when Audrey goes," I said, and although Katie said nothing, I could see the wheels turn at the mention of her best friend.

"You're going, and there will be no more talk about it," Mom said.

Katie rolled her eyes.

* * *

After breakfast, I stumbled to my room, where I stretched my tired limbs and dropped my clothes. The fall air chilled my skin, and I wrapped my arms around my chest. Standing in the middle of the room, I gazed down at George's bed for the second time that morning.

Just then, a figure swept past the window, swearing. It was Jack, who walked over to dip some water from the well. He had cut his thumb, and he muttered to himself as he washed it off, then studied it. After washing his thumb, Jack shook it in the air, then he suddenly stooped down, grabbed a dirt clod, and flung it with all his strength into the well. Then he stopped, and with his back to me, raised his hands to his head. Both hands landed palm down on top of his head, and rested there for a moment. Then they clamped down, clasping the hair on his head. He raised his eyes toward the sky and stood there like that for a long time, his hands tangled in his hair.

Because my head was still foggy, and because I simply didn't think about these things much at the time, it didn't occur to me then that Jack was now next in line to take over the ranch. I'd heard stories through the years of battles for land among siblings. But I thought that would never happen in our family. We were a family first and foremost. Little did I realize that the history of my father's family was anything but harmonious.

I turned away from the window, and sank onto my bed, where I spotted George's baseball cradled in a hollow among the blankets. And I struggled to accept the standard practice of my family and the people around me—the pragmatic, realistic approach to death, where you move on and do what's in front of you, recognizing that there's little time for mooning around thinking about things you have no control over.

I circled George's ball with my fingers and laid down, falling immediately into a deep sleep, and when I woke up hours later, still lying in exactly the same position, the ball had fallen from my hand and rolled across the floor, resting against the bedroom door.

2

summer 1917

"Blake, take me fishing tonight." Katie stood next to my chair, bouncing up and down, her sausage curls unfurling with each bend of the knee. "Pleeeeease."

I slowly scooped fried potatoes into my mouth. My hands were so stiff and blistered that I could barely hold my fork. I had spent all of the previous day clearing a pasture of sagebrush, using a grub hoe. Today would be more of the same. It was a tedious, grueling job, not one I enjoyed, and for the first time in months, I was regretting my decision to leave school.

"Nah, Katie. I'm sorry, but I'm not going to be able to take you tonight." I poked another bite of potatoes. "I won't be home until dark. Besides, I'm going to be pretty worn out."

Katie clenched her fists and punched downward, stomping one

foot. She had just come off a week-long bout with the flu, and although she was still weak, and chalk-white, she had never been patient with inactivity. Mom came in from the barn, lugging two full milk buckets. She kicked the door shut.

"Mom, Blake won't take me fishing tonight."

Mom stood up, sighing, and looked at me with a raised brow. I ignored her, going back to my breakfast.

"You really shouldn't be going out yet anyway, Katie," Mom said, but it was clear that she knew that this line of reasoning would not work with her headstrong young daughter. "Maybe you ought to wait and ask him again when he gets home," she added, to my relief. I hoped that by evening, Jack and Dad would be back from Belle Fourche, where they had taken a load of grain the afternoon before. Then she could pester one of them.

"We'll see how I'm feeling when I get back," I said, which barely pacified my sister. But Katie was soon occupied with something else, and as I prepared to leave, she was filling a bucket from the well to go water her garden. I carried the bucket for her, and studied the twisted, withered plants that bent with their own weight. Katie began pouring the water, holding the bucket awkwardly in her tiny hands. The water poured unevenly, but she didn't seem bothered by this, moving down the line.

"Everything looks great, Katie. Looks like you're going to have a good crop this year."

She blushed.

As was usually true, I felt better about the job ahead of me once I got out into the open air. It wasn't as hot as usual for July. I rode at a leisurely pace, studying the thick grass. We'd had a fairly cold, snowy winter, which meant a big spring runoff. The country had not looked this good for several years, with bright green grass and fat, healthy livestock.

My horse Ahab and I wandered along the river, following a two-rut dirt road until we came to the crossing, where the ruts descended at an angle down the slope into the muddy waters of the Little Missouri. I had to coax Ahab down the bank, as the black mud was moist, and slippery. He eased into the river, which just washed his belly. He hesitated midstream, and I found myself kicking him, harder than necessary.

George's body had still not been found. And each time I crossed the river, I was well aware of the possibility that my brother was probably hung up beneath that rush of muddy water somewhere. The image gnawed at me whenever I crossed. And although I always glanced quickly to each side, my heart would rise into my throat, hoping that I wouldn't catch sight of a bobbing foot, or a patch of hair poking from the water.

In the tradition of our region, we did not speak of George, and a debate raged within me about whether this was the right thing to do. I thought of him every day. Often. In the morning, I would sometimes look at his empty bed before I was fully awake and wonder why he'd gotten up so early. But the time I felt his absence the most was when I was out in the open, where the silence was magnified.

It wasn't until a few days after the fire that I remembered the bundle of papers I'd discovered under George's mattress. One day I tucked the papers under my shirt and snuck off to the barn, making sure I wasn't followed. I climbed into the hayloft, settled into a comfortable spot, and piled the papers on my lap. On top was a thin paperback book—a book about the fundamentals of baseball. I leafed through it, studying the sketches that displayed proper technique for fielding a grounder, and the correct batting stance. I was drawn to sketches of a hand gripping a ball, with the fingers in different positions along the seams. This chapter explained all the various twists and downward turns you could accomplish with these grips, and by flipping your wrist at just the right moment.

I was surprised I'd never seen George reading this book, and wondered why he'd kept it hidden, as we all knew how much he loved baseball. But when I got around to the remaining papers, the reason became clear. I unfolded what turned out to be letters, which were stacked in chronological order. They were from a man named Stanley Murphy who lived in St. Louis, Missouri. And he was a baseball scout.

It seemed that George had met an assistant of Mr. Murphy's in the fall of 1914, on one of George's trips to Omaha, where Dad sometimes traveled to sell calves. That year had been the first that he'd allowed George to make the trip for him. Mr. Murphy's assistant had given George a tryout, and George made a big impression. In the last letter, dated just two weeks before George's death, Mr. Murphy spoke of George's pending trip to St. Louis. "You'll notice I have enclosed a train ticket. That's how much faith I have that we're going to like what we see." The yellow ticket was still tucked into the folds of the letter—its price, $2.10, prominently displayed in one corner.

I sat with my eyes closed, trying to comprehend what these letters implied. There was no one I knew who seemed more suited to living on the ranch than my brother George. I thought. I thought he loved it out here. Like everyone in our county, I had expected George to take over the ranch when my folks were too old or too tired. No other possibility had ever entered my mind. And I didn't understand. The mystery haunted me enough that for a short time, I considered going to St. Louis myself. After all, Mr. Murphy had never met George. I could pretend to be George. They would eventually figure out that I wasn't, of course. But by then, maybe I would understand the attraction.

A week or so later, I wrote to Mr. Murphy. I explained who I was, and told him that George had drowned. I returned his ticket, and after pondering whether it was appropriate, I asked whether George had told him for sure that he was interested in playing pro ball. A month later, I received this letter:

Dear Mr. Arbuckle,

I'm very sorry to hear about George. I believe he had a lot of promise. And I wondered why we hadn't heard from him. I am returning the ticket. I want you to keep it. And if you ever wonder what being a professional ballplayer might be like, please write to me. I'll give you a tryout. My condolences to your family.

Stanley Murphy

The letter disappointed me. He didn't answer the most important question. I wanted to hear Mr. Murphy report that George had changed his mind, that he couldn't stand the thought of leaving the ranch. I ended up stashing the letters in a coffee can, along with the ticket. And I buried the can in a corner of the barn.

"C'mon, boy." I buried my heels into Ahab's flanks, and he reared and heaved forward twice. His front hooves caught the bank with the second lunge, and the momentum carried him right up the slope, into the pasture, where he settled into a comfortable trot. A light dew brightened the grass. Blue-white clumps of sagebrush, immune to the moisture, squatted stubbornly, as unchanging as stone.

I came to the top of a ridge where the view always left me breathless, with our world opening up in front of me. I climbed from Ahab's back and gazed out across the flowing sea of green. Only the distant, square brown outline of a homestead cabin, an occasional lone tree, and a cluster of cattle broke up the expanse of green. The deserted cabin reminded me of the day that the wife of the young couple marched up to our front door and defiantly dropped a basket of food my mother had prepared for them on the stoop.

"We don't need anybody's charity," she declared, turning proudly on her heel. We knew then that they wouldn't last.

The silence was so strong that when I walked, the rustle of my boots against grass sounded as if my head was right between my feet. I looked at the land around me, at the wheat field I had plowed the previous spring, and at the stack of hay George and I had pitched a month before.

Even before George's death, every time I was in this pasture, I recalled an incident that happened when I was ten years old. One day Dad, George, Jack, and I were stacking hay in that pasture. It was a hot day, a rare muggy day in this dry part of the world. After lunch, Dad had shocked the three of us by suggesting we take a little break. We were even more surprised when he pulled a bat and ball from the back of the wagon, meaning that he had planned the diversion ahead of time. So we laid out a couple of bases, and George and I took on Jack and Dad.

The game started out light, with cutting remarks tossed between each pitch. George had his usual running monologue going, teasing Dad about his swing, which was pretty bad, and telling Jack he threw like a sheep. Jack laughed, and made a bleating noise. But after a few innings, something shifted. Both George and Jack had always been competitive. When we played against other local teams, they were both there to win. But their competitive natures showed in different ways. George was cool but relentless. He never appeared ruffled, and he kept the same patter going on the baseball diamond as he did in the fields. He talked to the first baseman after he'd gotten a single, he talked to the catcher when he was batting—always trying to bait them into an argument, trying to rattle them.

But Jack was out to prove something. Playing baseball didn't come as naturally to him as it did George. So he clenched his teeth and turned each play into a personal war. He never spoke. He stood at the plate squeezing his bat until his knuckles turned blue, his lips pursed, eyes raging. And he fought. About once a year, he would get into a fight during a game, and someone would have to tackle him and calm him down.

But they had rarely been on opposite sides of the field. We usually didn't have time to play outside of the local fairs. So as the game progressed, their competitive tendencies kicked in, and it was like the weather had changed. George's banter became more pointed. Jack's mouth tightened. The laughter stopped.

With Dad and Jack just a run down, George stepped to the plate with two out and peered out at Jack, who was pitching. "Hey, Jack, you got something between your teeth there." He pointed to his own teeth. "Something stuck in there."

Jack smiled at him and fired a pitch. I was catching, and I was afraid to get in front of the ball, he threw it so hard. But I blocked it and tossed it back.

"Really, Jack," George continued. "Right in the front there." He pointed again to his mouth. "Looks like . . . I don't know . . ."

Jack threw again, his smile gone now, this time buzzing a fastball close to George's knees. George dodged the pitch, chuckling calmly to himself. He turned and winked at me. "He's getting rattled," he muttered. I didn't respond. I didn't want Jack throwing one of his fireballs at me.

Jack took my toss back, and got set to throw again.

"Oh, I think I see what it is now," George said just as Jack began his windup. "It's chicken, Jack. You got chicken in your teeth."

The words left George's mouth just as Jack was about to throw, and when he let the pitch go, he threw it as hard as I'd ever seen him throw a ball. The pitch came in so fast that George didn't have time to get out of the way, and it nailed him right in the ear. The crack of ball against bone flew across the prairie. And George went down.

Dad rushed in. I shouted, bending over my brother. And Jack rushed up to George, falling on his knees next to George's head. George was conscious, holding his ear, growling in pain. Blood trickled between his fingers.

"I'm sorry, George," Jack muttered. His face was so pale, I thought he was going to faint. The sweat soaked his shirt, and he ran his hand across his forehead so many times that the skin began to turn red. "I didn't mean to hit you in the head. I was just trying to scare you."

"Goddamit, Jack, I was just kidding around," he muttered.

"I know," Jack said. "Like I said, I'm sorry."

George had some trouble with his balance for a few weeks after that, and he sometimes couldn't hear very well from that ear. That was the last time we took a break to play baseball.

But the incident told me something about the relationship between my brothers. George had always been protective of us all, but particularly Jack. The buffer George provided between Dad and the rest of us was particularly thick in Jack's case. I don't think I realized how much this meant to Jack until that day. It was the most frightened I've ever seen him.

I climbed back on Ahab, and we passed through the field where we had planted oats the previous two springs. This experiment—Dad's idea—had raised a few eyebrows around the county. The general feeling was that we didn't get enough moisture to support an oat crop. And I could tell by Dad's pinched brow when we checked on the oats that he wasn't entirely sure himself. But he had proven to be a prophet, as we'd been blessed with consecutive wet springs. The extra money provided enough to buy the McCarthy place—three thousand acres added to the six thousand we already had.

I arrived at the big meadow, which formed the northwest corner of our property, and I went to work. I let Ahab drift, free to graze, while I wrestled with the grub hoe, which consists of two handles leading down to a blade across the middle. I hacked away at the solid, twisted plants, trying to break through the hard gumbo to their roots. I rested every now and then, breathing hard, gazing at the scene around me. At my back, the ground was clear except for the drying clumps of sage that I'd extracted from the hard ground.

By mid-afternoon, I had cleared several acres, and my hands were sore and bleeding inside my gloves. My back felt like a clenched fist. The corn bread and jerky Mom had packed were gone, as were the dried apricots I'd pilfered from the root cellar. I watched the sun closely, wishing it would sink a little faster. I even took a guilty break, pulling George's baseball from my saddlebag. I threw it at the trunk of a cottonwood a few times, but I got tired of fetching it when I missed. So I started winging rocks instead, winding up and kicking high with my left leg before letting each stone fly. I had been practicing a lot, so I was getting pretty good, and I hit the trunk more often than not.

I had painted two stick figures on the back barn wall—one right-handed—one left-handed, along with a rectangular strike zone between them. And I threw George's old worn ball against the gray planks almost every evening, studying his book until I learned to throw a respectable curveball. Occasionally, the old milk cow complained from inside the barn, telling me she needed some sleep.

Around four o'clock, I heard an odd sound from the direction of Hay Creek. I stopped hoeing. But after waiting a moment, and hearing nothing, I went back to work. A minute passed, and I heard the sound again. It sounded like a cow. The third time, I decided I'd better check on it. So I called Ahab, and we sauntered toward Hay Creek. I dismounted and led Ahab cautiously along the creek's edge. The ground was soft in places, but I didn't see anything. We strolled along the bank for several minutes before a low moan filled the air, growing into a rich "mooo" that climbed higher and higher upon itself. The sound was coming from behind us, so I turned Ahab around and stalked, still cautious, toward the noise.

At a sharp bend, the ground pulled at my boots, and I led Ahab away from the water, around a stand of willows. Behind the willows, a cow held her head just above the mud, where she had sunk to the base of her neck. I approached, leaving Ahab behind. The cow's head dropped to the ground, weak from the strain of her cry. Her tongue hung loose and dry. Her eyes were wild. The thick gumbo behind her was stirred up and thrown around in a way that indicated she had escaped one trap, only to find herself closer to the water, in still softer mire.

I didn't even think for a moment that I had any option about what to do with this cow. I knew it would take several hours to free her. But the value of every single head of livestock to the operation of a ranch like ours was immeasurable. It meant a source of calves for the next several years. It wasn't just one cow.

So I filled my sheepskin flask in the creek. The cow rolled her head away from me as I came closer. Although she fought, she was weak, and I cradled the weary skull in my lap and poured water into her mouth. But this made her choke, a deep hollow wheeze that shook the ground around her. I realized that if I didn't keep her head upright, I could drown her.

I tried pouring water into my cupped hands, but it leaked through my fingers faster than I could get it to her. I tried my hat, holding my hands underneath, but the water also seeped through the straw. Finally, I swung the saddlebags from Ahab's back, emptied them, and laid one in front of the cow's broad, panting nose. I placed my fists in the center of the bag and leaned into it, forming a hollow, which I filled from the flask. The cow pushed her nose into the water, and emptied it in seconds. I trotted back and forth, wearing myself out trying to keep the leather bowl filled. The cow sucked it dry faster than any man could run.

After many trips, I decided she'd had enough. I rested for a few minutes.

The cow faced the creek, so I positioned Ahab on the opposite bank. She didn't have any horns, so I had to tie a rope around her neck. I tied the other end to Ahab's saddlehorn.

"Okay, old girl. Get ready." The cow gazed up at me, her eyes startled, her breath racing. I smacked Ahab's flank and yelled. He plunged forward, the rope twanged, and the cow squeezed out a strangled

"Maaaaaaw." She rose like a mythical creature, the black mud flying, her bawl climbing. But she managed only a few feet of progress before she was exhausted. And she sank back to her chest.

Ahab was spooked, and straining at the rope, so I grabbed his reins to calm him, talking softly in his ear. "Easy, boy. Whoa. Easy. Easy." I stroked his neck, holding the reins taut a foot below his nose.

When a person can see for miles around them, it's not often that something unexpected happens. And because you tend to feel as if you can't be surprised out in the middle of nowhere, the unexpected scares you ten times more than it would if you were in an enclosed space, or in the woods, where you might be on the lookout.

So when a gunshot rang out from behind, my heart felt as if it would beat right through my ribs and dive into the creek. Ahab reared to full height, and I dropped to the ground, trying to make myself small. Ahab wanted to run, but the rope held him back, so he bucked from one side to the other, his hooves stabbing the earth in frustration each time he came down. On one lunge, I rolled to one side just before his front hoof plunked me in the hip.

I jumped up and groped for the reins, managing to catch one of them. But another shot sounded, and Ahab reared again, whinnying, trying to bolt, throwing his head from side to side. The rope jerked like a fish line, and I could hear the cow choking. I ran to Ahab's flank, pulling the single rein as hard as I could to twist his head to one side. I yelled until my throat hurt, not really thinking about what I said, but hoping my shouts would give the sniper something to think about.

Finally, I was able to pull Ahab back just enough that I could slip the rope from the saddlehorn. Without the rope holding him back, he lunged and jerked the reins free of my aching fingers. He took off, kicking his hind legs high into the air.

I chased him for a few frantic strides, until I realized how useless that was. Then I stopped, staring after the dust, so caught up in wondering what to do next that I forgot that some bastard was out there shooting at me. Another shot rang out, echoing across the plain, and I fell to the ground. I scrambled back down into the creek bed, my heart pounding into the earth.

The cow rested her muddy nose on the mud, looking near death. I crept to the top of the bank, scanning the prairie for signs of life. I saw nothing.

"What are you doin' on my land?"

A voice boomed from behind, and I went stiff, expecting a shot in the back. But nothing happened, and I turned slowly, peering across the creek to see the lean, craggy figure of Art Walters.

Now I'm always amazed at how a person can feel two things at once—two very opposite things at that. When I saw a familiar face, I was so relieved that a part of me could have hugged Art. But at the same time, it was hard to overlook the fact that he'd been shooting at me. But the second emotion was a lot stronger than the first, so I responded to that one.

"Art, what the hell are you doing?" I walked toward him, right through the creek, arms outstretched.

Art studied me carefully, eyes scrunched, still aiming the gun right at me. His thick handlebar mustache hung down over his mouth, tickling the barrel of his rifle.

As I waded through the creek, arms still straight out from my side, I didn't even consider that he would shoot again. I shook my head, the boil rising in my blood. "Goddamit, Art, you just ran my horse off and scared the hell out of me, and I'm not even on your land. This is our land. What's gotten into you?"

Art remained poised as he was, the gun on his shoulder, and to my complete shock, another shot rang out, and a puff of dust jumped from the ground three feet to my right.

I was paralyzed for a second, but as soon as I recovered, I rushed him. I lowered my head and ran straight at him, and I was just about to take him down when everything went black.

I think I was only out for a half minute or so, because when I came to, it only took me a few seconds to remember where I was, and what had happened. I was lying facedown, and I rolled over, ready to defend myself, but Art was crouching down over me, a wet kerchief poised above my face.

"You okay?" he asked.

My arms were wrapped around Art's slight torso, gripping the front of his overalls as we rode his horse in search of Ahab. I could feel Art's ribs, about to push their way through the threadbare cotton. My wet clothes were cool against my skin. There was a knot on my forehead, and a dull ache in my skull.

I was still angry, or maybe more exasperated, trying to decipher the contradictions of the man in front of me.

"Art, why in hell's name were you shooting at me?" I asked. "You trying to murder me?"

Art didn't answer right away, but after a deep breath, he turned to talk over his shoulder.

"I ain't no murderer, Blake." He shook his head, and kept shaking it, as if he needed to assure me, and keep right on assuring me. "Don't be starting rumors like that." The head continued to shake. "There's been too much of that going on already."

I frowned. "Too much of what?"

The head shook. "Rumors. Murders and rumors."

Again I frowned. "Murders?" I asked. "What the hell are you talking about? I haven't heard any rumors about any murders."

Art shook his head. "I ain't saying no more."

I puzzled over this strange comment, reviewing the recent history of our little community. There hadn't been anyone killed in our county for

many years, and the only death I could think of that was even accidental in a while was George's. And then it hit me. And a sudden anger rose
up in me again.

"Art, are you saying what I think you're saying?"

Art's head rotated again, back and forth, back and forth. "I ain't saying," he repeated.

"Well, what the hell is it that you ain't saying?"

His jaw tightened, as if he was preparing to fight against any
attempt to pry the words from his mouth. "I'm not gonna tell you
what I ain't saying."

"Goddamit, Art." I got worked up, wishing there was a way to force
him to tell me what the hell he was talking about. But I knew nothing
I said would prompt any more information out of him. "So what the
hell . . . goddamit." I thought about what people might say, and the
only conclusion that made any sense was that there might be speculation about Jack. But it was just so absurd to me at that moment that I
hardly even thought about it.

Then, out of the blue, Art decided to address something completely different. "Blake, I'm going to tell you something. Something
important."

"Oh?" I refrained from saying something sarcastic. "Okay."

Art cleared his throat, in a great show of guttural gacking sounds.
"Now listen here, Blake. I'm not a smart man. Everyone knows that."

He paused. I bit my tongue.

"But I watch. I pay attention to things. More than people think
I do."

I said nothing, letting Art set his own rhythm.

"I never thought for one minute that I could go nowhere else, or do
nothing else." Art cleared his throat and spat. "But some people . . . some
people are too goddam smart. Do you know what I mean, Blake? This
place, this land, it beats hell out of people. Have you noticed that, Blake?
Beats the holy hell out of folks. Do you know what I mean?"

I didn't really know what to say. This was a side of Art Walters that I'd never seen before, and I'd known him all my life. I'd never seen him, even with other adults, show any inclination toward carrying on a serious discussion about life. And I had a feeling that this was a rare occasion, that maybe nobody else had ever seen it before, either. It didn't exactly explain why he was shooting at me, and yet I think in his mind, it did.

"I'm sorry," Art said after a moment of awkward silence. "I'm outta line talking to you about this. That's your business, and I ought to know better."

"No, no. It's okay, Art. Don't worry about it. I'll think about it. Really."

"Will you?" he asked, and he sounded genuinely surprised.

"Yeah, I will. I mean it now."

"Okay," he said, and I could hear in his voice that this pleased him. I was glad I had managed to look past my anger, and figure out what he wanted to say.

Neither of us spoke again while we rounded up Ahab and went back to finish freeing the cow.

For the next two hours, Art and I tugged, rested, watered, and tugged, rested and watered some more. Art had plenty of experience pulling cows from the bog, so he was full of good suggestions, like stuffing grass under the cow's nose to give her some strength but also to firm up the mud a little. We secured ropes around each front leg, with one tied to each horse, once we had the cow's torso clear of the mud. I don't know if I would have been able to get the cow out without him. The ache in my head didn't get any weaker, but it didn't get any worse either.

Once she was free, the cow stood unsteadily for a moment, her legs shaking. Then she lumbered across the pasture, giving a weak kick of her heels. We stood watching her, and I felt the warm satisfaction of pulling a life from the brink of death. But then I noticed her brand, which had been covered when she was in the mud. I started laughing.

"I'll be damned, Art," I said, pointing. "That's your cow."

Art squinted, checking the old cow's flank, and turned, laughing, showing his toothless smile under that thick, drooping mustache.

By the time I returned home, the bottom of the western sky was smeared bright orange as the rest of the sky darkened to blue-black. The sound of the river brushed my ears as I rode back toward the house, almost putting me to sleep with its soothing flow. The wagon was out in front of the barn, so I knew that Dad and Jack had returned from Belle Fourche.

After feeding and combing Ahab, I went inside and sat up to the table, where a plate of food waited. I could hear Muriel playing outside, and I figured that Katie must be with her. Bob was wrapped in a blanket, curled up in a chair. Like Katie, he had been battling the flu. But unlike her, he didn't show any sign of recovery yet.

Mom had torn the whitewashed flour sacks from the walls to wash them, and she scrubbed one against the washboard. Dad dug at his thumb with a pocketknife. From the moment I entered the kitchen, I felt tension, and I knew my parents had been arguing again. Ever since George's disappearance, they had fought more than I could ever remember, sometimes raising their voices to the point that the only relief was to go outside.

"I was just about to come looking for you," Dad said, his voice tight.

"Yeah?"

"How'd it go today?" Mom asked. But her voice was also strained, and I knew I was only being addressed as a diversion. A wisp of red floated from one side of her head.

"All right. I found an old cow caught up in the bog over at Hay

Creek." I decided not to mention what happened with Art, thinking it would only add fuel to a combustible situation.

"You got her out?" Dad pulled a splinter from his thumb, then studied both. I bit into a chicken leg.

I nodded. "It was Art's. He helped me out. Where's Jack?"

"He took Katie fishing," Mom answered.

"Good." I wiped grease from my chin. "What time did you guys get back, Dad?"

"Around three." Dad sucked blood from his thumb. "What's that?" He pointed at my forehead.

"Oh, nothing. Just banged my head against the hoe." I touched the knot.

Mom squeezed murky water from a flour sack and shook it out with brisk, angry strokes. She hung it on the line she'd stretched across the kitchen.

"Did you stay at the road ranch, Dad?" I asked.

"Yep. That second Roberts gal, Sophie, I think it is . . . she ran off to Oregon to marry some older guy."

"Really?" Despite her mood, Mom's ear for gossip was strong.

"Is she the tall one?" I asked, knowing perfectly well that she was. Sophie Roberts, the second daughter of the couple that ran the ranch where people could bed down for the night on their way to or from Belle Fourche, had been a striking figure from the time she finished grade school. She had the kind of flour-white complexion contrasting her shiny black hair that, when she entered a dance, everyone lost a step.

Dad nodded. "God, son, you should see all the honyockers moving in. There must be twenty new homesteads between here and Belle, and those are just the ones I could see from the road." He shook his head.

Mom dipped another sack into the tub of water. I was glad that Dad brought up this topic, as it was something my parents were in complete agreement about—empathy toward these newcomers. By this time, the prime land, along the river and bigger streams, had all been claimed. Everyone knew that these latecomers were working against odds they hadn't anticipated, lured by ads from the railroads claiming five times more production from 320 acres than anyone could expect.

I noticed a tiny white dress draped over one of the kitchen chairs. "What's that?"

Mom glanced up. "That's for Jenny's baby."

I nodded. Jenny Glasser, Gary's son Steve's wife, had lost her baby a few days before. "When's the funeral?"

Mom stopped what she was doing, her eyes shifting from side to side. I studied her. "Mom?"

"Wait!" She held up one hand. "Quiet! I heard screaming."

Muriel suddenly burst into the house. "Mom, Katie is running up the road. And she's screaming."

We ran outside, where we saw a shadow flying toward the house. I raced ahead to Katie, who collapsed into my arms. Her hair was matted against her head from the sweat. Even her dress felt moist. Mom and Dad arrived just behind me.

"What is it, honey?" Mom brushed the hair back from Katie's sweaty forehead. "Is Jack okay? Where's Jack?"

"Where's Jack?" Dad asked, his tone more impatient than Mom's.

But Katie was breathing so hard that she couldn't speak. I carried her to the house and set her down in a chair. Mom knelt in front of her. "Katie, what happened? Where's Jack?" Now her own tone was more urgent, more desperate.

"Give her a chance to breathe," I said. "Give her some room."

"What happened?" Dad insisted, ignoring me, moving closer to Katie.

"It's George," Katie finally said, coughing. "Jack found him." She burst into tears, and the coughing intensified. We all stood, stunned, silent, for several minutes. Dad muttered softly, his head rocking from side to side, eyes to the floor. Mom's eyelids clenched together.

My throat closed. I couldn't have made a sound if I needed to. I found myself trying to imagine what George would look like after six months frozen underwater, but I stopped short of a picture, horrified that I would be thinking such a thing. Bob and Muriel started crying, and tears pushed toward my own eyes, but I blinked them back. I squeezed my eyes closed, wondering what Jack was doing. Was he fishing George from the river? If so, he'd no doubt need some help.

"Let's go, Dad." My voice was deep and thick in my throat, barely recognizable. I started for the back door. "Come on. Let's go."

Dad nodded.

We found Jack two hundred yards downstream from the crossing, sitting on the bank with his head on his knees, in his hands. One bloated leg, nearly bursting the seams of its overalls, jutted at an angle from the water, bobbing gently with the current. The boot was gone, the foot blue. Upstream, about ten yards, Jack and Katie's fishing poles were planted in the bank. One of them jerked with the weight of a fish.

Dad prepared a lasso and inched down the steep bank.

"Dad, shouldn't we just go in and get him?" I asked.

He didn't answer, swinging the lasso above his head, then tossing it out over the rushing water. He missed the first time, but on his second toss, the loop flopped over the foot. I scooted down the bank behind Dad, sitting, and hooked my hands into his back pockets. He pulled. I pulled. Jack remained folded up on the bank, still hiding his face.

The body broke free. We strained, dragging my brother's mutated form onto the bank. Our racing breath was nearly as loud as the rush of water.

George's face was bloated beyond human proportion. His arms puffed from beneath his sleeves, bleached from months in ice. His skin looked like a cow's bag—pale, almost transparent. Dad and I hauled the body further up the bank, struggling with the weight. Dad collapsed once we reached level ground. He rolled onto his back and stared up at the slate-gray sky.

As much as I wanted to, I couldn't avert my eyes from my brother's distorted expression. His eyes and mouth were wide open, his cheeks swollen until they nearly hid his ears. One hand was clenched into a fist, the other lay innocently open, its fingers sausage thick. In a way, his appearance was a relief, because it didn't look like him. This wasn't my brother. The river had swallowed up George and regurgitated this strange form in his place.

Dad and Jack were useless, I realized. Neither of them moved. Although his expression was as stoic and straight as always, tears ran down Dad's weathered cheeks, something I'd never seen. I tried to keep the air moving through my lungs, recognizing that if anything was going to get done, I had to hold my emotions in check.

I cleared my throat. "Come on, Dad." My voice broke. "We've got to get back to the house. Mom's going to be worried."

Dad had pulled his hands together against his chest, where they were clenched, as if ready to defend against an attack. His pinched, red-rimmed eyes met mine, and he nodded.

"Right. Okay, son." He lifted himself to a sitting position. I helped him stand. "All right. Let's get him on one of these horses." He sniffed. "Jack, give us a hand here."

Jack had still not moved. But at Dad's command, after lifting his head and staring blankly for a moment, as if clearing his mind, he stood, his arms dropping to his sides. I got ahold of George's arms, and Dad grabbed his legs. We hefted him up off the ground, and Jack stepped in, lifting the bulk of George's torso. George's skin was cold and soft, slightly sticky, like bread dough, and with his wet clothes and bloat, he was damn heavy. The feel of his skin made me feel cold myself, on the inside.

Getting George draped over Ahab's back was difficult, as his torso did not bend. But we balanced him on his stomach, then stretched a rope from his hands to his feet under Ahab's belly. I noticed that the flesh on George's leg had torn where Dad roped it. There was almost no blood, and the tissue inside the cut was as white as the surface. We did all this wordlessly, avoiding each other's eyes.

I finished tying the knot. Dad and Jack had already mounted their horses. I climbed up behind Dad, and held Ahab's reins, leading him behind us. Ten minutes later, we approached the house. Mom stood on the stoop, both hands clamped to her mouth. Muriel clutched Mom's skirt, and Bob stood behind her. Mom dropped her hands and moaned, disappearing inside the house when she saw the body, leaving the two little ones racing after her, clutching for her skirt.

Despite the long day, and my tired muscles, I had trouble sleeping. Although George's bed had been empty for more than a half year, I kept waking up and looking over at it. And each time I managed to drift off, my dreams were invaded by wolves, tearing into George's body, which we had laid out in the barn. Dad was certain that the stench wouldn't get too bad before morning, but I was worried that it was already strong enough to draw the attention of some predators.

The wolves in my dreams were screaming, like humans rather than animals. The screams half woke me several times, until they sounded so real that I was fully awake. But in the time it took me to pass from being vaguely aware to waking up, I realized that I really did hear screams. I jumped out of bed, pulled on my overalls, and raced toward the barn. But halfway across the yard, I heard the screams behind me, in the house. Confused, I turned back, and went inside.

I smelled kerosene, and saw a muted light leaking beneath the closed door of the girls' room. I opened the door carefully. Dad stood at the foot of Katie's bed. Mom sat on the bed, bent at the waist so that her face nearly touched Katie's. She held a wet cloth to my sister's forehead and spoke gently. "It's okay, sweetheart. It's going to pass. Just relax." Her voice sounded soothing on the surface, but I could hear the fear in it. Mom's hair drifted out away from her head in a tangle of copper and white flags. I saw the strain on her face. It scared me, as this fear was rare for Mom.

"What's wrong?" I asked.

"We don't know," Dad answered.

"Should I go for the doctor?"

"Jack already left to see if Doc Sorenson is in Capitol."

"Where's Muriel?"

"She's in our bed," Dad answered.

I approached the scene, half not wanting to, preferring the thought of sinking back in my bed and covering my head with a pillow. Katie arched her back and screamed, her mouth stretching into a frightening rectangle. It looked as if the skin might tear around her teeth. I felt my own teeth clench together. One of Katie's knees rose and fell time and again, thumping softly against the mattress. Her eyes, when they were open, darted around the room, without focus. It looked as if she could die at any moment, and I couldn't imagine that life could be so cruel as to take another of us on the very day we'd found our brother's body.

"How long has this been going on?" I asked.

"A couple hours," Dad said. "We heard her moaning, and we came in to see what was wrong. She started screaming about a half hour ago." Dad looked completely beaten down.

Katie screamed again, her head bent so far back that it looked as if it could break off. She panted frantically, her chest as busy as boiling water.

"Easy, baby," Mom said softly. "Where does it hurt?"

But Katie couldn't hear her, and I realized that her condition was worse than I thought. She repeated a staccato "oh, oh, oh" between breaths.

Katie screamed at regular intervals, her voice weakening each time. Dad brought a pot of steaming water from the kitchen. Mom dipped a cloth into the pot, wrung it, and laid it across Katie's forehead. Mom tried to feed Katie a spoonful of hot tea with whiskey and honey, but she wasn't conscious enough to drink. She knocked the spoon from Mom's hand with a jerk of her chin. The sheets had turned gray with sweat.

The fits eventually drained Katie so that she fell into an exhausted sleep between each spasm. Her eyes would close peacefully, sending a shiver of fear through me each time. But after a minute or two the pain would wrench her from slumber, back to the struggle, and the pain in her face made me wince right along with her.

At four in the morning, she uttered her first words of the night. "Pull 'em in, pull 'em in," she pleaded.

Mom panicked, trying to figure out what to pull in, what she could do to ease her daughter's misery. She tugged at the blankets, then looked at Dad, puzzled and scared. Then she turned back to Katie and pulled her lips inside her mouth. Her brow pinched. Dad and I studied the floor.

"The fish?" Dad said. "She probably means the fish."

"Or George," I offered.

One of the last times that Katie and I played homesteader in our little prairie house, Katie approached me with her arms wrapped around the blanket-swathed figure of her favorite doll.

"Blake, honey," she announced in a strong, steady voice, a voice very much like my mother's. "We need to get ahold of the preacher."

"Oh?" I answered. "What for?"

"The baby's dead," Katie said matter-of-factly. "We need to bury the baby."

Katie was six years old at the time.

"I'll put the baby in the barn," she told me. "And I'll send a note to the preacher. And then I'll get some supper ready. Can you start on a coffin, honey?"

* * *

I guess we all knew, or suspected, how the night was going to end, although we tried to hope otherwise. We looked to the door whenever any small sound echoed through the night's silence. But soon after she spoke, the final gripping vise squeezed the life from Katie. She died eyes, mouth, and hands open to the ceiling, her last sound so weak that it was little more than a groan, followed by a sigh.

Jack and Doc Sorenson arrived an hour later to find us in a silent vigil around the body. Mom wept, while Dad and I simply sat in exhausted amazement at what had taken place that day. I hurt so bad inside that I couldn't hold my head up. It seemed that I'd been awake forever, and that a year's worth of life had been packed into the past twenty-four hours.

Jack barely responded when he learned that Katie was dead. He turned and left the room, going directly to bed. Doc Sorenson examined Katie and determined that what we thought was the flu was actually spinal meningitis. He said that he couldn't have done anything even if he'd gotten there sooner, which was a very small consolation at the time. But a relief nonetheless. He checked Bob, and determined that he just had a cold, and not meningitis. Dad thanked Doc for his trouble, offering him a bed for the remainder of the night. But it was only a few hours before his first appointment, so he had to hurry back.

Because of the state of George's body, the funeral had to be hastily arranged for two days later. There wasn't time to make Katie a funeral dress, and none of George's clothes fit his bloated torso. So we wrapped him in one of his blankets, and we laid Katie out in her favorite frock— a calico with lace. Pastor Ludke from the Little Missouri Lutheran Church performed the service the afternoon after he had buried the Glasser baby.

The coffins looked strange side by side—one too large, to hold George's swollen corpse, the other seemingly too small to hold any corpse at all. Pastor Ludke stood behind the odd pair, his thinning hair oiled in parallel lines across his scalp. His ruddy cheeks shone with sweat.

"We come to this barren world with high hopes," he said. "And then the land takes our children from us, and we ask why. We ask how a just God could let this happen. And I say that perhaps it is a price of risk, of adventure. Perhaps if we remained safely in our old worlds, we would not have to pay this price. Perhaps God is telling us that the earth will not yield unto us what we ask without first asking that we yield unto Him. It is a question I have searched this book for answers to . . ." He held up his Bible. "And I have yet to find one that satisfies me."

He bowed his head, showing a certain guilt about not being able to provide the kind of hope or comfort that someone in his position might be expected to provide. "Let us simply pray, then."

Mom and Dad stood very close to each other, their hands only an inch apart, their brows low over their eyes. Neither of them shed a tear. No one in the crowd showed any sign of tears. Jack eased off to one side, as if he wasn't invited.

I held my face still but felt the full force of a sadness and loneliness that were new to me. I had been to more funerals by this time than I had weddings, birthday parties, or Fourth of July picnics combined. I knew the routine. And I had always felt a little strange about the stoic demeanor that was common among our people. I had always looked around at the faces at these funerals and wondered how everyone could appear to be so unaffected, unmoved, by death.

I studied my father's face. And I thought about his favorite bit of philosophy, the one and only phrase he repeated with a sense of religious conviction. "Always expect the worst, and you'll never be disappointed," he'd say. He said it about everything. I had never been comfortable with the phrase, and although I didn't then, I now understand why. Because my father didn't live by it. Although he did expect the worst, expecting the worst had never prevented disappointment. In fact, my father not only experienced disappointment, day after day, but he had built his life around it. And I see now that it was a common quality among our people, to live with a wary knowledge that things could always get worse. To not enjoy accomplishment because of the certainty of more disappointment. It was an attitude born of experience, as a bumper crop of wheat, and a bountiful year, could change to failure in the time it took for a hailstone to bounce off your head. We expected the worst because it often happened, and the disappointment was buried deep in all of us. For some, it served as a motivator. My father was a perfect example. He acted on the disappointment by working harder. It was all he knew.

On this day, I looked around at the faces, and for the first time in my life, I did not see stony, lifeless expressions. I felt the loss of my siblings. I thought of Katie's pathetic garden, and her unwavering dedication to it. I thought about our little homestead house, which I had ceremoniously burned the day before. I hadn't even bothered to clean out the trinkets before I doused it in fuel and held a match in it.

I thought about my brother, and realized to my horror that I had held some hope that he would show up again someday. Part of me hadn't allowed myself to accept that he was gone. I pictured him in the barn. I thought of how he loved lingering there after we'd unsaddled the horses, telling jokes or wrestling in a pile of straw. I thought about him lacing a single to right. And as I thought about these things and looked at the faces around me, I realized for the first time in my young life that there was something behind those stoic expressions. I looked at the people there and realized that there was only one family among them that had not lost a child. The Purdys, who didn't have children. The Glassers had just buried their baby that morning. And I saw in the eyes of these people a sympathy that only someone who shared their experience could see. I had never seen the pain because I had never felt it. I was now part of the community. I was one of them.

And I realized that despite the fact that our homes were so far apart, the open space between us was much smaller than I had always assumed.

I stayed and watched while Gary Glasser, Art Walters, and others lowered the coffins into the graves. The holes bookended the graves of my grandparents.

Dad stepped forward, reaching for a shovel.

"George, goddamit, we'll take care of this," Gary said. "Did I help you bury my granddaughter? You stubborn old bastard. We got it."

Dad backed up, still watching our friends. He stood next to me, hands behind his back, jaw set. I studied him, his narrow face drooping, blue eyes squinting and moist.

Looking at his face, I wondered what could be worse than outliving two of your own children, watching the earth swallow them up when your own body was still strong, healthy, and full of life.

"You coming?" Suddenly Dad's arm fell heavily across my shoulders.

"Nah, I'll be along in a second," I said.

I watched him walk away, his eyes lowered to his boots. Three men shoveled dirt, heavy scoops of soil thumping against wood. I stood between the graves, digging through my jacket. The smell of damp soil filled my nose. I gazed at the open pits, and before I turned to join the rest of my family, I dropped a fishhook into Katie's grave, and the piece of chalk into George's.

3

winter 1918

I opened one eye, feeling the cold air against my eyeball, wishing dawn would put off its arrival just a little longer. I pulled the blankets tighter around my ear, which was numb. A still, warm body lay next to me, and I knew that Bob had crawled into my bed again to get relief from the cold. A square of dim sunlight broke the frozen air, casting a faint glow into the sparcely furnished bedroom. I heard animated voices and smelled bacon and coffee, and after savoring a few last moments of relative warmth, I crept from my bed, adjusted my union suit, and dressed.

When I entered the kitchen, the conversation between my parents stopped. Mom sat at the table, her hands wrapped around a cup of coffee. She was bundled in her coat and hat, having just come in from the milking. Dad scrambled eggs in our iron skillet. I immediately knew two things—they had been fighting, and Dad was the one who was angry. It was the only time he cooked. I winced as I sat, thinking about his undercooked eggs, with glistening slugs of whites oozing between what managed to get cooked.

"Mornin'," I said.

"Morning, son," Mom answered.

Dad didn't say a word. I poured myself a cup of coffee from the saucepan on the stove and stood with my back to the heat. Outside, the snow fell steadily, as it had for a week—soft flakes the size of downy feathers.

The next several minutes were silent aside from the simmering eggs. I finally decided to prompt whatever discussion I'd interrupted and leave it to them to tell me to mind my own business. "Well?" I said.

Dad responded immediately. "Your mother volunteered to go to Alzada to help with the balloting."

I looked at Mom, then back to Dad. "The election's today, right?"

Mom nodded, sucking her upper lip under her lower one.

I shrugged. "So what's wrong?"

Dad turned, glaring at me, indicating that I should know—which of course I did. He shifted his gaze outside, indicating the storm. Then he wrapped a flour sack around the skillet handle and lifted it from the wood stove. He scraped helpings onto three plates.

"It's not that bad out," I offered. "We've traveled in a lot worse."

"Not alone," Dad muttered. This was true.

"I'll go with her," I said.

They both raised their brows at this suggestion. I actually knew before I even said it that I couldn't go—that I had to stay and help with the feeding. I shrugged, then sauntered to the table.

"Why don't you go, Dad?" I sat down.

Dad set full plates in front of Mom and me, then one at his place, where he settled. "Son, you know it's going to take both of us and Bob too to get the stock fed in this storm. We'll be most of the morning just finding a place to water them."

"I'm going," Mom said, scooping a bite of eggs. "If I can't vote, I'm going to at least do what I can, especially with Jeanette Rankin on the ballot."

My mother's reputation for being tough and independent was well chronicled, and well deserved. It actually began with an event that occurred on the day she met my father. She was in her mid-twenties, and her outspoken, direct manner had apparently scared off several potential suitors, a situation that would have devastated many young women of that time. But Mom had taken a job as a bank clerk in Spearfish. She liked the job and was in no hurry to find a husband.

One day in the fall of 1897 three men came into the bank and drew guns, announcing a robbery. They demanded that all the cash be stuffed into the worn saddlebags they tossed across the counter. Mom happened to be in the back when they came in, and she ducked down and crept over to the bank manager's desk, where she knew he had a small derringer stashed in a drawer. She quietly retrieved the gun and stood up, drawing the gun, telling the robbers to get the hell out. They took one look at that little gun and busted out laughing. They told the other clerk to keep bagging the cash. So Mom pulled the trigger. But the gun wasn't loaded, and the harmless click only amused the robbers more. They laughed louder, and one of them called her Wyatt Earp. So Mom threw the gun at him, nearly smacking him in the head.

They got away, of course. But the story gave Mom a legendary status. A status that was enhanced when they found out later that the men who robbed the bank were none other than the Hole in the Wall Gang. It was Butch Cassidy and his boys.

Coincidentally, there was a young ranch hand in the bank who was quite taken by the character of this clerk. Dad had also been informed by his boss just a couple of weeks before that he would give himself a much better chance of moving up to the foreman job if he could find himself a wife.

Little did Dad realize when he married Mom a few months later that she would inspire him to seek more than the position of foreman. They filed their first homestead claim a year later, and the Arbuckle Ranch was born.

We ate silently, Dad and I both aware that the decision had been made. I tried to keep my eyes away from my plate and swallow quickly so that I didn't see the runny whites mingling among the scrambled eggs.

"What about Muriel?" Dad asked in a last-ditch effort. "What are we going to do about her?"

No doubt anticipating this, Mom answered without a pause. "I'll drop her off at Glassers'. She'll be fine."

Dad nodded—a concession of sorts.

I hefted a sack of corn onto my shoulder, my gloved fingers stiff after only fifteen minutes in the cold. I carried the sack out of the barn, then flopped it into the wagon bed. Back inside the barn, I dug George's baseball from inside my coat, pulled my right glove from my hand with my teeth, and flung a pitch toward the stick figure I had white-washed on the inside wall for winter practice.

As much as I was convinced that I would never consider doing what George had planned, I had been thinking a lot since Katie's death about the train ticket buried in the corner of the barn. And of what Art had said about life out here beating hell out of you. I had noticed more than ever how right he was. I practiced my pitching whenever I had a spare moment. I started a scrapbook, collecting box scores from major-league games. I had one section devoted to the Cardinals. And I began sending away for whatever I could get my hands on about the cities in America that had baseball teams. I had a box filled with pamphlets about New York, Chicago, Boston, and Philadelphia. And I read through them time and again, trying to imagine what it must be like walking among thousands of people.

The ball bounded back to me. I tucked it back in my pocket, put my glove back on, and retrieved a second sack of corn, flopping it next to the first.

Dad hitched the team to the wagon. Bob loaded the pitchforks and a couple of axes.

"Where were Mom and Muriel going?" Bob asked.

I was worried that Dad would be brooding about Mom's decision, so I shot Bob a warning look, shaking my head. But Dad answered him, although his mood was far from happy. "Your mother's gone to Alzada to help with the election. And Muriel is at Glassers' for the day." His tone was dismissive, and Bob looked at me with wide eyes, wondering what he'd done. I shook my head again, trying to convey with a look that I would explain later.

Bob and Dad climbed into the wagon, where our dog Nate was waiting. I mounted Ahab. Dad clucked his tongue, and Pint and Ed started their trot toward the haystacks, as they had every morning since the first winter snowfall.

It had been a dry year, the first in ten, leaving us with less than our usual amount of hay. It also followed the worst winter we'd had since 1896, with temperatures consistently lingering around twenty degrees below zero. The snow came in great flurries, throwing itself against the east side of everything that had sides, piling in hard drifts as high as horses. We lost almost fifty head of cattle, and we were among the more fortunate. Many families left once the thaw came. The new home-steaders had their first introduction to what Montana winters could be like, and the loneliness got to many of them.

Riding along behind the wagon, I had so little feeling in my limbs that as I maneuvered Ahab's reins, it felt as if I was watching someone else's hands. Streams trickled from the corners of my eyes. I had to wipe my nose every few minutes to keep the moisture from freezing on my upper lip.

At the stack, Dad and Bob wordlessly pitched clumps of hay into the back of the wagon. The stack was crowned with a thick blanket of snow, and as they tore chunks from the stack's belly, tunneling into the core, the top hung down, and sheets of snow slid to the ground. I grabbed a pitchfork.

"Dad?" Bob paused and looked up at him from beneath the brim of his hat.

"What?" Dad answered brusquely.

"When's Jack coming home?"

I groaned at the mention of this topic, as I suspected this was the last thing in the world Dad wanted to talk about that morning.

"I don't know, Bob. Let's just get this job done, what do you say?"

A year and a half had passed since the funeral. And in some ways, it seemed like only a matter of days. The silence in the fields became more profound every time we were out there. And any effort anyone made to break up this silence only reminded us of who used to provide that distraction. So we remained silent, bending our backs to our work, keeping our heads low, eyes averted.

Katie was missed more around the house. Her absence pervaded our home, nibbling at our spirits. From early on, Katie had been the idea person, the one full of suggestions for how to fill what little idle time we enjoyed. It didn't faze her at all that we ignored most of them. She simply kept firing new ones until something stuck, or until we gave in just to keep her quiet. She seemingly never tired of card games, or crafts. I remember her spending an entire day building a giraffe out of matchsticks. The finished product looked more like a piece of farm machinery than an animal, but she was as proud as a bantam rooster.

Mom went into a self-imposed exile in her bedroom. She came out only when she had to milk the cow, or gather the eggs, or prepare the next meal. She never missed a meal. But other than those times, we rarely saw her. She often took her supper into the bedroom, eating alone.

Even Dad was afraid of disturbing her. One afternoon I watched him come into the house after he had somehow fallen into a puddle. His clothes were soaked and muddy. He started to go into the bedroom, but stopped himself as he reached for the doorknob. He paced back and forth a few times, brow furrowed, head bowed, and finally left the house.

We seldom heard anything from behind that bedroom door, but she sometimes emerged with swollen eyelids, and red rims, her hair in a wild frizz of pink.

And then it stopped. About three months after it began, the exile ended. Outwardly, it seemed that we were back in the old routine. But it soon became apparent that Mom had changed. The patient, calm assurance was still in her voice most of the time. But the measure of patience that had once seemed to have no threshold now had a moveable ceiling. Mom had always been gruff, blunt, but her frankness now had an edge.

The deaths had driven Dad further into the fields, where he worked with his head down and mouth closed. He absorbed Mom's attacks with the same posture, never fighting back, seldom arguing.

Muriel, who had never liked going outside in the first place, also retreated to her bedroom, trying to avoid the tension. She found books, and sought refuge from the stories within. But she became a fragile little thing, susceptible to every hint of conflict around her. She watched the world with a gentle curiosity, at the same time as if she expected to be hurt by it.

But because Jack was now the oldest, he bore the brunt of this family crankiness.

When George Jr. was alive, he had been Dad's foreman. When something needed to be done, Dad told George. When something was done wrong, Dad yelled at George. And George passed these commands and complaints to the rest of us with a gentler hand. George was the buffer, and the job suited him, because when he'd had enough, he let Dad know. He yelled back, sometimes standing toe to toe with the old man until they'd both emptied their lungs.

But contrary to his indifferent demeanor, Jack's skin was as thin as boiled lettuce. When Dad talked to him the same way he had with George, the words seeped through to Jack's soul, pounding, bruising him inside. And it only got worse when it was busy, when Dad's only concerns were that the work get done and that we had fewer backs to do it. When Dad gave orders, his eyes were out on the fields. He didn't see Jack's lips tighten and his eyes grow narrow and cold. But I did.

So I was the least surprised the first time Jack disappeared. It was early June, and we had just finished docking the lambs and branding the new calves. The hay wasn't ready to cut, so we had a bit of slack time. So Jack's three-day absence, after Dad yelled at him about a saddle Bob had left out, didn't have the impact it could have. Dad didn't even seem that upset when Jack dragged himself home with a new shirt and a headache.

Jack didn't get off so easy the second time. Toward the end of summer, things got hectic. We were finishing up with the haying, so the crew was underfoot, keeping Mom frantic with the cooking. Harvest loomed just around the corner, and Dad and Jack planned to take a small herd of heifers into Belle Fourche for a sale. Dad apparently hadn't learned anything from Jack's first disappearance. Day after day, he ordered Jack around, scolding him like a child. There were several times I considered intervening, but I just didn't have the backbone. The night before they were supposed to leave for Belle, Dad asked Jack whether he'd packed his saddlebags yet. When Jack said no, Dad said, "Well, when are you planning on getting around to it, after everyone else is asleep?"

The comment, though biting, seemed harmless enough, but it was apparently the last straw. Jack went outside, and we just assumed he was packing his saddlebags. We didn't see him for another three days.

So Bob had to join Dad on the trip to Belle, and we were a hand short on the haying crew, which was in my charge. Each stab of pain in my back as I pitched hay that day reminded me of his absence. We were all dead tired, not to mention furious, by the time Jack showed up that third evening.

We had just finished dinner when the door swung open very slowly. Jack ducked in, and although we were all sitting right in plain view, he turned and closed the door as if he had just entered a room filled with sleeping children. Then he walked on the balls of his feet toward our bedroom, not acknowledging us, not even looking our way. As an added element to this strange attempt at being inconspicuous, he was wearing a brand-new, bright yellow shirt.

He didn't make it halfway across the room before Dad pounced from his chair like a bobcat from the bushes. He lowered his shoulder, head down, and barreled into Jack. Dad's arm began pumping like a flywheel, and despite the fact that I acted as soon as I realized what was happening, Dad had dealt Jack several blows before I wrapped him up and pulled him back. Dad's taut, wiry muscles strained against my arms. His face was blood red, veins swollen. But Jack slowly and deliberately climbed to his feet, like someone just getting out of bed. He wiped blood from the corner of his mouth. Dad's elbows thumped against my chest.

Jack's eyes never did connect with Dad's, or anyone else's, but I don't think it mattered. I'm sure he felt what I saw in Dad's look, and I realized that night how useless words can be sometimes. Dad's glare said it all.

Jack simply turned and walked out.

It would not have surprised me if we didn't see him for another three days. But the next morning, Jack was out in the fields before any of us, sporting a nasty bruise on one cheekbone. Nothing was said, and in

Dad's case the words that went unspoken solidified into a wall. He stopped talking to Jack. Instead, he told me what to tell Jack. I became the new buffer. And I resented hell out of it. For one thing, I was just as angry with Jack as Dad was. I didn't want to talk to him. But the work had to get done. So I gritted my teeth. I endured. But each time Dad called me over, my shoulders tightened up around my neck, and my jaw clenched.

Jack started sleeping in the old homestead house, where our haying, harvesting, and shearing crews slept when those seasons rolled around. This upset Mom, who simply wanted peace.

"You need to sit down and straighten this out," she told Dad. But she might as well have been talking to the wood stove.

For the rest of that summer, and into fall, Jack worked harder than ever. He ignored whatever temptations drove him to leave, and he only went to town when work required it. But the minute we sewed the last sack of wheat from harvest, he was gone. This time, his disappearance had a more permanent feel to it. We didn't hear a word for a week, then two.

For a brief time, I was relieved. But it didn't take long to see that the tension caused by Jack's presence was nothing compared to what his absence brought. With more work, Dad became a tyrant in the fields. We needed help, but for months, instead of hiring an extra hand, he held out hope that Jack would return. And Mom felt the same way. So we worked seven days a week, dawn to dusk, and still couldn't keep up. The worry that we were all accustomed to in my father transformed into anger at the slightest wrong turn by a cow, or the appearance of a rain cloud. His weathered face became drawn, the tanned skin sagging, his blue eyes murky.

I suppose I was too young to see that after losing two children, my parents simply couldn't bear the possibility that something tragic had also happened to Jack. All I could see was that now that I was the oldest, I was catching the worst of whatever evil now inhabited my family.

The worse it got, the more I questioned my decision to stay. The more I sneaked off to the barn and rocketed fastballs off the wall, or dug up the ticket to St. Louis, and the pamphlets of other cities. And eventually, the more I hated my brother.

The first news finally arrived in the form of a telegram.

> **Joined the army. Don't know where I'll be stationed. I'm fine.**

When Mom read this, her initial reaction was to storm from the house, grab a chicken, and chop its head off. But over the next few days, her smile came a little easier, and I even caught her humming to herself one morning. She was clearly relieved to know Jack was all right.

It was harder to tell how Dad felt about it. "At least he's fighting for his country," he said one day, to himself. So I guess he was relieved in his own way. But he remained as grim and focused as he had been. Always expect the worst.

I was furious. First of all, the telegram asked nothing about how my parents or any of the rest of us were. But most important, Jack made no apologies. He must have known how his disappearance and this news would affect us all. But he apparently didn't care. It seemed to me that in Jack's mind, he'd left with best wishes and a handshake. The one good thing that came out of it was that Dad finally hired another hand. I was temporarily soothed.

But we heard nothing more for another six months. We had no idea where Jack was. We scanned the *Ekalaka Eagle* each week, taking a more vested interest in news about the war, which until then had seemed almost fictional, like a novel in installments. And we held our breath each time we opened the mail sack.

Finally, an envelope in Jack's tiny, deliberate hand arrived from France. The letter was short, a half page, and again it contained very little news. The line that drew the most interest was, "Don't worry. I'm not close to the fighting. I'm stationed in a supply unit miles from the front."

Mom began writing regularly—she sat at our worn dining room

table and crafted long, detailed letters filling Jack in on the livestock and the crops, and news about our neighbors—who had died, or left, or been discreetly shipped off after a case of loneliness. She asked him questions, probing for information. But we only received one more letter from Jack. Although it mentioned nothing of Mom's letters, and answered none of her questions, he did ask how everyone was doing. And he mentioned a girlfriend, which made a big impression on my brother Bob.

Bob buried his pitchfork into the haystack, then jumped, putting all his weight on the handle, prying a tangle of gray hay from the center. "You think Jack's going to marry that gal?" he asked.

"Hard to say," I answered.

"She sounds real nice." Bob pressed on, and I realized that he had invented this detail, as Jack hadn't said a word about the woman other than that she existed. We didn't even know her name.

"Bet you a nickel he marries her," Bob said to me.

"Blake, you goin' on ahead?" Dad muttered impatiently.

"I was just about to do that." I tossed one last forkload of hay into the wagon, then planted my fork in the hay.

"Bet you a nickel Bob's going to marry that gal," Bob said to Dad.

"If you had a nickel, I might take you up on that, partner," Dad answered brusquely. "Let's just get this work done. What do you say?"

I whistled for Nate, who trotted out from behind the stack.

Ahab inched gingerly across the frozen river. I led him, keeping the reins taut but not hurrying him.

The cattle huddled close to the river, their tails to the wind, their backs covered with snow blankets. Some lingered along the bank, looking for a break in the ice. I pushed the herd toward the river, covering my frozen nose with a gloved hand. The snow had let up, but a few thick flakes wafted to the ground. I chopped holes in the ice, and the cattle pushed their noses into the freezing river. Steam rose from their nostrils.

Mounting Ahab, I heard the clatter of the wagon. I looked downstream to see the straining team climb the bank. The sound perked the cattle's ears. They lumbered toward the wagon, some trotting, their heavy skulls swinging from side to side. They crowded around the clumps of hay that Dad launched from the bed. I guided Ahab through the cluster of snow-covered backs, dismounted, and tied the reins to the wagon. Then I joined Dad in the bed, grabbing a pitchfork.

I caught Dad glancing toward the house several times, although we couldn't possibly see that far through the drifting snow.

"She'll be all right, Dad."

He didn't answer. But for the rest of the morning, he tried to disguise his frequent glances.

We scattered hay along the river, leaving clusters of munching cattle. I hopped off the wagon, running in place for a second or two to warm up. I pulled myself into Ahab's saddle, then galloped toward the next pasture. Nate trotted alongside, tongue hanging loose, steam rolling from between his teeth.

For every bit of plodding predictability that you get from a herd of cattle, you can expect twice as much skittishness and lack of common sense from a flock of sheep. I found all seventy of ours tightly crowded into the corner farthest from the river, completely exposed to the wind. They had drifted with the breeze, although thirty yards from where they stood was a small grove of cottonwoods that would have provided perfect shelter.

I cut between the flock and the fence, telling them how stupid they were, but mostly hoping I wouldn't find any corpses crushed by the cluster. The sheep milled away from the fence, their thick woolly coats dirty gray up to the snow on their backs. They moved along the fence line like a low fog bank. Thankfully, none had been trampled.

About halfway to the river, a young lamb on the opposite side broke away from the flock. She scampered unprovoked toward the middle of the pasture, her rear hooves pounding the powdery snow. I was pinned against the fence, so I couldn't make a move to go after her. But I assumed she would stop and wander back to the flock anyway. However, Nate started after her, and instead of turning her back, he scared her further away. I whistled for Nate, but six more ewes followed the lamb, and this got Nate excited. He chased after them. I swore, nudging Ahab through the flock. Then I took off after the lead.

Ahab snorted, trying to catch his breath as we cut through the icy air. We overtook the six, who turned back as soon as we passed them. Nate cut back to herd them toward the flock. I hoped the lead would follow, but she was too far ahead to notice. As we closed in on her, Ahab picked up speed. Within ten yards of the ewe, I shouted, and a rush of cold air filled my chest. I coughed and pounded my ribs, trying to relieve the burning in my lungs.

Ahab overtook the ewe, but the minute he did, she skidded to a stop. She circled behind us, then took off in the same direction. I gritted my teeth, prodding Ahab's flanks, although he'd already jumped ahead. "Get back here," I shouted.

But the ewe raced on, unaffected by the cold. Ahab grunted with every stride as the freezing air stung his lungs. It took another thirty yards to catch her again. I tried approaching from the opposite side. But the second we drew even, her head dropped, and her front legs stiffened. She cut behind Ahab, and bolted ahead again before I could even tug at the reins.

The ewe emitted a confused, gurgling "Baaaah" as she rushed by our left side. Ahab shook his head, as if he took the utterance personally. I swore, because I did take it personally. Then I raked my boots along Ahab's ribs.

We went through the same routine twice more, with both sheep and horse slowing a little each time. Usually, I would not have bothered with this chase. Deep down, I knew it was a waste of time. With so much around me feeling so much out of my control, I was determined to prove I had control over this one small situation. But this determination weakened as my face became more numb. I wiped snow from my eyes and couldn't even feel my glove move across my skin.

The fourth time the ewe circled behind us, I reined Ahab in sharply and shouted, "All right, run away, you bastard. And don't come back." I felt like a fool yelling at an animal out in the middle of nowhere. But the anger burned like a chunk of coal in my chest as I turned Ahab around. And then I heard laughter.

Next to the flock, Bob stood in the wagon, buckled over and pointing. As I approached, his laugh echoed past me, and my ears warmed. But when I looked up, I realized he wasn't pointing at me, but behind me.

"Blake, you got yourself a friend," he shouted.

"Quiet, Bob," Dad told him.

I didn't even have to look. I realized from Bob's laughter that she was following me back to the flock. "You stupid goddam sheep," I muttered. I wheeled Ahab around and chased the ewe for a few strides. Then I stopped, turned around, and continued my humiliating return to the flock, with the ewe trotting along behind me.

I buried my shovel deep into the pile of corn and flung the feed out over the sheep's backs.

"Blake!" Dad scolded.

I ignored him, filling my shovel again. I sniffed and heaved the second shovelful out over the flock, dotting their snow-covered backs with yellow pellets.

"Son, you're not going to do much good taking it out on those poor animals."

"They don't know the difference."

"Well, they don't give a damn about your problems, either. But we don't need them digging in the snow for every kernel of that feed. It's going to freeze their noses up and keep 'em hungry besides."

I buried my shovel one more time and cocked my arms.

"Blake!" Dad warned.

I swung the shovel, and just as the corn flew out in a yellow arch above the sheep, Dad grabbed the shovel, shouting, "Stop it now. Goddamit!"

The shovel jerked from my grasp, and because I was already off balance from the motion, I nearly fell. I caught myself by propping my hand against the side of the wagon. Dad glared at me, and I met his gaze head-on. We stared each other down for thirty seconds, and the anger swelled a little more in my chest as each second passed. Dad shook his head.

Bob, who was sitting in the driver's seat, clapped a glove to his mouth, trying to muffle a laugh. "Little Bo Peep," he muttered.

I went for him, and the next thing I knew, a gloved hand smacked me across the cheek. I froze. I couldn't move. My cheek stung, and I wanted like hell to hold my hand to it. My father had never hit me before. My jaw stiffened. I heard Bob sniffle behind me.

"I'm sorry, son. But goddamit . . ." Dad stood there looking at me, but he finally turned his back, unable to continue. "Goddamit . . ." he repeated.

"Your turn." Bob lay sprawled on the floor, an old coffee can full of marbles in front of him.

I lowered *The Red Badge of Courage* from my face, still angry from that morning. "You think I can't keep track of a two-man rotation? I know it's my turn." My jaw was sore, stiff, my pride still bruised. Dad had not mentioned the incident again.

"Boys!" Dad was planted at the window, looking toward Alzada.

I stood and laid my book down, then bundled up, donning my

wool coat and cap, and my gloves. I grabbed our two largest wooden milk buckets and stepped outside. The snow had stopped for the moment, but it had snowed off and on all day, and would likely start again. Our pastures glistened with white, and the clouds mirrored the downy blanket they had created.

I took a deep breath, smelling nothing but the sweet scent of clean, cold air. But I was in no mood to appreciate it. I tromped into the yard, set the buckets down, and scooped snow into them. Once they were full, I straightened my back and turned an eye toward the road. I saw no sign of anyone, so I hauled the buckets inside, setting them with a clump next to the wood stove.

Dad paced, making a strained attempt to not look out the window. Finally, he gave up pretending and parked in front of the frosted pane.

He had reason for concern. In that previous brutal winter, several people had frozen to death in the county. In the worst of conditions, the trip from Alzada took a couple of hours. Mom had planned to stay until noon. It was now four o'clock.

Because Dad and I had not exchanged a word since that morning, I didn't let it show, but I was just as concerned as he was. I scooped snow from the buckets into two large pots on the stove. Then I added wood to the fire, bent my head over the pot, and watched as the cast iron warmed. The snow turned a dull silver around the edges before dissolving.

"Here comes somebody!" Dad shouted, half standing. His body coiled, as if he was going to run right out the door. But he didn't move. He studied the horizon. "There's two horses," he announced.

"Two?" I couldn't maintain my indifference at the prospect of Mom returning. I moved to the window.

"Yeah." Dad took a step, and I thought he'd really leave this time. But he stayed at the window, rubbing his neck. "Gary must have decided to ride along with them to make sure they got back all right."

"Probably," I agreed. Bob joined us at the window. "Does that look like Gary?"

Hard to tell," Dad said. "They're not close enough." The snow started drifting across the window again.

Dad rushed over and grabbed his coat, with Bob right on his heels. "You comin', Blake?"

"Nah, I'll wait." Although I was happy Mom was back, I didn't see much point in rushing out into the cold just to say hello a half minute sooner. I pulled my gloves on and emptied the pots of boiling water into our big metal tub. Then I dumped snow into the pots, which hissed on the stove.

Outside, moments later, there was a hell of a chatter, then feet stomping, and a round of laughter. A rush of cold air hit me as the door flew open. Dad burst in.

"Look who's here!" Dad's cheeks were as red as a bad sunburn. He stepped to one side.

"Jack?" I stood transfixed. Jack stood proud and tall in an olive-green uniform, his cheeks flushed, his nose running. As much as I hated my brother, I didn't realize how deep it was rooted until I saw him standing there in our doorway. I turned back to my pot of water to hide my face. Nevertheless, the sight of my older brother also sent a strange thrill through me. The mixture of these emotions left me paralyzed.

"That's a hell of a welcome," Jack said. "Come on, little brother." I heard his footsteps moving toward me. "I been out there protecting you from all those enemies." Jack's jovial, lighthearted tone was completely new, unfamiliar, and hard to gauge. "Come on, Blake. Didn't you miss me?"

I shrugged.

"Ah, don't worry, Jack. Blake's had a bad day," Dad said. "Come on, Blake. Don't spoil a good thing here."

I kept my back to the whole scene, feeling betrayed by my father. Mom and Muriel came in, stomping the snow from their boots. They made a beeline for the wood stove. I moved out of their way, and Jack joined them. They all warmed their hands.

I was overwhelmed by the power of my anger. For the past year, every blister, every pulled muscle, and every bruise I'd sustained in my work on the ranch had been magnified by the knowledge that Jack's absence was partly to blame. My tongue was lodged hard against my teeth. I felt as if I would be better off leaving the house.

Jack's olive-green overcoat stretched to his knees. His earlobes were shiny red beneath his watch cap, and the uniform made him look taller, although we still stood eye-to-eye. His left arm was in a sling.

"What happened, son?" Dad asked.

"Ah, it's nothing," Jack said, lifting the arm slightly. "I'd rather not talk about it."

"Oh, sure, sure." Dad nodded.

I felt dizzy. We had just endured the most horrendous year and a half of our lives, a year and a half of lost livestock, frayed nerves, strained backs, and constant worry, and here stood the cause of much of it, receiving a hero's welcome. I thought of how often I had tempered my desire to lash out at my father, and that while I had quietly devoted my life to this place, my brother had betrayed us all, and now he was the savior.

"Who's ready for a bath?" Dad asked as he dumped the last two pots of boiling water into the tub.

"You must be reading my mind," Jack said, laughing.

"Muriel, you go after Jack," Mom said. "Then I believe I'll have to take a turn. That hot water would feel awful good about now."

Jack pulled the old cotton curtain around the tub, and his clothes dropped to the floor. I resented even this, his gall of climbing into the bath, as it had always been traditional in our family that the kids went first. Not only was he not paying for his betrayal, but he was asking for special treatment, and getting it. Dad fired question after question at Jack, as we listened to the water splashing, and as Jack answered them in his new character—this confident, joking manner—the laughter filled the room, pushing me further into the corner.

Steam rose above the curtain. Mom and Muriel shed their coats, and huddled closer to the fire as Bob tromped outside and filled the wood buckets again, then emptied them into the pots. Mom took a couple of bricks from the top of the wood stove and laid them on the floor. She took off her boots and laid her stockinged feet on the bricks, lifting a toe that stuck through a hole in her sock. "Mmmm," she sighed.

Jack stayed in the bath forever, and the banter continued.

"So was there a good turnout?" Dad asked Mom.

"There sure was." Mom rubbed her hands together. "Especially considering this storm."

"I even got a chance to vote," Jack shouted above the sloshing water.

"Who'd you vote for?" Bob asked.

"I'll tell you one thing, I sure didn't vote for that Socialist Rankin."

I looked at Mom, who idolized Jeanette Rankin, the first woman ever elected to Congress. But the mood could not be spoiled by anything.

"That woman voted against the war, can you believe that?" Jack shouted. "Of all the crazy things that happen in Washington, that's got to rank right up there with the craziest. She was the only one."

Mom shook her head again, but she had a slight smile on her face.

"Anyway, enough about politics," Jack continued. "I'm just giving you a hard time, Mom. I know she's your hero."

"Yes," Dad agreed. "Yeah. Let's talk about something else."

"All right . . . well, since you opened the door there," Jack said. "How much land we got now? You guys buy any more land?"

The question seemed odd, and out of place, but the pause that it brought was only brief, as it seemed that everyone was willing to over-look everything on this day.

"Yeah, actually," Dad said. "Yeah. We did get some more land."

"The reason I'm asking," Jack said, "is that I got an announce-ment." He paused, amid a flurry of splashing water.

"Well, don't keep us hanging here. What is it?" Dad scooted to the front of his chair, like an anxious kid.

"You're gonna marry that gal, aren't you?" Bob squealed.

Jack laughed loud and long. "You got it, Bob. You're right. She'll be here in a few weeks."

"That's great!" Dad exclaimed. Muriel started jumping up and down. And Mom was beaming, her face flushed.

But I didn't really hear the part about the wife so much. I was more focused on the part about "a few weeks." Up to that point, I assumed that Jack was just home for a visit, on leave.

"Are you staying?" I asked. "Are you planning to stay?"

"Hell, yeah," Jack said. "I'm done. I'm home."

I turned to Dad. "Are you going to let him stay here?"

There was a short pause as my father frowned at me, and everyone else stopped what they were doing.

"Why not? Blake, what's gotten into you? Of course we are. You know as well as anyone that we can use the help. Besides, he's going to have a family."

Finally, we could hear Jack climb from the tub. "Damn, Blake, you are in a bad mood," he said.

A silence settled into the house. For several seconds, no one spoke or moved. Only a slight crackle of fire from the wood stove echoed through the room. But Jack started laughing, quietly, from behind the curtain. He pulled his clothes on, still laughing. "Damn," he said. "I forgot how grumpy living out here makes people. I might have to think twice about this."

Dad laughed nervously, and the rest of the family looked at me with wide eyes, as if they had no idea what to expect from me, as if I was a different person than I'd been that morning, and every other day of the sixteen years they'd known me. For the first time in my life, I felt like a stranger in my own home. I felt as if I was the only one there who was looking at the picture that was our family and seeing the opposite of what everyone else saw.

I now know that I was just too young to realize how much it meant to my parents that Jack had come home. I was too young to realize how many people didn't get to enjoy a similar scene during those years. I was too young to know how lucky we were.

So I stood in the middle of that room, staring at the floor, feeling all eyes on me, humiliated, with my brother's quiet laughter only adding to the humiliation. I turned and walked back to the corner.

There was little else said. Muriel took her bath. To my relief, when Jack went to bed, he said he would sleep in the old homestead house. As the water in the tub cooled, and Mom prepared to take her turn, Bob turned from his marbles.

"Your turn," he said.

I shoved a finger down between my neck and the new starched collar that rubbed like sandpaper against my skin. I loosened my tie.

Jack punched me in the shoulder. "You look pretty spiffy there, little brother."

I rolled my eyes, and turned away from him. The train station was quiet. Although the cold had broken, it was not a good time to travel with the heavy snow. It was also several weeks before the holidays. So our family accounted for almost half of the people waiting for the 47 Line to arrive from the East.

We were all wearing our finest clothes, as Jack and Rita's wedding was planned for just a few hours after she arrived. But because I had grown three inches, I was the only one with a new suit.

The three weeks since Jack's return had been horrible. Although the subject wasn't one I put much thought into at the time, Jack's absence had affected his position to take over the ranch. By the singular act of coming back home, Jack had stepped back in front of the line. Not only that, but by bringing a wife into the picture, he had strengthened his hold on the position. Subconsciously, I think I realized that the reward for my loyalty to the ranch and my family would be a polite, thankless escort to my old place in line.

On the other hand, it was the first time since we'd lost George and Katie that my parents seemed relatively happy. Jack's status as a war veteran inspired a sense of pride in them. And Jack surprised me by not taking advantage of his celebrity to avoid working. As soon as his unexplained wound healed, he took to the fields early each morning. But I was skeptical of the whole "new man" routine. I had a strong feeling that Jack wasn't giving us the whole story.

"How much longer?" Bob asked, tugging at his jacket sleeves, which were just barely long enough.

"Any time now," Jack said. "Just hold your horses there, partner." He scuffed Bob's head.

Moments later, the faint trail of smoke appeared in the distance. Jack moved to the end of the platform, leaning so far forward that he was in danger of falling. He stood on his toes. I'd never seen him so excited. My parents stood right behind him. And Bob and Muriel just behind them. Only I hung back, thinking that as unpleasant as this was, I couldn't let my mood affect an occasion that was so important to everyone else.

The train grew, its flag of smoke unfurling behind it. And the closer it got, the more animated Jack became. He bounced up and down at the knees.

The locomotive slowed, easing toward us, and then it passed, and then a few freight cars passed, and finally the passenger cars passed. Jack ran alongside, jumping to try and see inside. There appeared to be less than ten passengers on the train. It stopped, and the conductor opened the door, and two people stepped off, and then I saw why Jack was so excited. I understood immediately.

It wasn't that Rita was beautiful, although she was about as pretty as any woman I'd ever seen. Her face was round, with broad features, full lips, and big green eyes. A band of freckles crossed her cheeks, from one ear to the other. She wore a wide-brimmed hat, green with a tiny green rose tucked against the crown, lying along the brim like a tired baby.

Rita also had perfect teeth. But what got me was the way she looked at everyone. Her eyes had an open quality, a straightforward sincerity, that had a powerful effect. As Jack introduced Rita to each member of the family, her eyes took that person in like a warm pool. She engulfed each of us with a look that oozed with curiosity and a willingness to welcome, and to be welcomed.

I stood there feeling as if I had just run several miles. As if breathing was an ability I had been very capable of at some time in the distant past. A lost talent. And then it was my turn. Rita took my hand, saying, "Blake, I've been so anxious to meet you. I've just been so excited to meet all of you."

And she whirled around, turning those incredible eyes to each of us, in turn, and I had still not moved, or breathed, or spoken. From that first moment, I was hopelessly in love.

4

summer 1921

Pioneer Days was an annual event that drew a huge crowd, not only from Carter County but from the surrounding areas, including South Dakota and Wyoming. In 1920, nearly a thousand people made the trip, and we expected about the same the next year, despite the huge number of homesteaders that had packed up their belongings and moved on.

The Homestead Act and a vigorous campaign by the railroads had brought hordes of adventurous souls from the east to our little corner of Montana. And for a while, the land had played a cruel trick. From 1910 to 1917, all the propaganda that had been spread about this area's fertile soil was supported by record rainfall, as well as milder winters. A man named Campbell proposed a ridiculous theory that abundant years were progressive, with the abundance increasing each year. There were plenty of people naïve, or perhaps dreamy, enough to believe it, and the evidence had even the skeptics considering that he might be onto something.

So the honyockers rumbled out in massive numbers, made a few dollars, and while they carried on about how generous the land was, those of us who knew better could do nothing but nod and hope that once Montana showed its true face, it would be gentle about it.

Instead, in 1918 and 1919, we suffered through less than ten inches of moisture. That was hard enough on the people who were just hanging in there. But it was actually the winters that caught our new Montanans off guard. They were willing to work hard, and we rarely heard complaints about having to pound away at the rock-hard gumbo just to break a furrow or two. What they weren't prepared for was snow piled as high as their heads, or cold air that froze their tears to their faces. They didn't expect to spend days at a time just sitting, waiting for the subzero temperatures to break. And they didn't expect the devastating effect of being trapped in your own home—the cabin fever, the loneliness. Scores of banks—nearly half—all over Montana and the Dakotas had closed. The population of Carter County had decreased by a quarter. So we did what our people had always done during troubled times. We gathered.

Dad covered the two miles from our ranch to Albion quickly, parking the pickup amongst the herd of similar mud-splattered vehicles, and we piled out. Albion consisted of only three buildings—the school, the post office, which also had a small store and rooms in the back for the postmaster-storekeeper, and the town hall. But the buildings weren't even visible in the midst of several massive canvas tents. We entered a sea of hats, bonnets, and oiled hair. Bob and Muriel tore past me, toward the tent where the carnival games were set up. Muriel had a bow stretching out behind her head like wings, and it had already started to come undone.

Scanning the crowd, I spotted a bright yellow shirt, like a lemon drop in a bowl of chocolates. Jack was playing horseshoes with Art Walters, Gary Glasser's son Steve, and a fellow I'd never seen. I headed over, hoping that Rita would also be in the vicinity. Despite all reason, my attraction to Rita had become almost uncontrollable. I could barely speak when she was around, but instead of trying to avoid her, I migrated in her direction at the slightest hint that she was nearby. As I approached the horseshoe pits, I spotted Rita from the corner of my eye.

"Who's winning all the money here?" I asked the horseshoe pitchers.

Jack tipped his hat and tossed a shoe, laying it about two inches from the stake.

"Does that answer your question?" Art asked, smiling.

"Hi, Blake." The singsong greeting tickled my ears from behind, and my head went light. I turned.

"Oh, hello, Rita." I crouched down next to her, acting surprised to see her, my face immediately filling with blood.

"You going to play some baseball today?" she asked.

"That's probably the only reason he showed up," Jack said.

I swallowed, smiling shyly. Despite the fact that I was completely leery of Jack, we had settled into a fairly peaceable existence. And the main reason was Rita. From the moment she stepped off the train, and she and Jack exchanged vows, Rita had won the hearts of my family. And the effect she had on Jack was fairly dramatic. Jack built a small house for the two of them as soon as weather permitted. And Rita showed a decorative touch, making the tiny cabin a comfortable haven from our house when things got testy. The only drawback was that Rita loved cats, and she brought two of the mousers from the barn into their home, not paying any attention to their genders. Soon the place was overrun with cats.

Among the members of my family, I was the most skeptical toward my brother, but after a year of Jack working harder than he ever had, and even showing signs of sociable behavior, even I had to admit he'd changed. Still I wasn't convinced that it would last. For one thing, he had developed an obsession with the get-rich schemes that were often advertised in the *Eagle*, or in catalogues he'd pick up in town. Jack ordered pamphlets and books by the score, and it seemed that every week he had a new plan.

First he ordered a case of some kind of medicine—an ointment that smelled of oranges and supposedly provided instant relief for everything from arthritis to yellow fever. We all tried it, of course. I rubbed it on a knee I banged against the corral one morning, and it didn't do a damn thing. But Jack pressed several people into buying the stuff, and before long he'd ordered two more cases. I don't know whether he ever sold another bottle, but it wasn't long before he was on to the next scheme. He bought two cases of yo-yos, apparently overlooking the fact that most people could barely afford food for their kids, much less toys. He became a representative for a wool company, selling clothing and blankets. This was one arrangement that showed promise, but it seemed that even in the cases where he started to show a profit, Jack lost interest before he could benefit, moving on to something new.

That day, he had what he was sure would be the breakthrough item. He had ordered four boxes—ten in each box—of lightning rods. He was going to set up a table and sell them that afternoon.

To the rest of the family, Jack's interest in these schemes was a mild annoyance. It seemed to be wasted money in their eyes. But to me, it represented something more, something fundamentally unchanged about Jack. To me, it meant that at his core, he still didn't want to be here. That something about life on the ranch would never be comfortable to him. I suspected that his commitment to the ranch was only temporary.

Jack's return, and the events that occurred while he was gone, had also left me feeling very differently about being on the ranch, and about devoting my life to it. I had written a tentative letter to Mr. Murphy, the baseball scout, telling him that I was considering taking him up on his offer. He wrote back immediately, saying he would welcome the opportunity to give me a tryout. But I put him off, giving him whatever excuse I could think of. The real reason, of course, was that I couldn't just up and tell everyone that I was going to St. Louis to try out for the Cardinals. I had to have a reason to go down there. But the primary mental barrier was that I didn't want to make a fool of myself. I didn't know if I was any good. I managed to talk my neighbors into letting me pitch in a few of the local games. And I pitched fairly well. But I had a feeling that in order to make an impression on Mr. Murphy, I would have to be much better than anyone out here.

"I heard they're going to ask you to pitch today, Blake," Steve Glasser said.

"Yeah?" I didn't do a very good job of hiding my enthusiasm, my voice rising.

Jack chuckled. "The way Blake's been pounding down the wall in our barn, they better let him pitch or I'll have to drive him home right now."

I felt myself blush, trying not to look at Rita, as I could feel her eyes on me.

"You guys finished putting up hay yet?" Steve knocked his horseshoes together, cleaning the dirt off, then threw a nice spinning arch that landed like mud just short of the stake. Steve had one eye that was a little off center, staring absently off to one side. He aimed his good eye toward the stake. "Is that a point?"

"Don't think so," Jack said, bending over the pit.

"We got most of our hay up, but that's not saying much," I said.

"You're right about that," the stranger said.

"We haven't met, have we?" I stood and offered my hand. "Blake Arbuckle."

"Lawrence Andrews." Lawrence shook hands as if it was the most important thing he could possibly be doing at that moment, looking me square in the eye. I felt as though we'd just completed an important business transaction. He stepped back and settled his broad, bony hands onto his hips in an effort to look relaxed.

"So you two are brothers, are you?"

Jack and I nodded, not looking at each other.

I asked Lawrence Andrews the most common question heard around our county with so many newcomers around. "Where you from?"

"Nebraska, but we live just the other side of Belle now, near the river."

"Quite a trip from here," I said.

"Yeah, well, I left yesterday afternoon and stayed at the Roberts road ranch last night."

It was Lawrence's turn to pitch, and he planted his left foot even with the stake, stepped stiffly out with his right, then swung his right arm back and then forward without the slightest bend of the elbow, like a pendulum. It seemed that none of the joints halfway down any of his limbs worked. The wobbly shoe landed on its side then rolled away from the pit. It was, without a doubt, the least graceful act I ever witnessed. From the corner of my eye, I could feel Jack's gaze on me, and I had to turn my head, knowing that I would have to stifle one of those explosive bursts of laughter if I glanced his way.

"How is that road ranch doing, anyway?" I asked. "I wouldn't think they'd be getting much business with everyone either broke or buying vehicles."

Lawrence tossed his second shoe, this one soaring with less wobble but no better results. "As a matter of fact, not too well. They're talking about buying more land, going back to ranching." He stepped away from the pit, surveying his tosses with a calculating expression, as if he might figure out what he did wrong if he studied it long enough. "Or they might move to town. They were in Oregon for almost a year after Sophie's husband passed on. So they're having a hard time getting back into the routine anyhow."

"Sophie's husband?"

Lawrence nodded. "Cancer." He brushed his hands together, then looked them over. He spotted a smudge on the edge of his palm, and he licked his thumb and rubbed the spot clean. Then he took a sudden, almost threatening step toward me. A flicker of a smile flashed across his face. "I'm going to marry her," he said.

Lawrence came so close to me that I had to stiffen my muscles to prevent myself from stepping backward, and the others stopped what they were doing and turned toward Lawrence. We were not so much surprised by the announcement as by the peculiarity of its delivery. My first instinct was to ask whether Sophie knew about this plan, but I had a feeling Lawrence wouldn't get the joke. He was so proud.

"Look, Blake." Lawrence held his horseshoes out. "Why don't you take over for me here? I'm not much good at this anyway. And I want to go see what's cooking."

"All right." I took the shoes, feeling a sudden admiration for Lawrence's modesty. "Nice meeting you, Lawrence. And congratulations."

The others offered Lawrence good wishes.

"Thanks, fellas," he said.

I watched Lawrence, his long gangly frame teetering like a newborn colt's through the crowd. "Have you ever seen a prouder groom-to-be?" I asked.

Art Walters, who had been silent since the announcement, looked from the side of his eyes at me. "That fella is in for trouble," he said.

We all smiled, a bit uncomfortably, knowing that Art's one attempt at marriage had fallen short of a year. "Why's that, Art?"

"Any man who's that worshipful of his bride is gonna be gathering eggs before the ink is dry on the marriage license," he said.

We all laughed.

Art sniffed. "You can laugh, but take my word on that. Just wait and see." And with that, Art tossed a perfect ringer.

It was an ideal day for the fair. The temperature topped out at eighty degrees, with no wind. The mosquitoes were light. I bathed in the heat, playing horseshoes for a while before partaking in the tents bursting with homemade food. I wandered among the displays of livestock and children's art and always, always, maintained a vigilant awareness of where Rita was. I couldn't help it. Jack had even teased me about it on occasion, accusing me of being lovesick. He had no idea how right he was.

I noticed the endearing tilt of her head as she listened to my mother tell a story, and the way she relished a leg of fried chicken, or a piece of rhubarb pie. I noticed the elegant movements of her hands, no matter what she was doing. Even wiping the corner of her mouth with a napkin, Rita had a graceful air.

"You ready to play some ball, Blake?"

I dropped my horseshoe and followed Jack toward the two baseball fields that several of us had carved out of the sagebrush. We had stuffed six flour sacks with sand for the bases, and Steve Glasser cut a couple of wooden home plates. He sank them into the ground back-to-back, a little off center, so two games could be played in different directions without interfering with each other. He then rigged a couple of canvas tarps, like sails, to prevent balls from scooting past the catcher onto the other field.

There were coin tosses to decide which teams would play, and we ended up drawing Belle Fourche, while Capitol and Camp Crook took the other field. Our little community, which was about a fifth the size of Belle, had never beaten them that any of us could remember, so we stormed the field with a resolve to change history. I took my position at third base, and Jack started out catching.

Ever since I can remember, every baseball game between two of the communities out here starts out with an air of easy banter, with everyone acting as if they don't really give a damn who wins or loses. But nobody's really fooling anyone. The polite chatter usually lasts an inning or two; then the jaws set, the eyes narrow, and the spoken word takes on a harder edge.

Belle Fourche scored three runs against us in the first inning. We answered with three of our own on a solid, bases-loaded triple by Jack. And we scored two more in the second when Gary Glasser hit a grounder between the legs of Lawrence Andrews, who was as awkward in the field as he'd been in the horseshoe pits.

After Teddy Teagarten, Belle Fourche's blacksmith, hit a ball over everyone's head with two runners on, Belle Fourche led by a run, and our pitcher surrendered the ball, which took five minutes to find, to me. I trotted in from third base, and took a few deep breaths while I warmed up. I nodded to the next hitter.

I felt as if the desire of our entire community was being funneled toward me, and I discovered that I liked the responsibility. I liked the pressure. But in the fifth, my determination to live up to these expectations took over, and I started throwing too hard. I walked the first two batters, bouncing several pitches in the dirt. I took a short break, walking behind the mound, breathing deep, and when I returned to the rubber, I looked up to see Lawrence Andrews at the plate. He had shown little promise with the bat, so I felt myself relax a little. My first pitch to him was a good curveball, screaming toward the middle of the plate. Lawrence took a big swing, but when the ball broke down and away, he missed completely with a twirl that looked more like ballet than baseball. His bat was tipped at an angle, toward the sky, and one leg kicked up behind him. I had to bite my lip to keep from smiling as I took the throw from Jack.

I took a little something off the next pitch, and lost control of it, bouncing the ball a foot in front of the plate. The runners moved up one base, now standing on second and third. Jack held up his palm, encouraging me to relax, and I tried to talk myself calm before throwing again. The ball sailed toward the inside corner, and Lawrence twirled toward it. Somehow, the bat plunked its target, and the ball squirted along the bumpy ground, bouncing back and forth like a jackrabbit, toward Steve at shortstop. He crouched, but the ball caught the nub end of what had been a scrub of sagebrush. The ball bounded into left field, and both runners scored as Lawrence loped to first. In his excitement, he rounded the bag, looking bewildered about what he should do next. His pause gave our left fielder time to throw a strike to the first baseman, who tagged Lawrence on the thigh. Lawrence trotted off the field with a huge grin, not the least bit discouraged about getting thrown out. The Belle Fourche crowd was delirious, clapping him on the back and ruffling his oiled hair.

I took a deep breath, got my rhythm back, and retired the next two batters, striking out the last one. But with those two runs, we came to bat behind by one. Still, I was excited. The competition, the energy from the crowd, it all felt good. I was pitching well, and I knew that Lawrence's hit was a fluke. As I ran off the field, I glanced over at the crowd and saw Rita, who was clapping, and smiling at me. She waved when she saw me looking at her, and it made my heart swell a little.

"What the hell happened there?" Jack stood next to me, his face toward the ground. At first I thought he was angry, but a glance at his expression told me otherwise. He was laughing.

"I don't think that guy could hit his chest with his hand," he said, still laughing.

I chuckled. "Hell, his eyes weren't even open."

Jack spit into the dust, smiling, but his tone became businesslike again. "Yeah, well, let's beat these guys for once, huh?"

I nodded.

"Don't hold anything back."

A thin coat of dust gathered over the crowd as the game moved from inning to inning with no runs scored by either team. Jack, who had moved to shortstop, made an incredible diving catch of a shot up the middle by Teagarten. And we had a good laugh when one of my pitches got past Steve and hopped over the tarp, skipping onto the other field just as the batter there hit a grounder toward the second baseman. Both balls came toward him, from different angles, and he froze as if he'd just come upon a rattler.

But the highlight of the game came in the seventh inning, when Shag Tompkins hit a long fly ball to right field. Art Walters, whose legendary status in the community had nothing to do with his athletic ability, was standing out there with his back to the game, gazing at something. We all yelled, and Art turned just in time to see the ball coming right down at his head. His hands flew up in front of his face, and the ball bounced off his palms, and ricocheted directly into the front pocket of his overalls.

Art was looking around at the ground, crouching, trying to find the ball, when he suddenly spotted the dome of dusty white in his pocket. He plucked the ball from his overalls and held it up, proud as hell, as though he'd planned it that way. Our fans cheered as if a three-month drought had broken.

Shag argued briefly that the catch couldn't count, but he was laughing too hard to make a very convincing case for himself.

* * *

By the top of the ninth inning, I had not allowed any more runs, and we were ahead by one thanks to Jack's second triple of the game. Belle Fourche was up with one out and a runner on second. I walked the next batter, knowing that Lawrence was up after him. I felt confident that Lawrence couldn't repeat his earlier heroics, especially if I gave him my best curveball. So I took a deep breath, and bore down, snapping off a beauty. The ball dropped toward his shoes. Lawrence spun, his eyes clamped tightly shut. And in a miracle of almost religious proportions, the ball and the bat crossed the plate at the same moment, in the same place. A pock rang out, and the ball floated like a sick bird out over second base. Jack raced toward it and dove, but missed it by a foot. There was so much spin on the ball that it squirted past the charging center fielder. Both runners scored, and if Lawrence had run like anything other than a lame colt, he might have scored himself. But he stood with both feet on second base, too happy to care that he was perhaps the most comical sports hero in the history of Montana.

I shook my head, half angry but also amused. And as I tried to gather myself for the next batter, I caught a look from the crowd—an intense expression aimed right at me. Thinking it was Rita, I looked away immediately, knowing that a look from her right then would completely destroy my concentration. But as I wound up, my eyes quickly glanced that way again, and saw that it wasn't Rita at all. After I threw the pitch, and the batter swung and missed, I looked over again to see the same powder-blue eyes staring at me with an unnerving allure. I knew the face was familiar, but because I hadn't seen her for several years, it took me a second to recognize Sophie Roberts. She smiled, a smile so inviting that I blushed, quickly averting my eyes, remembering with some alarm that just a few hours before, I had learned that this woman was engaged to Lawrence Andrews. And then it occurred to me that he was standing behind me, and I realized that she wasn't even looking at me, but at her fiancé, the hero.

The whole exchange left me flustered, and I walked that batter. Jack trotted over from short.

"Where the hell are you?" He pointed at his head. "Is there something else you'd rather be doing?"

"I'm all right," I said impatiently.

"Yeah?"

I nodded. "Yeah. Come on. Let's get back to the game here."

Jack trotted back to his position. And maybe it was his intention, but I was annoyed enough that I struck out the next two batters with six pitches, firing the ball so hard that Steve kept taking off his glove and shaking his hand.

However, we failed to score in the bottom of the ninth, and lost by one run, much to the dismay of my teammates. To come so close to beating Belle Fourche for the first time ever was disheartening, and some of the players were angry enough to go off and pout for a while.

Despite the disappointment, I was feeling pretty good. I had pitched better than ever, and I was inspired by the experience. It had been a good, close game. And I felt confident enough now that I was ready to write to Mr. Murphy and let him know that I was ready to give it a shot. Part of me wanted to run home and write the letter that afternoon.

I saw a spot of yellow approaching from the corner of my eye, and I turned to find myself facing both Jack and Rita. Rita was beaming.

"Blake, you were great!" she said.

I nodded my appreciation, not wanting to look her in the eye and risk having all the blood in my body rise up into my head. "Not quite good enough," I said.

"Ah, hell," Jack muttered. "That guy's never hit a ball in his life. He just got lucky."

"That's right, Blake," Rita agreed. "You were great."

My face did turn red, and I was trying to think of something to say when an unfamiliar couple walked past us. The guy leaned toward his girlfriend, or wife, pointed at Jack with his thumb, and muttered, "That's the guy."

They kept walking, but Jack, after a confused glance at the guy, just pulled his mouth to one side and shook his head.

"Come on, Jack," Rita said, pulling at his elbow. "Let's get some food. We'll see you later, Blake." Jack walked away looking down, clearly chewing on what the guy had said.

I waved, standing quietly, shaking my head. But when I turned to get some food, I met the smiling face of Lawrence Andrews. His big, bony hand took mine and squeezed hard.

"Good game, Blake," he said.

"Thanks, Lawrence. I got to admit, I didn't think you had it in you." I smacked him on the back.

Lawrence laughed. "Thanks for hitting the bat for me," he said, and I found myself taking even more of a liking to him. Just then, Sophie Roberts sauntered up to his side, her head tilted toward her shoulder, one cheek rosy. She had hair the color of a crow's feathers, and it hugged her head in tight waves, sweeping just above one eye. I nodded to her, and was shocked to see her looking at me the same way she had been during the game.

"You know Blake Arbuckle, don't you, Sophie?" Lawrence gently placed a hand in the small of her back, and held the other hand out toward me.

"Yes, I do, although it's been a very long time," she said. "Nice to see you again, Blake. Nice job out there." She held out a hand that was slender but strong. And met me with that look—the inviting, vulnerable smile. After shaking her hand, I started to pull mine back, but Sophie held it for a second longer. She finally let go, but her fingertips brushed against my palm as I backed away, and a tingle skittered up my back like a waterbug.

"Thank you, Sophie," I said, blushing. "I'm sorry to hear about your husband. Lawrence just told me this morning."

She looked down and tipped her head to the other side. The sunlight flashed off her hair. "Well, it wasn't easy, I must say," she admitted. "But things are improving." She looked up at Lawrence, and smiled. He, of course, was beaming.

We exchanged a few more pleasantries, although I was unnerved by Sophie's intense gaze. I kept thinking it must be my imagination, but every time I let my eyes dart over in her direction, there it was—the suggestive, almost painfully suggestive, expression. My face felt like an oven, and I finally had to plant my eyes firmly on Lawrence, who seemed either oblivious or completely comfortable with Sophie's flirtatious manner. Finally, to my relief, he suggested that they go find something to eat. I stood, flustered, sweating, and watched them walk away, unable to stop myself from admiring the curve of Sophie's form. I tried one more time to believe that I was imagining things—that she couldn't have possibly been giving me the signal that I thought she was giving me. Just then, she turned her head, looking over her shoulder, and winked. I nearly fainted.

What followed was an evening of a delightful blend of food, dancing, and attention. I pondered the mystery of women—or more accurately, the mystery of love, and the dynamics between the sexes. I wondered how I could be oblivious to the smattering of single women in our county, but be completely smitten with a married one—not only a married one, but my sister-in-law. It made no sense to me that for the nearly three years Jack and Rita had been married, I had been unable to think of another woman. I had invented countless excuses to visit their humble house, despite my feelings about my brother, and often for just a brief glance at Rita. And now I wondered how Sophie, a woman who was seemingly happily engaged, would not feel strange about such bold attempts to flatter someone else.

My confusion was only confounded as the evening wore on. I gathered a plateful of chicken, roast beef, corn on the cob, and lettuce salad, and after I found a seat with my parents and started eating, I noticed that a lot of younger women slowed their pace as they walked by us. They smiled, or even spoke to me, complimenting my pitching, or they simply said hello. I was used to being fairly anonymous in crowds. People don't tend to notice a medium-height, round-faced, bowlegged man with thinning hair. So this newfound celebrity was uncomfortable.

But by the time the traditional Pioneer Days Dance began, I was starting to enjoy it. I shared a few snorts from the bottle under the seat of Steve Glasser's pickup, and when the dancing started, I was oiled up enough to overcome my usual shyness. I was thrilled to find that I didn't have to do much asking, which was always the hardest part for me. I danced until my legs ached. For a while, I forgot about Rita, and even lost track of where she was.

After a couple of hours of hard dancing, I needed a break, so I went out behind the hall to get some fresh air. I stood there, soaking in the pleasant sounds of the band from inside, and the shouts of everyone dancing, and the drunken chuckles from teenagers pulling bottles from under their dads' front seats, tipping them to their lips. I looked up at the clear sky and felt an inexplicable sense that this night was a turning point for me, with the confidence I'd felt on the diamond, and now this attention. I believed that my life was about to change. Oddly enough, just about the time that this thought entered my mind, I felt someone touch my arm. Looking down, I discovered Sophie and that alluring smile.

"Hello, Blake," she said, tilting her head. "Getting some air?"

I nodded. "Hi, Sophie."

She smiled, looking directly at me with those powder-blue eyes. I tried to think of something to say, but a series of prickly needles ran along my forehead, disrupting my efforts to think.

"Well, I hope you ask me to dance sometime before the night is over," Sophie said.

"Okay. Sure," I answered. "Yeah."

And then she leaned forward, rising to her toes, slipping her hand in mine as she also completely surprised me with a peck on the cheek. "See you," she said, twirling back toward the dance hall. She waved over her shoulder.

I stood there with my hand out, tingling from her touch. I didn't move for three songs. Until the blood had found its way back to my head, I didn't move. And of course, the minute I had my bearings back, I made a beeline back inside to find Sophie. But she and Lawrence were just leaving as I entered the hall. She waved discreetly. And I felt the force of disappointment, watching her back leave the building. But I floated on the current of that kiss, and I was eventually able to welcome the continuing invitations to dance.

For the first half of that evening, not only did I forget about Rita, but I didn't think about the ranch. Or Jack. I felt as if I had entered into a completely different world, and that I was the center of it. The dance lasted long into the night, and just as the band was about to wind down, I again felt a hand on my elbow. This time, I turned to find Rita's warm green eyes fixed on me with an earnest combination of fondness and curiosity. It took me back to the day she had stepped off the train.

"Blake, you haven't danced one single song with me."

"Well, let's go then." I pulled her to the floor, and we fell into an easy sway as the band played a waltz.

"What a day, huh?" Rita said.

I nodded, smiling. "It was great."

"You were great."

I blushed. "Well . . ."

"You were. Might as well enjoy it."

Suddenly a presence intervened, bumping me from behind. I turned to find the smiling face of my brother. "Hey, buddy. You having a good time?" he asked.

"Great," I answered.

"Okay," he echoed. "Me, too." He laughed, his head tilting back, and I could see from the droop in his eyes that he'd also had a few belts. More than a few.

Just then, the guy that had made a snide comment about Jack happened to swing by, his date in his arms. Just as Jack noticed him, the stranger said to his wife, "See what I mean?"

Jack whirled, and his mood immediately shifted. "Who the hell *are* you?"

The guy ignored him, dancing away. And when Jack started after him, I couldn't watch it happen. I let go of Rita.

"Blake, let him go."

But I grabbed Jack's arm. He turned and looked at me, not angry, but trying to pry himself loose. "I just want to know what he's talking about," Jack said.

The stranger, no doubt purposely, made his way within a few feet of us.

"People don't talk about people that don't do nothing," he uttered right near Jack's ear.

Jack's elbow jabbed me in the ribs, and he broke loose, lunging at the guy. I had a hand on my bruised ribs, so I couldn't respond right away. Jack got ahold of the stranger, and the next thing I knew, they were piled in a tangle of limbs in the middle of the dance floor.

Again, a hand gripped my elbow.

"Come on, Blake." Rita pulled. "Let's get out of here."

If it had been anyone else, I probably would have resisted. I probably would have worked myself free and tried to break up the fight. But I followed Rita without even thinking, and we zigzagged through the crowd, out into the clean, clear night. Word of the fight spread, and within thirty seconds, we were the only ones outside.

I leaned against the rounded fender of a Model T, holding a palm against my rib. Rita stood facing me.

"Are you okay?" she asked.

I nodded. "He caught me pretty good, but I'll be all right."

Rita folded her arms, looking with concern back toward the dance hall. It looked as if a part of her wanted to go back inside. But she forced herself to turn away, pointing her gaze down toward the dry ground. The music had stopped once the fight started, and it was actually quiet enough outside that I could hear the faint sound of the Little Missouri in the distance.

I thought it was odd at first that Rita wanted to leave, and that she brought me with her. I wasn't sure what to say, or do. I felt as if I was abandoning my brother.

Rita finally looked up at me, smiling a little sadly. She even looked slightly guilty. She shrugged. "I knew what I was getting into," she said.

But when she dropped her head again, I could tell that whether she knew it or not, Rita was at least partially blaming herself for what was going on inside. And again, I felt the need to say something, anything.

"He's always been this way," I finally muttered. "From as far back as I can remember."

Rita sighed, looking up again. She nodded.

"You all right?" I asked.

She nodded, taking a long, slow breath. "Yeah. I'm fine now. I just needed a few minutes. A little air." She rolled her shoulders a couple of times. And she looked up at me again, thoughtfully, as if she was trying to decide something. Finally, she spoke. "You know what that guy was talking about, don't you?"

I frowned. "No. Do you?"

She nodded, then tipped her head to the side and looked at me with a measured gaze. "You really don't?"

I shook my head.

"It's about George," she said. "Your brother."

I frowned again. "George?" My head was fuzzy from the booze, and I had to think for a moment. "You really think that's what he was talking about?"

Rita folded her arms, and looked down at the ground. She nodded. "I'm sorry. I shouldn't bring it up. But I thought you might . . . well, I thought you might know." She turned. "I think I should go back inside."

"No, wait." I grabbed her arm.

Now Rita broke free of my hold and turned again. "Blake, let's just drop it. It's just a rumor, you know? You know how people talk."

"No," I said again. "It's stupid. They shouldn't even be . . . I can't believe people would say that. I can't believe anyone would say that."

"Like I said, Blake. I shouldn't have brought it up. I'm sorry. Come on. Let's go back inside." She reached out for my hand. "Come on. Forget it."

I nodded. "Okay." But I walked in a daze.

And for the rest of the night, for the rest of the dance, although I still managed to have a good time, my mind kept going back to this rumor, baffled by the realization that people were still resorting to such cruel speculation about something that happened years ago. At the same time, my mind was reviewing the events of the evening we found George, and all that had happened since. And I hated the fact that, despite every part of me trying so hard to push the thought from my head, I couldn't.

That night, riding home in the back of the pickup, I lay on my back, staring at a coal-black sky that was filled from horizon to horizon with tiny stars. I felt the cool air wash over me, and smelled the sagebrush. And I lay there thinking that as much as I loved this land, this area that I called home, I wasn't sure how much longer I wanted to stay here. With the exhilaration of my experience pitching, and Jack's presence, and all that came with it, and considering the way I felt about Rita, I began to ponder the possibility that I would be better off somewhere else.

5

fall 1924

I've always dreamed of seeing more of the world. Despite my love for the land around me, I've always been curious about what else is out there. Some of my neighbors are content clinging to the prairie, with no curiosity at all about how other people spend their days. I suppose that most of these folks are simply happy enough or too busy with their lives to think about all that unexplored territory. But there are also those who talk with a sneer about city folks—rantings that are not usually based on firsthand experience, but assumptions, and hearsay.

I figure they're just scared—scared of a life they know nothing about. But it seems a waste to shut out half the world just because they wear softer pants. And I think it simply makes sense to say hello to someone who's sitting right next to you. As far as I know, there's no better way of getting to know them. So after my Pioneer Days experience, I looked for any chance I could find to make my way to St. Louis and meet up with Mr. Stanley Murphy.

My chance came in 1924, when we needed to ship a load of calves to Omaha. Neither Dad nor Jack was anxious to go, so I quickly volunteered. I contacted Mr. Murphy, who just happened to have someone else in Omaha that he wanted to get a look at that week. So once I knew the date I'd be there, he sent me the name of his hotel, and told me to contact him when I arrived. I told no one.

Dad and I moved the herd of calves to Belle Fourche, a three-day ride. We stabled them for the night at the stockyards next to the train station, and seventy-five calves and I caught the train at dawn the next morning. It was my first time on a train, and although I was twenty-two, I'm sure I was as big-eyed as a kid at his first fireworks show. I wore the suit I'd bought for Jack and Rita's wedding; the jacket was too tight, the sleeves a little short.

The trip took two days, with a stop in Chadron, Nebraska, to feed and water the stock. I barely slept from the excitement. Even during the dark hours, I pressed my face to the window, as the countless unfamiliar lives rushed past. The click, clack, pause, click, clack, pause of the wheels became such a part of the journey, like a heartbeat, that I didn't even hear it after a while.

I studied each town—homestead towns, mostly. There were usually just a few buildings—always a store, and a saloon or two, a post office, sometimes a hotel, a blacksmith, or a five-and-dime. But more interesting to me were the farms and ranches—the lone, miles-from-anything places like our own. I took a good look at each of these, trying to imagine as much as I could about the people who lived there. Some were easy—sod houses with chunks of earth hanging off, or crude ten-by-fourteen-foot shacks with oiled-paper windows, mud stuffed into the cracks, and a swaybacked mule out front. These belonged to the honyockers—the new settlers who were either already gone or nearly defeated, probably a winter or two away from being pushed eastward where they came from, or further west to another dream.

Soon after we crossed the border into Nebraska, the complexion of the land changed, as if state law demanded it. Pens filled with pigs crowded the grounds around tiny homesteads, and the fields were covered with either the stubble of freshly harvested cornstalks or the brown stalks themselves, wilting from too little water or too much sun. The rolling hills were gone. The land was completely flat, with such a lack of contour that the horizon seemed to be the only thing out there.

I ate in the diner car, eyes fixed on the panorama of scenery outside. The plates, silverware, and linen looked so delicate and fine that I was afraid of breaking them. So I ate carefully, feeling a bit sophisticated. I even ordered a glass of wine at dinner the first evening. But I didn't finish it, because I didn't want to fall asleep. I didn't want to miss a thing.

The stop in Chadron took nearly two hours. The calves stumbled down ramps, blinking in the daylight. But they were too tired to protest much, and the sight of water and hay shut up the few feeble complaints. They ate and drank at their leisure while I milled among them, checking for any sign of ill health while trying not to mess up my travel clothes. One calf had died, which made me angry, as I'd tried to talk Dad into leaving her behind. I hoped that whatever ailment had killed her wouldn't spread.

Halfway across Nebraska, I saw a house that made my eyes bulge. It was a big white clapboard house with neatly painted green trim around each door and window. A white fence made of broad planks surrounded the yard, and it had the first red barn I'd ever seen. In our country, no one had the resources to paint their barn, even if the idea occurred to them. I turned to the man next to me, who'd gotten on at Chadron and hadn't yet spoken to me. I pointed.

"Look at that house."

He glanced out the window with a look of utter boredom, his sagging, wet eyes hardly registering any sign of life. He shrugged. "I wonder how much corn whiskey that fella sold to pay for a place like that," he muttered.

I didn't realize he was joking, and I turned and studied the house. He couldn't be right, I thought. The house was not only big, but it showed the signs of care and grooming of someone who had great devotion to the good life. I thought about the only bootlegger I knew—Bert Walters, Art's brother, who lived in a ramshackle lean-to as far from the road as he could possibly get. And I secretly decided that this guy wasn't as smart as he thought he was.

"Are you from Nebraska?" I asked him.

"Hell no. I wouldn't live in this godforsaken country for all the steers in Texas." He laughed at his own joke, or wheezed, from deep in his soft chest. "I'm from St. Louis." He looked at me, only vaguely, and raised his forehead. "That's in Missouri."

I nodded. "Yeah, I know."

But despite being annoyed, the man's smug expression made me suddenly aware of my appearance. I realized that I probably looked and acted like exactly what I was—some young guy fresh off the farm, out in the world for the first time. I tugged self-consciously at my sleeves, at the same time resenting his superior attitude, and the fact that he made no effort to hide it. He wore a bowler and a well-tailored suit, complete with gold pocket-watch chain. His skin was as pale as milk.

"You a Dakota boy?" he asked.

I cringed at the word "boy," bit my tongue, and shook my head. "Nearly. Eastern Montana. Right in the southeast corner."

He nodded knowingly, his lower lip extended. "Nice country. Kind of dry, though."

"Yeah, more than ever the last few years."

"You know anyone in Broadus?"

"Sure. Quite a few people."

Well, despite the fact that he never dropped his little smirk, and despite my preoccupation with the scenery outside, my neighbor and

I ended up having a pleasant conversation. We had a few mutual acquaintances, and he shared my passion for baseball.

He was a farm machinery salesman, which explained why he'd been to my part of the country. His name was David Westford, and although I was a naïve farm kid, I had enough business savvy to sift through everything he said, to avoid falling into a line of questioning that might lead to promises I couldn't keep. But he didn't push me that hard anyway. Instead, we visited about our families, the Cardinals, and the upcoming elections.

David was from a huge mining family in Pennsylvania. He wasn't close to them, complaining that they all tried to take advantage of his success. He said he preferred St. Louis to his home state anyway. Before I knew it, we found ourselves in the outskirts of Omaha. Dusk had just settled, a very faint orange mist, and I could barely make out the silhouettes of buildings that were taller than any I'd ever seen. We climbed stiffly from the train, and David handed me his card with the name of his hotel scrawled on the back.

"This is your first trip to Omaha, am I right?"

I nodded.

"Well, I know some real nice girls, if you're interested." He raised his brow.

I blushed and thanked him, shaking his sweaty hand. And although I saw little chance that I would take him up on the offer, I tucked his card in my jacket.

That night I soaked in a city that was bigger than the combined size of every town I'd ever visited. It was a clear night, five or ten degrees warmer than it would be at home, and although I was exhausted, I wanted to absorb as much as I could before I collapsed.

I walked through downtown Omaha, and was struck by the shops—shops that sold only hats or only candy. I couldn't imagine how they stayed in business selling just one product. And the clothes on display in the windows! I wondered where people wore such clothes. But as evening fell, people wearing those very clothes filled the streets, strolling at a leisurely pace. I had to remind myself not to stare, especially at the women, who were glorious in their sleek dresses and stylish hats. I wanted to turn and follow them. Their faces were as smooth and clear as windows, as though they'd never seen an hour of sunlight. And their lips, painted red, looked like cherries in snow. I thought about David's offer, and the more of these beautiful women I saw, the more I considered calling him. But time passed, and my nerve faltered, and eventually I talked myself out of it.

On the streets, handbills were posted everywhere, and I stopped and read them all. Posters of Calvin Coolidge and John William Davis were pasted to walls and fences everywhere, as were pictures of the Nebraska gubernatorial candidates. And there were several other distinguished-looking candidates for lesser offices, looking stern and serious, with slogans circling their heads. There were bills for performances—music, theater, and dance, as well as ads for all kinds of household items, which reminded me of Jack. But one poster stopped me dead in my tracks. It was for a Negro League baseball game, a game between the Kanses City Monarchs and the Mobile Tigers, scheduled for eleven o'clock the next morning. I had a pencil and a notepad in my jacket, and I wrote down the details. I had called Mr. Murphy when I checked into my hotel, and we'd made arrangements to meet later in the afternoon. So I would easily be able to make it to the game.

Back at the hotel, I ate in the dining room—shrimp, breaded with crisp batter, and whipped potatoes, and buttery string beans. I'd never tasted shrimp, and although the slippery texture was strange at first, I immediately fell in love with the combination of intense fish flavor and butter-soaked flakes of breading. After a dish of chocolate ice cream, one of my favorite things, I retreated to my room bloated and content.

I took a bath in a real ceramic tub, and slid between sheets thick as cowhide. If I had wanted to make a phone call, all I had to do was go down into the lobby. In my room were electric lights, a toilet, and a sink with running water, none of which we had at home. And the next day, I would be handling the biggest business transaction of my life. But none of those things mattered that night. There were only two things on my mind as I lay on the verge of a deep sleep—my first professional baseball game, and my tryout.

At breakfast, the scrambled eggs looked as if the grease had been scrubbed off—they were as yellow as a new gold piece. I said a silent thank-you to Mr. Murphy for the dollar he had sent me to help pay for a little nicer hotel. The eggs tasted as good as they looked, with a hint of cheese. I held a copy of the *Omaha World-Herald* and reveled in learning yesterday's news rather than last week's.

I caught a carriage to the stockyards, where I met our buyer Mr. Tanner, a tall man with a friendly manner. He buried his fingers in the calves' coats, and lifted their upper lips, checking teeth. He kneaded their flanks and ran his hand along their ribs. I felt proud surveying the corral filled with plump calves pressed together into a massive brown hide. We had done well with this stock, thanks to a slight increase in moisture and some hard work. Mr. Tanner smiled broadly and nodded.

We weighed the calves, and after figuring the total, Mr. Tanner wrote a check. When I looked at the amount, my heart rose to my neck, and I pressed my thumb and forefinger hard together to make sure a sudden gust of wind didn't tear the slip of paper from my grasp. As soon as we shook hands and talked about what a pleasure it was to do business, I found a restroom, where I tucked the folded check into my boot.

I arrived at the baseball field nearly an hour early, so I got to watch the Tiger and Monarch players go through their warm-ups—stretching, running, and fielding grounders and fly balls. I sat in the rickety old bleachers and would have been a happy man if someone had instructed me to stay there and watch these guys for seven days straight. These professionals made every motion, from a diving catch to whacking the ball three hundred and fifty feet, look as natural as opening a door. For that glorious hour, I lost all desire to do anything athletic again. It felt as if any effort to emulate these men would be an insult to their gifts.

The Monarchs took the field first, but it was the Tiger pitcher that commanded all attention from the very first strike he threw. I couldn't keep my eyes off him, and I found myself grinning until my cheeks hurt. He pranced, he twisted his body into positions that would rip the muscles of mere mortals, and he threw the ball so hard I caught myself flinching along with the hitters.

On his windup, he sometimes froze in the middle of his motion, bringing his body to a standstill, as if some unseen camera was aimed at him, demanding that he strike a pose. He seemed to do this without thinking—never in the same position, and never enough to throw off his control. And he smiled. Always he smiled, a subtle curl of his mouth.

There were no programs, so I finally asked someone who he was. Even his name had a certain magic—Satchel Paige.

I sat with a sack of peanuts in my hand and forgot they were there, holding them as if I was waiting for their owner to come along and claim them. And I was sitting there like that—as motionless as the players were fluid—when a hand suddenly reached into the bag, plucking several peanuts from inside. I flinched, following the arm to its owner.

"Hello, Blake." The fleshy smile of David Westford greeted me. "You know, I thought later that I should have mentioned this game to you. I'm glad you found your way here." We shook hands.

"Good to see you, too, David. This Paige guy is something else, huh?"

"The son of a bitch isn't even human. He beats our St. Louis team every damn time. Or I should say kills us every time. It's never even close."

"Well, I feel privileged just to see these guys play," I said. "We don't see this kind of talent up our way."

He nodded. "Yeah. There's some good players in this league. I like watching these boys play. 'Course, they wouldn't be able to keep up with the major leagues. They might be just as fast, maybe even faster, but they aren't as quick, if you know what I mean." David smiled, pointing to his temple. I emitted a slight "hm," as unenthusiastically as I could, but I could tell from his expression that he assumed I agreed with him.

David told me he was going to get himself a beer, and offered to buy me one. I declined, thinking of my tryout.

Just as David predicted, the game was no contest. Paige had such control that the Monarchs only managed three base runners the whole game. I watched the catcher closely, and it seemed that no matter what kind of hitch Paige put into his windup, or whether or not he was looking at the plate when he threw, the catcher rarely had to move his glove. At one point, Paige turned his torso completely around, toward center field, in the middle of his windup. His head seemed to still be facing the fence when he spun and threw. And just as he reached his release point, his left foot tapped the ground quickly, then continued forward. But the pitch split the plate with the precision of a rifle shot. The batter swung so far ahead of the ball that he fell over. When he stood up, he was laughing. Even he couldn't believe what he'd just seen.

To my horror, David swore at Paige a few times, loud enough that people stared at us. But Paige didn't seem to hear him, or if he did, it had no effect. He pitched a two-hitter, walking only one, and striking out fourteen batters. And earned at least one fan for life.

David sat shaking his head, and drained the last of his fourth beer. "If the Cardinals had Paige, I do believe we could beat the Yankees," he said.

I smiled, declining a chance to point out the contradiction to his earlier comment. "I'm going to go talk to him," I said. "You want to come along?"

David looked up at me, and the smug little grin crept back into his expression. "You are?" he asked.

I shrugged. "Yeah. Why?"

David looked around him, and bent closer to me, lowering his voice. "You sure you want to be seen doing that? Maybe you could write him a letter or something."

When it occurred to me what he meant, I frowned. I looked around at the crowd. Although there were several white faces among us, they were separate from the rest. A few fans lingered on the field, but none of them were white. I just shook my head, starting toward the field.

"You go on ahead," David said. I could see that he was anxious to put some distance between us before I went down on the field. "I want to get cleaned up for a night on the town." He rubbed his palms against his heavy thighs and stood. "You're welcome to join me, you know, or should I say 'us.'" He winked. "Got a couple of real sweethearts lined up. But I think they could handle the both of us."

I reddened, nodding, unaccustomed to this kind of brash outspokenness about such matters. But I hadn't forgotten the women I'd seen the night before. "We'll see," I said. "I have to catch an early train tomorrow. And I want to do a little shopping, pick up a few gifts for the family."

"All right," he said. "But you still got my number, right?"

I nodded, patting my breast pocket. Then I started climbing down the bleachers. But I stopped, and called out, "Hey, David."

He turned.

"Do you know where this place is?" I dug in my jacket for the sheet of paper I had written Mr. Murphy's directions on.

David squinted, holding the paper at an arm's length. "Yeah. I know where that is. Why? You need a ride?"

"No, no. I just wondered whether it's close by."

"It's not very close, actually. But it's not far out of my way. Why don't I give you a ride? Why are you going there, anyway? It's just a little park—nothing special." He winked, with a hint of a smile. "You meeting someone?"

I shook my head. "Never mind," I said. "No, I don't want to put you out."

"No, really. It's no trouble," David insisted. "I got nothing going on this afternoon, and it's almost directly on my way to the hotel."

I thought, then decided I might as well take him up on the offer. "All right," I agreed. "I'll be back in a few minutes."

"Wait a second here. You've got to tell me what this is all about." He pointed at me. "That's the only catch."

I sighed. "I have a tryout," I said.

"A tryout?" David's eyes narrowed. "For what? A tryout?"

I nodded, looking toward the field, where Paige was starting to leave. "Yeah, listen. I'll tell you when I get back. I don't want to miss him." I started toward the field.

"You been holding out on me, Blake. Who's it with?" David called.

"The Cardinals," I shouted over my shoulder.

David stood. "The Cardinals? You definitely been holding out on me here. We been talking about practically nothing but baseball for the past two days and you haven't said a word about this." He was shouting, and I gestured to him to be quiet. "The Cardinals?" he shouted. "I can't believe it." And then, as if he suddenly remembered what I was up to: "I'll meet you in the parking lot," he shouted.

I waved.

Down on the field, my joints felt unhinged. Mr. Paige was not as old as I expected, younger than I was. I found out later that he was a rookie, barely eighteen years old. And so skinny he looked even younger.

I approached with a tentative posture, from the side. "Mr. Paige, my name is Blake Arbuckle." I stuck out my hand and he took it, looking at me with an amused expression, as if he either knew exactly what I was going to say, or as if no matter what I said, it would be amusing. I couldn't help but smile right along with him.

"Mr. Paige, I'm from Albion, Montana, and I just wanted to tell you what a pleasure it was watching you pitch. What you do out there is unbelievable."

He gave a little nod, still smiling. "Well, thank you very much, Mr. Buckle. It's mighty nice of you to come all the way down here from Albion to tell me that."

I nodded, chuckling. "Listen. I've just got to ask you . . ." I suddenly felt self-conscious about my hands, tucking them into my pockets. "I do a little pitching myself . . . and I'm just wondering . . . do you have some special grip, or a secret for doing what you do? How do you fool these batters? These guys are good hitters."

He smiled and shook his head, looking down at his well-worn cleats. Then he lifted his eyes, chuckling, still shaking his head. "They are good hitters," he said. "But I'm gonna tell you something, Mr. Blake R. Buckle—something I don't tell nobody."

I smiled, never having heard my name broken up that way before.

"I do have a secret." Mr. Paige looked over one shoulder, then the other, then back at me, smiling with the most marvelous twinkle in his eyes, and I knew that whatever he was about to tell me was going to be good. "The secret, Mr. Buckle, is to keep everyone thinking you got a secret." He laughed lightly, then put his hand on my shoulder. "That's the best secret of all." Then he shook my hand and sauntered off, still chuckling, his body following no particular rhythm but his own.

And I felt as if I had just met the wisest man in the world.

When I went out to the parking lot, David's demeanor had completely changed. Gone was the smug slant of his smile. I felt, just from the way he looked at me, as if our stations in the world had suddenly reversed.

"What did he say?" he asked.

I just smiled.

He tilted his head. "Oh, you can't do that to me. You just talked to one of the greats of the game, and you're gonna hold out on that, too? You can't do that."

I shrugged, knowing that I now had David Westford in the palm of my hand.

"All right. If that's how it's gonna be," he said, shaking his head. "You're the hot shot here." He opened his car door. "So when is your tryout? We got some time for lunch?"

"Three o'clock," I said.

David took out his pocket watch. "Okay. We got an hour and a half. So I'm gonna buy you lunch. Come on. It would be my honor to buy lunch for the next star of the St. Louis Cardinals."

"Don't get carried away now," I said. "It's just a tryout." But it was clear he wasn't about to take no for an answer, so I followed along without an argument.

At the restaurant, I could hardly eat. Between my nerves, which twisted my stomach into a tangle, and David's eating habits, my appetite was shot. David ate his food in great handfuls, like some character from a children's book. Grease coated his chin, and chunks settled into the corners of his mouth and lived there until they were crowded out by bigger chunks. I have no idea what he ordered, because I couldn't look after the first few bites. But I barely touched my steak. I also said very little. But David did enough eating and talking for both of us. While he went on and on about the Cardinals, my mind wandered, picturing the barn wall, and visualizing myself throwing pitches to those stick figures.

"A pitcher, huh?" David said, looking me square in the eye. "They could use some pitchers right now. They got a hell of a lot of good hitters. But they could sure as hell use some good pitching. I can't believe . . . boy, you really had me going with this whole farm kid routine."

Finally, mercifully, lunch was over. Mr. Murphy was waiting when we arrived at the baseball field, which was just as David described it—more of a small park, with a baseball diamond carved into the grass. There were no bleachers, or dugouts. Not even benches. Mr. Murphy was older than I expected, probably in his fifties. He was bald, ruddy-faced, and constantly squinting. His suit was worn at the elbows, and his shoes hadn't seen a polish brush for a couple of seasons. He had another young guy with him, a kid with a broken nose whom he introduced as Johnny Trumble. Johnny was decked out in catcher's gear.

"Did you bring your lawyer with you?" Mr. Murphy nodded toward David, who sat on his car's fender.

"No, he just gave me a ride. He's not a lawyer." I felt my face burn red.

Mr. Murphy laughed. "I was just kidding, Blake. Listen, are you nervous? Why don't you loosen up a little? Just play some catch with Johnny here. Don't think about pitching for a few minutes. Just relax, loosen your arm up."

He tossed me a ball. "Did you bring your mitt?"

My heart sank. I looked at my feet. "Actually, I don't have one."

He looked only slightly surprised, and it occurred to me that he probably scouted a lot of young country kids who couldn't afford equipment. "All right. Okay. Let me think. You know, I think I might have one in my car. No. Actually, I think I loaned—"

"I got one, Mr. Murphy." Johnny Trumble trotted off toward Murphy's car, and returned with a mitt while I took off my jacket and tie and unbuttoned my sleeves, rolling them up past my elbows.

Once I got loosened up, Johnny Trumble took his place behind the plate, and I climbed the mound. I felt as if I was towering over the world.

"You probably never pitched off a mound before, have you?" Mr. Murphy said.

And although there was nothing condescending about Mr.

Murphy's tone, I thought about lying. I didn't want to give him a reason to eliminate me as an option. But I shook my head.

"That's all right. You don't have to use the mound."

"No, no. It's okay," I told him. "I want to."

"Good. All right." He smiled. "That's the spirit. Just throw a few
easy ones to get a feel for it."

For the first few pitches, the angle threw me off, and the ball
bounced in front of the plate. But as I started to get more comfortable,
I saw how the mound could provide an advantage with the leverage. I
found a rhythm, and I began to put a little more effort into each pitch,
until I was throwing as hard as I could. Mr. Murphy watched from several different angles—from behind me, from each side, then from
behind Johnny. I felt pretty good, although my nerves never did settle
completely. Mr. Murphy's manner encouraged me. Not that he was
smiling. But he studied me closely. He wasn't bored, at least. But I was
worried about the curveball. Timing was so much more important for
that pitch, and I wasn't sure I could adjust to the new angle.

"You have any other pitches? You throw a drop? Or a curve?" Mr.
Murphy asked.

Okay, I thought. Here comes the hard part. "I throw a bit of a
curve," I said.

"Good. Okay. Let's see how you do with it from up there. On the
hill."

I took a deep breath. Then I fixed my gaze on Johnny, who held his
glove up, setting the target. He gave me a slight, encouraging nod, and
a wink, which I appreciated. I let her fly. Again, the first one kicked up
dust, landing just behind the plate. But it had broken off nicely, and I
closed my eyes, making a mental adjustment, picturing the stick figure
on the barn wall, and I imagined aiming just a little higher, at shoulder height instead of elbow. I wound up slowly and threw, and this one
also broke sharply, but far outside. But the distance was better, and I
used this as encouragement. Each pitch felt just a little better. I threw

curve after curve, breaking most of them off perfectly, just as they crossed the plate.

I was soaked in sweat, and I looked over at David. He was smiling.

"That's enough, Blake." Mr. Murphy walked toward the mound from where he'd been standing, behind Johnny. "That's good." He walked slowly, head down, hands behind his back. He didn't look at me. I got more nervous, my stomach floating. I took off the mitt, and my hand was sweating.

He didn't speak for a long time, stopping halfway between the plate and the mound, looking down, his hands still tucked behind. Finally, Mr. Murphy turned toward me and looked up.

"Well, what do you think?" he asked me.

"What do I think?" I scratched my head. "I'm sorry. I'm not sure what you mean, Mr. Murphy. What do I think about what?"

He took two more steps toward me. "How did you feel there? How were you throwing today? As well as you can? Better than usual? Worse?"

"Good," I said immediately. "I felt pretty good."

He nodded. "Well, you looked good, too, Blake. You throw well. That curve has some bite to it. And you've got a good fastball, too. It has a little movement."

"Yeah?" I suddenly couldn't breathe. "Really?"

"Yeah." He looked up at me. "There's someone else I'd like you to meet. My boss, actually. He's coming into town tomorrow. I'd like you to meet him, show him what you can do. What do you think about that?"

"Oh, no," I answered quickly, without thinking.

Mr. Murphy's brows rose. "No?"

"I mean, yes, I would like that. I'd like to meet him, but tomorrow isn't good. I have to catch a train, tomorrow morning."

Mr. Murphy stood right where he was, with one foot in the grass, one on the base of the mound. His eyebrows had jumped to the middle of his forehead, and he kept looking at me, as if he was waiting for me to tell him something different, to change my mind. But I couldn't think of anything to say. I wondered about coming down another time, but I knew that was impossible. It would probably be another three years before I had a chance.

"So?" Mr. Murphy finally said. "That's it, then? You can't stay one more day?"

I looked at my shoes. I suddenly felt ill. I thought about how long I'd been waiting for this chance—six years of hard work, six years of hope. There had to be a way.

"Can you just talk to your boss?" I asked.

"Talk to him?" Mr. Murphy shook his head in confusion. "About what? About what? If he doesn't see you pitch, I really don't have anything to talk to him about. See what I mean, Blake? What do I say to him if he's never seen you?"

I swallowed. I thought about harvest. They were starting harvest the day after my return. They needed everyone for harvest. I dug my hands into my pockets.

We all stood there, and for several seconds, nobody said a word, and I knew that all I needed to do was say "Okay." All I had to do was say, "All right, I'll be here," and I might have a chance. That was it. Mr. Murphy waited, knowing that questions would be rolling around in my head. The temptation sat, holding me hostage for those long, silent seconds, and he knew it. He was good. He knew that if there was ever a moment I would weaken, it was then. Finally, I saw that there was only one choice. Despite the price I would pay, and the trouble it may cause.

"Okay," I said. "All right. What time?"

And I heard a small whoop from the direction of David Westford.

Despite all my efforts to talk him out of it, David insisted on giving me a ride to the tryout the next morning. I sent a telegram to the Belle Fourche Hotel, knowing that whoever came to pick me up would be staying there. I just explained that something had come up, and that I'd be a day late. Nothing to worry about, I added.

I did manage to talk my way out of spending the evening with David. I wanted a good night's rest, and I had a strong suspicion that a night on the town with him would not end with a good night's rest. I was going to check out of my hotel, into a cheaper one, but again, David wouldn't hear of it, paying for my room while I tried talking him out of it. I could do nothing but say thanks. So once he was gone, I walked around town, shopping.

I bought a new pocketknife for Dad, some perfume for Mom, a leather belt for Bob, and some chocolates for Muriel. The hardest decision was what to buy Jack and Rita. But in a strange little shop that sold mostly cigars and magazines, I found a catalogue that was basically a list of all the catalogues in the country. And for Rita, I remembered that she used to wear a lot of hats when she first arrived in Montana. So I found a pretty, black felt hat with a brim that curled up the front and a fake diamond pin that held it in place.

As much as I enjoyed walking around again, it felt different than it had the first evening. I noticed things I hadn't that first night—such as the fact that people did not meet your eye. That they walked much faster than they did in Belle Fourche. And that almost every exchange I had with anyone outside of a salesclerk was negative. I started to experience some of the same stifled feeling that I did when I was living in Belle Fourche. By the time I got back to my hotel, I had a hard time breathing. I sat in the lobby for a few minutes, watching people walk back and forth, wishing there was some way to stop one of them and start a conversation. I watched people use the phone, and I wished that they had a telephone at home so I could call.

In the middle of all these people, I felt as lonely as I'd ever felt. I was happy to go to bed. And despite being as nervous as I could ever remember, I slept pretty well.

But the next morning, I was a wreck. I woke up early, with so much energy that after I ate breakfast and took advantage of the tub one last time, I had to take a walk. My mind raced as I covered blocks of downtown Omaha. I visualized pitching, imagining my motion, feeling it in my arm, and my body. But more than anything, I thought of my brother George. I remembered how horrified I'd been to find out that he was thinking of leaving the ranch. I couldn't imagine how he would even consider such a thing. Now here I was.

As my mind explored every angle of the situation, I looked up to realize that I had been paying no attention to where I was. I was in a part of town that looked completely different from the area where my hotel was. I noticed that it felt more dangerous, that people looked at you more suspiciously. There were people holding hats out for change, and the pedestrians were rougher, bumping into each other without a word of apology. I had to ask for directions, and to my surprise, I found that I was just two blocks from the hotel. It was a good thing, too, because I checked the time, and it was only ten minutes before David was supposed to pick me up. But I was struck by how abruptly the flavor of the town could change from one street to the next.

I hurried back, ran up to my room, splashed some cold water on my face, and waited in front of the building.

"You nervous?" From the amount of sweat pouring down David's face, he appeared to be the one who was nervous.

I shook my head. "Not too bad," I lied.

"God damn, I would be."

I didn't say much, and to my surprise, neither did David, somehow honoring my unspoken desire for a little time for mental preparation. When we arrived at the practice field, Mr. Murphy and Johnny Trumble stood on the field talking with a third man, a dapper, handsome man who was perhaps twenty years younger than Mr. Murphy, in his early thirties. And a good half foot shorter.

"Blake, how you doing today?" Mr. Murphy asked. He sidled up to me, shook hands, and handed me a mitt. I looked down and recognized it was not the one I used the day before. It was new. Mr. Murphy winked at me, and I realized that he had bought it for me.

"Good, fine," I answered, smiling. "Thanks, Mr. Murphy."

He simply nodded. "This is Billy Spinelli," Mr. Murphy said. "He's the head scout for the Cardinal farm system."

I nodded, shaking Mr. Spinelli's hand. But Mr. Spinelli showed right away that he wasn't interested in the social aspect of his job. "All right," he said. "Let's see what you can do, Arbuckle."

Johnny gave me an encouraging smile before trotting behind the plate, where he stood pounding his catcher's mitt while I took off my jacket and rolled up my sleeves. Mr. Murphy took a shiny new baseball from his jacket, rubbed it hard with the palm of one hand, and tossed it to me.

"Okay, Blake. Just remember how you felt yesterday. Just do the same thing you were doing yesterday." He sounded nervous himself, which immediately brought a fluttering energy to my body. I took a deep breath, adjusted my grip on the baseball, and threw a few straight fastballs, right down the middle. The jitters began to fade.

Mr. Murphy did as he had done the day before, checking my motion from several different angles. But Mr. Spinelli had the opposite approach. He stood ten feet behind Johnny Trumble, expressionless, his arms folded, his brow furrowed. After checking the look on his face a few times and seeing that it hadn't changed, I decided it would be better to avoid looking his way. Seeing that same rigid brow and the straight line in his mouth only worried me.

"All right, let's see that curveball," Mr. Murphy said. "Show him how you snap that thing off."

I adjusted my grip, running my first finger along one seam, and wound up. But I realized the moment I threw the first curve that something was wrong. The ball squirted off to one side, almost two feet outside the plate, not breaking at all. Johnny didn't even try to catch it, but stood up and trotted after the ball.

"That's okay," Mr. Murphy assured me. "Take a deep breath. Take your time. Just relax."

"I hope you're not wasting my time here again, Murphy," Mr. Spinelli said.

But I knew what the problem was. I wasn't used to a brand-new baseball. The leather was much slicker than the old, scuffed balls I was used to throwing. So before Johnny threw the ball back to me, I bent down and rubbed dirt on my hands. I caught the throw from Johnny and massaged some dirt into the smooth leather. I set my forefinger along the seam, laid my right foot on the rubber, kicked and threw. The dirt helped immediately. This pitch started toward Johnny's glove, then dropped off its line at the plate. It would have kicked up dust right at Johnny's feet, but he was ready for it, and caught it with his glove laid flat on the ground. Despite my vow, I had to shoot a quick glance at Mr. Spinelli. His eyebrows had jumped to the middle of his forehead. But it was the only part of his body or face that responded, and they quickly dropped back to their normal position, low over his eyes.

"Nice pitch." Mr. Murphy was behind me, and I was relieved to hear this bit of encouragement. "Let's see a few more like that one."

So I did what I could, throwing pitch after pitch, letting the ball spin off the tip of my forefinger as it left my hand. Most of them broke nicely, diving through the strike zone. Johnny smiled, and winked after four in a row broke across the outside corner of the plate. But Mr. Spinelli retained his rocklike demeanor. Not until I'd thrown about twenty-five curveballs did he speak.

"Is that it?" he asked, still standing firm, arms crossed, brow low. "Does he have any other pitches?"

There was a long pause. I was annoyed that he spoke to Mr. Murphy as if I wasn't there. Mr. Murphy cleared his throat behind me. I was just about to say "no," or shake my head, but a thought came to me. "Yeah," I said. "Yeah. I have one more pitch."

"Hm?" Mr. Murphy held back his surprise.

"What is it?" Mr. Spinelli asked.

"Well, I don't really know what you call it," I said. "It doesn't have a name."

This seemed to annoy Mr. Spinelli. "All right," he said impatiently, looking at his watch. "Let's see it. I don't got all day."

Mr. Murphy came out from behind me, circling around halfway between me and first base. He set his fists on his hips, and eyed me with a subtle look of amused confusion. I took a long, slow breath. Johnny established the target, and I positioned my fore and middle fingers right across both seams, just as I would for my fastball, and started my windup. I changed nothing about my delivery, throwing a straight fastball, except that just as I brought my right arm forward, I flipped my glove hand in a slight motion across my body. The pitch honed in on Johnny, splitting the plate, popping the leather on his thick catcher's mitt. He held the ball for a moment.

Mr. Spinelli looked up at me, and for the first time that morning, he shifted his glance toward Mr. Murphy. Again, his expression revealed nothing. But he did say, "Let's see that again."

I took the throw from Johnny, set my grip, and repeated the same motion. Again, I flipped the glove, and the pitch crossed the middle of the plate. The words of Satchel Paige ran through my head, and I acted as if I'd just done something nobody had ever done before. I took Johnny's throw with a confident flip of my wrist, and stretched my throwing arm above my head.

"You say you don't have a name for that thing?" Mr. Spinelli said. Considering his manner up to now, I was fully prepared for a sarcastic follow-up, or a challenge. I shook my head.

"Well, throw a few more of those." For the first time since I'd started throwing, Mr. Spinelli showed signs of life. His arms dropped to his side, and he stepped forward, so that he was just a few feet behind Johnny. He leaned forward, bracing his hands against his knees. Mr. Murphy moved closer to the plate.

I did as he asked, and the more I threw, the more comfortable I felt with the little hitch in my motion. In the end, I don't know whether this little flip of my glove actually affected the path of the ball, or if the best secret really is making people believe you have a secret. All I know is that after I had thrown this pitch another twenty times or so, Mr. Spinelli walked up to Johnny and reached for the ball.

"All right, Arbuckle." He gave a quick nod. "That's enough." He motioned to Mr. Murphy, and the two of them walked over across the third-base line and began a quiet conversation. Johnny trotted out to the mound.

"What the hell were you doing out there?" he asked.

I smiled and shrugged. I couldn't tell from Johnny's expression or tone whether he was impressed, or if he couldn't believe I thought I could get away with such blatant fraud. "I've never seen anything like that," he said with admiration.

"Thanks," I said. We shook hands.

I had not thought about David through the whole tryout. But I glanced over at him now. His ruddy face sported a smile that stretched from one ear to the other. He clapped his hands together a couple of times.

I watched the two scouts confer. It was clear from their body language who had the power between the two. Although Mr. Murphy was a half head taller than Mr. Spinelli, he was leaning toward him, his hands out, palms up, as if he was begging for a morsel of food, or a dime. As he listened, Mr. Spinelli stood with his arms crossed, his chin high. He pounded a fist into his palm when he spoke. Mr. Murphy nodded repeatedly, and it appeared as if no matter what Spinelli said, Murphy would agree with him. The discussion probably lasted a minute, but I wouldn't be able to guess, as my mind was racing. Finally, the two men turned and walked toward me.

"You're in," Johnny said quietly, but I didn't have time to ask how he knew.

Mr. Spinelli led the way, and Mr. Murphy was smiling at me from behind him. Mr. Spinelli took off his felt hat, plucked a handkerchief from his breast pocket, and wiped his forehead.

"Well, Arbuckle," he said, "what do you got going on next spring? You have plans?"

I couldn't breathe. "Um, well, besides doing my regular work, you know, on the ranch. No. Nothing."

Mr. Spinelli sniffed. He cleared his throat. "How does seven dollars a week sound? We'll start you out in A ball, and see what you do in game situations. Everything from there will depend on you. You mow 'em down in A ball, you can move up fast, start earning some real money."

"Seven bucks a week?" The voice from behind made me jump. "That's not right. Seven bucks a week?"

Mr. Spinelli's face suddenly changed completely. His brow lowered just over his eyes, and squeezed together. "And who is this?" He turned to Mr. Murphy. "Who is this?"

"Please don't pay attention to him," I said. "I barely know him. I just met him yesterday."

"Hey, I'm just trying to help. I don't want you fellas taking advantage of the kid. That's all." David stopped fifteen feet from us.

"David, please," I said, giving him a look. "This is none of your business."

"Are you a lawyer or something?" Mr. Spinelli asked David. I began to panic, thinking that David was going to ruin my big moment.

"No. I'm a businessman. And a baseball fan. And I just want to make sure you treat my friend right. That's all."

"David, please," I pleaded. "Mr. Spinelli, don't listen to him. I barely know him." I stepped in front of David, blocking the path between the two men.

"No, it's okay," Mr. Spinelli said. "He's just trying to help you out. Okay, Arbuckle. Here's what I'm gonna do. I'm going to offer you ten

dollars a week. But only if you promise not to tell any of the other players what you're getting. Except Johnny here, of course, who's getting
the same as you. You two can help each other keep this little secret." He
winked, and grabbed my upper arm. "What do you say?"

My head spun, and my jaw had fallen into a dumb slack. Despite all
the years of work, I don't think I ever believed it would come this far.
The offer came as such a surprise that I had no thought of the consequences of my decision. My mind was blank.

"Okay," I said. "Yeah. That sounds great."

Mr. Spinelli clapped me on the back, and Mr. Murphy stepped forward and shook my hand with an enthusiasm that confirmed my suspicion that his job might depend on this. Mr. Spinelli arranged to send
me a contract, and we all shook hands.

"I can't believe I'm sitting next to a future pitching star for my favorite
goddam team." David Westford chuckled like a little kid weaving
through the streets of Omaha.

"Well, I thought you were going to ruin everything for a second
there."

David laughed. "Yeah. I could tell you were worried. But hell, you
got to watch guys like that. They won't give you a dollar unless you ask
'em for it. And they won't give you an extra one unless you scare 'em
a little."

"Yeah . . . well, I guess I owe you a thank-you."

"Hell no. You don't owe me nothing, son. You earned it. You can
pitch. You're going to let me take you out tonight, aren't you? You got
to celebrate, right?"

"No, no. I've got to catch the train. In fact, what time is it?"

David pulled his watch from its little pocket. "You can't wait until
tomorrow morning?"

"What time is it?"

He looked at his watch. "Three-fifteen."

"Damn. I've got to hurry."

"What time is your train?"

"Four."

"I'll give you a lift."

"No, David. Come on now, you've done enough. Thank you, but you've already done too much."

I did catch my train, and of course David did give me a ride, and an hour later I was retracing the route home with a very different perspective from the one I had three days earlier. I ate an early dinner, but when I reached back into my pants for my wallet, I felt nothing there. I panicked. I searched my pants pockets, then my jacket. Then I searched them again. The waiter stood patiently watching, then impatiently watching. I looked up at him, my mouth slack. "I don't know . . . "I think I lost my wallet. I don't know . . . can I go back and check my seat?"

He nodded with a bored expression, and followed me. I searched my satchel, the floor, the space between the cushions, everywhere. We asked the conductor, and the passengers around me. Nobody had seen it. The tenth time I patted my palms against my chest, then my thighs, I flashed back to that morning, when I'd gotten lost. A man had bumped into me. Then another man had bumped me from behind. I hadn't thought much about it at the time, except that it seemed rude. But it suddenly hit me that my pocket had been picked. And my heart jumped up into my throat until I remembered that I'd slipped the check from Mr. Tanner in my boot. I pulled my boot off, and there it was, safely tucked away. I showed it to the waiter.

"I guess my wallet was stolen while I was in Omaha. Can I send a check when I get home? I'm very sorry. But as you can see, I have enough to cover it."

"This check is made out to you?"

I nodded, a white lie. But he agreed. I guess he didn't have much choice.

I sank into my seat, and felt an immediate change of heart about my experience in Omaha. The thrill of that first night on the streets seemed like weeks ago. The shrimp, the thick cotton sheets, the bathtub, it all felt like a façade, a setup. I was so exhausted from waking up early and from the strain of the day that I fell asleep before the windows were dark.

When I woke up the next morning, I had a whole day on the train, again studying ranches so much like our own, thinking about my decision, and considering the prospect of telling my family. And the more the miles rolled by, and the clicking and clacking beat away at my conscience, the more my resolve began to fade. When I had first gotten on the train, I would not have suspected that there was any possibility that I would change my mind. I was ready. I felt sure about what I wanted to do.

But now I saw these ranches racing by, and they made me realize how much I missed everything—the space, the smell of the grass, the feel of the warm wind that traveled unimpeded across miles of fresh nature. And the people. I missed my family. And as I thought about harvest, one of my favorite times of the year, and about watching the yellowing stalks of wheat being swallowed by the thresher, and about feeling a burlap bag swell with grain between my knees, I got excited about being back home. I hated thinking of the look on my parents' faces as I told them I was leaving.

For the first time, I had a slight understanding of why Jack would disappear the way he did, without telling anyone, to avoid seeing that look. And I wondered whether George had experienced this same hesitation, whether it might have had something to do with the fact that he never left. I changed my mind hourly, telling myself that I could always change it later. I could always come back to the ranch. I thought about ten dollars a week, and how I might be able to make even more, and maybe save some and come back with a little money put away. The next minute I was thinking about how lonely I felt in the hotel lobby that second night, and wondered how I could even consider moving.

By the time the train pulled into Belle late that evening, my head was muddled. The fact that I'd given Mr. Spinelli and Mr. Murphy my word weighed heavy on me—especially Mr. Murphy, who seemed to have a lot riding on my answer. As I expected, there was a message at the hotel:

> Couldn't wait. Had to get back for
> harvest. Jack

I went directly to the post office, where Annie Ketchal was just loading her truck. I dreaded another night with Annie and her stories, another night without sleep, especially with harvest the next morning. But as I climbed into the cab of her truck, it occurred to me that I could actually ask her to let me sleep. It seemed like a good idea, one that I was surprised I hadn't thought of on my last trip with her. But once we started out, I couldn't find a gap in the conversation big enough to wedge a word into. So I listened for a while, waiting for an opening, and as it turned out, she told me something important.

"I heard your brother was in town today."

I nodded. "Yeah. He was there to pick me up, actually. I was supposed to be here yesterday."

"Oh yeah? What happened?"

"Oh, nothing. It's a long story. I just got hung up."

I could tell that not getting a straight answer just about killed Annie, but she nodded, looking out the window. And I leaned back, resting my head against the seat, and closed my eyes. I was just about to tell her that I wanted to sleep.

"I also heard Jack was in the bank today," she said, "asking about your land."

I was so tired, and so unfocused on what Annie had to say, that this took a few seconds to register. But when it did, I lifted my head.

"He what?"

She wiggled in her seat, sensing that she had something good here. "He was asking about what it's worth."

"Our land?"

"Yeah. Your land."

"Are you sure?"

Annie nodded, squinting. She stopped to drop off a mail sack. "And I guess he was also asking how much money was in the account." And she got out, letting a cold wind blow through the cab.

And suddenly I was wide-awake. In the time it took for that cold wind to reach inside and slap me, I realized that there was no longer a choice. These rumors could mean nothing. And Jack's questions to the bank could be completely innocent. He might have just been curious. But I didn't trust Jack. I couldn't bear the thought of him even remotely considering the thought of pulling any of the land out from under our family.

Annie climbed back into the cab. "But I did hear it from Trudy Spears. Her husband works there, you know."

Any remaining doubts disappeared right then and there. I leaned back and closed my eyes. "Annie, if you don't mind, we've got harvesting to do tomorrow, so I need to get some sleep."

"Sure," she said. "Sure. Of course."

And I rested my head on the seat again, pretending to sleep, thinking about Jack, and about the ranch. And it didn't take long to realize that I'd made a decision.

For years, I convinced myself that the combination of the robbery and Annie Ketchal's news changed my mind about going to St. Louis. But I know better now. I know that when it came right down to it, I just used these facts as an excuse. As much as I liked the idea of exploring more of the world, I couldn't leave. The truth of the matter was, I didn't want to leave.

6

summer 1929

When I returned home from Omaha, with my dedication to the ranch rejuvenated, I took a good look around. And I'm afraid I wasn't happy with what I saw. It became clear to me within days, as we immersed ourselves in the harvest routine, that I had been so distracted in recent years by thoughts of Rita, and of baseball, and dreaming of far-off places, that I hadn't been paying much attention to the world around me. I noticed that although all the work was getting done on the ranch, most of us, and I include myself in the mix, were simply going through the motions. We walked around like a bunch of horses—waiting to be cornered and bridled before we'd finally do what we knew was expected of us. Then stomping our hooves until somebody stuffed some grain in our faces at the end of the day. The only exceptions—my parents. I saw that we had all gotten so accustomed to Mom and Dad doing most of the work, especially in terms of the business end of things, that we had no notion of how out of balance everything had become.

Although I knew the basic facts about the ranch—how much land we had (over ten thousand acres), and how much stock (three hundred cattle, nearly a hundred sheep), and a general idea of what it took to keep the place running, I knew very little else. Mom had occasionally made noises about teaching me how to keep the books, but I'm sure my lack of enthusiasm dampened her desire to make the effort. But now I asked, and she was thrilled for the opportunity to pass on the knowledge.

And one thing soon became clear. I didn't realize what a good business team my folks were. I knew we'd acquired some land here and there, but I assumed our neighbors were also picking up their share as more and more homesteaders packed up and moved on. We had a few more head of livestock than most folks, but I hadn't seen this as a big advantage. I guess I figured we had to put more money into the place to keep the extra stock fed, so that it evened out in the long run. And the small amount of farming we did led to unpredictable results.

But apparently Dad's extra half hour or hour every day added up, and through the years Mom squirreled away enough reserves that soon after I got back from Omaha, they laid out enough cash to build the biggest house in the county. But that makes it sound extravagant, which it wasn't. It was nowhere near the size of the one I'd seen in Nebraska, or a lot of the houses in town. It was just big for our area. Five bedrooms, to be exact. Two stories, plus a cellar. And a nice big kitchen, a dining room, and a living room.

The house was built to last, with the oak flooring that Jack and I had traveled to Bozeman for. Since we didn't have electrical service out that far, we had to buy a big wind charger, with a windmill twirling in one corner of the yard. And we dug a septic tank in the opposite corner. But we couldn't afford to shingle the roof. So when we moved in, the rain sang against corrugated tin on those rare occasions when it did rain.

Still, two years later, the house wasn't painted. It didn't look as though it would be for a while, either. Not only was paint expensive, but of course you have to paint in warm weather, and most of the important tasks that needed our attention had to be done when the sun was shining. And Mom insisted we paint it ourselves. Always saving.

We moved in on Mom's birthday, August 12, 1927, sleeping for the first time ever in rooms of our own. Jack and Rita and their first child, the newest George Arbuckle, even spent the night, spreading bedrolls on the living room floor. They eventually moved from their tiny house to the old house. The barn cats took over their house, multiplying in astonishing quantities until the house was literally filled with cats—close to thirty of them.

"Hey, Blake! We got a big bag over here." Steve Glasser waved to me from across the herd, then pointed down to a cow lumbering along, her hind legs wide apart, her bag swollen to the size of a month-old baby. She'd lost her calf.

"All right. Keep an eye on her, Steve."

"She's pretty swelled up," Steve shouted. "Too bad for that calf. He wouldn't have had to worry about food for a while."

Steve, Rita, Jack, Bob, and I moved the last bunch of our cattle in from the southeast pasture to the barn, where we would brand the new calves. Dad, Gary Glasser, and Art Walters were setting the branding gear up in the corral. And Mom, Muriel, Gary's wife Trudy and Steve's wife Jenny were at the house cooking. We had branded Glassers' calves the week before and would do Art's the following week, using the same crew, the same setup, but at different locations.

The July heat was thick, dry, and the mosquitoes were nearly as thick as the air, so everyone wore long sleeves. Art even had a sweaty kerchief around his neck. I felt for him. For some reason, mosquitoes never bothered me. Even if they did bite, I didn't feel anything or swell up at all. But Art got big ugly welts, the size of quarters.

The cattle moved with slow submission, their heads heavy from the heat, jaws working steadily, up and down, side to side, on their cuds. One calf had an extreme, inexplicable amount of energy, and kept racing off, away from his befuddled mother. His mother would stop, crying loudly, then swing her big skull to one side, and with a slow sweep of her neck, around to the other side. Eventually, she would find the lost one, and press her nose against him, making sure it was indeed hers, mooing more softly, a soothing "mmmm" that seemed to assure the cow more than the calf. Soon the calf was off again.

We kept the cattle moving at a slow but steady pace. With no water in the mile between the pasture and the barn, we didn't want them to get too dry. It would be a long day as it was.

Rita was happy to be back riding with us. The year before, she'd been pregnant with Teddy, their second child, and had to stay with the women and cook. Rita preferred riding. She had a straw cowboy hat broken down over her eyes, her dark hair in its thick ponytail down the middle of her back. She had taken to wearing baggy dungarees with suspenders, and she looked healthier than when she first arrived. Working outside had made her solid, her face browned by sun and wind. Her freckles had multiplied.

Jack was in danger of alienating himself from the rest of the family with his latest business venture. Because there were so few trees in our county, it was common practice, when people ran out of firewood, to use dried manure as a substitute. So Jack got the idea of collecting and selling manure. He built a box, like a coffin, with very narrow gaps between the planks. He would fill the box with manure, then add water, and while it was wet, he would compress it, stomping it down with rubber boots while the excess water leaked out between the gaps.

Once it dried, he turned the box over and dumped out the block of manure, which he then cut into bricks about the size of logs. It was a great idea, and people began stopping in to buy the "logs" which Jack sold for a nickel apiece, or six for a quarter. Soon the demand became greater. Jack built more boxes, and began knocking off a little early some days to gather and prepare his product. At first, he would just leave an hour or so before the rest of us. But he began to cut out earlier and more often, then showing up late. It bothered Dad; I could tell by the cool expression he always cast toward Jack as he departed. But in his typical fashion, he didn't confront the issue.

So while the rest of us worked harder to make up for Jack's absence, again, he was making a profit from ranch resources, and showing no interest in putting what he made back into the place. It went against what was considered ethical, not to mention traditional, for a ranch operation. And when it became clear that nobody else was going to do or say anything about it, I knew it was up to me.

So one evening, while Jack was working at his project, I went out to the corral, where he had his boxes set up. Jack stood in one box, his knees alternately rising and falling. Water seeped from the narrow crevices between the planks.

"How's it going?" I asked.

"All right." Jack eyed me with a hint of skepticism, and for good reason. I had been so annoyed with him that it had been weeks since I initiated a conversation. "Not too bad," he added.

Although I had rehearsed what I wanted to say countless times in my head, and although this was by no means the first time I'd studied Jack's little operation, I walked around the boxes, my hands locked behind my back, trying to settle my nerves before I spoke.

"Dad send you out here?" Jack asked. "Does he need something?"

I shook my head. "No." I cleared my throat, trying to dislodge a lump the size of a chicken.

"What's on your mind, then?" Jack asked. He didn't sound impatient, or testy. "Or maybe I can guess."

"Oh?"

"Yeah." Jack showed a little half smile, looking at me sideways. "I been wondering how long it would be before you spoke up."

I dug my hands into my pockets and faced Jack. "Me, or anybody?"

He stopped his stomping for a moment, his breath slightly labored. "You," he said. "I figured it to be you."

"Why's that?"

Jack's mouth curled into the half smile again. He winked. "Ah, hell, Blake. It's obvious that it bothers you more than anyone." Jack began stomping again, knees rising and falling. "And it's not hard to imagine why."

I frowned, not sure myself about the answer to that question. "Why?"

He grinned. He stopped the knees again. He put his hands on his hips. "Ah, come on, Blake. I don't really have to spell it out, do I?" Jack had gloves on and he lifted one leg, cleaning the excess manure from that boot. Then he stepped out of the box and did the same with the other. "You of all people." He eyed me, tilting his head. "Listen . . . there's no reason we can't both come out of this ahead. We can both get what we want here."

I was baffled by Jack's certainty that I understood what he was talking about. He scrutinized me, and apparently saw my confusion. He sat on the edge of the box. "All right, Blake. Let me put it this way. It's been obvious since . . . well, since I can remember . . . that if there's anyone who has the same feeling about this ranch as Mom and Dad, it's you."

I raised my brow.

"What? You don't think I see that?" Jack asked, smiling. "Come on, Blake. It's obvious. I don't have what it takes to run this place. I don't have the patience. I don't suffer well." He studied me. "So it's simple, really. I get what I can out of it while I'm here. Then I leave you alone. You get what you want. So do I." He shrugged. "Then I leave you alone."

I stood looking at the dry gray earth at my feet, and thought about what Jack was saying. Obviously, the conversation had gone very differently than I expected. In a way, I couldn't have planned it any better. I didn't even have to do anything. But I was uncomfortable with Jack's proposal, for a couple of reasons. I raised one of them.

"Have you talked to Rita about this?"

For the first time, Jack's eyes became guarded, and before he spoke, I knew the answer to my question. "That's my business," he answered.

And whatever slim chance there was of going along with Jack's little arrangement died. But it wasn't only the fact that Jack would keep such important details from Rita. In fact, when I thought about it later, I realized that I couldn't have gone along with the plan regardless of Jack's answer to this simple question. The whole conspiratorial nature of the idea went against all matters of principle that our family had built as a foundation. And it showed me just how far removed my brother was from those values.

I looked down at him, sitting expectantly on his creation, and I shook my head.

"Sorry, Jack," I said. "I can't go along with that."

Jack raised his eyes to me, squinting, looking at the same time confused and amused. "What do you mean, you can't go along with it, Blake? You don't even have to do anything. There's really nothing to go along with."

I nodded. "Yeah. You're right. That's the problem. I can't support you on this, Jack. As far as I'm concerned, if you're going to take from the ranch, you have to put as much into it as the rest of us. You've got to pull your weight. It's just the way it is, I think. It's the way it has to be." I shrugged.

Jack only seemed to become more amused. His shoulders shook slightly in a silent chuckle. "All right. So what are you going to do, then, if I don't? You going to force me?"

I sighed. "Nope. I'm not going to force you. Obviously, there's nothing I can do." Again I shrugged, pulling my mouth to one side. "It's up to you, Jack. If you can live with it, then I guess I'll have to. But I just got to warn you, I won't be happy about it. Never. It's not something I'll ever get used to."

Jack kept his gaze on me, and he retained his incredulous grin.

After holding my gaze for a moment, he shrugged, as if he didn't care one way or the other. But this exchange proved to be a turning point. Jack and I rarely spoke after that. But our silence did not seem to be born of animosity. Quite the opposite. It felt as if, now that our divergent paths had been established, any rivalry that might have been brewing was gone. There was no longer any need to compete, nor was there any need to be friendly. The pressure was off. Jack also rarely knocked off early after that, which gave me a sense of satisfaction.

But a new concern had come out of this conversation. My suspicion that Jack's return after the war was only temporary had essentially been confirmed. And the ramifications of this eventuality had changed. Now Rita was involved. Which meant I cared even more.

We pushed the herd over the rise a hundred yards from the barn. Then we ambled down the slope and squeezed the cattle through the gate into the corral, where Dad and Gary had a fire going, with three irons burning orange in the flame. Just before we reached the gate, the rambunctious calf took off one last time.

"Rita, watch that little guy over there!" Jack shouted, pointing.

"He's all right," Rita answered, calmly watching the calf kick up its heels. "He'll be back."

But Jack didn't accept Rita's assessment, and made a ridiculous show of pursuing the calf, first chasing him further from the herd before he finally got him turned around.

"Get the gate, Jack," I shouted as he guided the runaway calf into the corral.

He swung the gate shut, and the easy part was over. The cattle filled the corral, mawing and eyeballing us with an accusing look, as though we'd betrayed them yet again by bringing them there.

I twirled my lasso a few times and set my bead on the back hooves of a calf that was trotting along separate from the rest. I caught one leg and backed Ahab while Jack went after the front legs. He laid a loop down on the ground. I kept backing, and the calf stepped into the loop with both front hooves. Jack flipped his wrist and pulled, stretching the calf out. It fell to its side. Dad straddled the calf, sat, and held its head while Gary laid the glowing iron against the calf's right flank. The calf let out a bawl, and the smell and taste of burning hair filled the corral.

Gary lifted the iron and a wisp of smoke drifted from a perfect black "Rⵊ" in the midst of the furry brown coat. The calf was male, so Dad grabbed his pocketknife from his teeth, sliced the scrotum, and tugged the testicles from the open wound. He tossed them to one side, and the calf wriggled, bawling louder, his tongue hanging loose from the corner of his mouth. Dad sliced a notch out of the calf's left ear to mark it as a steer. And after Gary dumped disinfectant on the wounds, Jack and I nudged our horses forward, putting enough slack in our ropes for Dad to slip the lassos from the calf's hooves.

The little guy stood, dazed for a second, and I guided him toward the gate. When Bob opened the gate, Steve stood in the gap and waved his arms, spooking the unbranded calves to keep them in the corral. He then made a mark on one plank of the corral for each calf we'd branded, and a mark on another plank for each cow that got out. At the end of the day, we'd total these marks and figure the ratio of cows to calves. Each year a few cows would be dry, and a few would have twins. It generally balanced out to about nine calves for every ten cows, but some years, when the grass was thick, we'd have an equal number.

Nothing blocked the sun's path, and between the fire and the eighty-plus-degree heat, the air was as dry as hangover mouth. Dry enough that we almost didn't have enough water in us to sweat. Just within hearing distance, the Little Missouri River teased us with its rush of water. My rope was hot and stiff, worrying my hands until the nerves were tender. The heat encouraged the mosquitoes, too; the pesky little bastards kept us extra busy waving them from our ears. But the mood was light, as it usually was when we worked as a crew.

"Some nice fat calves you got here, George," Steve said.

"Not too bad," Dad answered.

Steve scrutinized Dad, his skewed eye aiming off away from everything. "You been letting these calves chew on our grass?" he asked. "I don't believe you folks could raise nice fat calves like these on that scrawny grass you got out here."

Dad eyed me with a mischievous smirk. "Should we tell him, Blake?"

"Hell no, Dad. I don't think we ought to admit to anything yet. Might give him reason to start looking for some kind of payback."

"What makes you so sure we haven't already?" Steve asked.

In the midst of our banter, Gary turned to say something, but he bumped into a cow behind him and dropped his branding iron, which caught his boot just enough to make him jump. One side of the R left a black curve on the toe of his boot. This sudden motion spooked some of the cattle near Gary. Bob was just opening the gate to let a newly branded calf out, and the rambunctious calf saw the opening and bolted. He was out before Bob or Steve could move to stop him.

"I'll get him." Rita was closest to the gate. She took off after the calf, her boots bouncing out and back against her horse's flanks.

"Now look what you done, George." Steve pointed at Dad, as though he was about to come after him. "Scared off one of your calves and damn near branded my dad at the same time."

"Maybe you ought to come over and brand this, Steve." Dad bent over and stuck his rump in the air, laughing and pointing at it.

"Get him, Dad," Steve yelled to Gary. "This is your chance."

"Rita's down!"

Our attention was so focused on the horseplay that when Bob shouted, it took a few seconds to register. We all looked at Bob, letting the words sink in. Then our eyes shifted out into the pasture, where Rita's horse galloped riderless in the opposite direction. We all moved at once.

Jack and Art barreled through the gate, their horses racing past Bob, who ran toward Rita's prone figure. Steve had the presence of mind to close the gate, but not before several calves had jumped on the opportunity to escape. I was the last one in the corral on horseback, and I had to shout for Steve to open the gate again before I could join the chase.

Rita was lying on her back several hundred yards from the corral. Her horse trotted off toward the river, stirrups flopping in all directions, reins dragging. Rita rolled over to her elbows and knees, trying briefly to pull herself to her feet, but she lowered herself to one side and rotated onto her back again.

Jack was the first to reach her, swinging down from his saddle before his horse even stopped. In fact, he was in such a hurry that his dismount pulled his horse to one side, and the horse nearly ran into Rita.

Art was right behind Jack, and by the time I got there, the two hunched over Rita, one on each side. Her face was pale, rimmed with sweat, and she held a palm flat against her side, at the base of her ribs. Her eyes were closed, clamped tight, and her teeth clenched, showing between her bloodless lips.

Jack and Art both held their hands helplessly in the air over Rita, as if they each wanted to touch her, heal her somehow, but weren't sure where to start or what to touch. A mosquito settled onto Rita's cheek, and in one of the most tender gestures I ever saw from him, Jack brushed the insect away, then pulled Rita's hair from her forehead.

"You okay?" Jack asked.

"Where does it hurt?" Art asked simultaneously.

Rita sucked air through her clamped teeth and pointed at her side. "Right here."

Art took off his shirt, rolled it up, and tucked it under Rita's head, inviting a cloud of mosquitoes to his bare arms. They even attacked his threadbare T-shirt. Jack unhooked Rita's suspenders and carefully unbuttoned her dungarees. He pulled her shirt from inside her pants, then peeled it away from her stomach, watching her face. She winced, but not enough for him to stop. Despite the serious nature of the situation—the possibility that Rita could be suffering from broken ribs, or some internal injuries—my vision was captured by this show of flesh. I felt my face turn red.

Halfway up her side, red and raw, was a hoof print, horseshoe shaped. The skin was scraped, not enough to bleed, but it looked damn sore. Jack placed his palm against Rita's forehead.

"You gonna be okay, sweetheart?"

She opened her eyes. "I think so. It hurts, though. It really hurts."

The others, who had run from the corral, gathered around, panting, asking what had happened.

"Looks like she's probably gonna have a few cracked ribs," Art said. "But I think she's all right other than that. You hurting anywhere else, Rita?"

She shook her head.

Looking at the raw spot made my side ache. "You think you can move?" I asked.

Rita's eyes got wide just thinking about it. "Give me a minute," she said.

"Well, it's about time for lunch anyway," Dad said, looking up at the sun. I could see he was thinking about the time we were losing. "We might as well all head back to the house when she's feeling up to it. You want us to get the wagon, Rita, or you think you can make it on horseback?"

"Dad, please," she said. "Just give me a minute. I don't know."

"I'm sorry, darling," Dad said. "I'm getting way ahead of everything here."

Jack continued to stroke Rita's cheek, and I could see that Rita was moved by this act. Lying there looking up at him, there was a softness in her gaze that was usually reserved for her boys. When a spasm rocked her, she reached out and grabbed Jack's hand. I felt a pang of jealousy. Jack looked down at her hand, as if it was the first time he'd ever held one. He put it to his chest.

"Well, somebody's got to catch those calves that got out," I said. "Bob, you want to man the gate while I round them up?"

Bob nodded, starting toward the corral.

"I'll give you a ride," Art told Bob.

We made a dramatic entrance into the house, with Jack and Art supporting Rita by each arm, and the rest of us explaining in bursts what happened. They led Rita to Mom and Dad's bedroom, and the accident brought out everyone's fundamental desire to do the one thing that would be most helpful.

Gary suggested that his wife Trudy drive to Capitol to get the doctor.

"No, actually, one of you men should go, otherwise supper won't get done in time," Trudy said.

"If one of us goes, the branding won't get done," Dad said. "We can wait to eat if it comes to that, but we got to finish the branding today."

"Maybe I should go," Mom suggested. "Trudy, you're right in the middle of making your bread. I wouldn't want to ruin it. You seem to be the only one who can get it right."

"No, no, no, Catherine," Trudy insisted, waving her hand. "You won't have any problem. A little more kneading, then it has to set for a couple hours. That's all that's left to do. I should go."

Jenny Glasser, who was so quiet that when she did speak, everyone looked at her as though they'd forgotten she was in the room, made her offering. "Who's going to watch Rita?"

"I'll keep an eye on her," Muriel said. "I can work on the pies and watch her too."

That covered everything, and Trudy left to find Dr. Sorenson while the rest of us went about the business of lunch. As we sat eating, Rita suddenly appeared in the doorway, bracing herself against the wall. Jack was out of his chair in a flash.

"Sweetheart, what the hell are you doing?"

"I'm hungry," she said. "I feel fine." Sweat covered her forehead, and she had to brace herself against the door frame. She was completely white.

"We'll bring you some food. You've got to stay in bed until the doctor gets a look at you," Mom said. She started to rise from her chair, but Jack motioned for her to stay put.

Jack wrapped his arm around Rita and led her toward the bedroom.

"I think I'm okay," Rita was saying. "I think I can go back to riding this afternoon."

Jack chuckled. "Oh no you don't."

We could not hear the rest of their conversation, but Jack's tone was insistent.

Steve sat shaking his head. "Who'd of thought someone from New Jersey would be the toughest one in this county?"

Mom prepared a plate for Rita and took it in to her. Mom and Jack came out talking quietly, their heads nearly touching. Mom had her hand in the crook of Jack's elbow, a show of affection I hadn't seen her show him in years.

We didn't linger over lunch, knowing that we were already behind, and short one hand. We hurried back to the corral, and after a short discussion about who would take which job, we were back at it. One person had to man the gate and also do the tallying, and Jack volunteered.

And as often happened, a near-tragedy brought our attention into a much tighter focus. We moved like one collective animal, with even the cattle seemingly in sync. The calves practically stuck their hooves in front of our lassos and lay down on their own. None bolted from the corral all afternoon. And the mothers gathered against the planks, as if they'd conferred and agreed to stay out of our way.

We hardly spoke. The heat didn't let up, nor did the mosquitoes, but those were the only nuisances of the afternoon. We not only finished, but we finished early. It was one of those rare, enchanted stretches of time when the world actually seemed like a pretty simple place.

The women were shocked to see us arrive back at the house, wearing smiles bigger than our faces and clapping each other's back. Jack looked worried until we found out that Dr. Sorenson had determined that Rita probably had a few cracked ribs, but no internal damage.

Once Jack heard this, his shoulders relaxed. I felt the same relief, but more privately, of course. Jack started toward the bedroom, but Mom gripped his arm. "She just fell asleep."

"All right," he said. "Of course."

We surrounded the table, which was soon covered with a huge beef roast, fried potatoes, fresh garden tomatoes, Trudy's bread—straight from the oven—and a thick, dark skillet gravy. And for dessert—pies. Apple, mincemeat, and a luscious sour cream–raisin. We ate like demons, leaving hardly a scrap. And we laughed. We laughed at everything, especially after Dad broke out two bottles he'd asked Art to bring along. We rarely had liquor in our home, but this day was obviously charmed, and we filled our glasses generously, as if for this one evening we were invincible even to the effects of alcohol. But I noticed that Jack drained and refilled his glass much more frequently than anyone else did. About halfway through dinner, his eyelids began to droop.

"Here's to the best damn neighbors in the county," Dad said, raising his glass.

We all seconded the sentiment, draining our drinks with a synchronized tip of the glasses. We moved into the living room after dinner, filled to the brim with food, drink, and the satisfaction of a productive day.

"Are there any dances this weekend?" Trudy asked.

"Camp Crook is having one," Bob answered.

"Is that Stillwell girl going to be there?" I asked Bob.

He gave me a hard look, blushed, and looked at his palms. "I wouldn't know."

"The Stillwell girl?" Steve asked, his lazy eye wandering. "You sweet on her, Bob?"

Bob rubbed his palms against his thighs. "Nah. I'm not sweet on anyone."

"She's pretty," Jack said, his voice a little too loud.

"Smart, too," Muriel added. "She was valedictorian when I was a freshman."

"I'm not sweet on her," Bob said, a little louder. He set his mouth in a straight line.

"Well, she's a nice girl anyway," Mom said. "Are you folks going?" she asked Glassers.

"Oh, you damn right," Steve said. "You know I don't miss a dance."

"How about you?" Jack turned to Jenny, deliberately, with a sly grin. "Are you goin'?"

Jenny lowered her eyes, obviously uncomfortable with being addressed. It was a strange question considering Steve had just said they would be going, and Jack's leering manner made it even more strange.

"'Course she's going," Steve said. "Jenny loves to dance." We all knew otherwise, and we chuckled, trying to make light of the situation.

"Do you really like to dance, Jenny?" Jack leaned forward in his chair, moving a little closer to Jenny. His eyes were nearly closed now.

Jenny stood up. "I'm going to see how Rita's doing." She emphasized Rita's name, looking directly at Jack. But Jack sank back into his chair, not the least put off, a dreamy grin on his face.

Steve got up and followed his wife to the bedroom. The rest of us sat in that sort of uncomfortable silence that numbs the brain, the kind that makes you feel as though you never have and never will carry on an intelligent conversation. I sat wishing Jack would disappear, or fall asleep, embarrassed that he would be so insensitive when Rita was lying injured just two rooms away.

Dad finally brought us out of it. "You get bit today, Art?"

Art was just then scratching away at his back. "The little bastards made a meal of me, all right," he said. "Left me just enough blood to keep me propped up in my saddle."

"You wearing some kind of perfume?" I asked. "I can't figure out why they all go for you."

"It's my pretty smile, I guess." Art showed his half-toothless, no-jaw grin below his drooping mustache.

"I think that face would kill 'em before it would make 'em want to suck on you," Jack mumbled, squinting at Art.

Art smiled and shook his head, making an obvious effort to believe Jack was kidding.

"Yep, you are a piece of work, Art." Jack tilted his sleepy-eyed face toward Art, and his cruel tone changed our laughter into nervous chuckles. Art gave him a long look, but didn't say a word. Steve and Jenny returned, and Jenny made a point of switching seats with Steve, who had been sitting further from Jack. Steve again tried to lighten the mood.

"Well, Rita's looking good, getting her color back. That bruise is going to be nasty, though."

Just then, Jack stood and left the room. We all breathed easier for a minute, thinking he was going to go look in on his wife. But he came back carrying a big fruit jar. The contents sloshed over the rim, and the smell of alcohol filled the room. And the seconds passed, and the tension built as Jack guzzled the drink, and we wondered whether he was going to do something more obnoxious than he already had, or if he would pass out before he had the opportunity. I gritted my teeth, despising the fact that anyone could take a woman like Rita for granted the way my brother had for so many years. How he could claim to love her and then show such blatant disregard.

But the fear of provoking Jack kept me in my chair, my teeth clenched but my muscles tense, ready to spring if something unexpected happened. Like most of us in the room, I did not look at Jack, but kept him in the corner of my eye at all times.

Jack settled back into his seat and drank deeply, looking pleased with himself, and drunkenly unaware that his actions were causing so much discomfort. Mom got up, her face flushed, and went to the kitchen. The sounds of clattering dishes and running water echoed through the house. Jenny followed Mom. Then, as if it was the most natural thing in the world, Jack stood and announced, "I guess I'll give them a hand in there."

It was the one and only time I remember Jack offering to help with the dishes, and I'm sure this occurred to everyone else in the room. I watched the stiff smile disappear from Steve's face as Jack staggered toward the kitchen.

We all sat with one ear aimed toward the kitchen, our mouths sealed shut with fear. Dad looked awful tired. We heard a steady drone, Jack's voice, mingling with the sounds of washing dishes. I finally resorted to the only thing I could think of.

"Wonder how long this heat's going to last."

The others merely nodded, and more minutes of quiet followed in what I think may be the only time in the history of Montana that even the weather failed as a topic of conversation. Finally, the silence broke. A rising, angry declaration bellowed from the kitchen, punctuated by the crash of a dish shattering against the floor. We jumped up, running to the kitchen.

Jenny stood with her back against the sink, her hands clenched into tight fists at her waist. Her mouth was pinched, and her face, which was generally white as chicken feathers, was dark red right up to her hairline. Mom stood between her and Jack, with a butcher knife in her hand, aimed right at Jack's chest. I couldn't breathe.

I don't think Jack even saw the knife. He still had that stupid grin on his face, and he looked right past Mom, at Jenny.

"Jenny, darling, are you rejecting my invitation?" he asked.

Dad grabbed Jack from behind.

"Hey," Jack muttered, looking truly confused. "What's the matter?"

"Let's take you on home," Dad said. "Come on. I'll walk you home."

"Oh, no," Jack said. "I ain't ready to go home yet."

"Yeah, well, I think it'd be a good idea if you did anyway," Dad insisted, his face straining.

"Jenny, do you want me to go home?" Jack raised his forehead and smiled at Jenny, trying to look sweet but falling far short of that objective.

"Shut up," Mom muttered. "Just shut your mouth, Jack."

My guts were tangled up like a tumbleweed as I stood watching my brother make a fool of himself. Part of me wanted to throw him to the floor and pummel some awareness into that murky brain. But he seemed so oblivious to his actions, and to the world around him, that he was almost too pathetic to be angry at. I took a deep breath through my nose.

"Come on, Jack." I stepped up and took him by the arm, and Dad and I started to lead him toward the door. "You don't want to do this."

"Jenny, you don't wanna go to the dance with that cockeyed joke-ster, do you?"

That was more than even Steve could tolerate. He started after Jack. Bob and Gary caught him, but Steve strained against their grasp, his veins bulging in his temple and his neck.

Through his teeth, he muttered, "Jack, I hope to God this is whiskey talk—that you don't know what you're saying." Steve's eye jumped from side to side as if it was being held back. "Otherwise . . . otherwise . . ."

Jack grinned. "Whiskey don't talk. This is my mouth sayin' you're a cockeye." Jack fixed a look on Steve that sent a chill through us all. It was a look that told us he was clearly too far gone to have any idea what he was saying. His eyes were apparently looking, in his mind, at something besides people—at some kind of vicious obstacles that stood in the way of getting what he wanted. He clearly hated us all at that moment.

This awareness seemed to hit each of us at the same time and together as we stared at the wild face, and the desperate, hateful eyes. Because the nervous, pumping energy that had been coursing through the room just minutes before melted away in an instant. Even Steve's anger abated, and his dad and Bob let go of him. We all stood looking at Jack, then not looking at him. We looked at our feet, because looking at him, or at each other, was too painful.

"Jesus," Jack declared, chuckling. "Who died?" He felt like an empty suit in my hands, but he shocked both Dad and me when he suddenly jerked away, lunged forward and ran from the house, slamming the door.

We were too shocked to respond at first, but when we heard Jack's truck start up and spit gravel as he roared from the yard, I thought of his condition, and rushed out into the warm summer air. Crickets chirped, and mosquitoes whirred around my ears, but Jack's truck was already a mile down the road. As irrational as it was, I grabbed a rock and heaved it in that direction. Nate bolted off toward the rock, then stopped and sniffed the ground.

Back inside, the mood was somber.

"Steve, Jenny," Dad said, "I can't tell you how sorry I am." His lips pursed.

"George," Steve said. "You know we understand. He's out of his head with the stuff. Nothing you could do. Nothing any of us could."

"You couldn't of stopped him with a firing squad," Art said.

"Well, I shouldn't have even brought the stuff out. I know it gets to him."

"Forget it, George," Mom insisted. "We had a good day. If there was ever a time when it seemed like a good idea, it was tonight." She laid her hand on Dad's back, and his body surrendered to her comfort.

"You want us to drive by the old house, see if he's out there?" Gary offered.

"No, no. If he's out there, he can just sleep it off. Him and the cats," Mom said.

This brought a weak, guilty smile to every face.

I don't know that a big, wonderful house full of people who love each other could ever be lonelier than ours was that night. After our guests left, we sat in the living room for a few minutes, but I don't think we could stand the sight of each other looking so sad and tired.

So we retreated to our rooms, each of us taking with us thoughts of what we might have done to prevent this terrible turn. I lay in my bed, staring out at the black sky, and finding the same darkness in my mind as I tried for the life of me to figure out how a man who was my brother, a man who grew up in the same house, with the same people, could be so different—so unhappy, so full of mistrust. How could he look at the life we had, the gifts the land had so abundantly showered our little family with, and find anything but good in it? I couldn't figure it out. And this didn't even include Rita.

I decided to check on her. I crept from my bed and tiptoed into Muriel's room, where they had moved Rita. She slept with a peaceful, calm expression. She knew nothing about what had happened, of course, and I sat wondering how she would feel about this latest escapade. What would it take for her to lose patience with him, I wondered. Muriel slept quietly in the next bed. And the scene took me back for a moment. To the last night I had reason to sit in the girls' bedroom. The night Katie died. I remembered her knee rising slightly, time after time, and thumping against the mattress. I remembered her face when

she'd reached the house, all flushed and soaked with sweat from running all that way.

And something occurred to me for the first time. I wondered why
Katie had been the one who ran home that evening. Why didn't Jack
run back to tell us that they'd found George? He could have covered the
ground in half the time, and he knew that Katie had been sick for a
week. And a horrifying thought hit me. It had never occurred to me
before that night that Jack actually had a motive for killing George.
Because he would be the next in line to take over the ranch, Jack actually had a motive. I dropped my head to Rita's side, resting it on the
mattress next to her.

Her arm rested on top of the blankets, and although I felt funny
about it, I reached out and took her hand. And as I closed my eyes,
I couldn't stop myself from sorting through the facts. I realized that
this could explain Jack's disappearances. It could explain his attitude.
It could explain a lot, when I really let myself think about it. But
still—I couldn't believe it.

I heard a noise, a shuffle. And I looked up. Rita hadn't moved. I
looked at Muriel. She hadn't moved either, and she was still asleep. I
heard it again. And I looked over at the doorway. And there stood little
George, looking like a tiny version of his father, his eyes wide and
moist. I wasn't sure what to do. I let go of Rita's hand. George started
walking toward me, and I wondered if I should leave. But when he
reached my side, he leaned his head against my shoulder. He rested his
head on my shoulder and held it there.

Book II

dust

7

spring 1932

There are a few events that can't be exaggerated—that no matter how much people talk or write about them, the full force of the experience can't be appreciated unless you were there.

From what I've read and imagined about living through a war, the Depression came as close to that particular hell as anything in terms of taking hold of people's senses and shaking the life out of them, day after day, until we weren't always sure where the sun would rise the next morning.

I guess death has a way of affecting you whether you know it or not. With our livestock toppling over every day, we had to become indifferent toward death to prevent it from overwhelming our spirit, and our will to survive. Carcasses were strewn everywhere, the bones pushing through withered hides, their necks twisted in unnatural positions. It was as if they, in their last moment, noticed something that would save them, reached for it, only to die a tongue's length away. There were also dead people, some walking beside the road, some showing up at the door, paper-thin hat in hand, begging to work for a meal or a bed for the night. And although we obliged them, often even giving them a few days' work, it felt as if we were only delaying the inevitable.

There seemed to be a part of us all that was dead, the part that would normally take note of death and ponder it for a moment, or feel something. It was as if this was energy we could not afford to use, as we had to work harder than ever just trying to keep ourselves and our livestock alive. As the grass became thinner, and the locusts became thicker, we had to rotate our stock more frequently, and make sure their sources of water hadn't dried up. And as our hay became less plentiful, we had to find creative ways to keep them fed in winter.

Our family was more fortunate than most. Ironically, I think George's and Katie's deaths played a role in that success. Because we tried to forget those deaths by working like hell, we had a little more reserve than most. Dad, Bob, and I also worked extra jobs during the Depression years, just to get by. We worked on the road crews up by Alzada, and Dad even tended bar from time to time. We were able to afford feed. But I heard that some folks had to peel bark from trees to feed their sheep.

We had to keep moving, and for this reason, as much death as there was around us, we were also more alive than ever. Both things were true, at once and together, and both were merely a result of being scared as hell. And it was clear that what killed a lot of people, in body or in spirit, was that they sat down and stopped. Like someone lost in a blizzard. They gave in to the fear, or to the loneliness.

The interesting thing about our county was that by the time the Depression hit, we had already experienced a difficult decade. In the twenties, half the banks in Montana had closed, rainfall had been well below average, livestock and grain prices were down, and many of the

honyockers that inundated our little corner of the state had gone
against conventional wisdom and used farming methods such as a
machine that pounded the ground until the topsoil blew away with the
slightest wind. Much of the topsoil in our county was gone before the
Depression even started. Because of this, the amateurs, the less dedicated, the disillusioned, were mostly gone by 1929. Most of us who
were left were survivors already, so we knew what it took.

But if we had known in 1929 that the drought was going to last
another ten years, we could have set our fields on fire, and shot three
quarters of our stock. It would have had the same effect.

We took four steps back for each step forward. But every now and
then, one foot crept out and made a mark in the dust just ahead of the
last one. An inch or two felt a lot like a mile. And each of these tiny suc-
cesses seemed to come just when we needed it. Just when we were about
ready to sit down. Every time the sky surrendered a few drops of moisture, or the price of beef rose a penny or two, we held that in the front
of our minds, running it over time and again for confirmation, and
straining our spirits to will this to be the point where things would turn.

We had to believe that each little step represented the beginning of
the end. And to help ourselves along, we had to create a few bright
spots of our own. A lot of people got married, and too many babies
were born. A woman in Capitol had eight babies during the thirties,
and told anyone who would listen that she was trying to force a little
mercy from God. Just doing her part.

Soon after Rita's accident, and Jack's disappearance, the Stillwell girl
that Bob wasn't sweet on became a regular guest at our dinner table.
And even more often, Bob spent the evening calling on her. On the
nights that he didn't eat at Stillwells', or she wasn't here, Bob would
attack his plate as if he'd never eaten before, then sit in the living room,
pretending to lounge around. His knee would bounce up and down as

if it was about to run out of the room on its own. And his eyes, which were already round, would get that wild, jerky look of someone who thought the law was after him. Finally, he would get up, stretch, and announce, to no one's surprise, "Well, I think I'll take a little drive."

About the time he stopped trying to fool anyone, Helen went back to Spearfish, where she attended the teachers college. And I've never seen a good hand go bad so fast in all my life. Bob's skill as a handyman saved his hide. Because once a week he ran some piece of equipment over a rock or into a ditch. After a few weeks of this, our team of horses even figured out that someone was in love. They'd get stubborn each time Bob took the reins, refusing to move. Thankfully, Helen came home most weekends, so he didn't completely lose his head.

Helen finished school the following spring, and in a stroke of good fortune for Bob, the teacher at the Albion school decided to move back to Missouri, so Helen got the job. She and Bob courted for another year, at her insistence, and they took their vows on a beautiful May afternoon, when the tips of the grass were just beginning to green. We had a reception at our house, and there just happened to be a dance in Alzada that evening. Around nine o'clock, a string of honking vehicles, led by Bob and Helen, snaked the fifteen miles from our place to Alzada.

The first few times Bob brought Helen Stillwell around the house, I thought she was the friendliest person I'd met in a good long while. She was curious—asking question after question. She made me feel as if my life, my opinion, were interesting to her. And I watched the effect of this ability on other people, too. She had a gift—people's guarded manner would melt away in a matter of minutes. Their arms would uncross. Their eyes stopped wandering to other parts of the room. And most significantly, their jaws loosened until it looked as if she'd have them talking all night.

And all the time Helen listened, intent, staring directly up at you. She was small, with short curly hair, schoolgirl cheeks, and soft blue eyes, all of which helped remove any sense of threat from her incessant questioning.

But her charm only worked on me for these first few meetings. I started to feel uneasy with her probing, and the long strings of compliments. There was an element of intrusion to her methods, and I began instinctively to slam the door when she started knocking. I was then faced with the problem of conversing with her without blatantly, rudely dodging her questions. I tried, but she was very aggressive, and I've never been a comfortable liar. It seemed the only way to avoid her questions was to avoid her. It wasn't long before I'd gotten on her bad side. I became close to invisible when she was around. Conversations would bounce around the dinner table, under her deft hand, touching on the events of each person's day except mine.

"You're awfully quiet tonight, Blake," Mom observed on one of these occasions.

"Oh, he's the deep one," Helen jumped in, smiling at me. "Still waters, they say. Right, Blake?"

And thus she shut me up before I could even respond. And at the same time charmed everyone else. But actually, I couldn't have been happier about it. Because verbally she was an expert, and that made me nervous. And because I had so little experience at verbal sparring, I knew I was no match for her.

"Blake, are you going to dance with your mother?" Mom's round face was shiny with sweat and pure joy. She stood in front of me, her hands clasped behind her back.

I grabbed her waist and swung her onto the floor. She squealed, then laughed, throwing her head back, her mouth wide open. We fell into a two-step, shifting and sliding our feet in unison, tilting from one side to the other. The back of Mom's dress was cool and moist, and I felt the moisture in my own shirt, under my suit jacket.

"So what do you think?" Mom asked, smiling up at me.

"I think I'm going to be the old maid in this family."

She laughed and nodded. "You are the steady one, aren't you?"

Mom, now in her fifties, still looked much the same as she had twenty years before, younger than her slender peers, who stooped from years of lugging kids, firewood, and buckets of milk and water. The creases in her face seemed to have always been there. She'd earned them, and they looked good and right on her brown, broad cheeks. Her hair was still the color of a muted sunset, and the color was striking set against the black cotton dress she had made for the occasion.

"Helen and Bob are going to need more space than he has in his room," Mom said, looking earnestly at me.

I dipped a little as the music did, but my mind worked, and I saw what was coming. "Yeah. I suppose they will." I looked down at her, but she wasn't about to say anything more. It was up to me to make the offer. "They can have my room. We can switch."

She nodded, but her distracted manner told me that this wasn't the answer she was looking for. She waited a few more bars before readdressing the issue. "I'm wondering if maybe Rita and the boys shouldn't move to the big house," she said.

The song ended, and we stood in the middle of the floor, waiting for the next one. Mom was looking at me, but her eyes were focused more on my forehead than on my eyes. I did some figuring. Bob and Helen in one room. Rita in another. The boys in the third. Muriel in the fourth. And of course Mom and Dad. This left only one person, and no more rooms.

"You want me to move to the old house?"

Mom threw her arms around me, and for a second I thought she was doing it out of remorse for this request, but in fact the music had started again.

"Just for a while," she said. "Until Jack comes back, or until Bob and Helen start having kids. Who knows? Muriel might even get married soon."

This seemed unlikely. Muriel was busy with college in Spearfish, and she hadn't mentioned any suitors. I was amazed to hear that Mom assumed that Jack would return.

I thought, and knew the suggestion made some sense. I even liked the idea of living alone for a while. But what gnawed at me was who had hatched the plan. I was certain it had been Helen, and the fact that she wanted to submit me to this little exile made me wonder what other tricks she might have up her sleeve. I had a feeling that my new sister-in-law was about to liven things up at the Arbuckle Ranch, and soon.

We had heard nothing from Jack. Nor from anyone else. No sightings, no rumors, nothing.

The initial effect of this on Rita broke my damn heart. Jack's behavior toward her when she fell off the horse had not gone unnoticed, of course. She had been moved by this rare show of tenderness and concern, and I'm sure it gave her brief hope of seeing more of the Jack she had fallen in love with. But when she woke up the next morning, and we told her he was gone, she rolled her head across her pillow, and tightened her lower lip against her teeth. We all crept from the bedroom except Mom, whose murmurings we heard from within.

As far as I know, no one told Rita what happened that night with Jenny. I don't think it would have mattered, anyway. Because after several months, it was clear that something else was keeping Jack away— something we'd probably never understand. By now, I couldn't help but wonder whether it was George, but I didn't tell anyone else that.

When it became clear that Jack wouldn't be back any time soon, we all expected Rita to pack up the kids and return to New Jersey, to her family. Not that we suggested it. We didn't want her to go. Especially me, of course. But we did discuss it briefly, and we all agreed that in the same situation, we would probably want to be with our family. So we waited for her to announce her departure. And because I was so sure she would leave, I gave little thought to the effect it would have on the dynamics of the ranch if she stayed.

One night when she and the boys came for supper, Rita was reluctant to leave, and it seemed the time had come. We muddled through lull after lull in the conversation, finally settling into a mutual silence that wouldn't have been unusual except for Rita's persistent fidgeting. She obviously had something she wanted to talk about. But she waited until the kids fell sleep.

After she had tucked Teddy into Muriel's bed, she sat down, folding her hands in her lap, and looked around at each of us. "Mom, Dad," she began, "I don't know what's going to happen with Jack. And I know things are difficult around here right now, that the boys and I are pretty much nothing but a burden. But if there's any way I can do something to make it worth your while, I would really like to stay here . . . if that's possible."

Because none of us expected this, our silence lasted a good minute, which no doubt made Rita wonder.

"What about your family?" Mom finally asked.

Rita leaned forward, resting her elbows on her knees and staring down at her tan, callused hands. She held them out in front of her, spreading the fingers, studying the backs of them. "My family . . ." She stopped, inhaling deeply, covering her eyes. "I've never felt as strongly about my own family as I do about this one." Her voice broke, and I felt a lump rise in my throat.

Again, our silence filled a long gap, and who wouldn't have thought just as Rita did? "I'm sorry," she said. "I shouldn't have asked. This is awful," she said. "I've put you all on the spot."

"Oh no, no, no," Dad said, bounding from his chair. He started toward her, but that was too much for him, and he paced the room. "My god, Rita . . ." He tried to go on, struggling to find the words, but his head moved from side to side and his mouth hung half open, making no sound.

Mom rose, walked over and sat next to Rita on the sofa, putting an arm around her. "Please stay," she said.

So Rita stayed, and it created an interesting scenario. As was common with most ranches of that generation, there were no written guidelines to determine who would take over our ranch, or how it would be split up among the survivors once my father and mother passed on. And because it was a source of potential conflict, it wasn't a subject that was discussed openly.

So what usually happened was that the siblings forged ahead year after year, each of them drawing their own private conclusions about how much of the ranch they were entitled to, and measuring their case against the others. And when the time came, when the owner died, and decisions had to be made, they fought it out. After years of silently creating their justifications, the reasons were strongly felt, and it often got ugly.

There were three major determining factors. First, of course, was age. The oldest was the natural heir—usually the oldest boy, or if the oldest daughter married someone who was interested in running the place. But it was rare for a woman to run a ranch in those days.

Second was need, which came in the form of dependents. The more kids you had, the bigger share of the ranch you could expect. And the third was investment, which was measured in time spent devoted to the ranch.

So in our case, if Jack had stayed, the decision would have been clear. He was the oldest, and he was also the only one with kids. But now that he was gone, each year that he stayed away would weaken his position, and shift it to me. Of course, I knew he wasn't interested anyway, but then I also knew that Jack was capable of changing his tune if it was to his advantage. But having Rita and the boys there complicated matters. How would they fit into the formula? We never discussed it.

The dance was crowded. And once everyone found out that there were newlyweds in the room, Bob and Helen were swamped with well-wishers, requests for the next dance, and invitations to step outside for a toast. Bob, who wasn't used to all the attention, spent his evening whirling around with a goofy grin on his face. He blushed and laughed and even talked a little.

But he was clearly not the eye of this little hurricane. The whirl-wind of activity and sound swirled through the small community hall, into the kitchen, out into the parking lot, and back, with Helen rotating squarely in the middle of the twirling fray. She wore the delicate white wedding dress she'd sewn herself, and its whiteness pulled the flow of browns and blacks and blues wherever she went. It was what everyone dreams their wedding day should be, and I was willing to put my feelings about Helen to one side long enough to grant her that. Especially for Bob's sake.

"When do you take the fall, Blake?" I turned to find Steve Glasser at my elbow, chewing a sandwich.

"Well, Steve, I guess I ought to find someone who's available before I start thinking about that."

Steve smiled and started ticking off names of single women around the county. He counted the names on his fingers, gathering the digits on one hand, then the other, into a bunch.

"All right, all right," I said, chuckling. "You made your point." I looked out across the dance floor, pretending to be searching for some-one. Steve kept his gaze fixed on me, the fingers in his left hand still gathered in the right. His good eye stared me down.

"So you done your calving yet?" I asked.

"Oh, ho," he laughed. "So we're changing the subject, are we?" He dropped his hands, then threw them in the air. "All right, if that's the way it's going to be. How about I buy you a drink?"

Steve and I wandered out to his pickup, where he reached under the seat. We handed the bottle back and forth a few times. I was hoping that Steve wouldn't bring up the subject of women again. It was not a topic I enjoyed discussing. Mainly because I had so little to talk about. From the time I left school, I hadn't been around women much outside of the occasional dance, card party, or rodeo. Between work and the years I had spent honing my pitching, I had found little time to even think about women, much less court them. And this lack of contact had made me much more bashful than I used to be. Each year, I thought that I would make an effort to get to know somebody in particular, or to talk to more girls at the next dance. But being alone got to be pretty comfortable after a while, to the point that the thought of making the effort was a lot more uncomfortable than being alone.

The one exception, of course, was Rita. She was the closest thing I'd found to someone near my age that I could talk to without stammering and feeling the heat in my face. But there was a slight barrier there, of course.

Steve's whiskey bottle was cool against my lips, but the liquor warmed them up soon enough, along with the rest of my body. Prohibition was history, so the bottles had real labels, better flavor, and less kick, but a few shots had me feeling pretty good.

"So you got your eye on anyone?" Steve asked.

I cleared my throat. "Ah, hell, Steve, I got so many offers I haven't been able to decide who to choose from."

Steve chuckled, shaking his head. "Well, I can see this isn't going anywhere."

We each took a couple more nips, listening to the muted sounds of the five-piece band, the whooping and hollering and stomping of feet from inside.

"So how long you figure this dry spell to last?" Steve asked.

"If I knew that, I'd give Hoover a run at the big house," I answered.

Steve nodded, tipping the bottle. His good eye was barely more focused than the other. "You never heard from Jack, have you?"

I shook my head. He shook his.

"That's a goddam shame," he said. "Runnin' off and leaving a wife and two kids over a little thing like that."

I nodded.

"Even Jenny knew he was too drunk to know what he was doing," Steve continued. "She doesn't hold it against him."

"Well, I think there's more to it than we'll ever know."

"Yeah?" Steve eyed me, squinting, waiting.

I reached for the bottle. "You done your calving yet?"

He laughed. "Blake, you sly son of a bitch."

I was holding out on Steve. Actually, I was holding out on everyone. I'd learned something about Jack that I hadn't told anyone, nor did I plan to.

What I'd found out was the truth about Jack's years in the service, and it happened completely by accident. Several weeks after he disappeared, one of the possibilities that occurred to me was that he might have reenlisted. So I wrote to the army personnel office, explaining the situation. I gave them all the information I thought might be useful, including the fact that he had served during the big war, stationed somewhere in France.

They replied a few months later. They were very sorry, but they had no record of a Jack Arbuckle currently enlisted. However, they did have a record of a Jack Arbuckle, from Montana, who served during the big war. But he had been stationed in New Jersey, not France.

My first reaction was—well, obviously they've made a mistake. After all, he'd written us from France. Their records must be botched up. But I got to thinking, and the more I thought, the more I considered another explanation. With Jack knowing that the folks would be mad as hell about him running off, what better way to win their favor than to come back as a war hero? It was the perfect strategy.

It made me think of Satchel Paige's advice: the best secret is to make everyone believe you've got a secret.

The brilliance of the ploy had carried over even after he returned. For years, despite my anger toward him, I had often stepped back from the urge to be critical of Jack, figuring he needed some room, some time, to forget the war. I figured that being in a war was one of those experiences that only the people who were there could appreciate, and that only those who shared the experience could provide comfort. For years I had given him the benefit of the doubt when he showed his temper, or disappeared for a few days. Now to realize that he not only didn't deserve this kind of leeway, but that he'd lied to get it, infuriated me. I wondered whether Rita was aware of this deception, and I considered talking to her about it. But I decided that if she didn't know, it would just add more unnecessary grief to her memory of Jack. I decided not to tell anyone else for the same reason. Jack had hurt them all enough. So I simply added this to the pile of secrets I held about my brother.

Steve and I stepped back inside, where with my spirits lubricated, I was ready for some dancing. I danced every song for the rest of the night, bouncing from Muriel to Rita to Mom to any other woman with two feet. I even dragged Jenny out for a few twirls around the old pine floor. And finally, I endured a couple of songs with the belle of the ball, Helen, who hardly gave me a glance, even a foot away. I didn't care. I was in it for the good time, and I sure as hell had one.

About halfway through the dance, as we all stood there sweating, waiting for the next song to start, Lawrence and Sophie Andrews came in, along with two little kids. I hadn't seen them for a couple of years, although from time to time I fondly remembered the kiss behind the

Albion Town Hall. My stomach folded up inside, and in the time it took me to walk from one side of the room to the other, I felt as if a dry washcloth had been stuffed down my throat. I said hello to them, and the butterflies rose up inside me just from this brief greeting. As with every other time I'd seen Sophie since that fateful day in Albion, she was cool. It was obvious that this was her way of putting that night out of her mind, by pretending it hadn't happened. She still looked terrific, though. So I was polite, and Lawrence was his usual friendly, oblivious self. But I didn't talk to them for long.

The next day was a Sunday. We had finished shearing, and our sheep were done lambing. It would be a couple of weeks before we started calving. So I did a few chores around the place. It was beautiful out, with the sky the deepest, cloudless blue. Despite a slight hangover, I was in a great mood. But my mood was undermined by the knowledge that I had an unpleasant task ahead of me.

I walked to the house, up to my room, where I began packing my clothes. I was stuffing them into the old leather satchel from my school days in Belle Fourche when little George appeared at my door.

For a while he just stood there, not looking at me, not even answering when I said hello. He was six now, and looked more like Jack than ever—with the same narrow face and hooked nose, small eyes. He kicked at the floor a couple of times, the dust flying off his little boot. Finally he said, "My ma wants to talk to you."

I set down the shirt I was folding and studied him, trying to imagine why he'd waited so long to say so. "All right," I said. I packed the last of my clothes and followed George outside, toward the old house. Nate trotted along beside us, smiling and barking, his tongue dripping into the dust. He got a little too close to George at one point, and George bopped him in the ear. The dog yipped and tucked his tail between his legs, but quickly trotted back near George's side.

"What did you do that for?" I asked.

George just shrugged, head down. He didn't need to look where he was going—he'd walked back and forth enough times that he knew the trail by heart. His hands were stuffed deep in his pockets, and a small tuft of hair stuck up like a feather on the back of his head.

We approached the old house, where Rita was out in Katie's garden, which she had brought to life. She drove a spade over and over into the ground, turning each shovelful back into its hole. Her movements were forceful and sure, with the blade disappearing well into the dry earth with each thrust. I wondered why she was spading by hand, when a cultivator would turn the whole square in a half hour. Teddy, who was three, was helping, following behind her, turning handfuls of dirt.

When Rita saw us, she buried the spade so it stood alone. She wiped her forehead with her sleeve. I noticed her rigid jaw and the fire in her eye, and I understood. She was angry, and using the activity to work off the raw emotion. She motioned with her head, tilting it quickly to one side, and she started for the house. I followed.

George grabbed the spade handle and tried pulling it from the ground, but he didn't make much progress. Teddy tried to give him a hand, but George pushed him away.

"Coffee?" Rita asked.

"You have anything cold?"

When Rita didn't even hear my question, I realized just how angry she was. She put the kettle on the old wood stove, then opened the door, peering inside. She stuffed kindling and a couple of split logs into the stove's belly. Then she struck a match against the stove and lit the fire. The flame spread through the blackness, and Rita slammed the door shut. I was glad it was a fairly cool day as the heat spread through the room.

Rita sat directly in front of me, just a few feet away, leaning one elbow on her knee. She rested the other hand on the table. A smudge of dirt spread across her forehead. Because she'd called me there, I assumed she was angry at me, and I tried to imagine why.

She fixed a steady glare on me. "Did Mom ask you to move out here?"

"Yeah, as a matter of fact." I watched, confused, as she leaned back in her chair and sighed.

"Are you and the boys planning to move to the big house?" I asked.

"No!" She slammed her hand palm down against the table. I jumped.

Rita didn't say anything for quite some time, turning her head to one side and breathing deeply in through her nose. In that silent moment, I realized that whatever had brought on this reaction probably had nothing to do with me. And I embraced the hope that she was angry for the same reason I was.

"What's going on?" I asked.

She continued to breathe in, real slow, through her nose, trying to calm herself, her eyes closed. She finally looked at me, but her eyes were slits.

"Blake, I don't know if I should get into it. I don't have much place talking about someone when I'm not really part of this family." She kept her gaze fixed right on my eyes, those deep blue eyes of hers showing a passionate desire to express something that she felt very deeply. I knew I needed to reassure her.

"Well, maybe you should go ahead and say what you need to say." I nodded. "I really think you should."

She had to think for a minute. She measured me. Then she took another deep breath and nodded once, as if giving herself the go-ahead. She spoke in a low, steady tone. "It just seems to me that when somebody's just starting out with a new family, they don't have any business trying to arrange things to suit themselves."

"I couldn't agree more," I said, feeling a tremendous relief that I had an ally. To me, Rita had even more reason to be upset. Because whether she wanted to or not, she had never thought of asking to move to the big house, much less suggesting that someone move out.

She turned her head to one side. Her hand fell again with a loud smack. "She asked Mom before the wedding, even!" She shook her head. "I won't live in the same house with that woman," she said, more quietly now.

I nodded. "Well, you ought to have some say in the matter, right?"

The water was boiling. Rita dumped some grounds in a pan, and after letting it brew a few minutes, she poured two cups.

I broke the news to Mom that Rita and the boys were going to stay in the old house. She took it hard. "Not a very good way to start things off with a new member of the family," she said.

"You might mention that to the person who suggested it," I said.

She looked hurt, apparently thinking I meant her. I realized that she had been taken in by Helen's charm a lot more than I suspected. And that angered me even more. Because I have known few people more immune to charm than my mother.

Now I could only wait and see. Because I suspected that once Helen's plans had been disrupted, there would be repercussions. I also suspected Helen would be subtle about it—something that wouldn't be obvious to anyone but me, and maybe Rita. I thought it would be difficult to pull off a scheme like that. This would be the last time I underestimated Helen.

"Blake, you were on fire today!" Dad stabbed the big roast on the platter in front of him and began slicing, laying the thin cuts on the plates piled next to him. We passed them around the table, where the whole family had gathered. "I've never seen anyone pitch like that in my life."

I blushed and looked down at my plate. It had been one of those days when the rhythm was perfect. I felt as if I could throw the ball clean through a wall. And the curveball spun through the strike zone like a diving mosquito. It was the first day in years that I had thought back to my tryout with a slight sense of regret. I dished up some mashed potatoes and corn on the cob.

Two months had passed since Bob and Helen's wedding, and we'd all traveled to Capitol for a Sunday-afternoon game. We were covered with dust when we returned, and even after beating ourselves until a cloud filled the air, we were all powdered and gray, the color of mice. Muriel was off in Spearfish, where she was now going to school, and decided to stay for the summer to work in the local drugstore.

The one thing that I had told people about my trip to Omaha was that I'd seen Satchel Paige pitch. I told them that I'd met him, and that he'd taught me a secret pitch. The effect was immediate. The first game I pitched after that, the other team came to the plate as if they were facing a firing squad. I did my little glove flip every now and then, and after each strikeout, the batter shook his head as if the ball had been invisible. And I wasn't doing a damn thing different. It was hilarious.

"I thought that scrawny little guy playing third was going to throw his bat at you after you struck him out the third time," said Rita, raising an ear of corn to her mouth.

"Could you please pass me some of that gravy, Mom?" Helen pointed with her delicate, respectful manner, and Mom passed the bowl as if it was filled with gold dust.

"How many times did you use that pitch ol' Satchel taught you?" Dad asked.

I winked. "You don't think I'm about to reveal my secret now, do you, after all these years?"

"Ah, come on." Dad chuckled. "You think we're going to sell it? Even if we wanted to, nobody's got any money anyway."

I kept my mouth shut, grinning at Dad, and after staring me down for a while, he shook his head. "All right," he muttered. "I guess this is just something we have to get used to, living with a genius."

We all laughed, then dug back into our food.

"Well, I think we need to drink a toast to both our heroes." Helen raised her glass. "After all, Blake couldn't have done what he did without someone to catch all those wonderful pitches." She looked over at Bob, whose ears burned red. I caught a glimpse of Rita, who rolled her eyes just enough for me to see.

We all lifted our glasses and drank. I kept an eye on Helen, wondering as I had so many times in recent weeks whether her plan for revenge would kick into gear. Every time she did something nice to me, my suspicions ran high.

"How's your hand?" I asked Bob.

Bob looked at his hand as if he hadn't thought to check yet, then shrugged. "It doesn't hurt too bad."

"I just don't know how you do it, catching those pitches over and over with that tiny little glove," Helen said, and Bob blushed again.

Helen's fawning started to embarrass me. "So when do you want to go after those cattle that got through Glassers' fence, Dad?" I asked.

"How many did he say there were?" Dad smeared a piece of bread across the gravy on his plate.

"About twenty head," I answered.

George reached over and took a stab at a piece of Teddy's meat.

"Hey," Teddy said, lunging at George's plate. George whacked him with an elbow, and Teddy wailed, holding his little hand over his head. Rita calmly stood up and switched places with Teddy, putting herself between the boys. She gave George a hard look.

"You two behave or you're going home."

Teddy protested, blubbering, "But I didn't do anything. I didn't even do anything."

"I swear, it must be such a chore, raising children on your own." Helen made a neat cut through the middle of her roast, pushing the halves apart with knife and fork, then cutting one of those in half, very deliberately.

Rita blinked, looking up at Helen with her eyes open wide. All other eyes also turned to Helen, and I thought, hoped, that she'd finally stumbled into such awkward territory that even she couldn't charm her way out of it.

"I just don't think I could do as well as you do, Rita, if I were in your shoes." Helen smiled sweetly at Rita, those bright blue eyes showing limitless compassion. Rita smiled back, but the anger showed in the tight arch of her lips, and in her eyes. Mom looked confused, and Dad was glancing from face to face as if he was wishing someone would explain what was happening.

"You know, it really isn't my place to say anything, but I just think it's just so awful that Jack ran off and left you like he did. It must be very hard." She kept her eyes on her plate, poking a very petite bite of meat into her mouth and chewing with the cool confidence of an assassin. "For all of you," she added.

The room was as quiet as night, and I sat dumbfounded, wondering what the hell she could be thinking. She had been around our family long enough to know that Jack was a subject we didn't discuss. And being a local, she also knew that voicing an opinion about another family's misfortune, so boldly, just wasn't done. I looked at Bob, whose eyes were glued to his plate. Unfortunately, my suspicion that she was just getting started was quickly confirmed.

"And it must have been terribly hard to find out, after all you've had to endure with Jack, that he was never overseas during the war. That must have been such a shock." She said this in such a sympathetic tone that I almost believed she felt bad about it. Then, in a look that would have fooled even the most perceptive, she scanned the startled faces around the table, then fixed a surprised, perplexed gaze on me. "Blake, you mean you haven't told the rest of them yet?"

I was completely thrown, humiliated that my secret had been revealed so publicly. My face was hot with shame, crimson, and my hand began to tremble. I was so embarrassed that I couldn't even address what was obvious—that Helen had rifled through my things and found the letter. I felt the eyes of my entire family, and although it probably wasn't true, what I thought those eyes were saying was that I had betrayed them.

"Oh, I feel just horrible," Helen continued. "Blake talked to me for the longest time one night about a letter he got from the government saying that Jack was never in France. Oh, Blake, I'm so sorry. I just assumed you'd told the others." She put a hand to her cheek, and her tone was sugar sweet.

I was paralyzed. Helen took another bite and chewed, looking directly at me.

"What on earth are you talking about?" Rita asked Helen, incredulous. "France?"

"Oh dear," Helen said.

I knew there and then that we were dealing with someone whose skills in the area of manipulation were far and above anything I'd ever imagined. The only mystery now would be what Helen wanted from us, and how far she would go.

8

winter 1933

—

It didn't take Helen long to establish a certain hold on the ranch. Ironically, Rita's decision not to move into the big house, in defiance of Helen's wishes, ended up working in Helen's favor. Because when I moved in with Rita and the boys, although we spent most evenings at the big house, a natural separation had formed.

But Helen was smart enough to realize that she had gained an advantage, and that treating Rita or me badly would only arouse suspicions of her motives. So she employed her considerable charm toward planning birthday parties for "the exiles," as we called ourselves. Because Rita usually worked out in the fields, Helen suggested that we should just plan on coming to the big house for dinner each night, which Helen helped Mom prepare after she finished her day teaching.

It became impossible not to wonder sometimes, despite the fact that Helen had so clearly invaded my territory to find the letter about

Jack, whether I was wrong about her. Rita and I talked about it often.

"Do you think that whole thing with the letter was just a bad decision?" I asked Rita during one of these discussions. "Maybe her family is more ruthless than ours. Maybe she felt like she had to do something dramatic to make a statement or something."

Rita sighed, looking up from her game of solitaire and shaking her head. "You are a trusting soul, Blake. You really want to believe the best about people, don't you?"

I raised my brow. "I guess so. I never really thought about it."

"Just look at it this way, Blake. If you were new to this family, and you wanted to gain an edge, who would you cuddle up to?"

I thought. "Dad," I said emphatically.

Rita looked surprised. "Really?"

"Sure. Of course. It's his ranch."

Rita nodded. "Okay. Yes. That's true. But . . . well, Blake, I don't mean to be callous, but look at it this way . . . think about your folks. First of all, who looks like they're going to be around the longest?"

That was easy. Because of Dad's smaller frame, the decades of work had taken a toll on him. He was stooped, thinner, his face taking on much the same haunted, ravaged, distant look that we saw in many of the disconnected men who drifted through our region looking for a bed for the night. "Mom," I answered.

"Exactly," Rita answered. "She's like the old water pump out there. When the rest of us are dead, and all the buildings have rotted away, somebody's going to come along and find that water pump still spitting gushes of that stinky alkali water into a bucket, and your mom out gathering the eggs."

I smiled, nodding in agreement.

"Your mom is the heartbeat of this place."

Again I nodded.

"And what's the quickest way to get through to your mom?" Rita then asked. "What is her biggest priority?"

"The ranch," I said matter-of-factly.

Rita looked at me with a slight grin, and tipped her head toward me, saying with a look, "Try again."

"No? God, I'm not doing very well on this test, am I?"

"Well, you're almost right," Rita said, laughing. "Your family, Blake. The family. Your mom would chop her arms off for her family."

"Well, maybe one of them," I replied. "She wouldn't be able to play cards without at least one."

Rita smiled. "Oh, if anyone could figure out a way . . ."

We laughed.

"But am I right?" Rita asked.

I nodded. "Yeah. You're right. The family."

Rita went back to her game. I picked up a newspaper, but my thoughts were still on the topic. "I guess the thing I don't understand is why she works so damn hard at it? With her charm, and her intelligence, she could have made an impression without turning it into some kind of competition." I shrugged.

Rita nodded, looking up at me sadly. "That's just it, Blake. That's where you're right, I think. Maybe her family is more ruthless . . . more . . . less trusting. If she doesn't keep trying, maybe she feels like she's falling behind. Some families are like that."

Rita's head dropped back to her cards. Her hair was up, as it usually was, the thick straight brown bands pulled tightly into a ponytail. There were a few gray streaks now, glinting subtly in the lantern's glow. Rita had never really talked about her family much, and it always made me wonder. Because she had become such a vital, positive influence on our family, it seemed odd to me that she didn't have more of a connection to them.

"Was yours like that?"

Rita lifted her head one last time, and studied me with an expression I hadn't seen from her before, a look that was even a bit frightening. I felt like a child who wasn't quite grasping a math problem.

"They were worse," she said, and her tone made me regret asking. She dropped her head, and the discussion ended there, abruptly. I never mentioned her family again.

"Frank, you see that?" Art Walters squinted into the sun, pointing just shy of the Finger Buttes. Art, in his increased sense of confusion, had been calling me Frank for several months. I tried correcting him a couple of times, but I soon saw it was pointless.

I shielded my eyes and looked in that direction. "What, Art? I don't see a thing."

"See that little bunch of pine trees there?" He pointed again.

I nudged my horse closer to his, then followed his arm. "Okay, yeah. I see those."

"Left of there." He waved his finger. "Just to the left and further along."

"Art, you're crazy. There's nothing out there but snow, and maybe part of South Dakota."

Art laughed and steam rushed from his mouth.

"No, by god, Frank, I swear there's a herd of antelopes out there. If you look a little harder, you can see a kind of shadow."

I buried my heels into my horse's flanks and yelled over my shoulder. "All right, buddy. If you're sure, let's give it a look."

It was warmer than normal for December, and the sun sparkled in shades of pink, blue, and yellow off the snow, which lay quiet and still. No wind. And although our breath showed, I could feel the sweat on my chest. The butt of my rifle, which rocked in its scabbard, bumped against my knee. My saddle creaked as we galloped through a shallow draw toward the buttes. Art caught up with me.

"Frank, if you're thinkin' about gettin' out ahead of me so you can get the first shot off, you got a surprise comin'."

"Sounds like a challenge, Art."

"You got that right."

I had suggested this hunting expedition to Art at a dance the previous weekend. It was common knowledge that Art was in trouble up there in his ramshackle, tucked-away ranch. His brother Bert, the former bootlegger, was dead four years now, one of many who couldn't wait the Depression out. He blew his head off, probably using the same rifle Art carried with him now. And Art's older brother Sam, the hardest worker of the three, had caught his arm in a thresher two summers ago. The machine had ripped the arm from its socket, and Sam would have bled to death if Art hadn't found him that afternoon.

With Sam's effectiveness diminished, most of the responsibility for keeping the place going lay with Art. And from what we could see, he'd made a hell of an effort. The fight to survive will bring the best out in a guy, I guess. But his efforts weren't enough, and Steve told me that on his last visit to Art's place, there was hardly anything to eat.

Art didn't realize I knew this, of course. In his mind this was nothing more than a couple of friends doing some hunting.

"You see 'em now, Frank?" Art pointed again, in the same direction.

I peered toward the buttes. "Art, I'm sorry, but for the life of me I cannot see what the hell you're pointing at. Either you've got an eagle eye or you've been dipping into the moonshine a little early today."

Art shot me a bit of a hurt look.

"All right, all right, I believe you, but I still don't see anything."

Art, who was nearly sixty, showed the strain. His clothes were torn and threadbare. Even the brim of his felt hat was torn, so that one side hung down close to his ear.

And the wind and worry had worked away at his face, cracking and drying it, pinching the skin around his eyes and mouth. He'd lost half his teeth, and his cheeks hugged his jaw so tightly it looked as though you could break the surface with your fingernail. It was a face common to many during the Depression, and although Dad still had his teeth, he shared many of the same features.

We came up out of the draw and still had several hundred yards to go before we neared the grove Art had pointed out. The heat of the sun's reflection oozed up from the snow, and I pulled my kerchief up over my nose to avoid getting burned. I kept my eyes glued to the spot where Art claimed to see the antelope, and after a while began to wonder whether he was hallucinating. We were close enough that a big herd would be easily spotted. Then we were close enough that a small herd would be easily spotted. And I expected if we did see any game, it would be a smaller herd, as the drought had also beaten down the wildlife in the region.

"Frank!" Art pointed again, thrusting his finger toward the buttes, a frantic gesture.

I squinted again, shielding my eyes. Finally—still a ways off, behind the trees—I saw, just barely, two antelope facing each other, their noses to the ground, where they fed on a small patch of green.

"Art, how the hell did you see those things from way back there?"

He laughed—a frantic, almost giddy cackle. "I ain't lost all my senses yet, Frank."

We decided to circle through the trees, hoping they would shield us. We took it easy, slowing the horses to a walk, and we unholstered our rifles. From the trees, we were just a little out of range, so we'd have to sneak out from our shelter and get closer before we could get a shot off.

Art whispered my name and signaled with his hands, waving and pointing to indicate that he'd wait there while I went ahead, so we could come at them from different angles. I waved and moved on, nudging my horse, wincing whenever she snorted or pawed at the ground. But the antelope weren't so easily spooked, and when I was as far as I could get from Art without losing ground to the antelope, I raised my arm, and we crept into the meadow.

They saw us immediately and took off, bounding in that four-legged, graceful way that makes most animals look stationary. Just as I started after them, a shot sounded, and I looked over to see Art getting set to fire again.

"Art!" I yelled as loudly as I could. But he shot once more, and I turned my horse toward him, pummeling her flanks. "Art, stop! Jesus, what are you doing?"

The antelope were not only out of range, but nearly out of sight. Art lowered his rifle, laying it across his thighs, then pushed his hat onto the back of his head. I caught up to him, and was about to tear into him, but there was something about his expression that stopped me. Something pathetic. He looked defeated.

"Well, that wa'n't too smart, was it?" he said quietly.

"It's all right, Art. Let's go after 'em."

He looked up and shrugged, holding his mouth to one side. "Not much use now, Frank." He threw a hand into the air.

"Come on," I said. I kicked my horse, and started in the direction the antelope had headed. I didn't look to see whether Art followed, because I was sure he would.

We followed the tracks until they led to a fence that the antelope had crawled through. We had to take a detour of about a hundred yards to get to a gate.

"Frank, we ain't never gonna catch up to these bastards," Art said.

"Art, you got something better to do this morning? We might as well give it a shot."

"Yeah, well, I guess. But I'm thinkin' it's too late."

"Art, shut up." I swung a leg off my horse to open the gate. "Just shut up and follow me. We have all day. And if we don't catch these two, maybe we'll find a few others."

Art set his jaw, his lower lip pinched up against the upper, sticking out a little. He nudged his horse through the gate, spitting into the snow once he was on the other side. I closed the gate and mounted my horse.

"You know, Frank . . ." Art looked thoughtful. He paused for quite a while. "You only talked to me like that one other time that I remember." He fixed an eye on me as we started back toward the tracks. "It was the day I helped you pull your cow out of the bog."

"Art, you pulled a gun on me!"

"Well, now, if I'm remembering right, there was some trespassing goin' on that day. . . ."

I groaned and waved him off.

"You thought I wasn't goin' to remember that part," he said.

"Oh, I remember. There was some trespassing going on, all right. And not only were you the one who was trespassing," I said, half mad and half amused, "but that was your goddam cow."

"Oh, no, you're just not rememberin' things too clear today, are you?"

I held my breath and decided not to continue the discussion, figuring that by the time we were through arguing, I'd be ready to leave Art out there to starve.

"Art, the last thing I want to do is challenge your fine memory. Of course you're right."

"Damn right."

After a silent half hour, we came up over a rise, and I spotted the antelope three-quarters of a mile away. I pulled up and put my arm out to stop Art, who was riding behind me. There was nothing but white, empty space between us and them, so we had to come up with a strategy.

A line of brush ran along the east side of the meadow. We agreed I would sneak along behind the brush while Art approached from the other direction. We figured he'd scare them toward me if they didn't see him too soon.

The sun shone nearly straight overhead, and the warm sweat felt good inside my clothes. Tromping through the brush, my horse's hooves unleashed the aroma of scrubwood and wild plum. I breathed deep. I kept a close eye on Art, trying to stay ahead of him in case the antelope jumped too quickly. I cradled my gun in my right elbow, the weight of its oily barrel heavy on my forearm. About halfway down, still well out of range, I heard a shot.

"Damn," I muttered. I was behind a thick bush and had to move forward before I saw Art, at full gallop, aiming at the bounding figures, again yards out of his range. He shot, then pulled his horse up. Art's head jerked forward and back, and I could imagine what he was saying. Or maybe I couldn't.

I resisted the urge to ask "What the hell has gotten into you today?" until I heard Art's explanation. I wanted to give him the benefit of the doubt. He'd been hunting since he could lift a gun, long before I was born, and was actually known as one of the better hunters in our parts.

"Those sons of bitches saw me and took off 'fore I knew what . . ." His eyes, desperate and wide, darted around me, over and under me, anywhere but at me, and it was then I realized how much Art's rabid desire to get one of the animals might be affecting his judgment. He looked frantic, hungry for something deeper, more crucial to life than food. He had the look of a man who had to get one of these antelope to prove something, to make things right somehow, to give him a reason to keep on. It scared the living daylights out of me.

"All right, Art. Let's just take it easy. I think we're okay. They're headed up toward that grove of cottonwoods near Hay Creek. If they go in there, it will give us a good chance of sneaking up on them and flushing them out." I slipped my rifle back into its scabbard. "Let's rest for a second or two."

Art nodded, his head bobbing unevenly. "Sons a bitches took off 'fore I even woulda figured they could see me," he said.

It was possible the antelope really did see him and take off, but the more he talked, the more I was convinced that he'd shot at them first. I decided if we caught up to them again, I'd better make damn sure I shot before Art did. He was in no condition to hit anything.

The tracks led exactly where I thought they would, into a grove of cottonwoods, an ideal spot. The cluster of trees was small and narrow, and it ended forty yards past where the tracks led into it, leaving us plenty of space to move around to the other side.

"All right, Art. I'm going to circle around the end there. Give me about ten minutes to get to the other side and go on in. Try and flush them from the north, so they're running past me, not away from me."

"I know, I know, Frank. I been flushin' since before you knew your name."

"Okay, Art. Just wanted to make sure."

Art had his hand on the stock of his rifle, although it was still in its scabbard. He held that thing like he was afraid it would run out on him, and I had a bad feeling I wouldn't get a shot off all day.

So I rode quickly, hoping to get out there before he did something boneheaded. I made it to the other side, heard nothing, and found a perfect spot to wait, behind a lone bush that was tall enough to hide me and my horse, but not tall enough to block my aim.

I didn't have to wait long. After a minute, I heard a rustling, then a whoop from Art, and both antelope bolted out into the open, less than fifty yards away. They were headed perfectly, running directly in front of me, from my right to my left. I shouldered my rifle, aimed at the lead, set my sights on his neck, and fired. The pop was echoed by another one, and I saw Art riding wild from the trees, rifle to his shoulder.

The antelope fell, its rear end tumbling forward, over its bowed, grounded neck, straight into the air, then twisting around the legs, following in parallel flight, until the whole torso flopped onto its side and slid forward, pushing the snow in front of it. The other animal darted to its right, angling back into the trees.

Art galloped toward the fallen antelope, whooping and hollering, his rifle above his head like a spear. I trotted toward him.

"I got him, Frank. I got the son of a bitch." He swung down off his horse and ran toward the animal, limping a little and laughing.

My pride almost got the best of me. I knew I was the one who hit the antelope, especially when I got there and saw the wound in the side of its neck, six inches above my aim. Art's bullet would have had to make a ninety-degree turn to hit him from where he shot. But he wouldn't have heard a word of it, and I was going to give the meat to him anyway. So I swallowed my tongue, nearly choking on the damn thing.

The antelope's side rose and fell, but just for a few seconds. His round, black eyes were wild, then sleepy, then dead, and he twitched, his legs jerking a few last spasms. Then he was still, stiff.

Watching death affects people differently, of course. Bob had never gotten used to it. When he was a boy, around twelve, he held a sheep's head while Dad slit its throat. Bob lost his breakfast and was never able to do anything like that again. Jack was the opposite, driving the blade of a knife into an animal's neck without a thought—not cruel, as if he was enjoying it, like some people I've known. But nearly heartless. I could butcher without thinking about it too much, but when the knife hit the hide, it always chilled my heart for a second or two.

I found death sad, but so peaceful that the sadness seemed secondary, almost insignificant. Since the night I'd watched Katie come to the end of that agonizing struggle with her body, I'd figured death could sometimes be a good way to end things.

* * *

The antelope was a buck, an older one. He was gaunt, his hide hugging his ribs, and he wouldn't have lived much longer. His meat would be tough, and sour, but Art rejoiced in the kill as if he'd never have to worry about food again.

"Let's go after the other one," he shouted. "We got to get one for you."

I shook my head. "No, Art. Don't worry about it. We have to haul this thing back to your place, then I have to get home. I don't want to work my horse any harder. We probably won't even find it."

I could see the relief in his eyes, but I appreciated the fact that he'd thought of me. After all, he had what he wanted.

We gutted the antelope and hefted the corpse up over the haunches of Art's horse, tying its front legs to the back ones. Then we started for his place.

It had warmed up enough that the surface snow was softening. It no longer had the slick sheen of ice, but looked rough, with shades of gray.

"You don't have to go with me, Frank. Really."

"I don't mind keeping you company, Art. Besides, I'm worried you might get lost." I winked.

"Smart aleck."

We rode silent the rest of the way. One of the nice things about winters during the Depression was that the snow covered the awful, bare ground, giving you a chance to forget how bad it looked. And the winter was free of the Depression haze of dust that kept us from seeing as far as we were accustomed. I liked to gaze out across the whiteness and picture the miles of waist-high grass that was once common and expected in Carter County. I'd close my eyes and imagine it that way again. But when the snow melted away, I knew that the gray, bald earth would resume its annoying habit of killing that fantasy.

I hadn't been to Art's for almost a year. One side of the barn had collapsed, and once we were inside it, I noticed he'd propped beams between the ground and the roof to keep the building from falling in on itself. We hung the antelope from the rafters, which made me nervous, then went into the house for a cup of coffee.

Art's brother Sam sat in a corner of their shanty, his torso unbalanced and incomplete with the empty shirtsleeve pinned to its shoulder.

It's a sad fact of life on the land that a large measure of a man's worth lies in his body, so that a mutilation like Sam's has the immediate effect of making him less valuable, less of a person than before. There is no way around it, and the results, except in cases of an unusually strong spirit, are predictable. If they don't move to town, they become exiles, usually hermits, because nobody knows what to say to them.

Sam had always been a loner anyway. He said hello, but that was all he said while I was there. A bottle sat on the table next to him, on the armless side. He didn't touch it that I noticed, and it seemed to be coated with dust. As though he'd quit drinking once he couldn't pour with that hand. He didn't seem to be doing anything, or preparing to do anything, or to have just completed anything. He looked to be in a state of suspension, between life and death, and much closer to the latter.

Art and I sat and drank weak coffee, had a cigarette, which I supplied, and played cribbage with cards that were almost white from wear. We didn't talk, but if I had said what was on my mind, I would have asked Art why he hadn't covered the broken window on the east wall, or why there were mice, both dead and alive, all over the floor. And once I saw the reason for that, I might have asked why he hadn't thrown out the dead cat under the wood stove. The place was freezing, but it stunk anyway, and I couldn't believe anyone could ignore and live with such a smell.

I kept my stay as short as was polite, thanked Art for the coffee, shook Sam's left hand, and took off, taking the dead cat with me.

"Oh, thanks, Frank. I kept on meanin' to get rid of that thing."

Riding back, I tried to focus on the fact that it felt good to help a friend. And I looked forward to seeing Muriel, who was supposed to be arriving in the next few days for a visit.

But as I approached the house, I had a sense that something was off somehow. For one thing, there was a strange vehicle parked out front. Not that this was unusual during that period. We often had strangers stop by, often families with their belongings loaded onto an old Model A truck, making their escape from failed homesteads. But this car was brand-new, a big black Ford sedan. And any time someone with means came by anybody's place in those days, it generally meant bad news. Foreclosure, or repossession. Something bad. So I didn't even bother to unsaddle my horse. I rode over to the car to check it out. It had Montana plates, but I didn't recognize anything else about it. I tied Ahab to the fence and entered the big house with a slight feeling of anxious irritation.

I entered the front door, and heard lots of activity toward the back of the house, in the kitchen. But there was a man sitting alone in the living room. He stood when I came in. He was tall, wearing a very nice black suit, his hair slick and flat against his head, with a knife-straight white part down one side. This guy was no drifter.

"You must be Blake," he said.

I'm afraid my assumptions about this man and what he might be there for brought out the mistrust in me.

"Yeah," I said, and I was just about to say, "Who the hell are you?" when he spoke again.

"There's been a murder."

"What?"

"Yeah. Up in Alzada."

"Oh, christ. You scared the hell out of me. I thought you meant here."

The man shook his head. "Oh, Jesus. I'm sorry. I didn't mean to scare you. Yeah. Of course you would assume . . ."

"I'm sorry, but do I know you?" I asked.

Just then, Muriel appeared from the dining room. I didn't recognize her for a brief moment. She wore a fashionable navy-blue dress, with a string of pearls dotting her neckline. And her hair had been cut short and curled. It was a dramatic change from the young girl who usually wore nothing but cotton print dresses, with her hair in a bun.

"Blake!" She looked pleased.

"Muriel, what are you doing here?"

"Well, we weren't planning to get here until Tuesday. But we were in Billings, and we heard about the murder. So we drove right up."

"What murder? Who got murdered?"

By now, others had begun drifting into the living room—Rita, Mom, Bob, until the whole family had filtered in from various rooms in the house. They all looked concerned, even scared.

"Somebody shot Harold Baldwin," Mom said.

"Really?" Everybody was looking at me, so I realized I was the last to learn this bit of news. "When?"

"Last night," Muriel said.

"Do they know who did it?" I asked.

Nobody answered, but several shook their heads. And then everyone dropped their eyes to their shoes.

"I'm sorry," I said, "but I never did figure out just who you are." I addressed the stranger. "Since Muriel keeps saying 'we,' I assume you're with her."

"Oh my goodness," Muriel said, stepping forward. "You didn't meet Stan?"

"It's my fault," Stan said. "I was so anxious to tell Blake here about the big news, I didn't think to introduce myself." He stepped forward to shake my hand. "I've heard so much about all of you that it's easy to forget that we've never met. Stan Grant." He reached out his hand, and we shook.

"We're engaged," Muriel said.

"Engaged?" I couldn't hide my surprise, as we'd heard nothing about a suitor of any kind, much less a fiancé. "Wow. Well, congratulations."

"Thanks," Stan said. "Thanks a lot."

"Well, dinner's ready," Helen announced.

"Yes. Let's eat," Muriel said.

We sat up to a table of fried chicken, cooked carrots, potatoes, and pan-stirred gravy. We learned that Stan was an executive for the Amalgamated Copper Company in Butte, and that he and Muriel had met several months before when Stan's car broke down in Spearfish. Muriel explained that she hadn't mentioned Stan sooner because she didn't expect anything to develop with Stan living five hundred miles away. But after traveling to see her several times, Stan had proposed. They were to be married in the spring.

I managed to extract this information despite a nervous energy, a palpable feeling that everyone else had something else on their minds.

"So they haven't caught the guy who shot Harold?" I asked.

"They don't have any idea who did it," Muriel said. "It could be a woman, you know."

"It probably was a woman," Dad said, prompting an elbow from Mom.

"No witnesses," said Stan.

"Did you guys come through Alzada?" Bob asked.

"No!" Muriel said. "Stan wanted to. But I was too scared. My lord, there's a killer out there."

"I bet no one's leaving their houses up that way," I said.

"No doubt," Dad seconded.

* * *

The discussion continued, spirited and laced with an element of fear. And as speculation bounced around the table, I was struck by two things. First was that Stan seemed to be as charming and likable as he first appeared. He had an unusual but infectious laugh—a singular explosion of joy, a "Ha" that economically conveyed as much delight as most people express in a good long belly laugh. My first impression was of a man who was hard not to like. But despite his natural manner, and the good feeling that both his presence and the news of their impending marriage brought to our table, there appeared to be two people in the room who were not happy. Both Mom and Rita were conspicuously silent in the midst of the banter. But Stan did not know them well enough to notice.

"Mrs. Arbuckle, this is a fine, fine meal," he declared.

Mom nodded—a single, curt bob of her head.

"We don't expect anything less from Mom," Muriel said. "She's a victim of her own standards."

"Oh, stop this nonsense," Mom insisted. "This certainly isn't anything special. And I didn't do it alone."

We who knew her were prepared to close the subject. But not Stan.

"Mrs. Arbuckle, your humility is admirable, but not necessary. I'm used to my mother's cooking, which I won't comment on because she's not here to defend herself."

We all chuckled, and I even caught a hint of a smile on Mom's face.

It actually wasn't hard for me to imagine the source of Mom's displeasure, although Stan remained blissfully unaware of it for the rest of the evening. Muriel represented the last hope for Mom's dream of a college graduate in the family. It now appeared she was going to come up just short. I'm sure the suddenness of the announcement was a big concern as well. It was clear that Stan had at least ten years on Muriel.

But for Rita to appear so distant, even depressed, was very unusual. I made several attempts to catch her eye, to question with a look whether she was okay. But she did not look my way.

"Now what exactly is it that you do at the mine, Stan?" Helen put a napkin to the corner of her mouth.

"I'm the business manager." He finished swallowing before he continued. "It sounds important, but all I really do is take care of the books."

"Now who's being humble?" Muriel softly slapped Stan's upper arm. "Stan started out as a clerk, and worked his way up. He's very good at what he does."

Stan tilted his head and smiled shyly. "Well, I also had an advantage. My father has been with the mine pretty much from the start. He's helped me a lot."

Muriel again jumped in. "But Stan works very hard." Then to him: "You didn't just have this position handed to you because of your father. You always make it sound that way."

Stan looked as though he needed to be rescued.

"Well, I don't think anyone here knows enough about mining to even ask an intelligent question about it," I said.

"I could say the same for ranching," Stan added.

"It doesn't seem that anyone knows enough about ranching these days," Mom said with a trace of anger. "It doesn't matter what you know when there's no water." Although she still sounded angry, I knew it was a good sign that Mom had voluntarily joined in on the conversation.

Stan nodded thoughtfully. "It's tough. We get more people coming through looking for work than I can ever remember."

I nodded. "I know what you mean. We have two or three guys stopping in every week, offering to work for pennies."

Stan turned to me, surprised. "Really? Out here?"

This brought a smile to everyone's face, except Rita's.

Stan emitted one of his "Ha"s. "I'm sorry," he said. "I didn't mean that the way it sounded."

"It does seem strange, I know," I assured him. "So far from everything."

Stan nodded. "It's got to break sometime soon."

If only he'd been right.

It seems that the laws of nature work against those of us who play cards so that we rarely end up gathered in numbers divisible by four. This was one of those rare occasions, and it was clear to all present that we had no choice but to take advantage of the opportunity. With Stan being a numbers man, I was a little surprised and disappointed that he wasn't as adept at cards as he was at turning a charming phrase. But the latter skill adds as much to a card game, if not more, than talent, and by the end of the evening, my stomach hurt from laughing, and my tongue was sore from too much coffee and cigarettes. Even Mom was loose after a few games. Stan also broke out a bottle that he had brought along to celebrate their announcement.

But Rita, who was my partner for most of the night, stared at her cards with wide-open, blank eyes. She constantly had to be reminded when it was her turn to bid, or to play a card. Even after downing several drinks, something she rarely did, Rita remained quiet.

Around eleven o'clock, when the black and red cards began to blur together, we stood and straightened our stiff knees, groaning, sticking our chests out and stretching our arms.

"Hey," Dad said, suddenly looking up at me. "I didn't think to ask . . . did you and Art get anything?"

"Yeah. An antelope. An old buck."

Dad nodded. "Did you go up there?"

I shook my head. "Yeah. Boy." I just continued shaking my head, and everyone dropped their eyes to the floor, understanding the state of the situation. "It was bad," I said.

A long pause followed.

"So . . ." Stan looked around. "Where do you want me to sleep? In the barn?"

Mom smiled, the skin around her eyes pinching. "All right. If that suits you."

"Hey, as long as there's a sheep out there that I can use for a pillow."

When Mom chuckled at his joke, it was clear that a remarkable transformation had taken place. I caught myself smiling broadly.

"More than a pleasure," Stan said as he shook my hand.

"For us all," I replied. "I look forward to more nights like this."

He nodded. "I'll need some time to practice my five hundred," he said, referring to our card game.

I carried Teddy out into the clear, clean night, my spirits buoyed by good company and a few glasses of expensive whiskey. A full, white moon dominated the sky. The light was so bright that it shone off the big weathered house, which was still unpainted, making the weathered gray siding also appear white. We walked along the path, just wider than a shoe, Rita in front, Teddy and I just behind, and George in the rear. The crickets called. As ridiculous as it seemed at the time, I couldn't help but think as we walked the hundred yards from one house to the other that someone had killed a man just fifteen miles from where we were walking. Someone who was still out there somewhere. I kept my ears alert. I also noticed that Rita was walking very unsteadily.

"How about that Stan?" I said to her, hoping to break through her mood. "He's something else, huh?"

"Yeah." She answered without enthusiasm. "He's great."

We continued wordlessly on to the house as I wondered about the source of Rita's surliness. Once inside, I sat quietly in the living room, smoking a cigarette, while Rita put the boys to bed. We generally sat and talked for a while before bed, and I hoped that she wouldn't sneak off to her room without following that ritual.

She did come out, settling into her rocking chair, picking up the socks she was knitting for one of the boys. She held the socks closer to her face than usual, and her eyes were unfocused.

"You okay?" I asked.

She nodded.

"You sure?"

Again she nodded. But in the next moment, she aimed one of those unfocused eyes toward me, winking through a narrow opening.

"What if it's him, Blake?"

I blinked. "What if it's who?" I asked. "What do you mean?"

"What if it's Jack?"

A slight, confused grin came to my face. "You mean the murder? You couldn't be serious."

Rita looked up with defiance. "Why not?"

"Oh, come on, Rita. Jack's not a murderer."

"No?"

I paused, thinking about what I was saying, realizing that I really didn't know, that it wasn't out of the question.

"I need another drink," Rita said, lifting herself to her feet.

"Are you sure that's a good idea?"

Rita stopped and turned, frowning at me. "Blake."

"I'm sorry. Actually, maybe I'll join you."

I watched Rita teeter toward the kitchen. "I didn't know you had anything around here."

She smiled over her shoulder. "Yeah, well . . . you don't know everything, you know."

I smiled.

Rita came back with a bottle and two glasses. She set one on the table next to me and poured, spilling a little. Then she returned to her chair and poured herself a glass. She drank a healthy amount, then turned to me.

"I think it's him, Blake."

I sighed, shaking my head, studying Rita. "You don't really think that."

Rita nodded. "I do, Blake. I really do."

She was actually too insistent somehow, as if she was exaggerating in order to convince me, or herself.

"I just don't think it could possibly be him, Rita. I mean, this is a very different thing than . . . than . . ."

"Than George."

"Exactly."

Rita drank more. "How? How's it different?"

"Well," I said. "I guess I always figured that whatever happened between George and Jack, if anything did happen . . . well, I just figured it was an accident. Either that, or a fight. I figured maybe they got into an argument, and that Jack . . . well, that maybe things got out of hand." I took a drink. "That's how I always pictured it."

Rita drained her glass, to my mild alarm, and refilled it. "But what if that isn't the way it happened, Blake? What if it was uglier than that? Did anyone check George's body? Did anyone look at it?"

I lowered my head. Of course all of this had occurred to me before. Of course I'd wondered about it. Nobody had checked the body. As far as I knew. But I was hesitant to tell Rita this. Instead, I decided to probe her a little more, for her own ideas about Jack.

"Rita . . . you know Jack better than anybody. You've seen him at his worst."

She blew a puff of disgust from her pursed lips. "That's for sure."

"So can you really say that you think he's capable of something like that? Honestly?"

Finally, Rita got thoughtful, focusing her eyes on the glass between her ranch-scarred hands. She shook her head slowly, sadly. "I don't know, Blake. Sometimes I think I know. I remember one time . . . one night before little George was born . . . Jack got mad at me for something or other. Of course, you can never remember what started it years later—things that seemed so important at the time. Anyway, he usually started yelling when he was mad. I was never very scared of him, really. It was mostly noise, you know. Like a baby crying. He wanted me to pay attention to him. Anyway . . ." She waved a dismissive hand. "That night was different. This time he got real quiet." Rita raised her eyes. "I don't know if I can explain why, Blake. But it was much more frightening, that quiet. He looked at me, and I don't even remember what he said. All I remember is that I was really scared, Blake. I was scared just from the way he was looking at me." Rita dropped her eyes again, back to her glass, which she raised once more, sucking half the contents into her mouth.

I didn't know what to say. The story sent a chill through me. But Rita wasn't finished. She raised her head once more, and her eyes had become bleary, drooping from alcohol.

"You know what the scariest part of that is, Blake?" She fixed a gaze on me, as glazed as it was.

I met her eyes, shaking my head.

"I didn't know about George then. I hadn't heard yet."

I held her look for a moment longer, then dropped my eyes. "Mm," I said, not underestimating the power of this fact, because although I didn't understand it, I knew how much this woman loved my brother. I could imagine how frightening it must have been to see this side of Jack.

We sat quietly for a while, with the only sound being the familiar click of locust wings outside, the almost clocklike ticking, as if they were measuring the time before the next victim packed up and gave in.

"You know, Blake . . ."

I raised my head, meeting the now bleary eyes. She had an odd, dreamy expression.

"What, Rita?"

"Sometimes I wish Jack was you."

I frowned. "What?"

"Sometimes I wish you were Jack. I wish he was himself but also you."

I shook my head, intrigued but assuming the booze was doing the talking now. "I'm not sure what you mean by that, Rita."

She smiled, her eyes bathing me with the warmth I had first noticed the day I met her. I couldn't help but smile back.

"Jack . . . well, Jack has a lot of . . . a big sense of adventure . . . of possibility."

She paused. I nodded, slightly insulted by the insinuation that I did not.

"But you . . . well, you, Blake . . . you are just so damn sweet. You're always thinking about other people . . . what might make them a little happier." She paused, still smiling. I felt my face fill with blood. "Not Jack." She shook her head. "He's a taker. He's a taker. He never thinks about me. Or you. Or these kids." She gestured vaguely toward the boys' room.

Although part of me, for some odd reason, wanted to convince Rita that Jack cared about her and her kids, I knew very well that she was right. So I said nothing, looking at my hands.

"I sometimes wish I'd met you first, Blake." I felt a hand on my own, and it was as if I had just been bitten by a rattler. I jumped to my feet, fumbling with my chair, trying to push it in, but somehow tripping over it, and mumbling about how it was time to get a little shut-eye.

Rita started laughing, a self-conscious chuckle. "Blake, you're like a shy school kid. You're as shy as a kid in school."

"Yeah . . . well . . . I think I need to get some sleep. Maybe you should, too. Huh, Rita? It's late."

I escaped to my bedroom, and I heard Rita retire to her own room. But I couldn't sleep, thinking about her. Or more accurately, I couldn't sleep thinking about what she said. Although it had always been obvious that Rita was fond of me, she had never given any indication, any slight hint, that she was fond of me in the same way that I was fond of her. And it seemed to me a cruel twist that this information would come out when she was in that condition. Now I could only wonder whether she actually meant it.

For the next week, questions of who and where the murderer was took our county hostage. Because we didn't have telephones yet, and because Annie Ketchal didn't want to deliver the mail in the middle of the night until they caught the killer, we relied on her to fill us in each day on the news. But there was little to report. In fact, the only reports she did have were rumors, most of which were absurd. It seemed that of the sixty-nine people who made up the population of Alzada, everyone over the age of fifteen was a suspect, whether there was any hint of a motive or not. But apparently, most people thought that Tex Edwards, the man whose first wife drowned in a mud puddle, was the guilty party. Although Tex's wife said he was home all night, there was much conjecture that she was scared to tell the truth. Johnny Berrenda even claimed that he'd seen Tex out that night, but everyone knew that if Johnny had been sober, it would have been the first night in several years.

It was a rough time for the drifters in the area. They were used to being fed and given a bed without question. But they were now sent on their way with a bundle of food under their arms and an evil eye at their backs until they were out of sight.

Stan and Muriel stayed an extra three days because she was too scared to leave. Stan finally insisted, because he had to get back to work. But they took the back road, through Ekalaka, just to make sure.

It was immediately evident that Rita had no memory of our drunken conversation. Aside from a headache, she acted as if everything was just as it always had been the next day. There was no sign of discomfort after that. So I found myself in the awkward position of living with the question of Rita's objectivity that night, as well as her revelations about Jack. The situation made me tense, and withdrawn, which only added to the stifling atmosphere.

Exactly one week after the murder, we gathered at the big house for Sunday dinner. The week of intense apprehension had permeated our homes. Every glance was furtive. Any unexpected sound had us all jumping a foot off the ground. We sat down to a table of tough antelope meat. The lettuce was tired, the carrots juvenile, almost yellow.

"Mom, this salad doesn't taste right," Teddy complained to Rita.

"You better just learn to appreciate what you have here," Rita said impatiently. "You better learn we're lucky to even have a garden right now. A lot of people don't even have gardens."

"A lot of people don't have any food at all," Mom added. "You've seen those men come to the door, Teddy?"

Teddy pouted, picking at his food.

"I think he gets the point," Dad said.

"George, don't interrupt now. We don't want to give the boy two different messages, do we?" Mom said, not looking at Dad, her head tilted.

"I'm not giving him a different message. I agree he should appreciate what we got, but Rita already said it once. We don't need to beat the kid over the head with it."

A tear leaked from the corner of Teddy's eye.

"Mom, Dad," Rita said in a warning tone. "Is this really necessary?"

There was a brief, fuming silence, during which Teddy ate slowly, the tears still trickling. It was Helen who broke the silence.

"Teddy, you know, I remember one time when I was just about the same age as you are now . . . we were eating supper, and my mother had cooked up some turnips, and I hated turnips. Oh, I hated turnips so much. I still . . . well, I shouldn't say that. But I did not like turnips at all. So I told my mother in no uncertain terms that I was simply not going to eat my turnips."

Helen had Teddy's full attention, and he forgot to cry. His eyes were wide, and a slight smile began to curl his lips.

"Well, Teddy, can I tell you what my mother did that night?"

"What?" Teddy asked. "What did she do?"

"My mother got right up out of her chair, right up from the table, and she went down to the root cellar, and she marched right back up into the dining room and she dropped the biggest, ugliest raw turnip on my plate. And she asked me whether I thought I could eat that whole turnip by myself, raw and ugly that way."

Teddy looked scared to death, imagining the possibility of what would happen next. His brow worried.

"Did you have to?" Teddy asked. "Did she make you eat it?"

"Well, thank goodness, no. But you know what she did? She held that big ugly thing right up to me and said that there were people in the world that would actually kill each other just to have one ugly turnip like that. I never forgot that."

"Do you think it's true?" Teddy asked.

"Oh, absolutely," Helen said. "I'm sure it is."

"Wow," Teddy said, and the effect of the story was quite immediate. He lowered his head and started shoveling the salad into his mouth as if it was a birthday cake.

But after a short silence, little George, who was nine and had been his usual mum self during the entire meal, mumbled into his plate, "It's still not very good."

At which point my mother stood up in grand fashion, her shoulders thrown back, and stalked out of the house. We heard the root cellar door clunk open, and we all sat in quiet anticipation, waiting to see what hideous foodstuff she would find to instruct her grandson with.

We all sat eating, heads down, Teddy looking wide-eyed around the table, George doing his best to appear indifferent.

"I like turnips," he said after a minute.

And although it was a great line, we were all aware of the seriousness of the situation. No one laughed.

But Mom did not reappear. Two minutes passed, then three, and there was no sign of her, and we heard nothing. If not for the image of the scathing remark I would have to endure if I went down there and she was fine, I would have gotten up right then and checked to see if she was all right. The worried look on Dad's face told me that he was thinking the same thing. But I hesitated, and just moments later, we heard the most horrific scream echo from outside. We were out of our chairs and through the back door in a flash. All except Dad.

"I'm going to grab the Winchester," he called out.

The root cellar was right outside, to the right of the back door. I was the first to turn the sharp corner, and when I stumbled down the steep stairs leading to the cellar, the first thing I saw was Mom's back. She was squatting on the floor, and a pair of denim-clad legs kicked away behind and beneath her. Mom was rocking a little, and when I got up close, I saw that she had a man pinned to the ground and had her hands around his neck. His face was too dirty to determine whether it was red, but his eyes looked as if they were about to explode out of his head.

"Mom, you're gonna kill him," I shouted, putting a hand on her shoulder. "Mom, you're killing him."

But she was in a trance, and she continued to rock six inches forward, then back, the muscles in her arms and neck taut, her mouth in a teeth-clenched smile of concentration. The man gasped for air. I dropped to my knees, and threw my arms around her and leaned to one side.

"Somebody get ready to jump on him," I yelled.

"I got him." Dad appeared behind me, rifle at his shoulder.

I pulled Mom as gently as I could onto her side and held her there, both of us breathing in steady, full gusts.

The man was choking, holding his own throat, trying to lift himself to his elbow. Dad held his rifle, aiming it right at the guy's head. There was a pistol lying on the ground, which Bob picked up. Food was strewn everywhere—potatoes, dried fruit, apples, some half-eaten.

"Mom, how did you get the gun from him?" Rita asked.

"What gun?" Mom said. "I didn't see any gun."

I chuckled, trying to imagine how this whole scene played itself out, and thinking about how this would only elevate Mom's reputation around the county.

"Mom?" Teddy peeked out from behind Rita.

"What, honey?"

"Is this one of those people?"

"What people?" Rita turned and looked at Teddy.

"One of those people that Aunt Helen was talking about. One of those people who would kill somebody for a turnip."

The silence that followed was brief but filled with revelation as we watched the skeletal figure in front of us try to find some air. It was as if we all suddenly realized that this was a human being—that despite the fact that he was a murderer, he was also someone who was simply desperate for food. It excused nothing, of course, but it made me think about how the death we had seen over these desperate years had numbed us. A moment before Teddy brought this to our attention, I wouldn't have considered this guy for a moment.

"Well . . ." Rita said. "I guess so, honey. Yes. I guess it is."

9

fall 1935

I stood in front of the mirror, trying to tie a knot in a string behind my head. A black cardboard disk covered my left eye, and I had a red bandanna tied pirate-style on top of my scalp.

"You guys ready?" I yelled.

"Just about," Rita answered.

This was the end of two weeks of preparation for Bob's thirtieth birthday party. I let my whiskers grow, and Rita and I had been sewing costumes for ourselves and the boys. Helen had shown a gift for planning parties, although Rita and I were reluctant participants for the dinosaur birthday party she threw for George. For that one, we dug for previously planted bones. For the Knights of the Round Table party she threw for Dad, we battled with cardboard swords, and the kids even jousted, charging each other on their horses with lances Helen had sewn. She stuck a willow pole into two long tubes of fabric, then stuffed them so full of wool that they held their shape but were still soft enough that they wouldn't hurt anybody. It was just one more example of Helen's innovative ideas.

It proved impossible to not have a good time at one of her parties. In fact, the parties had become a welcome relief from the relentless emotional pummeling of the Depression. The days between raindrop sightings increased, and instead of rain clouds, the sky filled with the foreboding shadow of locust swarms. The thick clay ground cracked and curled, and carcasses were left to rot away, eventually becoming just one more isolated arrangement of sunbaked bones.

It had become more difficult for Rita and me to be leery of our new sister-in-law. Even aside from these parties, Helen had become a positive influence around the house. She took a lot of the pressure off Mom by helping prepare meals and taking care of general household chores. And although Mom had shown little sign of wearing down physically, her face sometimes reflected the frightening, distant look commonly attributed to the loneliness. But Helen's arrival seemed to change that. Rita and I had made some discreet inquiries from people who knew Helen's family, and found out that, just as Rita suspected, their approach to family matters was much more cutthroat than ours. So I had reluctantly chalked up the incident with the letter about Jack as a miscalculation on Helen's part, an effort to establish herself as a worthy foe.

"You guys look great!"

The boys emerged from their bedroom, decked out in colorful, billowing pants and shirts. They had both rubbed charcoal along their jaws, and Rita found some black plastic and fashioned tubes around their calves that looked like knee-high boots. Rita had made herself a purple dress that was cut low in the front, showing her ample cleavage, and I couldn't stop myself from staring. She dug out some makeup that she hadn't worn "since I left New Jersey," and I had never seen her look so provocative.

"Blake," she said with a touch of amusement in her voice.

"Huh?"

"You're drooling."

"Oh. Sorry." My face got hot, and I turned my back to Rita as she started laughing. "Are we ready then?" I asked.

Helen had decorated the house brilliantly considering the meager resources of the times. She had found a worn-out fishing net, and hung it from the ceiling. She took a dusty old trunk and stuffed it with filler, then covered the newspaper with trinkets and cardboard coins painted gold. There was a plank mounted on the front porch, ready to be walked.

To my delight and surprise, everyone in the family was in costume—even Dad, who sported a homemade vest and a big gold earring. Mom and Helen wore dresses similar to Rita's, with less revealed. Helen's was blue, Mom's yellow.

But the birthday boy was the star of the show. Helen made Bob a shirt with thick red horizontal stripes. He wore blousy pants, and around his waist, Helen had wrapped a black sash as wide as a pillow. But the best feature was that he had tied one leg up behind and fashioned a wooden leg out of a chunk of cottonwood. We all started laughing the minute Bob came limping out of his bedroom, and it was the beginning of a day of much of the same.

"Happy birthday." I shook my brother's hand, and he sported a warm, happy smile.

"This is great, huh?" he said.

Sharing this fond moment with my brother seemed far removed from an experience we had shared just a few days before, a range of emotional zigs and zags typical of those years. We read in the *Ekalaka Eagle* that the government was sending some people to Belle Fourche to buy sheep at eight dollars a head. It was not much more than the average annual cost of keeping one sheep fed and healthy. But sadly, it was more than the market was paying. So after arguing with Dad about it,

I told him I was going to take some dry and older ewes in and sell them whether he agreed with me or not.

"Don't be surprised if they end up giving you less than advertised," Dad warned, and I frowned, annoyed by his growing suspicion toward the government.

So early one Wednesday morning, Bob and I roused twenty-eight head of sheep and eased them out of the corral, pointing them in the direction of Belle Fourche. It was a three-day ride, and we had to move slowly, as many of the sheep were lame from age. We took turns riding ahead to ask permission to cross the next property. The first night, we bunked with Ed and Betty Lee Sloan, who fed us and provided good conversation. Betty Lee even got up at five and cooked breakfast, although we had insisted the night before that she just leave some biscuits and coffee on the table.

The second night, we pulled up to the tidy farmhouse of a couple neither of us knew very well, although we'd heard plenty about them. His name was Lonnie Roberts, and he was the brother of Sophie, the first woman I ever kissed. Or the first woman who ever kissed me.

Lonnie was a tall, lean, long-faced man with the smallest mouth I'd ever seen, and teasing eyes. His wife Ruth was a beautiful woman, and knew it. Her mouth was as full as Lonnie's was tiny. Her lips and cheeks were always darkened with rouge, and she had a curvaceous figure that she made little effort to hide, wearing tight dresses that provoked many a stern look through the years. But she was, as my dad liked to put it, "a well without a bucket." Not too bright. The Robertses drank, and their reputation for infidelity was legendary. But nobody could deny that they were as hospitable as anyone around. They each had the kind of charm that made the rumors about them believable. I had always liked them both.

But when we settled into their living room that night, Lonnie seemed distracted, distant. I wondered whether he was one of those people who work so hard at their public persona that they can't sustain the energy when they get home. While we waited for dinner, Lonnie offered us a drink, which we declined. But he poured himself one—not his first, I'm sure—and sat facing a little away from us. The house was less than neat, with clothes scattered around, as well as items in various stages of repair, including an old horse bridle. Lonnie said little, tipping his glass every few seconds, then refilling it once he'd drained it. Bob and I exchanged a look, wondering if we'd interrupted a fight, or done something offensive.

"How's your hay?" I finally asked.

Lonnie sipped, staring dreamily toward the window. He looked at us as if he'd just remembered we were there. "Hm?" He sat up straighter. "My hay? I'm sorry, boys. I'm not too talkative tonight. We just found out this morning that my brother-in-law passed on yesterday. Had a heart attack loading some feed." Lonnie took a deep drink. "Worked himself to death," he added. "Only forty-two."

"You mean Lawrence?" I asked.

He nodded, then looked at me, surprised. "You know him?"

"Met him at Pioneer Days, probably fifteen years ago."

"Wasn't that the guy that cleaned your clock in the ball game that day?" Bob asked, smiling.

I nodded. "That's the one."

"That was you?" Lonnie showed the first sign of his usual charm, smiling, although his mouth barely stretched. "I remember that. I never saw Lawrence lay a bat on a ball before or after that day. He was the worst baseball player I ever saw."

We all chuckled, guiltily, eyes down.

"I'm sorry to hear that," I said. "He seemed like a good man. They had a couple of kids, right?"

"Four," Lonnie said. "Yeah, we're going to their place tomorrow. The funeral is the day after."

Bob shook his head. "Damn. Four little ones. What's Sophie going to do?"

"Sell the place, if they can find a buyer. She'll move to Belle, I think."

"Maybe I will have a drink, Lonnie," I said.

"Yeah, pour me one, too," Bob added.

The rest of the evening was a blur, although Bob and I only had a couple of drinks. The same could not be said for the Robertses, whose capacity surpassed their legend. I suppose some of their indulgence could be attributed to grief, but there was a routine to their drinking that was smooth, remarkable, indicating that this night was not out of the ordinary. Lonnie poured. And on every other drink that he poured himself, he held the bottle out and poured to one side, without looking. And Ruth's glass was there each time, ready, if a little unsteady. It was something.

But I was tired, and all talk began to run together, so I excused myself and rolled my sougan out on the floor of the guest room. But I could not sleep. The news of Lawrence's death had a surprising effect. Although I barely knew him, Lawrence had made an impression on me. I liked him enormously. But I think what hit me hardest was the fact that of all the people I had known who died during the Depression, he was the closest to my age who hadn't died of disease. And he was dead of overwork. At forty-two. Art's statement about this land beating hell out of people rang through my head. As did Annie Ketchal's question from so many years ago—what was he like? I wondered. What was Lawrence Andrews like?

And I realized that although I didn't know him well, I had a feeling that I knew what he was like. I had a feeling that he was a good man, who worked damn hard, and treated people with respect. I had a feeling that Lawrence was a solid husband and father. I had a feeling that Lawrence was a lot like me. And I think for the first time in my life, it occurred to me that working hard your whole life, and being a good man, and trying to do the right thing can sometimes lead to the same payoff that any other life can. That it's no guarantee of a damn thing.

Maybe some of it was the booze, but lying there on the floor that night, and seeing myself in Lawrence Andrews, a feeling of nausea entered me like a ghost. I had to run to the window, which I wrenched open, and I thrust my head outside, where I emptied my stomach.

Late that next evening, Bob and I pushed twenty-seven head of tired, limping sheep up to the stockyards in Belle Fourche. We'd lost one old ewe on the way. The office was closed, but one big fellow was just leaving. "Sure, you can corral them here for the night," he muttered. "I don't give a damn." He pulled his felt cowboy hat lower over his eyes.

Bob and I exchanged a look. "Must have had a bad day," I said.

We got up early the next morning. It was ten degrees warmer than the previous three days, and we could smell the stockyard a half mile away. We arrived around seven, and none of the government people were there yet. The sheep had gathered in a cluster in one corner, complaining in long, hoarse bleats. They were bunched so tightly together that they had to lift their heads above the backs of each other just to see. We sat on the top rail and waited.

An hour later, Bob turned to me. "They must not get paid by the hour," he said.

I chuckled, nodding. "That's for sure."

Bob sighed, staring off toward town. Among the children of George and Catherine Arbuckle, Bob and I had come to look the most alike. Besides the square, solid build of our mother, we also shared round facial features—head, eyes, nose. The one big difference was that I had our father's squinty, playful eyes, while Bob's drooped rather sadly, like a hound's.

The fact that we also shared similar personalities made it natural that we didn't find it necessary to speak much in order to understand each other. We had also inherited our mother's quiet watchfulness, with our father's tendency to accept things as they come, sometimes too readily, I suppose. Bob was more passive, but that may have been because he was younger, and married to Helen.

At any rate, the fact that we rarely spoke to each other had never been a source of discomfort for either of us—never, that is, until Helen came into the picture. Before her, I had always felt a solid, unspoken allegiance with my younger brother. But from the moment she unpacked her bags in the big house, even after the incident with the letter about Jack smoothed over, Bob's demeanor had shifted. Instead of sharing silences, we suffered through them. I felt as if he was always waiting for me to ask him a question that he didn't want to answer. He would glance at me with a shadow of dread in his eyes. And of course, this made me feel awkward. So in an effort to undermine this awkwardness, I often asked whatever came into my head, which almost always made him nervous. It seemed to be a no-win situation.

"So when are you and Helen going to start having some little ones?" I asked after an hour and a half of silent waiting.

I immediately wished I hadn't asked, as Bob, who usually sat pretty still, started twitching and jerking his head around like a chicken.

"Oh, I don't know," he answered. "I don't know. You can't ever tell with these things, you know. These things tend to happen in their own time, you know."

I nodded, but said nothing, hoping to let the topic die from lack of fuel.

"Just because other people . . . just because it seems to make sense, or because it would make somebody else happy . . . well, you can't make these decisions just because someone else . . ."

"Yeah," I said, trying to give Bob a reprieve. "Of course, Bob. I know what you mean." He seemed to be arguing with himself, or with Helen, I thought. And I didn't particularly want to get in the middle of either of those conflicts. "I understand," I added.

He was clearly relieved to drop the subject. And fifteen silent minutes later, a guy finally came along, walking right past us, although he made no effort to acknowledge our presence, even when we said hello.

"Not very friendly, are they?" I said.

"Well, hell, they pretty much got us by the nuts, don't they?" Bob said. "They don't have to worry about giving good service."

We chuckled, but it wasn't because we were amused.

The rest of the crew arrived, most of them showing the same head-down, eyes-averted indifference that the first guy had. Bob stopped trying to be friendly. But I greeted each of them with a cheerful "Mornin,'" wishing I could rattle them a little, I guess. It didn't work.

After ten big guys had ducked into the building, I began to wonder why they needed such a big crew. But I decided that with times so bad, they must be flooded with sellers. We waited another half hour before an older guy finally came outside. I recognized him as the one we'd talked to the night before. This guy, who had a ruddy complexion and big bags under his eyes, sauntered over and shook hands. We told him our names, and although he dutifully recorded them, he didn't tell us his.

"These yours?" He indicated our sheep with his head.

"Yes, sir," Bob answered.

"All right. Six dollars a head's the price."

"I thought it was eight," I argued. "The paper said eight."

"Six dollars a head. Take it or leave it."

I frowned, looking at my feet, and the guy studied us for a second or two. When it appeared that we wanted to think it over, he turned on the heel of a black shiny boot and headed back into the building.

"All right," I called to the guy.

"Blake," Bob said. "That barely covers a year's feed for one of these bastards."

I nodded. "I know. But do you want to turn them around and take 'em back now? They got us, just like you said. Right here." I grabbed my crotch.

Bob shook his head, and the guy called over his shoulder. "I'll be right back."

Bob and I stood waiting, heads hanging, as if we'd done something to provoke this indignity. Although the twist wasn't a complete surprise, especially with Dad's warning, I thought about expecting the worst, and wondered whether I would be less disappointed if I had anticipated this. I didn't think so.

The man returned with a metal box tucked under his arm. He didn't look at us, setting the box on a shelf mounted along the fence. He pulled a key from his pocket and unlocked the box, folding a black cover back to reveal a thick pile of bills.

"There's no give on that price?" I asked.

The man closed his eyes for a second, as if he couldn't believe anyone would ask such an ignorant question. "You sellin' or not? If not, you gotta clear out of here. There's bound to be more coming." He finally, for the first time that morning, looked at us, and I wished he hadn't.

The man wore dungarees that were worn at the knees. His hands were rough and scarred, his forearms thick. He was one of us, except for one obvious exception—his eyes. His eyes were hooded, cold, disconnected. And I wondered whether his heart was as cold and disconnected. And I wondered what had happened to this man to make him so hard and cold. Nobody comes into the world with eyes like that, I thought. Was he one of the many who had lost their places? Had he lost his stock? His family? Any of these was possible, but at that moment, I had no room for compassion for this man. Because to me, no matter what had happened to him, taking it out on his own kind was inexcusable. I hated this man.

"We got twenty-seven head," I said.

He dug into the box, pulled out a notepad and a chewed pencil, and figured while I did the same in my head. "Comes to a hundred and sixty-two by my count. You want to check it?" He held the pad out.

"That's right," I said.

He counted the money and handed me a wad of cold, greasy bills. Then he took another pad from inside the box, and wrote out a bill of sale. "I'll have to have one of the boys count, just to make sure."

I nodded.

The guy called into the building, and two big guys opened the massive sliding doors and sauntered outside.

"Give me a count on these," the guy shouted to them.

Ten minutes later, after they had counted our sheep and herded them inside, Bob and I were still sitting on the fence, unmotivated, immobilized. I felt humiliated. Another rancher came along on horseback, pushing about fifty head of sheep. I opened the gate for him. And standing there holding the gate open, I heard a loud bang from inside the building. Then another. It was a strange noise—very loud, and very penetrating, like two pieces of metal slamming together.

Bob and I approached a small, dirty side window. We held our hands to the sides of our eyes and pressed our faces against the glass. And what we saw still pains me.

Our sheep were lined up in a chute. The sheep we had spent years feeding, nursing, or pulling out of the mud and tangled wire. At the end of the chute stood two of the biggest of these many big men, with sledgehammers. And just as we peeked inside, one of these men swung his hammer in a giant, gleaming arch down onto the ewe's head, shattering her skull, sending her body into convulsions. Then two other men pulled the still-jerking torso from where it lay and heaved it onto a pile of dead meat, dead wool, where several other big men sheared the carcasses.

I felt ill. Bob swore through his teeth. I tasted salt in the corner of my mouth, and turned away from the window, running the back of my hand along my cheek. Bob hadn't moved, and I heard another slam of steel.

"Let's get the hell out of here," I said.

We went and got drunk, the first time Bob and I had ever done that together, and it helped us forget, but only for that evening.

To this day, I have never understood why, while people were starving along the roads of Montana, and starving in their homes, and piecing together meals from scraps, meals of hard moldy bread smeared with lard, or the tough, stringy meat of an unfortunate prairie dog, the government bought hundreds of sheep people had mothered and loved and doctored for the purpose of feeding people, and they slaughtered them and let them rot. They did nothing with the meat.

Helen had a treasure hunt set up for the boys. There was a map, which she burned around the edges for authenticity. Little George and Teddy studied that map closely, and went searching for several buried treasures—some baseball cards, bags of hard candy, some colorful marbles, and a brand-new book for each boy—*Treasure Island* for Teddy and *The Adventures of Tom Sawyer* for George.

The boys were thrilled by the whole affair, laughing each time they unearthed the next surprise.

"I thought this was my birthday," Bob complained.

"Bob!" Helen scolded, but they were both smiling.

We sat down to a birthday dinner of shark (actually catfish). The party had raised our spirits as high as they'd been in years. We laughed loud and often, sometimes just from looking at each other and our ridiculous costumes.

Bob sat at the head of the table lit up like a Halloween pumpkin. He said practically nothing, just smiling and absorbing the good feelings around him.

I sat watching Bob, grateful to have this diversion from the difficult realities we had just experienced days before. And as I scanned our little round dining room table, seeing the joy in those familiar faces, I struggled to find a way to measure the importance of this family.

There was, it seemed, only one certainty—that being the unwavering hold my family held as my most important source of strength. This would never change. What did seem vulnerable to so many things was my ability to remember this, and to keep it in focus. I realized how much I had been distracted lately, even before the trip to Belle Fourche. The years of drought, of falling prices and rising casualties, had quietly but steadily created a monster in my head—a monster that started as a small desire to stop the decay, but had grown into an obsession with figuring out a solution. I had somehow convinced myself that there was something that we were overlooking—some answer to our problems that, once we stumbled across it, we would all slap palms to our foreheads and say, "How could we have missed that?" It couldn't be so simple, I thought. It couldn't be that just because we weren't getting any rain, so many around us were on the verge of death. The obsession had pushed me into a mental storm shelter, I realized, where I'd locked the door, trying to protect myself from the damage. The problem was that I was alone in there.

That day, looking at my family, I vowed to remind myself that everyone else in the room was facing the same hardship that I was, and despite that, here we were—laughing, happy, together. I needed to remember that the solution to my problems was right here in front of me—we were it.

"A toast," I announced halfway through the meal. I stood and raised my glass. "To the toughest damn pirate on the high Montana seas. Barnacle Bob."

Everyone laughed, glasses high, and Bob turned the color of the stripes in his shirt. As I sank back into my chair, a tinking of spoon against glass turned all eyes toward the head of the table again. Although Helen was standing, she was so small that it wasn't immediately apparent. She cleared her throat, looking down for a moment. When she raised her face, her cheeks were shiny red. "I know that this is Bob's day. I don't want to steal any glory from old Barnacle Bob here . . ." She gestured toward him, laughing nervously. "But I do have an announcement to make."

Helen dropped her head once more. "I do hate to bring up something . . . well, something less than happy . . ." She ran a knuckle under her nose.

"Sweetheart, don't . . ." Bob reached for her arm, but she twisted her torso away from him, just out of his reach.

"It's okay, Bob. I want to."

"I don't want you to," Bob said quietly. "That's just it. Not now. I don't want you to."

Helen ignored him, and Bob's lips pursed as he watched her prepare to say what she was going to say. Helen lifted her chin.

"It seems that some of us don't have soil that is as fertile as others," she said, and she turned directly toward Rita, her blue eyes fixing on Rita with a brief, envious glare. I don't know if anyone else even caught it, but it sent a current down my spine, and Rita looked at me with a puzzled frown.

"Bob and I lost our baby," Helen said. "Just yesterday," she added. "We lost our little baby boy." And Helen put a hand to her eyes, squeezing them into a bundle of skin. Bob stood up and wrapped an arm around her waist, leading her from the room as her shoulders bounced against his chest.

The rest of us sat in a bewildered silence, staring at anything but each other. There were so many reasons to be uneasy about this turn of events, my mind swirled. First of all, this was not something our family usually did—announcing bad news in such a way, drawing such attention to misfortune. Especially something so personal and delicate. Something that most of us would hardly discuss privately among ourselves, and never in front of the kids. And for the very reason of the effect that this announcement had brought—the unease. But more than that, the timing of this was so hard to fathom—in the middle of such a joyous occasion, one of so few during that period. It was odd and unsettling, and finally, to add one more element—we had no idea that Helen was pregnant. She certainly wasn't far enough along to be showing yet, which wouldn't be far considering how small she was. So that was one more reason that her announcement seemed bizarre. Miscarriages, in early pregnancy, were pretty common in our country. In fact, they were common enough that they seldom rated very high in the realm of news or gossip unless there was some twist to it—if it was an unmarried teenager, for instance. But as difficult as they may have been for some of the women who experienced them, there were enough children under ten dying that it pretty much overwhelmed the dramatic effect of a miscarriage.

All of this together was enough to make everyone uncomfortable. But for me, the worst part of all was the look she gave Rita. The rest I could find a way to chalk up to the frustration of a woman who was distraught. But I could not forget that look, which was hard to describe as anything less than envious hatred. It left me with a very uncomfortable feeling that the Helen we had lived with for the past two years had been a calculated presentation of what the real Helen knew we wanted to see. But the real Helen was lurking. I was afraid that we'd just seen a glimpse of her.

10

winter 1937

"We should be back before dark." Dad tucked both arms into his coat, buttoned it up, and pulled a scotch cap onto his head. He had a strip of cotton cloth tied around his head, covering his ears, as did I.

"All right," Mom said. She shoved a fresh loaf of bread into the bag of food she had prepared for Art and Sam Walters. After the murder in Alzada, and Mom's dramatic apprehension of the killer, Stan and Muriel had shipped a big console radio to the ranch, to make sure we had more up-to-date news. The radio had become an immediate fixture, droning in the background all the time—providing news, ball games, and entertainment. We especially enjoyed listening to Jack Benny and *Fibber McGee and Molly*. But the radio proved to be invaluable as a source of something everyone in our family was interested in—information—weather reports, news, and the latest statistics on the devastating decline of the economy. As we prepared for our departure, the current stock prices drifted from the living room in a steady voice.

"You guys stay warm out there," Steve Glasser said. "Don't let Art sell you anything." He smiled. "And tell him to drop in sometime soon."

"We'll do that," I said, trying to believe that Steve's optimism was justified. No one had seen Art for about a month, which prompted this trip. Not that it was that unusual for him to be out of sight for that long, but he had continued to deteriorate, looking more skeletal each time we saw him. During each long absence, the concern grew a little stronger.

It was damn cold, and the walk from the house to the barn, with the snow crunching beneath our feet, worried me. Dad was also getting old, and these excursions, even our morning feedings in the winters, were not easy on him. The sky was gray, the snow gray, the trees gray, and our breath floated thick and gray from our mouths and nostrils. I felt the icy ground right through the soles of my boots, and the moisture inside my nose froze within minutes. My nose actually hurt from the cold. The wind was strong, directly into our faces, and I pulled my kerchief up to my lower eyelids.

"Feels like winter," Dad said.

"Yeah, must be just around the corner."

The barn wasn't any warmer, but at least it provided some shelter from the wind. We saddled our horses with stiff fingers. The horses fought the frozen steel bits, shaking and raising their heads, keeping their teeth clamped shut so we had to dig our fingers into their jaws. We rode out into the weather, and the six feet of horse put us higher, where the wind was stronger and colder. My joints felt stiff, and the exposed skin immediately lost all feeling. The leather saddle was cold against my butt and thighs. And it never did warm up.

We had lost more stock, but this winter hadn't been quite as bad as the previous few. For one thing, most of the sheep and cattle we had left were the strong ones, the ones that had made it this far. Unlike the men and women who tried to eke out a living on the land, the livestock had nothing to work with but bulk, muscle. Their smarts were limited to having enough sense to eat what they could find and drink when water was in front of them.

The ride to Art's place took us through the river crossing, which was frozen over, the thick ice covered with two- or three-foot cliffs of powdery snow.

The previous summer, near the crossing, Dad, George, Teddy, and I had stripped to our underwear for a swim one searing afternoon. At first, because of the heat, and a general lack of energy, we just wallowed around in the shallow water, submerging our torsos beneath the surface. But as our bodies cooled, our slumbering energy stirred. George started splashing water on his brother's head, and soon an all-out war broke out. Teddy endured his brother's abuse for thirty seconds, then jumped to his feet and pounced on George, pushing his head underwater.

The next thing I knew, Dad was on his feet, swinging his arms, fists locked together, sending great arcs of water over his grandsons. At that point, I couldn't just lie there and watch. I got up and grabbed my hat, and started scooping hatfuls, flinging them toward Dad. Soon we were soaked and laughing, in one of the few periods of pure joy we experienced during the thirties. It was a moment I had used to replace other memories of the river whenever I had occasion to maneuver the crossing.

We rode through the pasture where our cattle were wintering. They looked at us, in unison and forever, perhaps wondering why they were seeing us for the second time that day. The broken corpses of the dead lay off on their own, isolated and half covered with snow, like graves that had been uncovered by wind.

The trees that were still alive along the river looked thinner, more alone, because much of the brush at their feet had died during these hard, dry years. And of course the creeks, buried deep beneath the snow now, were dry, as they had been every season during the past fifteen years. The wind blew the dry, powdery snow just above the ground, making the sweeping air appear visible.

Dad and I spoke little, sensing each other's need to look, and think about what we saw. Although Dad and I had never talked much, it seemed that we had less than ever to say. It wasn't that we had little to discuss, either. There were plenty of things we should have been talking about. With Jack's absence, I was the natural choice to take over the ranch when Dad couldn't do it anymore. But aside from day-to-day operations, we seldom talked about the ranch. Dad kept his thoughts about the future to himself. And it bothered me. I couldn't help but wonder why. Did he expect Jack to return? Or did he not want to think about the fact that he couldn't go on forever? Was there something about my abilities that he questioned? As unpleasant as these possibilities were, there was one that was worse. It was hard to admit, but even harder to overlook the coincidence that this distance between us had started when Helen became part of our family.

In some respect, this behavior was consistent with my dad's attitude. He had always been more interested in doing the work than in discussing it, or planning it out. But he had developed a certain degree of gruff impatience behind his usual indifference. And it was this that led me to an unpleasant theory. Although I hadn't seen it happen, I could just imagine Helen turning her gift for inquisition toward Dad and his plans for the ranch. And it also wasn't hard to imagine Dad jumping to the quick and probably accurate conclusion that Helen's questions were pointed in a specific direction. From there, it was easy to see Dad move to a decision to ignore anybody and everybody's questions.

I tried not to think about it too much, and I ignored Helen, and she me, a much easier task than one would expect for two people who live on the same ranch, often sharing the same table.

But there was one occasion when Helen and I found ourselves alone in the big house for most of an afternoon and evening, a day that Rita had asked me for some time alone with her boys. Mom, Dad, and Bob had gone into Belle for some reason. I spent part of the day outside working, but it was very cold, so that didn't last long. So I sat in front of the radio for the rest of the afternoon, listening to a game between the Yankees and the Red Sox while Helen baked a cake and worked on a dress she was making. But we couldn't eat dinner separately without being downright rude, so we sat down at the same table. It was the most extensive conversation I ever had with her alone. She had apparently decided to accept the fact that I would never trust her, which I respected somehow, and that evening it seemed that our mutual mistrust could be set aside while nobody else was around.

She sipped quietly at a spoonful of soup.

"It seems we don't have much to say to each other," she said.

I rubbed the back of my neck, then broke some crackers into my soup. "That would be true," I said.

"I sometimes feel, Blake, that you didn't give me much of a chance."

I thought, gulping a spoonful of soup to delay my response. I crunched on the crackers, and swallowed. "That may also be true."

She brightened a bit at this admission, shaking out her napkin, then folding it neatly back into her lap. "I don't know if you realize it, Blake, but I had a very difficult childhood."

I studied her, nodding. Although I knew this was true, I didn't quite know how to respond to this information. It was not something people usually talked about in our world. I was also leery of her trying to use this to elicit some kind of sympathy from me, something I didn't feel. So other than the small nod, I didn't respond.

She didn't seem offended. "Well, no matter," she said. "The fact is this—to me, the most important thing in the world is having a good life for my husband and children."

I raised my brow. I knew that Bob and Helen were still trying desperately to have children. It was something Helen talked about incessantly. I wondered if she was suggesting that they had been successful.

"When we have some," she added.

I gulped the last of the soup from my bowl, then set it down in front of me. "Well, that sounds about like everyone else who lives out here, doesn't it?"

"Exactly," she said.

I eyed her, stopped short for a moment by this admission. It was the closest any of us had ever come to approaching the delicate topic of the future. And it was the closest she had ever come to admitting what she wanted.

"You figured it out, Blake," she said. "You're the smart one, you know. You figured this all out a long time ago, didn't you?" She smiled, and for a moment, I saw what Bob and so many others had fallen prey to. She really could be charming. And I couldn't help but admire her willingness to put herself right out there like that.

But we didn't talk that way again, ever.

Nearing Art's place, there was no smoke coming from the chimney, and a pool of dread started to gather in my belly, like a cold liquid splashing up into my chest. I held my hand over my mouth and nose, trying to warm some air and inhale some of that warmth back inside. It didn't help.

The rest of the house came into view, and it looked worse than the last time I'd seen it. The barn had given up, lying down on itself, and a big chunk of tin was gone from the roof of the house, leaving a section of the rafters naked. The inside of the house would be as cold as it was outside. Not a good sign.

"Uh-oh," Dad muttered.

We dismounted and walked to the door, which was ajar. Dad kicked the snow away so we could swing the door open, and our dread was confirmed. Sam was in the same chair as always. His head tilted forward, as if he'd fallen asleep sitting up, except that his eyes were open. His hand rested on his thigh. The dusty bottle still sat on his armless side. He was blue-gray.

Art lay on the bed, curled up like a cat, his knees tucked against his chest, arms folded under his head. He looked surprised, scared, and most of all tired. And he must have been tired, trying to fight off the relentless decay around him.

Things were strewn everywhere: clothes, plates, pans, and bones with the meat picked off. It all lay in a strange sort of arrangement—not like someone had come in and ransacked the place, but as though it had all been laid out to form a message of some kind. A code. Mice were frozen to the dirt floor, everywhere, and the snow had formed a drift in the kitchen. I knew from the look of things that death had been a good way to end things for the Walters brothers.

Dad and I speculated that they'd died when the weather was a little warmer, or that the tin had blown off the roof after they died, because neither of them wore a coat, and Art didn't have a blanket over him. In fact, he was in his union suit. There were no gunshot wounds, or knife wounds, no signs of a struggle, nor any reason to suspect suicide. It appeared they had simply died, about the same time, probably even the same day.

"We better go check on the horses," Dad said.

"Mm." I didn't look forward to that. The condition of the horses would depend on how long the Walterses had been dead. I almost hoped that the horses were also dead. Because there is nothing more gut-wrenching to me than a starving animal. The broken, fragile frame brings up all kinds of helplessness.

The horses were thin, but not dangerously so, which led us to con-

clude that the brothers had been dead less than a week. A few weeks'
extra feed would have the animals back to normal. I tried to pump
some water for them, but the pipes were frozen. So back to the house,
where I started a fire in the wood stove, and set two pails of snow on
top.

The horses drank thirstily, and I had to jerk the pails away from the
first two so there would be some left for the team. Dad had dumped
small mounds of hay in each stall, enough to fill their stomachs, but
not too much, as they would easily founder.

"The milk cow didn't make it," he said.

"Where is she?"

"One corner of the barn must have fallen since they died. She was
trapped."

He held a handful of oats to one of the team, who flipped his upper
lip open to scoop the oats from Dad's palm.

What was Art like? The question came to me when we went back inside
to retrieve the bodies. And it took me back to the day he'd taken a few
potshots at me down by Hay Creek. And looking at him now, it was
frightening to remember what he'd said that day, about this land beating hell out of people. It was frightening in its truth. Aside from Art's
mention of it when we were hunting a few years before, Art and I had
never really talked about that day until the last time I saw him. We
threw a card party one Saturday night just before the blizzard hit that
winter, and Art made a rare appearance, to my delight.

Late that night, after several games and probably a few shots from the
flask Art had started carrying, he cornered me in the kitchen and looked
up at me, pointing a bony finger in my face. His eyes had that vacant,
hollow stare of the loneliness, and he worked his mouth a few times, trying to get some moisture going, before he spoke. He still insisted on calling me Frank, a habit I never did determine the source of.

"Frank, I just wanna tell you something, something I been wantin' to tell you for a while now." He jabbed the finger, poking, poking, poking. "I knew it was you that day . . . when I was shooting at you. I knew it all along."

I chuckled. "Hell, Art, I don't know how you couldn't have known. It was our land, and . . . well . . . with your eyesight, I figured you knew."

"Well, now, just wait one minute here, because I want to tell you why now. I want you to know why I was shooting at you. Because I was mad at you, is what it was. I was mad at you, Frank."

I frowned. "Why? Hell, I was just a kid then. What did I do?"

"You came back, Frank. You came back to this goddam place when you had a chance to . . . well, maybe you didn't. I don't know. But you were young enough that you could've . . . maybe. I just hated to see it, that's all. 'Course I wasn't trying to hit you. I just thought maybe I'd scare you a little."

When we lifted Art off the bed, I found an old cigar box tucked under his arm. When I flipped the lid open, it nearly fell off, as it was connected by a skin-thin layer of paper. Inside, I found Art's personal papers and about eight dollars in cash. On top was a picture of a thin—skinny, really—woman holding a baby in her arms. I recognized the woman as Rosie, Art's ex-wife, holding his son, whose name escaped me at the moment. I set the picture back in the box, carefully closed the lid, and tucked it in my saddlebag.

We wrapped Sam in a blanket and tied him onto the back of one of the team horses, who appeared stronger than the other two. This method proved to be difficult in Art's case because of his fetal position. We couldn't get a blanket around him, so we decided to take him the way he was. We tried to balance him on his side on the horse's back, but he kept falling off.

The third time it happened, we both burst out laughing. We couldn't help it, and we shared a guilty look, then laughed some more.

"Stubborn as ever," Dad said, shaking his head.

The only way we could get Art to stay was to balance him sitting sideways on the horse and tie the rope very tightly around the horse's belly from Art's waist to his ankles. He looked like a king, perched up there in that position, as if he was ready to review his subjects.

The ride back was cold and somber.

"We'll go up tomorrow and get his stock . . . what's left of it," Dad said.

I nodded. It was all we said.

Back at the house, we stomped the snow off our boots before going inside. The scene that greeted us when we swung the door open and stepped into the kitchen was confusing. There was half-prepared food strewn across the counters and tables in the kitchen, with no one tending to the food at all. No one was even in the kitchen.

In fact, we couldn't see anyone within eyeshot, but there were footsteps and bumps and voices echoing throughout the house, a feeling of busyness that felt ominous. There was shouting, and at first I thought someone had turned the radio up too loud. But we could hear Mom's voice, and she was angry. She was clearly giving implicit instructions to someone.

Dad looked at me with a world-weary sigh. "What a day," he muttered.

Just then, Helen came roaring through the kitchen, wrapped in her winter coat, sniffling, and carrying a bundle of clothes. Bob was not far behind, also dressed for the cold, satchel in hand. As much as I wanted to know what was going on, I had a feeling from their hurried manner and their wounded looks that they weren't open to conversation. Helen looked furious, Bob bewildered. Dad and I stepped back, although we were well out of their path.

Soon after they had passed through the kitchen, Mom came charging through, mouth set, eyes ablaze. She didn't go outside, but went right up to the window and looked out, apparently assuring herself that they were headed wherever they were going. I peeked over Mom's shoulder, watching Bob and Helen tromp dejectedly toward the old homestead house. Mom seemed satisfied that all was going as planned, so she turned away from the window. Only then did she notice us. But she didn't speak to us, or even acknowledge us. I felt myself step back one more step, although I hadn't thought about it. Mom started out of the room.

"What's goin' on?" Dad asked.

"Nothing," was all she said. She didn't break stride, continuing right into the living room.

Dad and I looked at each other, both trying to decide whether to follow her or run off to Wyoming. He jerked his head toward the living room, and we crept off in that direction.

"I thought Steve and Jenny were going to stay for dinner," I said.

"They are," Mom said, sharp and dismissive.

I wondered where they were, but I didn't dare ask. Dad sat down, holding his head in his hands, and I felt the same way. There appeared to be no hope of a reprieve in store from the constant drama that this day brought, and I think my suspicions about Dad's withdrawal from the family were confirmed at that moment. It was too hard, it seemed. Too much.

We heard tromping and slamming outside the back door, and my first thought was that Helen and Bob had returned for more of their belongings. But when the door swung open, Steve and Jenny came in, followed by Rita and the boys.

Their entrance seemed to remind Mom that she was in the middle of making supper. She roused herself from staring out the window and marched into the kitchen, where the sounds of pans and the stove door and plates soon clattered through the house.

Rita and Jenny shared a tentative look, then ventured into the kitchen to offer their assistance.

Dad leaned across the table and said to me in a hushed tone, "You suppose anyone will bother to tell us what's going on?" He tilted his head. He shrugged, then threw his hands in the air, but I had a sense that he didn't really want to know. He certainly wasn't making any more of an effort to find out than I was.

The smells of supper soon swelled through the house. Steve and the boys joined us in the living room, where we sat talking about everything but what we were dying to talk about. Steve seemed especially eager to tell the story, but we knew it wasn't the right time. I knew that if Mom caught a drift of us talking, we'd probably be confined to the barn for a week.

For several days, I didn't even have time to think about finding out what happened. I didn't get a chance to talk to Steve. And Rita had no idea what had prompted the move. Mom was tight-lipped about it and always would be. And of course asking Bob was out of the question. So Steve was my only hope.

I finally made a trip over to his house one evening, telling everyone I needed to discuss some REA business, although I'm sure they weren't fooled. But I was disappointed. Steve didn't know what happened. All he could tell me was that at one point during the evening, while the women were in the kitchen and he and Bob were sitting in the living room smoking, he heard a slam "louder than a gunshot," he said. "The next thing I knew, your mom came charging out of the kitchen, into the living room. She told me to go get Rita and tell her and the boys to come over to dinner. Then she turned to Bob and said, 'and you'd better pack your things.' And she walked out."

Steve said Jenny wouldn't breathe a word about what was said. This didn't surprise me, not as any reflection on Jenny, but because of the code in our country. Some information that passed between women never crosses the gender line. The same holds true for men. We have always held firm to the belief that some facts belong only in one world or the other.

So with my visit to Glassers' that night, I had to accept the possibility that I may never know the complete story.

Once supper was ready, we all sat and waited as Mom whisked the food into the dining room, clunking the pans onto the table and refusing all help. Rita and Jenny somehow managed to set the table without offending Mom, and we dug into the grouse Dad and I had shot a few days before, green beans, and corn bread.

We ate as if we were late getting somewhere, heads aimed directly at our plates, eyes down but sometimes peering out from the tops at the others around the table. I enjoyed watching George and Teddy, who were wide-eyed with the excitement of the drama. And Rita was clearly pleased about this development. She glanced at faces from time to time, as though expecting someone to share in her subdued excitement.

I looked around, rejoicing quietly and to myself about having my family again. That was exactly how it felt. Helen had made a mistake, and I had a feeling once Mom came out of her spell, we would be graced with the Catherine Arbuckle we'd known before Helen came.

It wasn't until we were nearly finished eating, and several attempts at small talk had fallen flat, that somebody thought to ask how Dad and I had fared that day. The events of that morning hadn't left me, although they seemed distant. I figured either Dad or I would tell everyone once the drama had died down and everyone finished eating.

Steve, in the act of bringing a big spoonful of beans to his mouth, stopped suddenly after seeing the basket of food sitting by the kitchen door.

"Say, how's Art?" he asked.

I finished chewing, planning to answer once I'd swallowed, but Dad beat me to the punch.

"Gone," he said.

Everything stopped.

"So is Sam," Dad added.

No one moved. Except for hands lowering their spoons and forks to their plates.

After a silence of several minutes, a reverence of sorts, Mom was the first to speak. She took her napkin from her lap, and tipped her head back, breathing deeply. "My god, how could we be so thoughtless? I didn't even think."

And we sat quietly again, our heads bowed, so that if someone had come along who didn't know us, they would have thought we were praying.

11

spring 1938

If it's raining in Carter County, chances are that it's spring. Although fall sometimes brings some moisture, and we get an occasional summer shower, seventy-five percent of the yearly rain usually falls in the season of rebirth. And another large percentage of moisture comes in the form of snow, so that we rely on the spring thaw to give us our start on the growing season.

But that is under normal conditions, a term that would never be used to describe the Depression. Instead, year after year, the snow melted, and the sun sucked it out of the ground so fast that it seemed as if something underneath, some fire underground, was also at work. The sky, that beautiful expanse of deep blue, stayed blue and open, closing itself off from the intrusion of anything that would interfere with its blueness, like a cloud, for instance.

The ground withered and split, thirsty. It turned hard and tired, giving up less and less space to those water-sucking plants that tried to stretch their roots into its belly. Tufts of grass found their neighbors moving further away each year. Especially after lumbering beasts chomped at their blades, leaving only sagebrush, broken skeletons, and a few lonely clumps to stare at the empty space between them and far-off fences.

Finally, the dust looked around and, free of its usual restraints, danced. Dusty clouds and swirls frolicked between drooping, solitary plants, mocking and tormenting. The only sign of life.

Most springs, we moved the stock to pastures further from the river, because the creeks were filled with winter runoff. But each year of drought, as more and more creeks dried up, we had to keep the stock closer to the river, until the pastures that bordered it were chewed to nearly nothing. The stock weakened, their bones pushing against thinning hides, and their immunity diminished. Many cows and ewes went sterile. We lost several during labor, leaving so many orphaned calves and lambs that we didn't have time to feed them. Most of them also died. When the wind blew, and it blew often, it smelled of death.

But we usually couldn't smell even that, thanks to the dust. Our noses seemed to be constantly clogged with dust. And we had perpetual coughs. For over ten years we coughed, spitting gobs of dust into the dust.

"I'm going to check on the cows." Rita grabbed her felt cowboy hat from its peg and tugged it over her dark hair, which was in a bun. A few gray strands sparkled in the lantern's light. I nodded, looking up from my newspaper. It was calving time, and we had moved the few cattle left to calve into the small pasture behind the barn, where we checked them regularly.

"Did you boys feed your lambs?" Rita asked.

George and Teddy were in charge of the bum lambs, the orphans, which they fed by bottle every day. It was an unpleasant, difficult job, and getting bigger all the time.

"Yeah, we fed 'em," George said impatiently. George had become a source of nearly constant amusement to me. Although he was perpetually surly, it was a disposition that appeared to come more by design than by nature. His stony glare could be easily broken with a good joke, or a teasing comment, and he showed an excellent, dry sense of humor of his own. "We fed 'em and we changed their diapers," he said without looking up. Rita responded as she usually did, with a smile and a roll of her eyes.

"You think you could put some coffee on?" Rita asked me. "I'll be ready for some when I get back."

"Sure."

"Let me do it." George grabbed the pan before I could think about saying no, then rummaged through the split logs for some kindling.

Teddy tried to help, but George cocked his fist, ready to bring it down on Teddy's scarred ears. For once I jumped in before it happened.

"George, you hit him and you're doing the milking for the next two weeks, every morning. I don't care if you're late for school, you will milk the cow every morning."

George's hand fell to his side, still clenched. And Teddy shocked the hell out of me, and George, by clocking him right in the chin, a deft, accurate jab.

Even more surprising, George didn't hit him back. Teddy's hands immediately flew up to cover his head, but George's fist opened slowly, and he turned back to the stove, where he started loading wood into it. He wiped a slight trickle of blood from his lip.

It was hard to keep from laughing. Actually, I did laugh, but I kept it quiet, behind my newspaper.

* * *

Checking the cows sometimes meant pulling a breech birth, or unfold-
ing a front leg that was hung up inside the mother. If everything was
okay, a quick check took about a half hour. So after an hour, I was just
about to go out and see whether Rita needed some help when I heard
a horse outside. Rita came in, her face troubled.

"Blake, you better come out here."

She cupped her hands to the wood stove.

"What is it?" I set down my paper and slipped my boots on.

"I'm not sure," she said. "But we should probably hurry."

I was confused. Despite this statement, she didn't seem rushed at
all, and I couldn't imagine what problem could come up that she
wouldn't have encountered before.

"You're not sure?" I wrapped myself in a jacket and tugged on
my hat.

"No." She shook her head. "I've never seen anything like it." She
sounded terribly sad.

"All right," I said.

Out in the pasture, Rita wove through the cattle, some standing, some
lying down, one licking the fresh afterbirth from her shaky newborn.

"Shoot," Rita suddenly said.

"What?"

"Oh, she's moved. She was right around here." She pointed, then
jerked the horse's reins, guiding him at angles across the pasture. Five
minutes later, we came upon a lone cow, standing in a corner of the
pasture, facing us with a fearful, confused look. "There she is," Rita
said.

When we approached, the cow bobbed her head as if she was
going to run, but Rita pulled the horse up. I looked the cow over and
didn't see anything unusual. Rita seemed hesitant to move.

"What's wrong with her?"

Rita nudged the horse slowly around to the side, then behind the cow, who turned her head, watching us closely. When the cow's rear end came into sight, I saw the problem. There, hanging beneath her tail, was a mass of nearly white, bloody flesh. And I knew then why Rita hadn't been in a hurry to come back out.

"Oh, no," I said.

"What is it?" Rita's voice shook.

"She's prolapsed." I climbed slowly off the horse.

"Prolapsed?" Rita repeated the word cautiously, as if the sound of it might cause the cow more pain. "What does that mean? Is that her womb?"

"Afraid so." I started to walk, very deliberately, circling behind the cow. "We're going to have to get her to the barn. We're going to have to go easy with her. She's pretty jumpy."

The cow lowered her head, still eyeing me, ready to run. I raised my arms and waved them, not quickly, just enough to get her moving.

"I wonder where her calf is," I said.

Back in the barn, we studied the cow. "God, that looks painful," Rita said. We had gotten her into a stall, and we sat on the gate. I lit a lantern and hung it above the stall, and its soft glow gave us a clearer view of the cow's condition.

I recognized the cow by the twisted knob of horn on the left side of her head. She was one of our best mothers, one we could count on to take an orphaned calf each spring. It seemed ironic now. She'd been so anxious to see her new baby, she'd pushed too hard, exposing her womb and who knows what other organs to air they were never intended to see. It was also a strong indication of how much pain she was in that she had left her calf somewhere.

"What do we do?" Rita looked at me.

"We've got to push it back inside," I sighed.

Rita cringed. "Have you ever done that before?"

I shook my head. "I watched Dad do it once when I was a kid. It's not going to be fun. We'll need some water and a needle to sew her up."

"Oh, god," Rita said, her shoulders rising up to her ears. She shook off the thought. "Okay, I'll go get that stuff."

"I need to go out and find her calf."

Rita nodded, then climbed down from the gate.

With life on the ranch as difficult and strained as it was, Rita and I had come to rely more and more on each other to keep our spirits up. We had an odd arrangement, living like a family in every respect except the obvious. And although we worked well together when it came to planning our days and sharing in the chores, the awkward nature of the situation brought a natural arm's length to our relationship. We were very cautious about touching; even an accidental brush caused us both to flinch, jumping away from each other as if we'd singed our skin. And although our conversations sometimes veered close to the topic of Jack, we were both quick to make an abrupt change in direction at those moments. But as time passed, we did discuss other people, and politics—safe topics. But I had to be careful not to broach anything that stirred up my personal feelings toward Rita. They were too strong. And as long as Rita was holding out hope that Jack would return, I didn't want them exposed. I knew she was still thinking of him, because every once in a while she would retreat to her bedroom early some night, telling the boys not to bother her, and we would hear her crying quietly.

So the trust we developed was strong, but incomplete. Because of course the two topics that we never discussed were the most important ones in our lives—how I felt about Rita, and how she felt about Jack.

* * *

Because it was so dark, and I had no idea where the cow had given birth, finding the calf proved to be difficult. I started where we'd found the cow, and meandered back and forth across the pasture. I considered waiting until morning, but I knew that once the cold settled in, the calf probably wouldn't survive the night. So I gave the pasture one more round.

Finally I spotted a small, huddled figure, only twenty or thirty yards from where we'd found the mother. The calf's rump was in the air, and he was down on his front knees, struggling to pull one of his forelegs out from under him. His coat was slick with afterbirth. I wiped as much of the moisture off him as I could before slinging him over my horse and riding back to the barn. He had some trouble breathing, so I cleaned his nostrils and wiped my hand on my dungarees.

When I got to the barn, Bob was there.

"Where's Rita?" I asked.

"She went to put the boys to bed. She'll be back." Bob turned to the cow, who still looked scared and confused. "I've never seen anything like this before."

"Really? Weren't you there when this happened before, when we were kids?"

Bob shook his head.

"Hm. I could of sworn you were there." In fact, I remembered Bob being there, because he had been so upset by the whole scene that he had to leave.

"I don't remember anything like that."

I opened the gate just enough to squeeze the calf inside. The cow nuzzled him, then licked him clean, her big pink tongue smoothing his shivering hide. The calf kept trying to stand, but his mother's bath knocked him over each time.

"Did you bring water?" I looked around.

"Yeah. I got a bucket right here." Bob walked around to the next stall.

"Why did you put it in there?"

Bob shrugged. "Don't know. I guess I didn't want it to get knocked over."

I rubbed my chin. "All right, let's see what we can do here."

Replacing a cow's womb must be a veterinarian's worst nightmare, and since we weren't even veterinarians, I guess it would qualify as worse than our worst nightmare. It was like trying to push a balloon through a knothole.

We ducked into the stall, sneaking past the cow so she wouldn't get too spooked. But her eyes got wild, staring right at us, daring us to come near her.

"Set that bucket down in the corner," I told Bob.

We walked slowly, making our way behind her. She twisted her neck around to keep an eye on us.

"Mooo," she said, and I'm pretty sure she meant it as a threat.

I pictured what would happen when we touched the womb.

"We're going to have to tie her head," I said. "Otherwise she'll be all over this stall, and us with her."

Bob nodded. "I'll get a rope." He crept out of the stall and returned with the rope, which he'd already fashioned into a lasso. He straddled the gate and dropped the loop down toward her head.

The cow pushed her nose into the corner when she saw the rope, and Bob had to reach down and slip the loop over her head by hand. He slipped the other end through the gate's planks and crawled outside the stall, where he leaned back, pulling at the rope. I slapped the cow's flank, and she moved toward the gate. Bob gave the rope a tug to keep her momentum going. She ended up with her head about a foot from the gate, and Bob tied the rope.

Rita returned to the barn. "How's it going?"

"Well, we haven't gotten too far along yet." I heard the irritation in my voice.

I looked over at Rita, and the pained look had returned to her face as she studied the cow.

"Don't worry," I said. "It doesn't hurt as bad as it looks."

"How do you know?"

I shrugged. "I don't. I'm just trying to make you feel better."

Rita smiled. "You don't have to do that. Besides, I don't believe you. Speaking of pain, I brought the needle." She held up a big needle, one we used to sew up the ends of gunnysacks. I cringed, and she shrugged.

"Should do the trick," she said.

I nodded.

We washed our hands in the bucket and stood in a row behind the cow, staring at the glistening mass of flesh. I wasn't sure where to start.

"Well, somebody's got to break the ice here." Rita stepped to the cow's side, reached out, and placed her hand along the bottom of the womb, lifting it with slow deliberation. The cow bawled, a strangled, wheezing call, and one hind leg kicked, missing everything.

I stood on the opposite side and cradled what skin was left. We lifted the flesh, which felt like a big lung, up to the opening and held it there. The cow squirmed and grunted, fighting the rope.

"Hold the tail, Bob."

He pulled the tail to one side.

I slipped my hand inside the cow, taking some of the tissue with me, and Rita did the same. I slid my other hand inside, and a bubble of skin popped out of the opening. The womb slid from the inside hand, then from Rita's, until the whole thing was hanging down just as it started.

We tried again, moving slower, even more deliberate. I felt my jaw tightening. I pushed a handful of flesh inside, but the cow suddenly clenched. I had expected she might do this, but I wasn't ready for it to hurt like it did. She clamped down on my forearm, and my sympathies went out to every calf ever born. I groaned, loudly, and Rita looked at me with alarm.

"What?" she asked.

I couldn't talk. My hand went numb, and I pictured the arm turning blue, stiffening like a corpse. But the cow let up a bit, and I whipped my arm out before she could grab it again.

"Whoa." Rita jumped. "What are you doing?"

"I guess she thought she needed an arm." I massaged my forearm.

"Oh, she gave you a little hug, did she?" Bob said, chuckling.

"She likes me, all right." I shook the arm out.

The calf, inching forward on shaky legs, groped toward his mother's udders, sniffing through his damp little snout. His tongue slipped out and took hold of an udder, pulling it between his jaws. He began sucking, and we couldn't have come up with a better anesthetic if we'd tried every drug known to man. After the calf suckled for a half minute, the cow stepped forward, putting a bit of slack in the rope.

Rita and I smiled at each other.

"Okay, let's try her again," I said.

We followed the same procedure, with my left arm inside this time. "Bob, why don't you thread that needle in case we ever get this thing in there."

Bob stared at the tail, contemplating what to do with it. He let it drop, then came back with a hunk of twine and tied the tail to the stall.

For the next two hours the three of us tried to solve this puzzle. Several times we nearly had the whole womb back inside when the cow squeezed it out. She kicked me once, right in the shin, and she got Rita later, prompting a punch in the flank.

The calf finished nursing, lay down, and slept. I was jealous.

Our arms felt like the muscles had been pulled right out of them.

And because we had to stand with our knees bent, to get the right angle, we fought intense, gripping cramps in our legs. It was good there were three of us. One could sit and rest while the other two strained at the birth canal.

Bob was sitting on top of the gate, stretching his legs, when we heard a rustling outside. Then footsteps. Helen appeared. We all looked at her, questioning, wondering if something was wrong.

She fixed an eye on Bob, and he looked down at the ground. Helen showed no interest in what was happening in the stall. Rita and I had about half the womb back inside the cow. Rita looked at me, making a fierce face. I almost laughed.

"I just wondered if everything was all right out here," Helen said, her tone pleasant on the surface but strained in its core.

I don't know what she meant by "all right," but with Rita and me grunting away, and the three of us covered with sweat and blood, and one miserable cow trying to figure out what was going on at her south end, things were clearly not all right. Bob just shrugged. He couldn't look Helen in the eye, and I wondered whether it was possible that she actually expected him to come inside.

Helen stood squarely facing Bob. He mumbled something we couldn't hear, something that didn't satisfy Helen as she made no move to leave. In fact, she didn't make any move at all.

"How are your legs?" I asked Rita, talking a little louder than necessary.

"Pretty tight."

Two or three feet of flesh hung from behind the cow. She was getting tired and hadn't pushed anything out for a while.

"You need a break?" I asked.

Rita took a deep breath. "I think I'll make it."

This wasn't the answer I was looking for, and I tried to get the message across with a look, but Rita was intent on her work.

"You sure?" I asked.

She nodded.

"How much longer you think this will take?" Bob's question annoyed me. I can't describe how much Bob's question annoyed me.

"You know I can't answer that," I said after a pause.

"Did you get the needle threaded?" Rita asked Bob.

"It's right here."

"Well, if she doesn't push again, we could be finished before too much longer," Rita said.

There was a long silence, with only a slight rustling from where Helen was standing.

Bob cleared his throat. "You guys think you can handle it?" His voice sounded as if it would crack.

The silence that followed this question was even longer. Rita and I inched the womb up, sneaking a little at a time back into its cavity. A few inches slipped out. Two steps forward, one back. My legs were burning. Neither of us answered Bob, and I guess it became obvious we weren't going to.

I heard a brief, guttural "Hmph," then the crunch of heels against dirt and straw. To my surprise, Bob didn't follow.

"Need a break, Rita?" He stepped back to where we were. "Whoa, you guys almost got it."

"Better get the needle ready," I said, impatient.

Bob, who seemed pleased with himself, was anxious to help. He plucked the needle from his pant leg and stood at the ready.

"So you're going to stick it out after all, huh, Bob?" I didn't expect this from Rita, but I guess she was as tired and at least as annoyed as I was.

Bob ignored the remark, directing his attention to the job. Helen's visit got Rita and me angry enough that it renewed some of our strength. After a few minutes, we worked the last of the womb into the opening and held her closed.

"Ready?" I asked.

"She's not going to like this," Rita said.

We braced ourselves, but it didn't help. Bob inserted the needle, and the cow reacted as if we had shoved a branding iron into her. She cried out, and her body tensed, pulling at the rope. The gate shook. She kicked Bob, and the womb sloshed out, falling to its full length. Rita collapsed, rolling out of range of the cow's heels, and I sat down myself, exhausted, leaning against the stall.

"Damn!" Rita shouted in a tired, husky voice. Then she repeated herself, several times, harder each time.

Once we recovered, it took another half hour to get the damn thing back inside. This time, we were smart enough to put a few stitches in beforehand so we'd have a start once we got to the end.

Bob kept twisting his neck around, looking out toward the barn door, expecting Helen to show up again. The first few times he did this, I didn't think twice about it. But after a half hour of Bob turning every minute or two, even in the middle of this job, I lost my patience.

"Bob, why don't you just leave, get it over with. You're not doing us any good here." Once I started talking, I was surprised how angry I was. "If your mind is somewhere else, you might as well go there before someone gets hurt."

I felt Bob's eyes on me, and felt his hurt, and probably for that reason, I didn't look at him. But I was too tired and angry to worry about him. And by that time, I was willing to finish the job with just the two of us, no matter how much longer it took or how painful it was.

Bob walked away wordlessly and climbed from the stall. After several footsteps, we heard a loud smack, and the barn shook. The cow jerked, but not enough to affect our job. Bob had either punched or kicked the wall, and the fact that he knew the sound could have made us lose the womb again made me angrier.

As we huddled behind that poor cow, struggling to stuff this fleshy balloon through the fleshy knothole, we pressed against each other, and I felt Rita's breath on my cheek. At times our heads touched, and we were so focused on the task at hand that we didn't pull away. The sweat ran down our faces. Our cheeks slid against each other. Rita's hair brushed against my neck, and my nose. I smelled her, and felt every movement she made—each time she bent her knees and pushed upward, and each time she twisted to one side with her hip. Physically, it was the closest I had ever been to Rita, and it was distracting. It made my heart race a little, and the blood pounded in my head. And the longer we worked, the more I thought about being so close to her, and the more I liked it. A half hour after Bob left, we finally tied the final stitch into a knot. We sat in the back of the stall, leaning our heads against the wall and looking at the raw, sealed opening. Our breath beat through slack mouths, showing a little in the dim light of the lantern.

"We did it," Rita said.

I nodded and held out a hand. She pressed hers into mine, and as we shook, our hands slid against each other in blood.

Back at the house, covered with blood and slime, Rita and I were both in need of a bath. We usually alternated evenings, but this was clearly a special case. I heated up the water and filled the tub while Rita warmed the coffee that George had made earlier. I let her go first, and I sat and read a book while listening to the water slosh behind the curtain. I noticed this splashing and the motions of Rita's body more than usual that night, listening to each ripple of water, and occasionally watching the shadow of Rita's arm, or the silhouette of her head as she let her hair down from its bun.

"Blake?" Rita asked from behind the curtain.

Her voice was so unexpected that I didn't answer right away. I had to clear my throat. "Yeah?"

"I forgot a towel."

"Oh. All right. I'll get you one." I stood and fetched one, and held it over the cotton curtain, where it was snatched from my grasp. But the towel got hung up on my thumb somehow, and when Rita pulled a little harder on it, and I simultaneously tried to jerk my thumb loose, we ended up pulling the curtain down. And there stood Rita, naked and wet.

She immediately covered herself with the towel, but for a brief moment, our eyes locked. I had never seen a naked woman before, not even in photographs. Despite the tauntings of my friends, I had passed on the occasional trips to a discreet house in Deadwood. Actually, I had gone once. But when we got there I got so damn nervous, I had to leave. I ended up waiting in a bar down the street, where I was greeted with a razzing that was unmerciful.

Now I stood before Rita, and although she had covered herself, I still pictured her as she had been seconds before. She was solid, her breasts large but still firm, the nipples dark and stimulated by the moisture and the cool air. I was struck by the curves—the way the lines slanted in from her breasts to her waist, then eased out again to form the lovely shape of her hips. It was a vision I would not soon forget, and its impact on me was powerful.

I felt a physical sensation that I had never experienced before. My erection was painful, as if every drop of blood, especially from my head, had rushed to my groin. I was dizzy. I felt as if I was falling toward Rita, and that I had no way of stopping myself. It was overwhelming, and almost entirely physical, as if the lower part of my body had a will of its own, separate from the rest of me. My head, my mind, was irrelevant, completely uninvolved in the process.

"Blake, maybe you ought to put that curtain back up before you faint." Rita held the towel tightly around herself.

"Yes." I suddenly jumped into action. "Yeah. Of course." I fumbled with the curtain while Rita patiently waited, still covered. I didn't look her way, and eventually, after much fumbling, I got the curtain hung. But when I went to sit down, the feeling stayed with me. And it got stronger. The image of her moist skin lifted a lump to my throat. It affected my breathing. I felt as if the weight of Montana was pressing down on my chest. And despite all my better judgment, and what I believed, and how much I respected Rita, and everything about my life that spoke against it, I found myself speaking to her.

"Rita?" I said, and I didn't even know what I was going to say next. I had no idea.

But something about my voice must have revealed all that I was thinking, or all that I was subconsciously thinking, because I wasn't thinking. There must have been nothing hidden in the way I spoke her name, because Rita didn't respond. She simply dried herself and disappeared into her room, never coming out from behind that curtain, never acknowledging that I'd spoken to her.

When I lowered myself into the tub after dumping one more bucket of hot water into it, I thought about the fact that this same water had brushed against Rita just moments before. The realization made me hard again, and dizzy. I began scrubbing, rubbing the grime and slime from my skin. I washed quickly, then relaxed for a moment, taking advantage of what heat was left in the water. I flexed my arm, the one that the cow had squeezed earlier, and thought about the fact that the only females I'd ever felt inside were animals. And this thought brought on a chilly loneliness that had become a familiar companion in the time that I'd been living with Rita.

I would sometimes lie in bed, feeling as if Jack was still there, as if no matter how long we lived together, Jack would always interfere, even if we never saw him again. It seemed I would never escape the power he had over some of the things in my life.

I ducked my head under the water one last time, and enjoyed the confined silence for as long as I could hold my breath. And then I came up, brushing the water from my face. My efforts to stifle the vision had failed, and after I finished drying, I ducked into my room and pleasured myself to relieve the pressure. Still, I was awake for another hour.

Two days later, I came back to the house late one night, just past sundown, after a long day tilling. My throat was sore, filled with dust, and my arms were heavy from working the reins all day. When I walked in, Rita was bent over the washtub, scrubbing dishes. George and Teddy hunched over open schoolbooks at the table, scratching math figures onto yellowed paper.

On the floor next to the table, I noticed my worn leather satchel. I didn't think much about it, as my mind was on the cup of cool water I'd just drawn from the well. But after drinking, as I filled a plate from a panful of roast beef and potatoes, I saw my suit hanging on my bedroom door. I looked at the satchel again and realized it was stuffed with clothes—my clothes.

I turned to Rita, who was watching me, waiting for me to notice. I heard a sniffle, and saw that Teddy was crying. I looked back at Rita.

"It doesn't have anything to do with the other night," Rita said. "Or you. It just doesn't seem right anymore, Blake."

Teddy cried openly, and George slumped off to his room

"You're probably going to have a family of your own before too long. . . ." Rita took a deep breath and turned away from the washtub, wiping her hands on her apron. Then she held them to her eyes, pressing firmly against the lids with her fingers, so her palms covered her mouth. She held this position for a full minute, then lowered her hands and took another breath. "And the boys and I might as well get used to living alone."

I stood looking at her for a while, and I felt the corners of my mouth falling. Part of me wanted to argue, to put up a fight. Part of me was thinking about one night when Rita told me she still missed Jack, and realizing that, as impossible as it seemed, this was still true.

And I resented the fact that even though I'd been there every night, and listened to her complaints about Helen, and shared some of my own concerns, could it be possible that she still felt more for Jack than for me? I thought about telling her how I felt. But just about that time, she looked up at me with an expression of slight pleading, and I could tell just from this look that she knew, and that she didn't want me to tell her.

And I knew that I had just been a guest in this house. That this was Rita's house, and my stay had ended. It seemed I should say good-bye, but that didn't make sense, considering where I was going. So I picked up my satchel, draped my suit over one arm, put a hand on Teddy's heaving shoulder, and left.

The big house looked a long ways off that night. It was dark, with the smell of meadows muted by dust, and quiet except for the clicking of locusts. Just before I took that long walk, I decided to pay a visit to some old friends. I headed for the barn, where I dropped my satchel by the door.

The old whitewashed stick figures had faded with age and weather and from animals rubbing up against them. I dug one of my baseballs out of the bin where we kept the oat buckets and spare bridle parts. And I started throwing pitches against the wall. I threw and threw, and the more I threw, and the more my body warmed up and the blood coursed through me, the angrier I got at my brother Jack. I thought about all the anguish he had caused his wife, and my parents, and all the extra work he'd heaped on us all, even when he was home, and I thought about how callously, even after all that, he could just up and run off again.

I started throwing my curveball, but it had been a while since I'd used those muscles, and I began to feel it in my elbow. So I went back to burning fastball after fastball against that wall, belt-high to the stick hitters. And I pictured Jack's head on the batter, and I gritted my teeth and whipped a fastball, and I don't know whether it was intentional or not, but that ball went right for that poor stick bastard's head, and it broke clean through the wall.

As fate would have it, Helen—the reason I'd moved out in the first place—just happened to be walking back to the old homestead house as I headed satchel in hand toward the big house. She looked at the satchel, and I swear her eyes lit up like a goddam forest fire.

"Hello, Blake." It was the best reception she'd ever given me.

"Helen, do me a favor, will you?" I said. "Mind your own damn business for a change."

To my dismay, the command had very little effect on her. She just smiled, looked down at the satchel again, and said, "Okay, Blake. Whatever you say."

12

summer 1939

In the absolute middle of a clear blue sky, the sun sat with great satisfaction, spreading its heat and light and a slight, undulating buzz through every square mile of open space in Carter County. The ground lay tired, beaten, surrendering its skin to the feet, hooves, and wheels that trundled over its increasingly bare surface. The topsoil had long drifted away, and what remained was hard, gray clay that, in those rare instances of rain, formed deep, unforgiving ruts. Footprints stayed molded into the earth for months, reminders of a mid-shower trip to the outhouse, or to the pickup for a snort from the bottle under the seat. If you hit a footprint or a rut just right, you could break an ankle. The creek beds curled up like dried leather, and the grass turned yellow, smelling as if cooked.

We, the residents, were also beaten, and tired, and our skin was weary of the sun soaking into it, baking it deep brown and pulling the moisture from us until we could sleep twelve hours a night, with a nap during the day—along the riverbank, or under one of the few trees still bearing leaves, or under a wagon. We only wanted water. That was all. Everything we needed depended on water.

During the thirties, the banks of the Little Missouri River had lost touch with the flow of water. A thin band of current trickled through the middle of the waterway, leaving a gap of ten feet on either side between the wagon-wide ribbon of brown water and the riverbank. The lowest I ever saw it was the summer of '37, when the river was below my knee. If it was a foot deep, then it was twelve inches exactly. When we took a herd of cattle or a flock of sheep to the river to water them, you could almost see the level of water drop as they drank. I remember crossing the river once, and wishing it would become the threat it had been when it sucked George beneath its surface. The thought shook me for a moment, although it made perfect sense when I considered it.

As it turned out, the spring of '38 brought some rain, and although we were hopeful, we didn't get too excited. But '39 was also wet—still far below average, but better than we'd seen for almost two decades. There was indeed hope.

I drove our tractor around and around, circling the big meadow, pulling a heavy rake with teeth as tall as a child, gathering hay into mounds. The dust followed, also gathering, a cloud that grew as the morning passed. I wore a kerchief over my face to keep the dust from filling my nose and mouth, but nothing could keep it from my eyes, and I had to squint. I could barely see where I was going.

My thighs ached from working the pedals, and I could feel the hot metal through my boots, as though there were no soles. The engine roared between my knees, its heat drifting up through my legs, through my clothes, boiling my skin until I felt almost feverish. I carried a jug of water, wrapped in damp burlap, which I stopped to drink from and pour over a kerchief, rubbing the damp cotton across my face and inside my shirt. But the water was warm as tea by noon.

Dust and short stalks of hay settled inside my clothes, causing an itch here and there. These I learned to put out of my mind. Otherwise I would spend half my day reaching inside my clothes to scratch or dig out a piece of hay. I needed my hands—the right to steer and the left to pull the lever that lifted the rake when its belly was filled with hay.

Behind me, Dad and George followed with the team and wagon, pitching mounds of hay into the wagon bed. Their figures fluttered in the waves of heat—bending, jabbing, tossing, bending, jabbing, and tossing. I would trade jobs with Dad later, in the afternoon.

George was a teenager now, fourteen, and whether it was the age or the nature of his temperament I don't know, but he was still sullen, with a dash of dry humor. He had developed a sudden desire to spend time with Grandpa, his namesake. The two of them were an interesting pair, playing silent hours of gin or cribbage or trudging off wordlessly to drop a fishing line in the river. They had less to say than any two friends I'd ever seen, which was probably what they valued most about each other.

Teddy, at eleven, was his ever-enthusiastic, curious self. Most of his time was spent alone with a sheepdog named simply Pup, whom he trained to do tricks that left us gaping. At one point, Teddy decided to teach Pup to walk along the top plank of the fence around our yard. We smiled, watching him lift the shivering dog up onto the inch-wide plank time after time. She would stand whimpering and shaking, four feet from the ground, take a few tentative steps, and then tumble into Teddy's waiting arms. But Teddy was persistent, and after only a week, he had Pup hopping onto the fence herself, stepping carefully along the plank, then smiling and barking when she was back on the ground.

As for Helen, the conflict that had occurred between her and Mom had never been resolved. Helen had taken it badly. She would sit, quiet and tight-lipped, an injured look permanently carved into her face. Bob found himself in the unfamiliar, uncomfortable position of having to speak for both of them. If anyone directed a question to either of them, Helen would turn to him. She only spoke—in clipped, terse tones—to correct him when his facts were confused.

I found her behavior more infuriating than when she had been completely artificial, but the whole situation provided endless delight for Rita, who would direct all of her questions pointedly toward Helen, still looking at her while Bob fumbled through an explanation. Although I understood Rita's pleasure in this, and I found it amusing at first, I thought it was unnecessary to keep it going for as long as she did. I was worried about consequences for Rita.

Meanwhile, Bob and Helen had decided that the tiny old homestead house wasn't big enough, especially with her obsession with making a few babies. Bob started building a new house near the river. He didn't ask for help, although I considered offering. But a few weeks after he began work on it, Steve Glasser became a regular fixture there on the weekends. Unfortunately, by the time Bob finished the house, Steve and Jenny had become cool to the rest of the family. Obviously, Helen had gotten to them somehow, probably placing the blame for the blowup on Mom.

After several hours of driving, around and around, turning forward to check the direction, turning back to watch the rake, the engine roaring until the sound consumed everything around me, it seemed as if the tractor and I were the only things that existed. My mind wandered. I had been daydreaming a lot, ever since the trip to Belle Fourche with Bob. I often found myself thinking about other places, other lives, wondering whether the twenty-odd years I'd dedicated to the precious land around me would ever amount to anything besides more work. I sat in front of the radio at night, listening to news from places I had heard about but never been to, and I tried to imagine them—what life would be like as an autoworker in Detroit, a teacher in Boston, even a congressman in our nation's capital. I read letters from Muriel and Stan, and sometimes considered pulling up stakes and moving to Butte, where Stan said he could always get me a job working in the mine.

On this day, I thought of Omaha, a trip that was still fresh with images, smells, and texture after fifteen years. I remembered the delicate, white-faced couples with tailored clothes and rosy cheeks, chattering and walking casually, their gleaming shoes clicking against the sidewalks. And again I wondered what those people did for work, what job would allow someone to spend any night of the week out dining, dancing and drinking instead of resting your weary body. I thought about Satchel Paige and the other players, and how exciting it must be to play baseball for a living. Although I had often reflected back to my tryout, I had made a concerted effort not to do so with regrets. Lately it had been harder.

All these thoughts filled my mind, shifting and jumbling among themselves as the tractor shuddered beneath me, my body functioning unconsciously, steering and lifting the rake, lowering the rake, lifting the rake, lowering the rake, until I suddenly felt a presence very close to me. I nearly fell off my seat when I turned to find George standing on the running board not three feet away. I cut the engine.

"My god, you scared the hell out of me, George."

"Sorry, I been running alongside of you for five minutes. I guess you didn't see me."

"My mind was drifting a little, I guess. Is something wrong?"

He shook his head. "Lunch time. Hungry?" George's voice cracked. It was beginning to change, and he talked carefully, trying to hold it in the lower register. But whenever it jumped up to the boy voice, he grimaced, as though he'd made a mistake, letting it get away from him.

"Sure. Have you ever known your Uncle Blake to work through lunch?"

He shrugged and didn't smile, indicating without words that he didn't care one way or the other. He was just the messenger, and he'd already failed at that by letting his voice break. I stepped down from the machine as he dropped off the opposite side, and we walked toward the wagon, where Dad pulled food from a saddlebag, spreading it out in the wagon bed.

"Looks like we might finish this meadow today," I said.

"Yeah." George nodded, looking behind him.

"How's your back holding out?"

Shrug. "All right." He answered softly, as though that would help keep his voice in check. "For an old man," he added.

I chuckled, but decided not to subject him to any more of the torture of conversation. We walked silently, kicking up dust with every step.

"Dad, you ready to take over for me after lunch?"

He nodded. "How's the tractor running?"

"Fine. No problems at all."

"Looks like we'll finish this meadow today," Dad said.

I smiled at George, who almost grinned.

We polished off the bread and leftover fried chicken in a few jaw-grinding minutes, gulping warm water from a jug to push the food through our dust-dried throats. Then Dad and I rolled cigarettes and smoked, sitting in the wagon bed, swinging our legs and gazing out at the prairie.

"You checked the wheat lately?" I asked Dad.

He shook his head. "I'm afraid to." He chuckled, his head wagging back and forth, and took a long pull on his smoke.

Because we now had a tractor, we decided to take a chance and try the first wheat crop we'd planted in several years. And although we did get a little rain, we weren't sure it would be enough to support the crop. It looked as if harvesting the wheat might be a waste of time. Dad let out a long, high-pitched sigh, smiled up at the sky, then put his arm around George's shoulder.

"George, my boy, if you can help it, any way at all, find something to do with your life besides living off this godawful dusty country. Sit behind a desk and count beans or stand in front of a bunch of hayseed kids and scribble on a chalkboard, but don't be a rancher."

George kept his eyes out in the distance, and they narrowed just a little. Then he frowned up at Dad, squinting into the sun. "I want to be a rancher, Grandpa." His voice broke on "want," and he immediately dropped his eyes to his boots.

Dad opened his eyes like someone had just brought him a birthday cake, and looked first at George, then at me, then back at George.

"Did you hear that, Blake?" He turned his eyes back to me. "This poor misdirected kid wants to do this for the rest of his life." He took his arm from around George's shoulder, shook his head, and rested his hands on his thighs, turned inward so that his elbows stuck out like wings. "What did we do wrong? I never slipped up and told you this was fun, did I?" Dad smiled at George.

George blushed and looked straight down at the ground. He shook his head. "Nah."

"Well, that's good." Then, as if it had just occurred to him, he turned to me. "Blake, you never told him this was fun, did you?"

I snorted. "Not a chance."

Dad nodded, pinching his lips together.

I could tell that despite the show he was putting on, Dad was damn proud that George wanted to stay on the ranch, and it made me kind of proud myself, even if I didn't understand it coming from a kid who'd been through what George had.

"I love pain," George said, deadpan.

* * *

For the rest of the afternoon, George and I hefted hay into the bed of the wagon while Dad manned the tractor. When the wagon was full, we pulled the team around to a stack Dad and George had started that morning. There we pitched from the wagon onto the stack, piling the hay higher and higher, until our forks fell short of the heap, when we started another stack on the opposite end of the meadow.

Late that afternoon, I noticed a cloud of dust in the direction of the main road. This wasn't unusual, except that the cloud lingered for the next couple of hours, moving slowly across the horizon, as if the vehicle causing it was only going about three miles an hour. It moved much slower than a team of horses, or a tractor, even in low gear. I pointed the cloud out to George, and even he was intrigued, glancing from time to time for the rest of the day. There was one explanation for the cloud that frightened me, a flashback from a few years ago. Locusts.

Dad finished raking the meadow around seven, and rather than move on to the next meadow, he came back and helped stack what was left.

"Did you notice that cloud moving along the road, Dad?"

"No, what about it?" He looked toward the road, shielding his eyes from the setting sun.

"It's been there for a couple hours, creeping along."

"Really?" Dad reached back into his shirt and scratched his back, pulling a stalk of hay from inside. "Hm." I saw a hint of fear creep into his eyes. "Well, let's finish up here," he said, turning his back to the cloud.

We piled the last of the hay onto the top of the stack about an hour later and flipped our forks into the back of the wagon, stretching our stiff backs before we climbed up, Dad driving, George and I in the bed, and headed home. The sun was just shy of setting, and the heat had let up. I tipped the jug to my lips and savored the wetness, even though the water was almost too hot to swallow. I passed the jug to George, who drank, then replaced the cork before passing it up to Dad.

George shook his head. "Whew, that's hot," he exclaimed. "Like drinking from the kettle." He shuddered.

Back at the barn, we watered and fed the horses before walking back toward the house. I noticed the cloud still floating from the road. It was a mile or so from our house, and I was relieved to see from closer up that it wasn't dark enough to be a locust cloud. It was obvious from this distance that the opaque formation was nothing more than dust.

"Look." I pointed.

"Hm," said Dad, who I could see was also relieved. "You want to drive up and check it out?"

I thought. "Nah. It should get this far before too long. Besides, I'm hungry."

George looked disappointed.

"You can wait fifteen or twenty minutes, can't you?"

We went inside and washed up; then the three of us went to the living room and stared out the front window, waiting for the cloud to come up over the last rise. Rita came in from the dining room and stood behind us.

"What are you guys looking at?"

"Well, we're not too sure," I said. I pointed to the cloud and told her that we'd been watching it for a few hours.

Teddy ran up to the front door, with Pup right behind him, carrying something in her mouth. Teddy pointed down at her, obviously telling her to stay, then he flew through the front door. Pup dropped her treasure between her paws. It was a gopher.

"What's going on?" Teddy asked when he saw us staring out the window.

I explained, again pointing out the cloud. And it was only a matter of minutes before Mom's curiosity was piqued, too. We all stood gazing out the front window until we couldn't stand it any longer and went out into the front yard and gathered in a bunch, looking in the same direction, as if we were waiting for fireworks to start.

Finally, about the time it seemed this damn thing was never going to show up, a pickup came creeping over the ridge. We all looked at each other, confused about why anyone would drive their pickup so slowly, until a minute later, when something followed the pickup over the tiny ridge. The first we saw of the second vehicle was a big, gleaming silver blade, slick and shiny so that it looked white in the sunlight. It was a bulldozer. The big tracks along its sides rolled along the road, throwing dust straight into the air, forming the now-familiar cloud. The driver sat exposed, working the steering levers and occasionally reaching up to pull his hat down over his eyes.

And as they came close to our turnoff, the driver of the bulldozer waved to the pickup, indicating the turn. And somehow, from the way he moved, the shape of his body, and maybe just because it's the way things are sometimes, I suddenly recognized him. It was Jack.

And at the very moment I recognized him, I heard Rita behind me. "Oh, my god."

Mom inhaled a quick, gasping breath, and Teddy started looking around at all of us, gazing up into our faces with questioning eyes. "What's wrong?" he asked.

"It's your father," Rita said to him.

"It is?" Teddy looked out at the lumbering machine in disbelief. George turned and barged inside the house, slamming the door.

My heart pounded and I felt my tongue swelling up in my mouth, as if it had been stung by a bee. The sweat gathered around and on my forehead, under my arms, and on my upper lip. I wiped my mouth with my sleeve.

We stood frozen in fear or anger or whatever each of us was going through as we watched this man we hadn't seen for ten years maneuver the huge piece of machinery through the gate, which was barely wide enough, then guide it off the drive and kill the engine. The pickup, which was brand-new, pulled right up to the yard and stopped. The fattest man I'd ever seen poured from the cab, causing the pickup to tilt to one side.

Jack hopped down off the bulldozer and strode toward us as if he'd just come in from a long day in the fields. He wore a big smile, and his walk was confident, anxious. The other man waited for Jack, then turned and joined him.

They stopped about twenty feet from us. Jack held his hands out as though he expected us all to run up and fall into his arms.

"The troublemaker is back!" he announced.

The other man laughed, not noticing that none of us did. Then the fat man looked us all over, moving his head around as he looked at each face, and walked toward us, then particularly right toward me.

"That you, Blake?" he asked.

I was completely baffled as to who he was, and how he would possibly know my name. But there was no denying that he knew who I was. He held out his hand and stood right in front of me. I shook it.

"David Westford," he said. "We met in Omaha a long time ago."

"I'll be damned," I mumbled. I never would have recognized him. He must have weighed a hundred pounds more than he had fifteen years before. "So how you been?" I asked, but I wasn't really looking at him or interested in what the answer might be. Once I knew who he was, my attention was back to my brother, and everyone's reaction to him.

"Fine," David Westford said. "Never better."

Teddy stood right out in front of us all so he could get a good look at his father. Mom straightened her spine. Rita took a step back, crossing her arms. Dad made the first move, stepping forward, not all the way, but within a couple steps. He put his fists on his hips and lifted his chest a little, taking a deep breath.

"So, what exactly do you expect us to do, bend down and brush the dust off your boots?"

Jack let his hands drop to his sides. He stood like that for a second or two, just standing, not showing anything in his face. He looked off to the side, out into the fields, and took his hat off, rubbing his other hand through his hair. Then he put his hat back on and faced Dad again.

"I guess I didn't expect nothing except that I wouldn't get drawn and quartered, that I might get a chance to sit down with my family and have a meal and maybe give them an opportunity to benefit from my success."

He turned and held his hand out to the bulldozer. "I come to offer my services to my family. If there's anything this country needs right now, it's water, and if there's anything that's going to help people get water from where it is to where they need it, it's irrigation. And if there's one thing that's going to make irrigation easier . . ." And again he turned and gestured to the machine.

The whole speech was so pat, so polished, that I knew he'd been practicing it all the way from Belle Fourche or wherever he came from. That bothered me. He sounded like one of the guys that came through trying to sell things—carpetbaggers. He sounded like the same old Jack.

Dad turned to Mom. "You s'pose we got enough to feed a couple of swindlers?"

David laughed, again not noticing that none of us did. Or maybe it just didn't matter to him.

Mom shrugged. She looked over at Rita, whose arms were still crossed. Rita looked down at her shoes, and for the first time, Jack turned his eyes toward her. Without thinking, I moved in Rita's direction, taking two steps to the side until I stood in Jack's line of vision, directly between him and his wife. He eyed me, his lids lowered, then a slight grin curled his lip, and he turned his head to the side.

"Is this Theodore?" he asked, moving slowly toward his younger son.

Teddy stepped a few steps closer to his father, his hands behind his back, and stood up straight. "I'm not real fond of that name," he said. "I like Teddy better."

Jack laughed, and I noticed his teeth were shiny white. He'd had some work done on them, either caps or false teeth. He looked as though he'd done fairly well for himself, which went against most every scenario I'd imagined during his absence. I had generally pictured him either parked in some dingy small-town bar or riding the rails, working odd jobs. But under the coat of dust, I could see that the dungarees and work shirt he wore were new, with no holes. His boots were also hardly worn, and the band on his hat was leather, and polished. His stomach was flatter than it had been last time we saw him.

"Well, shall we eat?" Mom said, turning quickly toward the house. Dad and David Westford walked close behind, then Rita, who took one last glance at Jack before going inside. Jack's eyes followed her, measuring. Then he turned to Teddy, who stood unwavering, studying his father up and down.

"So how old are you, Teddy, nine or ten?"

"Eleven," Teddy answered with conviction.

Jack looked at me, a touch of amazement in his eye. "Has it been ten years?"

I just stared at him.

"It sure has," Teddy said with no hint of bitterness. I felt a great swelling of pride for this kid, who had as much reason as anyone to hate this man but who seemed ready to forgive everything right on the spot. I thought back to Jack's return from the army, and to how angry I had been. And I knew that most of the credit went to Teddy's mother, whom I'd never heard speak badly of Jack in all the time he'd been gone.

"God damn," Jack said into his shirt. "Ten years. Time sure does pass quicker than you think." He looked back at Teddy, whose steady gaze seemed to unnerve him. He patted him awkwardly on the shoulder, then turned to me. "So should we go on inside?"

I didn't respond at first. The range of things I could have said, wanted to say, questions I would ask, covered such a wide swath that it was impossible to focus on any one thing.

"Hey, I didn't expect a big hug or nothing," Jack said. "I might do dumb things sometimes, but I'm not that stupid."

"We'll see about that," I muttered.

"Fair enough." Jack nodded.

We walked inside, where Mom and Rita were getting the food ready while Dad set the table. George stood off to the side, away from the nervous energy, in the corner. David was the only one already seated at the table.

"Where's Bob and Muriel?" Jack asked.

I answered after a moment in which nobody seemed anxious to. "Bob's living in his own house near the river with his wife. Muriel lives in Butte. She's married, too."

Jack shook his head once, absorbing more new information. "And how you doing, George?" He nodded toward the mirror image of himself crowding in the corner. He moved toward George, a little more sure than he had been outside, feeling more comfortable in his old home, as minutes passed and no one told him to go away.

When he got within a few feet of George, he held out his hand to shake. But instead of shaking, George hit him, a fist right to the jaw, a crack of bone that happened so fast that even those of us who were looking right at them didn't register the act for a second or two. A collective gasp rose like a chorus, and those of us who weren't looking turned their heads toward the sound of the punch. Everything stopped. George whirled and marched out of the room, not appearing to fear retaliation so much as having finished what he intended to do.

Jack stood motionless for a full minute, sixty seconds of him standing with his back to us, and us first staring at him then looking at each other, dazed. Would he leave? Would he go after George? Or turn on us all, and start in about not being wanted? But when he turned, he had his head tilted to the side and he let out a big, heavy sigh that puffed his cheeks out. He started nodding.

"Well, I guess I had that coming," he said, with no trace of humor. He said it sadly, and truly. He held his hand to his jaw, resting it there as if preventing the jaw from falling off his face. And he stepped to the table, where he sat down next to David, who seemed oblivious to the world around him, acting as if people hitting each other was a daily occurrence.

Jack's response, or lack of one, set everyone back into motion again. Dad finished setting the table, Mom and Rita placed the food in the center, Teddy and I walked into the kitchen to see if there was anything else that needed doing, while David Westford rubbed his hands together, staring at the food. He cast a couple of quick glances at Jack, and it made me wonder what Jack had told him to expect from this homecoming.

"Where did you get the dozer?" Dad asked Jack as we ate. It was the first anyone had said since we sat down.

Jack tilted his head toward David Westford. "Bought it from David."

"That's right. You were selling farm machinery even back when I met you," I said to David.

His pink face brightened, and he nodded. "Ah, so you do remember me." He smiled. "That's right, Blake. That machine out there has made me a very rich man, even with things going the way they have the last few years."

This seemed pretty obvious, considering most people in America couldn't afford food to maintain the bulk he carried, much less gain a hundred pounds. His bravado embarrassed everyone, and silence again fell over the room. We focused on our portions of canned venison, mashed potatoes, gravy, and cooked carrots.

"You didn't drive that thing all the way from Omaha, did you?" Dad finally asked.

David laughed loud and long, much too long, making everyone uncomfortable again. "No, no," he said. "We shipped the machine by train to Belle Fourche, and drove Jack's pickup up there to pick it up."

"That's your pickup?" Dad asked Jack.

Jack nodded, eyes down.

There's little doubt in my mind that everyone at that table was going through the same thing I was that night. The questions asked were not what we wanted to know—not even close. Nobody gave a damn about where the bulldozer came from, or how they got it there, or how Jack and David happened to meet, although that was quite a remarkable coincidence.

What we really wanted to know, nobody asked. But the questions were there, sitting on the end of our tongues, waiting to be sprung, to have their shells cracked open so some things could be explained. But we couldn't do it, and we all knew that. There was no chance of asking Jack where he'd been for the last ten years, or where he'd gotten the money to buy not only a bulldozer but a new pickup, and some new teeth. Even Teddy, whose curiosity was without bounds and who probably wanted to know worse than anybody, knew the rules. He did not ask. Instead, we resorted to small talk, chitchat.

"Weren't you from St. Louis?" I asked David.

He answered immediately, talking right through his food. "Yes, I am from St. Louis, Blake. Still live there. Just happens that Omaha is part of my territory, as it was when we met." He shoveled another forkful of venison into his mouth, without pausing to take a breath. He somehow managed to chew and talk very quickly at the same time.

"You seen any good baseball games lately?" he asked me.

"No, no, you couldn't really call anything we play around here baseball compared to what we saw in Omaha," I said.

I was just about to change the subject, thinking that David might bring up something that I didn't want to have to explain, when he asked, "How about that tryout? You had a good deal there."

I shook my head, not elaborating. "I've tried to keep up with that

Paige fellow through the years," I said quickly. "He's not still pitching for Mobile, is he?"

"Satchel?" David said. "Oh, no . . ." as though everyone should know. "No, Satchel hasn't been in Mobile for a long time. I think he pitches for a team down south now, Charlottesville or something like that. I don't follow the nigger league like I used to."

David Westford plowed right on ahead with his patter and his chomping. Jack looked embarrassed by David's behavior—not to mention his manners—and I concluded that he probably didn't know David very well. Might have even met him just long enough to make the deal for the bulldozer. I thought I had perhaps managed to maneuver my way around the topic of my tryout, but the delay was only temporary.

"What tryout is he talking about?" Mom asked.

"Yeah." Dad looked at David, then at me. "What's he mean?"

David looked up at me, and Jack started chuckling. "Looks like somebody's got himself a secret," Jack said. "Somebody besides me."

"It was nothing, really," I said. "I just tried out with a guy when I was in Omaha that summer. It was nothing."

"Nothing, hell," David said. "He invited Blake here to play for the Cardinals' farm club. You never went?" he asked me.

I shook my head. "It's not really worth talking about. I don't want to talk about it."

"The Cardinals?" Jack asked. "They offered you a contract?"

I nodded, eyeing Jack, telling him with a look that I didn't want to talk about it. He saw the look and dropped his eyes.

"I can't believe this," Mom said. "You never said a word about this."

"Like I said, it's not really worth talking about. I didn't go." I was surprised to hear quite an edge to my voice, and it had an immediate effect on the momentum of the conversation. We were all quiet for a while, just concentrating on our food. But the longer dinner went on, and the more David talked, the more uncomfortable everyone got. In a way, as obnoxious as he proved to be, it was good that David was there, as a distraction. Even George's entrance, about halfway through dinner, went fairly unnoticed because of the attention on David.

I watched David and remembered my first instinct, when I met him on the train to Omaha, had been not to trust him. On that trip, I'd grown to like him, and my memories of him had always been rather fond. But he'd changed. By the time Mom brought out the pan of cookies she'd baked for dessert, we had conceded all conversation to David. We didn't have to ask questions. We just sat and listened to his unsolicited opinions about everything from the New Deal to *The Grapes of Wrath* (he thought that Steinbeck was exaggerating). He really brought the hair on our necks up when he stated that if he had owned a farm or ranch during the past ten years, he not only could have made money, he could have become even richer than he was.

A slight grin turned up the corner of Dad's mouth, and I could tell he was barely able to hold back his laughter. But Mom was not amused. Her head jerked back as she took a deep breath in through her nose and pulled her mouth to a point. Rita shook her head. And Jack stood up dramatically, picking up his plate and carrying it toward the kitchen.

"Well, I have to drive David in to Belle tomorrow to catch the train, and I'm pretty well tuckered out from wrestling with that big machine, so I think I'll turn in. Where do you want me to sleep?" he yelled from the kitchen, poking his head in, looking to Mom.

"You and David can sleep in your old house. Nobody lives there anymore."

"Okay. Great," Jack said, reentering the room. "Thanks so much . . . all of you. It's really good to see you all." He looked down at George, who was seated closest to the kitchen. Jack nodded to him, and to everyone's surprise, George turned his eyes toward Jack. He didn't acknowledge him or say a word, but he did look at him. And those of us who knew him well realized that in his subtle way, George had turned a corner.

Jack and David were gone when we got up the next morning. Rita looked worried, and I felt as if I should talk to her, but I had to get out to the fields. I wasn't sure what I would say anyway. That day, Dad and George and I fumbled through our work with stunned expressions, getting about half what we would normally get done, trying to adjust to the presence of this person we'd spent ten years trying to forget.

Dad looked old that day, and spent a lot of time wiping his brow with his kerchief. George's attention was everywhere but on his pitch-fork. As we dragged ourselves back to the house, all I wanted to do was sit in front of the radio for a couple of hours, then go to bed. I wasn't even hungry. But when we got there, Jack had returned, Bob and Helen were there, and the mood was spirited.

Most of the talk passed between Bob, Jack, and Mom, and it reminded me of Bob's almost reverent admiration for Jack when we were younger. He would be the happiest to see him, I thought, and I tried to believe that their bond would help ease us all through the adjustment.

Helen and Rita were both quiet, focusing their attention on matters in the kitchen. Rita was tense. She turned to look at Jack now and then, only brief glances, as if she was making sure that he hadn't snuck off again, or wasn't trying to come near her. It was hard to tell which, and I wanted very badly to know. It bothered me to think that she might be even remotely happy to see him.

We ate a big dinner without incident, and as everyone retired to the living room, I announced, "Well, I need to turn in. I didn't get much sleep last night."

"Blake, just a second before you go to bed." Jack pulled me into the kitchen, and everyone followed us discreetly with their eyes, curious, as they walked in the opposite direction, into the living room.

It was the first moment Jack and I had been alone since his return, and I prepared myself for a showdown. I was ready for a confrontation. I imagined all kinds of things Jack might have to say to me, and I had comebacks ready for every one of them. I was ready. I was ready, and even hoping that he would start something. Because for the first time in my life, I felt like I wanted a fight. But when Jack looked at me, he was smiling in a way that was disarming—it was friendly, even playful. There was no sign at all of the usual underlying smugness in his eyes, which made me more nervous.

"Hey, I ran into Lonnie Roberts today when I was in Belle," Jack started, a little glimmer in his eye.

My first thought was that Jack could probably use a few more positive influences than Lonnie right now, but I pushed that into the back of my mind and heard him out.

"He tells me that his sister . . . you remember Sophie?" He looked at me, smiling big, those new teeth shining.

"Yeah, sure, of course," I said.

"Well, Lonnie says that ever since you came by his place a couple of years ago, you and Bob . . ."

I nodded.

"Ever since then, she's been asking about you until he's about sick of hearing it. Always wondering if you've been by again, or whether he's seen you in town lately, that kind of thing." Jack put his hand on my shoulder, still smiling, and I couldn't hide my intrigue. A slight smile came to my lips.

"Aaaah," he said. "You like that, huh? Well, brother, maybe you oughta do something about it."

I blushed and said nothing, dropping my eyes, and Jack laughed. "Well, well. I didn't know if you had it in you, old buddy," he said.

* * *

I regretted going to bed early that night as I wasn't a bit tired. Eventually I had to get up and take a walk, hours after I'd lain down, a couple of hours after everyone else had gone to bed. I went and sat on the bulldozer, pushing and pulling the levers, then lighting a cigarette and smoking it slowly, watching the orange glow in the dark.

Pup ran over and romped around the machine, trying to bring herself to jump up onto the tracks. But the dozer was too frightening, and she whined, staring up at me, her head tilted to one side. I told her I was too tired to come down and see her right then. Eventually she gave up and trotted away.

I sat for nearly an hour, my head full of questions. Questions about Jack—was he up to something, or did he really just want to be part of the family again? The potential for heartache, especially for Rita and the boys, made me sick to my stomach, and I tried to think about Sophie instead. But thoughts of her also made me nervous. Thoughts of her had always made me nervous, which was part of why I hadn't allowed myself the luxury of thinking about her much. I was amazed and thrilled that she asked about me. But I couldn't decide what I should do about it. Or I knew what I should do, but wasn't sure when or how. Especially how. The whole process, the rules of that part of life, were such a mystery to me. I knew nothing.

So I rolled another cigarette and stared up into the black sky at the stars, breathing in the smell of baked grass and dust. And I breathed in deeply, maybe hoping to inhale some wisdom from the cool evening breeze. I laughed to myself, thinking that just that morning, riding in circles on the tractor, my only complaint about my life would have been boredom. That problem had certainly taken care of itself with no help from me. It looked as if I wouldn't have to worry about being bored again for quite some time.

Book III

water

13

spring 1940

Romance happens one of two ways on the prairie—very fast, or very slow. The reason is simple. When two people meet, they generally live at least a couple of hours away from each other. It makes courtship worse than hard, especially without telephones. The only way around this is to get married and live in the same house. But for those who don't want to rush into things, getting to know each other takes a long, long time.

This was one reason that, at thirty-eight years old, I had never come close to marriage. I had yet to meet anyone besides Rita whom I would consider marrying in short order. And of course there were a few obstacles there. But I couldn't see the sense in a quick marriage anyway. Getting to know my wife after the wedding sounded pretty damn frightening. And I was always working too hard to put much time into courting someone who lived far away. The idea of driving to some girl's house several nights a week, as Bob had done with Helen, didn't appeal to my sensibility. Sleep and rest were too rare, too valuable.

As the result of all this nonsense, when Jack told me that Sophie Roberts was interested in seeing me, I had no motivation to pursue the possibility, especially with her living in Belle Fourche, more than an hour's drive away. So for almost a year, despite constant prodding and reminders from Jack, and a couple of encounters with Lonnie Roberts, who confirmed Jack's reports, I didn't do a damn thing. Except worry it over.

The road to Belle Fourche was slick and muddy, with light brown puddles dotting the darker brown every few feet. The rain was still coming down, flowing down the windshield in little rivers, right over the wiper blades. I drove Jack's Chevy pickup, and I was stiff as new leather in my white shirt with pearl snaps and my cleanest dungarees. I kept looking down at my boots, which were fairly worn, and coated with mud.

On the seat next to me sat a fresh-baked chocolate cake Mom had made, insisting I take it with me "for the meeting," she said with a wink. I hadn't told anyone except Jack what my intentions were after the REA meeting that afternoon, and although I was convinced he told everyone, I don't think he had to. I suspect all the attention I paid to my appearance gave me away. I even combed what was left of my hair, which must have been the clincher.

The grass sparkled green with moisture. The fields were still more brown than they were green, but the previous winter had dished out a generous helping of snow, and we already had more rain that spring than we'd been accustomed to getting for an entire year. For the first time in two decades, the air smelled alive, like the skin of a baby just out of its bath.

I peered through the blur of water at the swirling brown and green countryside and smiled a little hopefully. There was no reason to believe this season was anything but a fluke, and that within a year's time, I would be staring once again at miles of gray dust clouds. But I chose to ignore this possibility for the moment, and enjoy a bit of optimism. I waved gladly to each passing vehicle, not able to see if my greetings were returned, although I assumed they were. Only out-of-staters didn't know to wave on a country road.

Gravel bounced off the bottom of the pickup's floor, like an echo of the rain tapping the roof. I came to a muddy stretch, and although I slowed to a crawl, I hit a bump hard enough to send the cake flying. It landed on its side and stuck, on the floor. I swore. But the cloth wrapped around it didn't come off, and after pulling the pickup off to the side, I lifted the cake with both hands, trying to retain its shape. Still, I could feel it breaking into chunks inside the cloth, and I groaned.

I approached Belle Fourche, where wisps of chimney smoke fought upward through the downpour. The town looked scrubbed, the dry wood buildings sparkling with water, every vehicle free of dust, and dogs romping through the streets, their hair slicked down against their hides. The people outside either held something over their heads or let the water run from the brims of their hats, like the stream from a pump. I didn't see any umbrellas. Nobody'd had reason to own an umbrella for some time.

It was ten minutes after the scheduled meeting of the Rural Electrification Association, which was generally when they started. I stomped my boots on the porch of the Belle Fourche Town Hall and ducked inside. Sure enough, the president was just calling the meeting to order. I took off my hat and brushed the water from it as I sat down.

My mind was not on electricity that day, and I had a difficult time following the discussion. My concern was with what to say when I got to Sophie's house. She wasn't expecting me, so I needed a believable explanation for showing up. But I couldn't think of anything that made sense. The original plan had been to tell her that Mom had baked the cake for her and the children, but using the cake was out of the question now.

Behind the various ideas jumbling around in my head, I heard something about reports. Members began to stand and talk briefly, turning halfway where they stood, then settling back into the folding chairs. After the third one, I realized that the president of each regional chapter was giving a report on their last meeting. And I was president of the Albion chapter.

I got my thoughts together enough to remember what we'd discussed at our last meeting, and when they called my name, I was able to stand and sputter what I remembered. I sat down, happy I hadn't been first. Following these presentations, I heard little of what was said. The organization had done wonders during the late thirties, nearly doubling the number of rural homes with electrical services, but for those of us fifty miles from the nearest center, the wait would be a long one. Knowing this sometimes made the meetings an exercise in futility, and I justified my inattention with this knowledge. As they wound down toward the end of the meeting, I pictured myself walking to Sophie's door, and tried to imagine her expression when she saw me. I envisioned everything from the most beautiful, pleasant smile to frantic confusion.

I heard something about elections. The next thing I knew, my name was called from the back of the room as a nominee for something. I almost asked the guy next to me what I'd been nominated for, but I didn't want my inattention to be obvious, so instead I listened as I was voted the new vice president of the Black Hills Rural Electrification Association. I nodded when they asked if I accepted the position, and acknowledged the applause. By this time, I couldn't wait to get the hell out of there. The meeting was adjourned, and I tried to sneak out. But people offered their congratulations, and the next thing I knew the outgoing vice president was at my side, telling me he wanted to go over a few things before I took off.

I tried to dodge him, telling him I was in a hurry, but he insisted it would only take a minute or two. Fifteen minutes later, when he still wasn't done, I told him I couldn't stay.

By the time I got back in my pickup, I had forgotten every excuse I invented for showing up at Sophie's. So on the way over, I decided I had to use the cake. The rain had stopped, for which I was grateful. I hadn't been to her house before and was worried that I would have a hard time finding it in the rain. Still, I couldn't find it. Jack had given me directions, but he'd never been there either, and I found myself sitting in front of a house with "Gregory" on the mailbox. I went to the door to ask.

The woman looked me up and down with a slight grin once I told her whose house I was looking for.

"You a friend of Sophie's?" she asked.

"Well, not exactly. I met her and her husband years ago."

She stood quiet, and raised her eyebrows, waiting for more of an explanation. I didn't want to get into it, so I looked down the street, as if I might try another house.

"Her husband passed on, you know," she said.

"Yes, ma'am, I did know that. I have a cake for her. My mother baked a cake for her and the children."

"Well, isn't that nice," she said, crossing her arms under an ample bosom.

Under the best of conditions, I don't have much patience for someone who makes people's business their own. I felt myself about to say something uncharacteristic for me, something rude. But I held my tongue. "Ma'am, I'm in quite a hurry, if you don't mind," I said.

"I see." She chuckled a little, a nasty sort of laugh that irritated me even more. "Well, what you want to do is go to the end of this road . . ."

She gave me the directions, making every effort to not hurry about it, pointing and repeating each thing two or three times. I nodded politely until she finished. But I couldn't endure her request that I repeat the whole thing back to her.

"Thanks much," I said, racing back to the pickup.

"Well I never," I heard her mutter.

And finally I sat in front of Sophie Andrews's house. My first thought was to leave before she saw me. My second thought was to forget about the cake altogether, and walk up with no plan at all. But I changed my mind about both, cradling the fragile cake in both hands and stepping from the pickup. I swung the door shut with my foot and walked cautiously toward the house, stepping off the muddy path and onto the shining wet grass. I slid my boots through the lawn, trying to wipe the mud off.

The climb up the steps was the worst part. I knew I had most likely been seen by then, that my options were down to one, and I almost ran out of breath, although there were only four steps. I walked across the porch, trying not to let my heels tread too heavily on the wooden floor. But boots against floors only make one noise—loud—and I shivered at the door, wondering how the hell I would knock without half the cake falling out of its wrapping. But I didn't have to worry, as the door suddenly swung open.

There, just above the lower half of the screen door, was a round head framed in blond hair straight as straw. A little girl smiled, showing a missing tooth. She pushed on the screen, bumping my arm with the frame before I stepped back. She opened it.

"Hi, mister," she said. "Are you here to see Albert?"

I blinked, holding the cake in front of me like a small puppy. "Albert?" Must be her brother, I thought.

"Yes, Albert. He's inside if you want to see him, talkin' to Mother."

"Oh, all right. Well, I really came to see your mother, not Albert."

"Well, she's talking to Albert." The girl looked to be about five, and wore a blue-and-white cotton gingham dress with a blue sash tied around her waist. She twisted one hand in the other, then lifted her arms in front of her body. One wrist was bent backward in a position only children can manage without breaking a bone.

"Do you think you could tell her that there's someone here to see her, or do you think she doesn't want to be bothered?" I asked.

She thought about it, squinting with one eye. "I think she doesn't want to be bothered," she said. "Because every time I try to talk to her when she's talking to Albert, she tells me she doesn't want to be bothered while Albert is here and that I should wait until Albert leaves to ask her." She let go of the one hand with the other, and began swinging them at her sides. Then she clasped them behind her back.

It was then that I realized Albert must be another gentleman caller. I was miserable. I wondered if I should leave, just scoot on back to the pickup and drive away. Or if I should somehow let Sophie know I was there, maybe leave the cake with the little girl. But I knew the girl would never be able to manage the cake, which was about to crumble in my hands.

"What's your name?" I asked.

"Laurie," she said. "Laurie Andrews."

"Okay, Laurie. Do you think you could just show me where the kitchen is, because I have a cake here that my mother baked for you and your mom and your brothers and sisters."

"I only have one sister," she said.

"All right, your brothers and sister. Laurie, if you could just show me where the kitchen is, I'll put the cake in there and then I'll go."

"That's where Mother and Albert are," Laurie said. "Mother and Albert are in the kitchen."

"Laurie? Who are you talking to?" A voice came from within the house. It was a woman's voice—Sophie's. I whispered to myself, "Please come to the door."

"A man with a cake," Laurie shouted.

"A cake?"

"Yeah, a cake for me and you and Wade and Andrew and Millie," she shouted.

And she appeared.

"Blake!" Sophie held her hand to her collar, gripping the lace and reaching with the other hand to push the screen door open wider. "My goodness, what a surprise. Laurie, why didn't you tell me it was Blake Arbuckle? Blake, I'm so sorry. How long has she kept you waiting out here?"

"He never told me his name was Blake Arbunkle anyways," Laurie said.

"It wasn't that long." I stepped inside and wiped my feet. "I have a cake here from my mother," I said. "It fell on the drive in, so it's a little busted up, but it shouldn't taste any different."

Sophie reached for it, but I pulled it back.

"Maybe I should just set it down somewhere," I said. "I'm afraid if I give it to you, it'll fall apart right there in your hands."

She looked a little unsure about what to do, and I remembered Albert in the kitchen.

"Listen, Sophie, I know I shouldn't have dropped in without giving you some notice, so if you have some company, I'll just come by another time. I'll leave this cake here and you can worry about it later." I started to put the cake on a table in the entryway.

"Oh, no no no, Blake. No, please don't go. It's only Albert. He's a friend of the family. No. Come on into the kitchen and we'll take care of that cake. Have a cup of coffee." She led me, lightly touching my arm, which tingled, back through the hallway and into a small, crowded-with-chairs kitchen. At the table sat a handsome, black-haired, brown-eyed man about my age. He had a dark mustache that looked to be made of wax. The top of his head was too short, as if someone had ground off a couple inches. He had no forehead. And from the subtle, unfriendly look he gave me, I could see he was not just a friend of the family.

"Albert," Sophie said, "this is Blake Arbuckle. He lives out by Alzada. Blake, Albert Carroll."

I set the cake on the counter, then reached out to grip the hand waiting for me. Albert's hand was soft and a little damp, and he loosened his grip the moment I tightened mine. "How do," we both said.

Laurie stood on her toes at the counter and with her thumb and forefinger lifted the cloth to look at the cake. A chunk fell out and tumbled onto the floor, first hitting Laurie's shoe. "Oops," she said.

Albert laughed, a big, boisterous "ha ha" that had a harsh edge to it. I had a strong notion I was not going to enjoy this man's company. Laurie bent to pick up the piece of cake, but it crumbled in her small, pudgy hands. This made Albert laugh even harder.

"Albert!" Sophie said.

The more Laurie tried to pick up the lump of chocolate, the more it crumbled, and the more restless I got. I crouched down and began to scoop up the crumbs.

"Let me!" Laurie said.

"Okay. I'll just help," I said. "You get the big ones, and I'll get the little ones."

As Albert continued to chortle, Laurie carefully plucked a chunk of the fluffy cake in each hand and stood up, keeping her eyes fixed on them, like cups of tea. She set them on the counter. I brushed the remaining crumbs into one hand and dumped them into a slop bucket under the table.

"Thank you, Blake," Sophie said. "Can you say thank you to Blake, Laurie?"

"Thank you, Blake," Laurie echoed, without enthusiasm.

"That cake looks like it's seen better days," Albert said.

"It had a rough ride into town," I said through my teeth.

* * *

What followed was the most stilted, unnatural half hour of conversation I've ever been party to. Sophie did her best to keep things moving, asking each of us questions, but I was so flustered I could hardly talk, and Albert thought himself quite a wit. Each time she asked him something, he made a joke of it, which annoyed the hell out of me. My curiosity and sense of humor were absent, bludgeoned by embarrassment and Albert's lack of charm.

His smart-alecky remarks made Sophie uncomfortable, more uncomfortable than she already was, and I couldn't believe Albert didn't see this. I wondered why she would even be interested in someone like him. But after he told me what he did, that he was the vice president of the First National Bank, which he reminded us of several times, I began to understand. Here was a widow, twice over, with four small children and no visible means of support. How could she not consider the interest of a man of Albert's position? The thought made me miserable, thinking what little I had to offer.

But I fumbled through the conversation, spending most of the time studying Sophie from the corner of my eye. She looked older, but she hadn't aged that much considering what she'd been through. Her hair was still crow black, and the creases around her eyes made her look wiser, more worldly. The joints of her slender hands were swollen from farm life, but otherwise she looked much the same. I only wished I could talk to her alone. My discomfort finally got the best of me.

"Well, Sophie, I've still got a long drive ahead of me, so I think I best get going," I said. "Good meeting you, Albert." I almost choked on this lie, hoping my insincerity showed.

"Oh, do you really have to go already?" Sophie asked. I figured she was just being polite, so I insisted.

"Hey, the poor guy wants to go," Albert said. "Let him go."

I glared at him for just a second, not long enough that Sophie would notice, but hoping Albert would get the message that I didn't appreciate much about him. But he didn't seem ruffled. He was the kind of guy who wouldn't catch something so subtle, I decided.

Sophie showed me to the door, and Laurie followed right behind, licking chocolate from her fingers.

"Blake, thank you again for the cake. The kids will love it."

"Where are the others, anyway?" I asked.

"They're not home from school yet," she said.

"Oh, of course." Just one more reason to feel foolish.

"I'm going to school next year," Laurie said. "When I'm six."

"That's good," I said. "You should go to school as much as you can. Because you never know when you might have to start working."

Laurie looked up at me, her blue eyes not comprehending, and I realized I was talking way over her head. I decided I'd said enough.

"Well, see you again," I said without conviction.

"Yes, please stop by any time you're in town." Sophie shook my hand and grabbed the back of it with her other hand.

I nodded, but knew I never would, and I tipped my hat before turning to weave my way through the puddles in the grass.

The last thing in the world I wanted to see at that moment was a rainbow. But when I pulled out onto the main road, every color that had been missing for the last ten years was smeared across the sky in broad, rich strokes. The beauty was blurred by water gathering in my eyes. I wasn't crying, but I was so angry that my eyes were leaking like an old rusty bucket.

I couldn't imagine the visit being any worse. Everything had gone wrong, and in my head I listed every reason I'd ever had for not bothering with marriage. First and foremost, I had no time for romance. There was too much to do. This I knew, had always known, and now I was angry at myself for forgetting, for having to learn this lesson once more. I vowed to never forget again.

Besides the rainbow, I failed to appreciate one of the most beautiful spring evenings we'd had since boyhood. I drove home faster than necessary, jaw set in the direction I drove and no other. I did not let myself dwell on the sky as the light faded and the western half caught on fire, glowing a glorious red.

My other senses were also shut down for the night. I ignored the fresh smell of damp grass, and damp ground, and the damp, clean air. And my skin was coated with leather, unable to feel the cool freshness of that moist air. I tried to convince myself that the hope I'd had on my drive in was ridiculous, that it would only be a matter of time before the ugly, gray dryness returned.

At dinner, I averted each question from the family with a scornful glance. Jack was the only one who didn't give up after the first try.

"What? It couldn't have been that bad," he said.

"Guess again."

He looked at me, head tilted forward, eyebrows raised.

"There was some guy there already," I said.

"Oh, hell."

"Yeah."

Jack shook his head.

To my surprise, Jack's turnaround had proven to be the real thing. He wasn't a completely different person, of course, but nobody expected anything that drastic. I wouldn't even say he was happy. His moods were still unpredictable, changing often and for no apparent reason. But he worked hard and had put a lot of thought into what could be done with the bulldozer. I had yet to see him take a drink since his return. But of course we'd seen a similar turnaround from him before, and I for one assumed he would turn again.

He showed impatience with any skepticism, especially as the months rolled by. But instead of refusing to work when he was insulted, or disappearing, he set his jaw and worked harder, which seemed to me the most impressive change.

The biggest skeptics, predictably, were Rita and George. Mom and Dad didn't exactly warm to Jack's return, but they seemed too tired to make anything of it. They appeared ready to put the years of dealing with family drama behind them and concentrate on work. Dad still tended to take things out on Jack, but not often and not as harshly as before.

But Rita would not let Jack near her. Not even in a crowd. She would not sit next to him at the table, she didn't dance with him at the dances, nor would she ride in the same vehicle unless she had no other choice. She didn't make a spectacle of it. She just made damn sure these things didn't happen, and once everyone figured that out, we helped by sitting next to her, or making certain they never ended up in the same room alone. To my delight, Jack didn't seem to mind any of this. I couldn't figure out whether he had no desire to regain his status as her husband, or if he was just showing a hell of a lot of patience.

Jack made more of an effort with George, trying to talk to him from time to time, usually with the same results the rest of us had gotten over the years. Teddy seemed immune to the history of the situation, and gave his father every chance to make up for lost time. In fact he insisted Jack take him fishing, something that Jack had never enjoyed much, especially after George drowned. But to his credit, he often went.

The biggest surprise to me was that Bob and Jack did not hit it off. Not because they didn't try. But Helen didn't trust Jack, and in her subtle way, she managed to keep them from spending much time alone. I noticed that even when they were together, Bob talked tentatively, as though Helen might be able to hear him.

"All right, here's what you have to do," Jack said. We sat in the barn, Jack on a rail, peeling a potato with his pocketknife, slicing off strips thin as shoelaces. "You have to send her a note, some kind of apology, or thank-you note, something like that, just to let her know you're still interested. 'Cause she's going to think that because this other son of a bitch was there, you probably don't want to see her again."

"She'd be right about that." I scooped handfuls of oats into a galvanized pail and carried it over to one of the horses.

"I don't want to hear that." The peelings gathered at Jack's feet, a pile of strips that looked like a bird's nest.

"She sure would be right about that," I repeated.

The horse dipped her nose into the pail, and a hot snort blew a hollow into the oats. Her upper lip grabbed at the oats and she began munching. Jack stopped his peeling and turned to me, tilting his head and his shoulders and dropping his hands. "Are you serious? You're ready to give it up because of one bad afternoon?"

I nodded. "It's not worth it, Jack. I've lived almost forty years without a woman."

Jack turned back to his potato, sliding the silver blade across the rough brown surface and lifting a string of peel. The meat of the potato turned brown from the dirt on Jack's hands. "There's some damn nice things about being married, Blake. I know I'm not exactly the one to be giving advice about it, but there's some things about it that are real nice."

This was a remarkable statement, I thought, considering how easily Jack had given up on his own marriage. And it made me think. But only for a minute or two. "I guess I'm just not sold on it myself." I picked up the pail, now empty, and filled it again, ducking into another stall.

"Well, I'm not about to try and talk you into anything," Jack said.

We sat silent for several minutes, his knife working away at the potato. I stood there wanting to ask him about things—everything. The letter from the army, where he'd been the last ten years, what he'd done, what he'd seen, and of course George. Jack was the only person in our family whose life I knew nothing about. Everyone else had lived their lives in front of each other, unable to hide. But Jack's secrets were out of reach.

"We all have our secrets, right, Blake?" Jack said, as if he'd read my thoughts. He smiled, then nodded at the barn wall. "Even you. Even the king of morality."

I was annoyed by this sudden anointing, but also a little amused, and I had to smile.

"I just about swallowed my tongue when David told me about your tryout," Jack said. "He said you were great."

I shrugged. "I think I did pretty well, actually."

"You must have, if the guy offered you a contract." He chuckled, looking at me and shaking his head. "Damn, I would have liked to have seen Dad's face if you told him you were going to go play ball. That would have been something."

I sat soaking this all in. And I thought of questions again, and almost did the same thing I'd always done with Jack—that is, keep it all to myself, just thinking about what I wanted to know, but not asking. Not opening my mouth. But before I could talk myself out of it one more time, I spoke.

"Did you know about George trying out, too? Did you know he tried out with the same scout?"

Jack's smile disappeared. His head dropped. He went immediately into deep thought, and I suspected he wouldn't even answer the question. But he did. "George?" he asked. "You mean Junior?"

"Yeah."

Jack's narrow eyes opened, then fell, but for the brief moment that they were open, they revealed an emotion I had rarely seen in Jack. It was fear. "No. He did?"

I nodded. "You didn't know?"

Jack shook his head.

His silence had an impenetrable air, and again, I almost backed down. But I was pleased about going as far as I had, and I went with the momentum. I knew Jack was lying, and suspected there was little hope of getting an admission from him. But I wanted to try. I felt as if I had to try. "So you never knew, huh? He never talked to you about it?"

Jack's whole body tensed up, and I could almost see his mind working away, old wheels whirling, picking up speed. He started cutting the potatoes into quarters. "He may have mentioned it. I don't remember."

The pained look on Jack's face was hard to read. There were so many things that it could mean. He could be bothered by the mere mention of George, and the reminder of the painful day that he found him. Or he could be bothered that I was treading on an unpleasant secret. Whatever the case, I could see that nothing was going to push this conversation any further along. This suspicion was confirmed when Jack cleared his throat and made an abrupt shift in the conversation.

"Listen, Blake." Jack dropped his head, locking his fingers together, studying them intensely. "Maybe this is a good time to talk to you about something. I don't know. Maybe not."

Jack stared at his hands, thinking, for quite a while. And I sat there wondering whether I wanted him to continue. If this was going to be some kind of confession, I wasn't sure I wanted to hear it. Although part of me wanted to know what happened the day George drowned, I had my doubts about what purpose this revelation would serve now, nearly twenty-five years later. Would an admission of guilt just drive a bigger wedge between Jack and me? And what would my responsibility be if he told me? Would I be obliged to share this information with anyone? The law? My family? All of these thoughts blew through my mind in a matter of seconds.

"I just wonder, Blake . . . well, it doesn't seem like you think much about the future . . . about how things could play out." Jack turned toward me, sideways, eyeing me from that angle. "You know what I mean?"

"Well, I think so. Yeah. Actually, I do think about it."

"You do," he said—a statement. "Okay. Then tell me something."

I nodded.

"Let's say you never get married. Let's just set up a little scenario here." Jack held his hands out like he was cradling a baby. "You never get hitched, and Bob knocks up Helen a few times, and Rita stays here, and I stay here." He looked up at me, still holding his hands in the same position. "Who's going to take over the ranch in that situation?"

I thought about it. "I don't know."

"Exactly." Jack nodded enthusiastically. "That's my point."

The unknown quantity of all this, of course, was him, Jack. What did he want?

Jack threw his hands in the air and let them come to rest in his lap. He shook his head. "As far as I can see, Blake, it's up to you. I'm not in any position to take charge. But if Bob could get some babies pumped out, he might have an argument there. Don't tell me you haven't thought about that."

I couldn't say I hadn't, but I wasn't sure I wanted to tell Jack this. I sighed. "Well, it's not that easy to just go out and find a wife, you know."

Jack snorted, and shook his head. "Goddamit, Blake, you annoy the hell out of me sometimes. You got a prospect all lined up . . . she's even got kids. You manage to hook Sophie and you're set. A wife and four kids? There's no way Bob can get a hard-on four times in his life." Jack laughed, and I couldn't help but smile myself. "Just give it some thought, buddy."

"I will," I agreed. "Believe me."

A week later, I received an invitation to have dinner at Sophie's home the following Sunday. My throat closed up. I would go, of course. I didn't think otherwise for a moment, and I was amused by how quickly I discounted all the reasons I had carefully laid out, like Sunday clothes, for never going back.

The appointed day was another rainy one. This time the sky was blue-black, covered with clouds, although the rain didn't fall as hard— more of a persistent mist, a drizzle, unusual for our region. We were used to two or three hours of driving, roof-pounding drops that left spots the size of quarters in the dust. But this mist started in the early morning, and was still drifting when I left at two o'clock in the afternoon.

Jack gave me a sly smile as I left the house in my suit and oiled hair. "Not worth it, huh," he said. I blushed and smiled.

Halfway to Belle Fourche, the quiet whisper of rain against the roof was interrupted by a loud tick, followed by another, and another, then several.

"Damn!" I muttered as a gust of wind brought a patter of hail against the windshield. The pellets built up quickly, and a sudden blast poured down onto the pickup, as though a wagonload of corn had been tipped from about ten feet above the roof. I pulled off to the side, waiting for the storm to pass. I rolled a cigarette and tugged at the string of the tobacco pouch with my teeth. I smoked and stared at the little frozen stones beating against the glass. A burning smell filled my nose, and I looked down to see an ember resting in the middle of my tie. "God damn." I brushed the tiny pellet of orange onto the floor and examined the kernel-sized hole, rimmed with brown, right in the middle of a white stripe.

The storm lasted twenty minutes, blasting the steel roof with unfailing persistence, like a prairie wind. I would be late.

The sky cleared almost immediately, as if the clouds had given everything they had. I drove as quickly as I dared, slowing to forty miles an hour after I slid toward the ditch a couple of times. I was late anyway. I buttoned my coat, trying to cover the hole in my tie.

Sophie came to the door, her lips wet and red with rouge. She wore a navy-blue dress with tiny flowers of different colors, and white lace all around the edges. My chest filled with air, and I felt as if no amount of exhaling would empty my lungs. She smiled, opened the door, and gripped my upper arm. Her touch brought a blush to my cheek and a skittering shiver up my arms.

"Sorry I'm late," I said, my voice pinched.

"I figured you would be. I half expected you to turn around with that storm!"

Not a chance, I thought. She led me to the kitchen and I was happy to see no sign of Albert. Laurie sat at the table, pouting and snapping green beans in half, tossing them angrily into a bowl.

"Have a seat," Sophie said. "Say hello to Blake, Laurie. You remember Blake?"

Laurie pushed her lower lip out and said nothing, giving me a brief, unpleasant look.

"The children take turns helping me with dinner. Today is Laurie's day," Sophie said, winking by way of explanation.

I smiled. "That's nice of you to help your mother out, Laurie."

She continued to ignore me.

"Laurie, you're being very rude," Sophie said.

"No I'm not."

Sophie shrugged and sighed, and I smiled at her.

"So are the others outside?" I asked.

"Yes, they couldn't wait to get out there the minute the storm was over. No doubt they'll come back all covered with mud."

I smiled. I was impressed with Sophie's amused ambivalence about the prospect of her children coming in muddy with a guest in the home. I had a sense that she wasn't just acting as if it didn't matter for my sake. A pan of meat sizzled on the stove, crackling and spitting its juices, and Sophie filled another pan with water, dumping the green beans into it, and placing it on another burner, where the flame burned the moisture from the pan.

"Laurie, go call the others," Sophie said.

The prospect of putting an end to her brothers' and sister's fun brought Laurie out of her snit, and she rushed out the back door, yelling before the screen slapped shut.

"Blake, I'm very happy you accepted my invitation," Sophie said. "I wasn't sure you'd want to come back after that last visit."

I had been standing ever since I walked into the house, and I suddenly felt foolish. I sat down. "Oh, no. It wasn't that bad," I lied.

She smiled knowingly. "Albert is a very good friend, but he thinks because he is rich and good-looking, he can say anything and everyone will think he's charming. Let's just hope it goes better this time."

I breathed out, a rush of air that came from way down, below my lungs.

It did go considerably better, of course. The food was delicious and Sophie proved to be a gracious hostess. The children were as well behaved as one could expect. I could tell they didn't like having a strange man at the table. Only the younger boy, Andrew, showed any interest in me. However, he also told me that it was time to go home after dinner. I didn't take it personally. I teased them a little, but they acted bored, or tried to hide their smiles when they couldn't help but laugh.

"What grade are you in, Millie?"

The older girl, who was tall and shy, also blond, looked at me with indifference, her cheeks reddening. "Seventh," she said.

"Do you like school?"

She shrugged. I thought of George.

"What about you?" I asked Wade.

He looked serious, thoughtful, as he carefully cut a corner off his steak. I could see the same deliberate, meticulous manner his father had. "I'm in fourth grade. I think I'll like school better next year," he said, "when I'm a fifth-grader."

"I'm in second grade," Andrew volunteered. "I hate school!"

The other kids giggled, and Sophie gave Andrew a stern look. But she raised her brow and turned up one side of her mouth, looking at me. "He does," she said. "But I think he'll get over it."

"I'm going to school next year," Laurie said.

"When you're six?" I asked.

She looked surprised, then mad. "How do you know?"

I smiled and tilted my head. "Just do," I said.

The rest of the evening was fairly easy, and I felt the muscles in my neck and shoulders loosen as time passed. The kids ran off to play after dessert, and Sophie and I sat in the living room, drinking coffee and talking until dark. It was mostly small talk, about common acquaintances and such. But I couldn't stop looking at her. I was surprised to find that she was a little bit unsure of herself. She mentioned being twice widowed several times, and it occurred to me that this would probably be a much bigger deal than I imagined. There would be men who wouldn't come near someone like that, thinking they were jinxed or something. Or worse, there would be those cruel enough to consider her some kind of harlot. I'd heard that kind of ridiculous talk before about other widows. I thought it was strange that none of this had entered my mind before, but I realized later that in my own private view of the world, I probably saw Sophie as the same person I had met nearly twenty years before. It was hard for me to separate that brash, forward young woman from the one who sat before me now, saying things like "It's hard to imagine who would want someone like me."

"Blake, do you think you'd like to come back next Sunday?"

I said yes without hesitation.

"Good," she said, reaching out and resting her hand on mine. "I'd like that."

* * *

Driving home that night, I understood for the first time in my life why people get married within weeks of meeting. I felt like going home, packing my things, and driving right back. I had to laugh at myself. Was it possible to change your mind about something so quickly, I wondered, or would this feeling pass in a couple of days?

It didn't, and before long, I was doing just what I'd always found so strange in others—driving to Belle a couple of times a week, sleeping on Sophie's couch and rising before the sun to drive home in time to get to work.

Sophie was hesitant, cautious. I suspected losing two husbands would give a woman cause to hesitate about talking freely. But she made the effort, fighting the reservations, which I admired. She was very thoughtful about what she said, but it was clear that once she made up her mind, she had strong opinions. She wasn't saying what she thought I wanted to hear.

I loved her house. It was small, but filled with delicate, decorative things. Nothing fancy, but she'd managed to brighten her home without extravagance. It was quite a contrast to the practical, efficient home my mother had laid out for us. No frills there. I found the difference appealing.

One Sunday afternoon, after we had fixed a fence that a bull had torn up, I sat at the dinner table with the rest of the family and ate as quickly as I could, thinking that I still needed to clean up before the hour-and-a-half drive to Belle Fourche. The clock showed two o'clock. It was an unusual day in that everyone was at the table—even Jack, Helen, and Bob. About the time I planned my getaway, Jack took a look over at me, sensing my intention, and cleared his throat.

"Hey, Blake, before you take off . . ." Everyone laughed, and I reddened while Jack paused to allow the laughter to fade. "I've got something I want to put out here . . . something I need to tell everyone. Or maybe I should say . . . well, it doesn't matter how I say it, actually."

Everyone stopped eating, although there was little sense of urgency or drama about it. For all we knew, he could be announcing that he was going to buy a new pair of boots. But it was unusual for Jack, or any of us, to request this kind of attention. So our forks hit the table, and we were a captive audience.

Jack cleared his throat again, looked down at his plate, and took a deep breath.

"I been trying to think of a way to ease my way into a little matter that's been on my mind, but I think it would be best if I just come out with it. I know I'm not the most popular member of this family, and I don't have any hard feelings about that—I understand the reasons—but I also know this place could use some help. I know that there is a lot of work that hasn't gotten done just because money's been a little short—things like painting the house." Jack seemed to run out of breath about this time. So he took a big gulp of iced tea while we all sat in rapt attention, wondering what he could possibly be leading up to. He cleared his throat one more time. "Anyway, what I'm trying to say is that I put quite a lot of money away while I was out there fooling around, and what I'd like to do is . . . to buy the ranch. I want to buy it."

"Are you out of your mind?" The words jumped from my mouth, for once, before I had a chance to even think. "No. Absolutely not. No." The next thing I knew, I was standing up, my sense of betrayal throwing me into an emotional response that caught me completely off guard. But it was suddenly so clear to me that when Jack talked to me in the barn that day about finding a wife, he wasn't thinking about me. He didn't have my interests at heart. He just wanted to make sure he had me on his side. He didn't want to have to contend with Bob and Helen. He wanted an ally.

"You can't be serious," Mom said to Jack.

"I am. I am serious." Jack's mouth was slightly open, conveying his shock at our response.

"Do you honestly believe that after all we've put into this place, and all the work we've done while you were out there doing whatever the hell you were doing, that we would be willing to hand this place over to you just because you've got some money tucked away?" I had never been so angry. I couldn't stop myself. The thought of stopping myself didn't even enter my mind.

Jack held his hands out, palms up. "But I can help. I can help this place."

"No." This final, firm word came from Dad. "No, Jack. You're out of line here."

"That's right," Mom seconded.

"What makes you think—" I said, but Dad held up a hand.

"Let me finish," he said, and I nodded, clamping my teeth together, and pressing my tongue against them. It felt as if my tongue might cramp up.

Dad bowed his head for a moment, and closed his eyes. His lips squeezed together. Finally, he looked up, and there was a look in his eye I hadn't seen in years—a fire, a conviction. "I'm so goddam sick and tired of the games that go on around this house. I'm so goddam sick and tired of it." Dad's voice was shaking, he was so angry. His head quivered. "I've gotten to the point where I don't give a damn if none of you get this ranch. I've got a good mind to sell it to somebody else . . . somebody outside of the family because I'm just so goddam sick and tired . . . I'm sick of it." He pounded his fist on the table at this last phrase, and we all jumped. Dad stormed out of the house. He slammed the back door with such force that the building quivered.

My family sat in a stunned silence. Nobody's eyes met. I sank slowly into my chair. I hadn't seen my father act with such violent force since the day he hit me, and I can only guess that if anyone else was feeling like I was, they were thinking hard about what he said, or maybe more about the way he said it. It was the first indication any of us had ever seen that Dad even noticed what was going on in our family. And it was certainly the first indication we had of how strongly he felt about it.

I left the house as soon as I could get cleaned up and get the hell out of there. Sophie noticed right away that I was distracted, that something was bothering me. And the result of her concern was a very pleasant surprise. She fed the kids, hustled them off to bed early, and came out of the girls' bedroom pulling the pins from her hair, letting it fall to her shoulders. She came and sat down next to me on the couch, and put her head against my shoulder. Then she touched my chest with one hand, pressing her palm against my heart.

"Are you okay?" she asked, her mouth close to my ear.

I was immediately aroused. "Yeah. Actually, I'll be fine. This thing with Jack just came out of the blue, you know. It makes me nervous. We never know what to expect."

Sophie nodded, and the next thing I knew, her lips were brushing against my neck. The muscles in my shoulders collapsed, and my head tilted back involuntarily. I felt the goosebumps spread from my neck, down my arms. My body surrendered to a brief shiver. I let out a soft moan.

"What do you think you're doing?" I asked.

"You don't like that?"

"Oh, I didn't say that. I didn't say that at all." I laughed, an airy exhale of air and sound.

Sophie tugged at my earlobe with her teeth, and her lips lightly touched my cheek.

And then she moved to my mouth, and my insides melted. Of course, this was not the first time we had kissed in this new incarnation of our relationship, but it was the first time we kissed like that, with our mouths grafting together in a meeting of skin and feeling that sank into my chest, flooding me like a blast of sunshine when you come out from under a shade tree. It was also the first time we retired to Sophie's room, and it was about to be the first time that we made love, except that by the time we had our clothes off and crawled under the covers, I was such a nervous wreck that I could barely stay in the bed. The energy nearly bounced me out of the room.

"Are you okay?" Sophie finally asked after I sighed deeply for the third time.

"I'm sorry," I said. "I'm really not okay." My hands were trembling, and I suddenly felt a clammy sweat cover my body.

Sophie lifted herself up on one elbow and looked up at me, her expression one of confusion. "Am I doing something? Is there something I can do differently?"

I cleared my throat. "I don't know, actually, if there's anything you can do. Maybe I just need to relax a little here. Let me just lie here for a second." I closed my eyes, taking deep breaths.

Sophie pulled her head back from my chest, studying my face. "Blake, don't tell me you've never done this before."

I turned my face away.

"Really?" she asked. She reached around and pulled my face toward her so she could look at me. "Seriously?"

I smiled shyly. "It's true. I'm a goddam rookie."

She measured me, her eyes narrowing to tiny slits. "Really?"

I nodded my head.

"My goodness. I've never heard of such a thing. How old are you, Blake?"

Now I was more than embarrassed, and my cheeks flushed. "Well, now, you don't have to make such a big thing about it," I said.

"No. I'm not. I'm sorry. I don't think it's strange in a . . . in a . . . strange way or anything. It's just so unusual for a man, you know."

I nodded. "Yes . . . I know."

"Oh, I should just shut my mouth. I'm sorry. I'm just making it worse. Here . . ." She leaned up against me, and the warmth and soft velvet of her skin soothed me, calming my stomach. "We'll just lie here," she said, and we did. We held each other into a quiet, calm sleep. And then, in the middle of the night, I woke up to a soft touch, a rhythmic caress, and then the slow descent of a snug, moist embrace lowering down onto me as I lay on my back. Sophie sat still for a moment, sighing when I was as far inside her as I could go. And she leaned forward, resting a breast against my mouth. I licked, then sucked. Her skin looked even whiter in the still darkness, and her eyes seemed to shine as she looked down at me. A smile curled her lips, and then her eyes drifted slowly and peacefully closed.

She moaned, and began moving. The undulation was gentle, perfect, like a dance without music. A perfect dance. The sensation was excruciating in its perfection, and I exploded quickly, of course, although I didn't know that until later, after more experience. Sophie didn't seem to mind. She pressed her face into my neck, and sighed happily, opening her mouth and biting gently just below my jaw. "Mm," was all she said. It was all either of us said.

I learned a few things about myself as time passed and my visits became more comfortable. I learned that I was good with kids—firm but patient. My time with Rita and the boys had no doubt contributed to that. Sophie's children finally took a liking to me after a few weeks. They were pretty easy kids to like, and Sophie had raised them well, with manners that were admirable, but also a playful sense of fun that was contagious. When I walked in the house, Laurie would run into the room and jump into my lap, squealing my name, and it made my heart swell every damn time.

But most important, I learned I had been lonely. I was amazed I had managed to keep this secret from myself, and it made me wonder what other things I didn't know about myself. It seemed that my obsession with the ranch had closed off some part of my mind, or my heart. At the same time, I wondered whether I would have been able to enjoy somebody's company any sooner in my life, whether I would have been too preoccupied with work to appreciate a wife and kids. It was hard to say, of course. I would never know.

All I did know is that six months after my first dinner with Sophie, I drove to Belle Fourche, my mood cheerful but nervous, my heart flooded with clean, pure blood. Because nearly twenty years after first catching Sophie Roberts's, now Sophie Andrews's eye, I had decided to pop the question. I knew I was ready, and I felt certain that she would say yes. In fact, I was thinking more about the logistics than I was about asking the big question. I was more consumed with the details of when we should get married, and where we should live, and whether we should have a big wedding. I was thinking about what Jack had said, and how this marriage, and the kids that came with it, would leave no doubt at all about who had the upper hand in taking over the ranch. With my mind so focused on these details, it isn't surprising that I was too preoccupied to notice that Sophie was also distracted. I was talkative when I arrived, although the topics I brought up were far from what was on my mind. It wasn't until halfway through dinner that I began to notice a distance in Sophie. In the past, this mood usually indicated that she was having some trouble with one of the kids, so I assumed the same was true this time. But when I mentioned that I was worried about whether the recent hailstorm had ruined our wheat crop for the year, and she answered, "Really? That's great, Blake," I knew that she had something on her mind.

So I put all thoughts of a proposal to the side, and I was just about to ask her if something was wrong when she looked up at me with a wide-eyed, fearful expression—so fearful that I stood up, starting toward her.

"Blake . . ." She dropped her eyes immediately.

"What? What is it?"

* * *

A half hour later, on the road out of Belle Fourche, the scene was again blurred by the rainwater flowing down my windshield. I pummeled my steering wheel, slamming one fist then the other against my inflexible, unfeeling victim, yelling as loudly as I could, filling the cab with sound. I finally realized that I was dangerously close to injuring my hands, so I stopped pounding. But I yelled once more, trying to extract the pain of hearing from the woman I thought I loved that she was going to marry Albert Carroll. And as I reviewed her reasons, hearing them as if I was still sitting there in front of her ("I'm too tired, and too old, to live on a ranch again. And I have to think of my kids."), I cursed the fact that I had allowed myself to stray from what I had always known. I reminded myself yet again that the land had claimed me all those years before, when George got sucked into the current of the Little Missouri River. And I derided myself for getting seduced by the belief that I was able to devote time to anything else.

I suppose I was too angry to admit that I was really mad at Sophie. Or maybe it was just easier to take it out on myself. After all, I was the only one there. But for whatever reason, I didn't think about this development coming out of the sky, with no sign of Albert, not even a mention of him, in the six months I'd been busting my butt to see Sophie twice a week. All of that finally did hit me after a few days. But what didn't hit me until weeks later was something about my own motives—something that wasn't easy to admit. It started when I noticed that my feelings for Sophie actually faded pretty quickly. This confused me. I thought I'd been in love with her. I was certain of it. But when I thought back to that day I planned to propose, recalling my thoughts about positioning myself at the ranch, I realized that even though I liked Sophie well enough, I had probably never been in love with her. I realized to my horror that when Dad made his speech, I had been righteous enough to believe that it didn't apply to me—that he was talking just about Jack and Helen and Bob. But here I had been plotting to marry a woman I didn't love. He was also talking about me.

14

spring 1942

The sleek, varnished coffin, dark as a strong cup of coffee, sat closed and pristine in the living room. Light glanced off the silver handles, and three roses lay on top with their stems crossing and looping between and around each other.

Callused, awkward ranchers' fingers held cups, tipping them to chapped lips, then lowering them to their saucers, with a slight tremor, afraid of doing something that would draw attention, such as dropping the cups or spilling coffee on their owners. The men stood in suits that didn't quite fit and hair that wouldn't quite stay down, even with oil. The light shone off only the tops of their foreheads, where the skin, starting in a straight line halfway up, was bleached from hiding under a hat.

The women did wear hats, colorful ones that matched their dresses, with netting draped from the brims, covering half their faces. They held white lace handkerchiefs to their eyes, dabbing along the bottom lid. Many wore cloth gloves, hiding their own swollen, red hands.

And the smaller children ran among the stiff legs, immune to grief and confused about why this gathering was different from any other except for the beautiful wooden box in the front room.

Lonnie Roberts approached, holding not a cup but a glass with amber liquid and ice.

"Blake, I always thought your mom was someone who would live to be a hundred. She never looked any older or worse for wear, any time I ever saw her." We shook, then he laid a hand on my shoulder. The alcoholic aroma washed over me.

"I've thought that myself, Lonnie." I sipped from my coffee, staring at the coffin.

"How do you think your dad's taking it?"

"Hard to say." I recalled Dad's face when I returned from the barn two days before. I'd found Mom slumped against the milk cow, the tips of her fingers dipped in the bucket of milk. Dad hadn't reacted, as if he already knew. His eyes had just gotten narrower, and his head bobbed once.

"Yeah, it takes some time before you can tell with something like this," Lonnie said. He paused, taking a long look at the coffin. "It should be a little easier for him with you and Rita living here. Those fellas that live alone after their wife passes on, you can sometimes watch them die right before your eyes."

I could think of plenty of examples, and I nodded, suddenly glad we were living with Dad. I thought about asking Lonnie about Sophie, about how she was, but I decided I didn't really want to know right then.

Lonnie drained his glass, then looked inside it, to make sure. "Well, can't let this thing stay empty too long," he said. "Never know when they'll run out." He smiled and patted my shoulder again. "I'll talk to you later."

"Yes, good," I said.

I watched Lonnie waltz through the crowd in his dignified manner, pressing hands and bending to the women. He had lost Ruth two years before when she stormed out of the house during one of their legendary arguments. She froze to death trying to make it to a nearby farmhouse, walking in a dress and heels. But Lonnie was definitely not dying before anyone's eyes. His response had been just what everyone expected. He buried in the bottle whatever guilt or sorrow might have been lurking, causing some hand-wringing nights for husbands waiting for their wives to come home, or wondering why they had been outside the dance hall for so long. I was amazed every time I saw Lonnie at how he maintained the charm, the appearance. He didn't look to be tormented. It might be the death of him, I thought, but there's something admirable about his tenacity, his determination to wring the life out of whatever time he had left.

The noon hour approached, and the service was to start at two or two-thirty, depending on whether Muriel and Stan had arrived yet. They were driving from Butte. Already, we had a houseful of people. Several of the neighbor women had taken charge of serving drinks and sandwiches, shooing anyone from our family out of the kitchen when we tried to help.

Jack stood in a corner, removed from the crowd, cradling a cup and watching everyone. When someone approached to talk or offer their condolences, he shook their hand and bowed politely, lowering his eyes. But he didn't encourage further conversation, and nobody stood next to him for long before getting uncomfortable.

Dad sat in the dining room, his hands resting lifeless on the table. He talked to anyone who approached, his eyes shifting uneasily, as though he was having a hard time paying attention.

Rita moved easily among the guests, sad but gracious, and I couldn't help but think that if anyone in the family would take this well, without long months of anguish, it would be Rita, who had made peace with Mom in their last years together in this house. Nearly every night before bed, the two of them sat in the kitchen and talked quietly, each flipping cards in their own game of solitaire. They had become friends, best friends, and I imagined Rita's sense of loss must run deeper in some ways than any of ours. But she had the satisfaction of reaching a part of Mom that most of us never had.

"Where's Bob? And Helen?" a neighbor asked me in passing. "I haven't seen them."

"Oh, they're at their place. They'll be at the service," I said.

He eyed me, puzzled, and I couldn't think what else I could say. "They'll be at the service," I repeated.

He nodded, walking away with the same puzzled look.

I was a little surprised that anyone wasn't aware of the rift in our family. For as much regard as I have for the people of our county, I do know that news doesn't travel slowly here.

The conflict had come to a head due to an unlikely source—the death of Art Walters. It had taken the authorities several months to track down Art's ex-wife, and when they did find out where she was, it turned out that she had also died. So they had to find his son, and that took several more months, as he turned out to be quite a rover himself.

When he was informed of his inheritance, his decision was apparently a quick one, and the place was put up for sale. Because it bordered our place and Glassers', we were the logical prospects, and the only ones seriously interested. So Dad and Gary settled on a fairly even split, and the deal was struck.

I went to Belle Fourche with Dad to pick up some feed and to draw the check. It was a Tuesday, so the town was quiet, as was the bank.

Dad told the teller that we needed a check for thirty-five hundred dollars—1,750 acres at two dollars an acre.

"All right, Mr. Arbuckle. Let me just check on your balance then, and make sure you have enough money." The teller, whom we knew well, winked.

Dad smiled, nodding, but it was clear when she approached us again that something was wrong.

"I'm sorry to have to tell you this, Mr. Arbuckle, but it turns out that you don't have enough in your account. Your balance is about seventeen hundred dollars."

Dad smiled at her. "Gloria, now, don't fool around with me. That's just downright cruel."

But Gloria shook her head. "I wish I was fooling, Mr. Arbuckle. But it's true."

Dad just stared at her.

"Can we see the books?" I asked.

"Yeah," Dad echoed. "Give us a look here. There's got to be a mistake. That can't be right."

"Certainly." Gloria retrieved the balance book, spinning the cloth-bound ledger around on the counter. And there, plain as day, were three withdrawals, totaling over twenty-five hundred dollars, from Bob Arbuckle.

I don't know whether I've been more afraid of dying than I was on the drive home that afternoon. Dad was pushing his old pickup to its limit, swerving on the curves. When we nearly fishtailed off the road a few times, I finally yelled at him to slow down. It was uncharacteristic behavior for both of us.

He pulled right up to Bob and Helen's stoop, and we raced for the door, bursting in. Helen was alone, and she looked shocked at first. But Dad and I both started yelling at the same time, and once she realized what we were there for, her face took on a completely impassive expression, as if she didn't hear a word we said.

"You are never welcome in our house again," Dad was yelling. "Don't even think about coming in that door."

At the same time, I shouted, "You could have had a nice piece of this place if you'd just shown a little common sense."

We both ranted for a few minutes, and the whole time Helen acted as if we weren't even in the room. And it was as if we both realized at the same instant that we were wasting our breath. We stopped yelling, and just glared at her for a moment. She still didn't bother to acknowledge us, and looking at her expression made me tremble with anger. I couldn't stop shaking. Dad turned and left.

"Don't think for a minute that you got away with something here," I said, looking around at the nice furniture and decorations that were the fruits of their extortion.

Finally, she looked up, and a slight smile came to her face. She shook her head. "That's okay, Blake."

I gritted my teeth, feeling as if I could strangle her on the spot. I had to leave to keep from acting on my rage.

Bob was no more apologetic than Helen, although the first time I saw him after that, his face did a horrible job of hiding his guilt. But none of us had been to their house since that day. Nor had they been to the big house.

"Blake?" I looked up to see Rita standing before me, her forehead twisted with concern.

"Yes?"

"Muriel and Stan just pulled up."

"Great," I said, looking at my watch. "They made good time."

"Blake?" Rita rested her hand in the small of my back.

"What?"

"Are you all right?" She rubbed my back lightly, and I looked down at her.

"Yes, I'm fine. Why?"

"I just wondered. You looked like you were thinking, or worrying about something."

"Yeah, I guess I was thinking, but I'm all right. Just trying to keep track of everything that needs to be done."

"Blake?" One of the women came from the kitchen. "We're running out of cups. Do you have some more somewhere?"

I thought. "Teddy!" I yelled across the room.

Teddy came over, his face uncharacteristically unhappy. "Hm?"

"Get some of the other kids, run down to the your dad's house and bring back some cups." I held his arm, stopping him from running off, and turned to the woman. "Is there anything else we need?"

She shook her head. "I don't think so."

I turned back to Teddy. "Okay."

He walked away, a slouch in his narrow, teenage shoulders. His pant legs stopped a few inches short of the tops of his shoes.

Rita was next. "Blake, Pastor Ludke wonders if you want to start early since Muriel and Stan are here."

"No, I don't think we should. I'm sure there are other people who aren't planning to come until the service." I was thinking of the house down the way, the second gathering.

Rita nodded. "That's what I was thinking too," she said. "I just thought I'd better make sure." She turned and walked back over to Pastor Ludke, who nodded as she explained.

I made my way to the back door, hoping to catch Muriel and Stan so I could greet them privately, without an audience. But they were already in the door. I shook Stan's hand and held Muriel, who cried softly.

"Where are the kids?" I asked.

"We decided to leave them with my folks," Stan said. "It's going to be a quick trip anyway. I have to get back to work day after tomorrow." He shook his head.

"Sorry to hear that," I said. Muriel pulled back from me, still holding my forearms, and smiled, her cheeks wet.

"How are you, Blake?"

"I'm holding together all right," I said. "What about you?"

"Oh, Blake, it's so strange. I never thought about Mom dying. I've always been so worried about Dad, I didn't even consider her."

"She's just always been there," Stan said. "She's been there for so long, we always expected her to be there." I saw a glimmer of moisture in the corner of Stan's eye. "You're a lot like her that way, Blake." He looked right at me as he said this, and I felt a lump rise from my gut, right up past my heart, through my throat, and against the back of my teeth, sitting like a mouthful of oatmeal on my tongue. I knew if I said anything at that moment, it would come out in tears, and I looked down, swallowing hard. The blood ran to my neck, and needles of sweat tickled my forehead.

"That's right, Blake," Muriel said, pulling me against her again.

I relaxed into her arms, breathing deep, and felt a lone stream trickle from a corner of one eye. But I quickly wiped it away before stepping back and asking, "What do you two want to drink? We have coffee or stronger stuff. Might even be able to dig up some castor oil if you want."

Stan laughed, and as always, his single, cheery "Ha" lifted my spirits.

It felt strange, wrong, not to have Bob among those of us who lifted the coffin to our shoulders and carried it out to the pickup. We drove the half mile to the hill where the other graves were and, once there, the same six unloaded the coffin, setting it next to the hole some of the neighbors had dug the day before.

Within minutes, the other, smaller group arrived. Bob and Helen led them to the site. They gathered to one side, so that there was an empty space between. Helen looked more distraught than anyone in either group, her mouth stretched into a frown. She cried when she saw the coffin, and Bob and their friends, including Steve and Jenny, closed in, surrounding her, putting their arms around her. I had to look away, and I fixed my eyes on the coffin until Helen was able to pull herself together enough for the service to begin.

The day was, in a word, glorious. A very light, warm wind whispered from the hay meadows, and the smell of alfalfa and sweet clover washed over the funeral. Soft, clean white clouds moved slowly across the sky, hiding the sun from time to time, shifting the light between a warm dusk and a pleasant afternoon. And the green rolled away from us like carpet in every direction, the gift of another wet season.

Pastor Ludke cleared his throat, and he captured Mom's spirit nicely, talking of her tough, practical nature. He related the Hole in the Wall Gang story, and the murderer a few years before, which brought smiles to our faces. People grieved privately, with restraint, except for Helen.

Rita held my arm and sniffled, and Dad, just in front of me, bowed his head until the end, when he looked briefly up at the sky and pushed a sigh from deep within his chest. His shoulders lifted nearly to his ears and then fell as he exhaled.

None of us lingered. Once those designated began to lower the coffin into the ground, we left, the crowd splitting in two again, driving in different directions, to two different houses on the same tract of land.

The guests stayed for another cup of coffee and a snack. Everyone had brought food, and we had enough to feed the family for a week. Once the first of the guests found it an acceptable time to leave, the rest followed in short order, having one last brief word with the family. I was struck by the respect Mom had among those hundred or so in attendance. What was she like? I wondered. Mom had ruffled her share of feathers in her life, but many of the people she'd been in conflict with were there.

Whatever others thought of her, there was no denying that Mom was her own person. She spoke up when many women were afraid to, and on this day, even those who disagreed with her seemed willing to concede that this was an admirable woman.

But here's what's interesting to me about my mother. More than anyone else that I've lost in my life, I have reconsidered this question of what she was like as the years pass. In fact, the question has changed in her case to "What would she have been like?" Under different cir-cumstances, what would my mother have been like? Because the word that I heard bandied about during the reception for my mother was "tough." She was tough, all right. But was that really what she wanted to be remembered for?

I think not. I think more than anyone in our family, my mother's personality was shaped by her life. She knew nothing but work, and because she did not question her lot in life, she probably didn't think much about whether she was missing out on anything. She shouldered her load and carried it with a dignity that was almost invisible. But it wasn't until years after she was gone that I wondered whether there were dreams she had never pursued. Perhaps dreams she had never even given voice to. I wondered whether she and Rita had ever talked about such things. And more than anything, this is what I grieve about my mother. She lived a good life. She was a good person. But what would her life have been like if she'd had more of a say in the matter? We'll never know.

The worst part of these occasions, for me anyway, is when they're over, when the guests are gone, and there's still a good portion of the day left. For whatever reason, I always feel like I should be doing some-thing with all that time. But it isn't exactly appropriate to jump into work clothes and rush out to the fields. So the time crawls like the Little Missouri on the hottest day of summer. We sit in our dress clothes, the most painful part over, and nothing left to say.

If I were to revise the rules of grief, I'd say everyone should spend this time doing what they like instead of what's appropriate. The prob-lem with that, of course, is the same as with anything else. When other people are involved, if you do what you like, somebody will take it wrong, or think you're avoiding them. It's the price of having a family, I suppose, following these unwritten rules.

Jack, who normally ignored such rules, stuck around this time, although he looked as if he wanted to tear the clothes off his body. He sat fidgeting in the dining room. The rest of us settled into the living room, stretching our legs out.

"That was a real nice service," Muriel said.

"Yes, it was," I said. "The old fella surprised me. I think that was the first time I heard him give a service for a woman when he didn't say 'she was an obedient wife.' Made me think he actually knew her."

Dad smiled, sadly.

"Blake," Rita admonished me gently, "it's not exactly a time for jokes."

"It's all right," Dad said. "I'd rather laugh than cry."

We all nodded.

"How was your drive down?" Rita asked Stan and Muriel.

"Real nice. Such a beautiful day," Stan said.

"It really was," Muriel said. "I love the mountains in spring. The trees are so green and the animals are coming out of hiding."

A silence settled for a few moments, as we all looked at the floor.

"So what have you been reading about the war?" Stan plucked a cigar from the pocket of his jacket and bit the tip off. He held it toward me, and raised an eyebrow.

"No, thanks," I said. "Never have liked the taste of those things."

"Dad?" Stan asked.

Dad shook his head, but reached into his pocket and pulled out his pouch of tobacco and papers. I decided to have one too.

"Pearl Harbor was something, huh?" Muriel said.

"It's pretty frightening," Stan said. "The Nazis are willing to do whatever it takes, and now that they've got the Japs working with them, I just don't know."

"We should have jumped in sooner," Dad said. "We waited too long."

"I don't think so," Rita said. "I don't think Roosevelt knew how serious this was until Pearl Harbor."

"But the Germans!" Stan said. "They've been marching across Europe like someone taking a walk through their backyard. How could he not have known? He should have done something to stop that!"

"I think he did what he could without declaring war," I said.

"But he should have declared war," Stan insisted. "He should have declared war the minute they started bombing London. Because you know once they're after England, they're going to want us next."

We all sat chewing that thought, drinking and smoking.

"What do you think, Jack?" Stan yelled into the dining room. "You were in the first war, right?"

A silence settled over the room that I could feel, like a cold winter wind. Everyone's eyes dropped, and Stan looked around the room, sensing the chill. I waited for Jack's reaction, wondering if he still believed we didn't know. He had to realize that Rita's presence made it impossible to lie. I glanced at Rita, who was glaring toward the dining room.

I heard a rustling, and heels against oak, heading through the kitchen, then out the back door.

"Oh, no. Now I've done it," Stan said. He looked around, and Muriel looked puzzled.

"What is it?" she asked. "Is he still upset about the war? That was twenty-five years ago."

"He was never in the goddam war." Rita spat the words, her anger over years of secrets, worry, and fear fueling a raw, harsh voice I couldn't remember ever hearing from her.

"I thought . . ." Muriel's voice faded. "I thought he was."

I thought back to the day that Helen revealed Jack's secret at the dinner table, and realized that Muriel had been off at school in Belle Fourche by then. She wasn't there.

"Muriel always told me he was. That you used to get letters from France," Stan said.

"We did," Muriel said. "What about his injury, his arm?"

Rita again spoke bitterly. "He hurt his arm in a bar fight. That's why he was discharged early, before the war was over. And friends he met in boot camp mailed those letters from France for him."

"It's a long story," I said. "Well, not that long. But maybe not worth going into right now."

"Like Bob and Helen?" Muriel asked. "Is that not worth going into now too?" She looked around at each of us, and her face started to lose its color, a pale white covering her skin like paint. "What's going on with this family?"

"Muriel, honey, simmer down," Stan said. "Jeez, I didn't mean to start something here."

"I just want to know what's going on." Muriel spoke in a careful, measured tone, keeping her voice low. "That's all." She looked around at each of us.

Dad breathed deep, holding his hands over his face, so that his nose showed from between. He lowered them, then reached up with the back of one and wiped his eyes. He shrugged. "I can't imagine why you want to know, but it don't matter to me."

"Why don't I tell them," I said.

"Yeah, that's fine," Dad said, leaning back in his chair.

So, after taking a moment to collect my thoughts, I proceeded to tell Muriel and Stan everything they didn't already know about Jack, Helen, and how all the stories fit together. It was actually the first time I'd told anyone about the letter Helen had stolen from my room, way back when, and when Dad heard this, he shook his head, his eyes closing with a look of dismay. When I told about the argument that prompted Bob and Helen to move, I had to admit I didn't know the cause. I looked at Dad to see if he could help me out, but he shook his head again.

Stan and Muriel sat and listened to the whole story, he puffing on his cigar and shaking his head from time to time, she with her hands folded in her lap, clenched tightly together. Now and then, one hand would flutter away from the other, up to her face, where she brushed back a strand of hair or scratched behind her ear.

And I was surprised to find my body tensing up, my muscles tightening with each word. The emotions that had accompanied each event came back as I recounted them. I felt myself going through all the anger, hurt, embarrassment, and an overwhelming sense of sadness. Telling about the money Bob and Helen had stolen, I looked down to see that both hands were clenched into tight fists, recalling the indifference on Helen's face. It seemed impossible that this was our family I was talking about.

Muriel and Stan asked few questions, as I left out few details. And when I finished, they both sighed and looked down at the floor for a while. Stan twirled his cigar in the ashtray, forming a point with the burning ashes.

"I had no idea," he said.

Muriel turned to him as he said this, then looked back down at the floor, as if contemplating whether she had suspected any of this. She lifted her eyes to mine, and they looked very sad.

"Neither did I," she said. "You sure do keep a lot to yourselves."

"Well, there's not much you can do about it from out there," Dad said, a little irritably. "There's not much anyone can do about it."

Stan leaned forward, looking past Muriel at Dad. "She wasn't criticizing you, Dad. Were you, Muriel?" She shook her head. "It's just that we, especially Muriel, sometimes worry about you folks out here. I've always said I'd be glad to help you out any way I can, and you've never asked. We don't know if it's because you don't need help, or if you just aren't saying."

Dad looked away, squinting through the smoke from his cigarette. "There's still not much anyone can do about any of this."

Muriel threw her hands in the air, and turned her head to one side, her nostrils flaring. "So that's it, then," she said. "Is that all there is to it? Because we can't do anything about it, we don't have a right to know what's happening in our own family." She turned to Dad, who did not meet her gaze.

I felt the need to jump in. "I think all Dad's trying to say is that we don't see any reason to worry all of you out there when you have problems of your own. Isn't that right, Dad?"

Dad remained in the same position, his eyes distant and narrow, his whole body turned away from us, legs crossed. "Well . . . not exactly," he said.

"So what then?" Stan asked. "If that's not the reason, then I don't get it."

Dad took a drag off his cigarette, the paper burning down to his fingers, and crushed the butt in the ashtray. He exhaled through his nose, a thin stream of smoke drifting from each nostril up toward the ceiling. "The way I see it, if a body decides to move away from their family, well . . ." He lifted one weathered hand, as if that explained everything, and he said nothing more.

Muriel lifted her chin, taking short breaths in through her nose and clamping her hands together, the knuckles white. "I see." She nodded. "I think I understand," she said. She stood up, slowly, and walked from the room.

Stan ground his cigar into the ashtray and leaned forward, resting his elbows on his knees. He locked his hands together, the fingers relaxed, curved slightly. He held this position for a long time before he spoke. "Dad, I'm sorry this came up today. It wasn't the right time to talk about family matters. But I'm hoping that your grief is affecting what you say. And I hope you didn't mean that the way it sounded." He said this in his deep, steady voice, speaking directly at Dad without a pause. Then, without waiting for a response, he rose and went to the room where Muriel had retreated.

Now it was just Rita, Dad, and I, and if there was ever a time I felt helpless, it was that moment. I sat exhausted, as if I had just relived the last twenty-five years of my life.

"Dad, is there anything you want, some coffee or anything?" Rita asked.

He shook his head, and I said a silent thank-you to Rita as the gesture made it somewhat comfortable for us to leave the room. I stood and stretched my arms out in front of me. Rita stood beside me.

"I think I could use a nap right now," I said.

"Actually, that sounds pretty good to me too," she said.

So we went to separate rooms and lay down, leaving Dad alone, staring out the window. It seemed to be what he wanted.

I woke up an hour later, and I rolled out of the bed, sweating and nearly choking on my twisted dress clothes. I wondered why I hadn't taken them off before I lay down. I quickly changed into dungarees and a work shirt.

Drifting into the dining room, I sat down with a deck of cards, laying out a game of solitaire. It seemed that every adult in the house had been napping, as they emerged one by one from their rooms, hair mussed, yawning and scratching. All except Jack and Dad.

"Anybody seen Jack?" I asked.

"He's down at his house," Teddy said.

I nodded. "What about your grandpa?"

They all shrugged and shook their heads. "Haven't seen him."

"I think he's sleeping, too," Rita said. "I heard snoring from that direction."

The kids laughed.

"Well, I suppose we should get something going for dinner," I said. "We have a bumper crop of food here."

Rita, Muriel, and I went to the kitchen and surveyed the icebox.

"This looks good," Muriel said, pulling the lid off a beef casserole.

Her spirits seemed to have improved with a little sleep.

"I think all we need to do is warm up a few of these dishes," Rita said.

We filled the oven with the casserole, some scalloped potatoes, and a vegetable dish. We also found a beautiful chocolate cake and set it aside for dessert.

We sat down to eat. Teddy ran to the old house to get Jack, but Dad had still not come out of his room.

"He probably needs sleep more than he needs food," Stan said.

"This all looks so good," Muriel said.

"It certainly does," Rita agreed. "It would be nice to eat like this all the time without doing any of the work."

Stan had a good "Ha" for that one.

There was a strange sort of giddiness to our mood, as if we had forgotten for the moment that we had just buried our mother that morning. Or as though we were all relieved to have some of the secrets out in the open after so many years trying to protect each other from them.

Teddy came huffing into the house, probably having sprinted the whole way. "Dad says he ain't hungry."

"Ain't?" Rita said.

"Well, you know what I mean," Teddy said.

"Ain't?" Rita repeated.

"It means the same thing as isn't," George said in his droll, low voice.

Rita's eyes flashed, but she couldn't help smiling. "You, young man, are a smart aleck," she said to George, grabbing for his ear.

George smiled into his shirt. We were still laughing when Dad emerged from the bedroom, rubbing the back of his head with his knuckles. He passed right by us as if we weren't there, and our laughter died a quick death. We all turned our attention to our food, not looking at each other. Dad rummaged around in the kitchen.

"Dad, do you need help finding something?" Rita called.

"I'm all right," he answered. We heard water running, filling a glass. Then Dad appeared in the doorway.

We were stricken with rusty joints, all of us at once. We moved slowly, cutting and lifting our food as if each forkful weighed several pounds. None of us looked directly at Dad, but you can bet we had him in the edge of our vision.

He walked into the room, straight over to Muriel, tipping the glass of water to his mouth as he walked. He bent at the waist and whispered something into Muriel's ear, then gave her a peck on the side of her head, right in her hair. And she burst into tears and threw her arms around his waist, nearly knocking him over.

15

winter 1943

In the corner of the living room, a fresh pine stood thick and shining green, strung with popcorn, cranberries, candles, and the gleaming colored balls that Muriel and Stan bought in Billings. The radio played Christmas carols softly, so that we could still talk at normal volume. The smells of pine, wax, and a raging fire filled the house. The bottom three-quarters of the windows sported an intricate frost, with an arc in the icy coating. And small glass and paper figurines littered the mantel, shelves, and tables. Since Mom's death, Rita's decorative eye had transformed our once-functional house. Her touch made the house seem more like a home, and I was pleased with how much more comfortable, relaxing, it felt. The decor helped compensate for the absence.

Toys lay like battle victims across the floor—a red metal car with rubber wheels, a doll with wiry blond hair and a hole in her mouth for her plastic bottle, a wooden train, each car painted a different, bright color. Dad slept in his overstuffed chair, snoring lightly, a pair of new wool socks resting in his lap. Stan, George, and I had just come in from feeding. We gathered the wrapping paper, which we used to feed the fireplace. The women created the aroma of Christmas, working their magic in the kitchen, and the kids had been sent upstairs to play, where they wouldn't disturb Grandpa (or at least that's what we told them).

"Well, did you get what you wanted?" Stan asked me.

"Santa was very good to me," I answered.

"Ha." Stan balled up a wad of wrapping paper and tossed it into the fire. "I didn't know you still believed in Santa, Blake."

I held a finger to my lips. "Quiet, Stan. You don't want to disillusion young George here."

"What, you mean there's no such thing as Santa?" George adopted a shocked, hurt expression, and Stan and I laughed.

Just two months past his eighteenth birthday, George was trying to decide whether to join the army. Rita jumped on any and every opportunity to talk him out of it, showing him articles in the newspapers that gave casualty totals, and telling him that he probably wouldn't even get to fight, but would end up like his father, stationed somewhere in the states, shuffling papers around. "I wouldn't mind," he'd say. "I just think it's my responsibility."

But I think he was more drawn to the glory of fighting than he let on. When his mother wasn't around, he pored over the descriptions of battles, or read books like A *Farewell to Arms*. It was easy to imagine him putting himself in the place of Hemingway's wounded soldier, being tended by a beautiful, sympathetic nurse. And as much as I also hoped that he wouldn't enlist, I could understand the romantic allure.

"Well, whatever they're cooking in there sure smells good," Stan said.

"Sure does," I agreed. "And I'm getting hungry. Seems like breakfast was yesterday."

* * *

We had just sat down to Christmas dinner, said grace at Muriel's request, and begun to pass the food around the table, when the sound of stomping echoed from the back porch. A pocket of cold air blew through the house. Jack entered the dining room from the kitchen. He cupped his raw hands up to his mouth, and his shoulders hunched up around his neck. I was sitting at the head of the table, a position I had taken since Mom died. One evening, I came to the dinner table and found Dad sitting in my chair. He nodded toward his, indicating that I should sit there. I never asked why. But it had been that way ever since. And now, everyone looked at me after seeing who it was.

I noticed that Stan had been dipping rather more frequently into the egg nog than he usually did, and when Jack appeared, Stan bellowed, "Merry Christmas, Jack."

Jack grinned slightly and said thanks before looking down at his boots. None of the rest of us said anything, and Stan looked around at everyone, trying to understand the silence.

The cause this time was an incident that occurred the previous summer, at the Belle Fourche Roundup on the Fourth of July. Before that, Jack and Rita had shown signs of renewing their romance. He had begun shyly courting her, and had somehow managed to overcome a healthy skepticism on her part. And to everyone's surprise, and my dismay, they spent several evenings a week strolling out into a grove of trees behind the old house, where they would sit and talk for an hour or so. I have to confess that I spied on them from time to time, feeling sick to my stomach as I wondered each time whether I would find them wrapped in each other's arms, or locked in a passionate kiss. But Rita apparently wasn't ready for that.

But at the Roundup, Jack showed up parading around with another woman. This blatant disregard for Rita destroyed whatever goodwill he had developed among his family. Rita filed for divorce, and he didn't fight it, although that evening was the only time we saw the mystery woman, who we later found out was from Sundance, Wyoming. It was almost as if Jack wanted it to happen. He had the opportunity to renew what had been a pretty good life, and he threw it away for one day with some woman that apparently wasn't even that important to him.

To further his exile, Jack had moved out of the old homestead house, asking the boys to help him clean out the little cabin he and Rita had first lived in. The cats that once swarmed the house were long dead, but nobody had ever had any reason to clean them out. So according to Teddy, "the place smelled worse than a chicken coop." But Jack moved in, and we hardly saw him other than out in the fields. He focused on his dirt work, erecting a series of dikes and ditches that allowed us to flood our meadows, and he finished building two reservoirs, damming the creeks so we could use those two pastures for summer grazing. He had also hired out to the neighbors on the weekends. But this time, he was careful not to take time away from the ranch.

And in one final stroke of defiance, Jack had begun to spend a lot of time at Bob and Helen's. To me, this was the most confusing part of his arrival that morning. We just assumed he would be spending the day with them.

"What is it?" Dad asked, not bothering to look at Jack.

Jack shrugged. "I thought I might be welcome to spend Christmas with my family, at least for dinner."

Dad looked at Rita, whose mouth was a straight line, with little creases above the top lip. "You've got some nerve, Jack Arbuckle," she muttered, but her tone was fairly indifferent.

"Oh, come on, everybody," Stan said, his palms smacking the table on each side of his plate. The silverware shook and rattled. "You can let things be for just one day, can't you? Every man should be able to spend this day with their children, if they've been blessed with any."

"Every man who gives a damn about 'em," George muttered.

This comment stung Jack, I could tell, and he looked suddenly pathetic and lonely to me. Although I didn't want him there, it seemed obvious that he hadn't come to cause any trouble. "Sit down, Jack," I said.

"What?" Dad said.

"Ah, let him eat, at least," I said.

"Yeah," Stan agreed.

I looked at Rita, who gave a curt nod.

Because nobody wanted the situation to turn into a conflict, there were no protests. But the silence had the feel of unhappy submission, and as Jack took off his coat, went to the kitchen for a plate, and pulled an extra chair up to the table, between Teddy and Stan, the tension was impossible to ignore.

As dinner progressed, I began to wish I had kept my mouth shut. Jack's presence sucked the festive spirit out of the gathering like a tube siphoning gas. Everyone ate as though they couldn't wait to finish and move on to the next thing. There was almost no conversation, and if Stan hadn't been at the table, there might not have been any.

"So how's the mining business, Stan?" I asked.

"Better all the time." Stan finished chewing before continuing. "Of course, the war doesn't hurt us any."

"Ah, yes. The war." I nodded. "I've heard something about a war going on."

"I wish that wasn't the reason business was better," Muriel lamented.

"Yeah, well, we didn't start the war," Stan said.

"Of course not," Muriel said, "I just wish nobody had. It never solves anything."

Talk of the war made me think about the last time the subject had come up in Jack's presence, and I studied him. He looked placid, not really interested in what was being said. His face was drawn, and I wondered whether he'd been eating enough.

"Well, I think Hitler is going to self-destruct," Stan said. "He's trying to do too much. Even with help from the Italians and Japs, he's taking on too much."

"Let's just hope to God you're right." Muriel raised her glass to her husband.

"George, you're about that age. Are you thinking about enlisting?" Stan asked.

This brought the first reaction from Jack, who looked up from his plate in alarm, fixing his eyes on his oldest son. It looked as if it had never occurred to him that his son had grown up.

"He is," Rita said. "And any help in talking him out of it would be appreciated."

"George, I hope you decide not to join," Muriel said. "You just don't know what can happen." She shook her head.

"The boy has to decide for himself," Stan said.

"Leave the boy alone," Dad grumbled.

"We're discussing," Stan said. "We're not riding the boy."

"It's all right, Grandpa," George said. "For one thing, everybody stop calling me boy. I'm not a boy anymore. I don't have to listen to what they say."

"Well!" Muriel said.

"He didn't mean it that way," Rita said to Muriel.

"Let's change the subject," I said.

"Good idea," Rita agreed.

"No," George said. "No, I want to talk about this. I think I have the right to make up my own mind. And if I want to join the army, I shouldn't have to worry about whether my family is never going to talk to me again if I do."

Rita looked stricken. "Son, who do you think wouldn't talk to you? Why would you say something like that?"

George sighed, shaking his head with an expression of someone carrying a much bigger load than he had any business taking on. "Maybe we should drop it. I didn't mean to offend anyone. I'm just saying that it's about time somebody realized I'm a grown-up now."

Rita looked down at her plate, her face slightly older. But I thought George made a good point—it occurred to me that maybe Jack wasn't the only one who hadn't been paying attention, that maybe we had all been so wrapped up in our own lives that we hadn't noticed that he was a man now.

We talked about less controversial topics as we finished our main course and went on to dessert. Jack never did speak, and by the time we finished eating, his presence had lost its power. I could feel the room slowly relax.

After dinner, we decided to play cards. Between the adults and George and Teddy, we had eight people, so Rita and I sat down in the living room, teaming up against George and Dad. In the dining room, Muriel and Jack paired up against Teddy and Stan, who continued to indulge in his share of eggnog. The candles on the tree had long burnt down to nothing, the wax coating the pine branches, and the fire had to be fed to keep it from dying to a smoldering pile of ash. A chill filled the air even with the fire as the light outside began to fade. And as the temperature dropped, the cold air leaked in through the cracks under the doors, and around the windows. It soaked into the wood floors and walls. We all put on sweaters before we sat down.

"Blake, I don't know what you're trying to do to me, but these cards are terrible," Dad said.

"I don't feel bad at all," I answered, smiling.

"Well, you could have dealt your partner a decent hand," Rita said.

"Looks like George and Blake have the cards this time around," Dad said.

"Don't look at me," George argued. "I couldn't win Old Maid with this hand."

Indeed, I had an incredible hand—three aces, and a string of seven hearts including the ace, king, jack, and ten. I took the bid easily, at eight hearts, and ran the table, taking every trick. This was the beginning of a streak of luck that I've never known in all my years of playing cards. I ended up with at least two aces in nearly every hand, and if I didn't have a strong suit, I seemed to have just the right cards to complement Rita's hand. Dad got so disgusted, he asked if anyone at the other table wanted to switch partners. But there were no takers.

"Blake, what are you doing to those poor folks over there?" Muriel asked.

"I'm not too sure what's going on here," I said. "Living right, I guess. The cards are definitely falling my way tonight."

"Well, you take it easy on my nephew," Muriel shouted.

"Hey, if I get the hands, I have to play 'em," I said.

"You're coldhearted," Dad said, shaking his head. "Cruel and cold-hearted."

Over the course of the evening, as we played game after game of five hundred, the conversation from the dining room got louder a little at a time. And due to his overindulgence, Stan's voice dominated, along with much laughter.

"Hey, how much longer you guys gonna play in there?" Stan's voice boomed from the dining room. "We're about ready to quit in here. You gonna play all night?"

"Yeah, we're gonna play all night," I yelled.

"Yeah, Blake is gonna play all night. But he'll be playin' solitaire before too much longer," Dad shouted.

I laughed. "Dad, I never knew you were such a sore loser."

"I never lost this bad before."

"Well, if you guys aren't gonna quit, we're just gonna have to come in there and bother you," Stan shouted.

A few minutes later, Stan weaved through the door, with Jack, Teddy, and Muriel following. Stan held his arms straight out at his sides and bowed his head slightly. "Here we are!" he announced. He had a glass in one hand, half filled with eggnog, tipping precariously, and a big smile on his face, with deep creases on each side of his mouth. His cheeks were red right up to his eyes. Jack lingered behind him, his face giving no sign of his condition.

"Here we are," Stan repeated, then started giggling, which sounded strange coming from him.

Stan and Jack made their way to the couch, which they caved into. And Teddy and Muriel settled into the easy chairs.

"All right," Stan said. He turned to Jack and made like a whisper, holding his hand on one side of his mouth. "We gotta be quiet. They're playin' cards. Gotta keep it down." Stan laughed conspiratorially, holding his hand against his stomach. "Besides," he continued, "Blake's on a roll over here. We don't want to ruin his lucky streak."

We continued playing, watching this scene with amusement. Except for Muriel, who was not happy to see her husband in such a state. She became distracted from the game.

I had my eye on Jack, who hadn't said a word. I had yet to see him drunk since his return, but I couldn't read his condition. He appeared a little slow, but it was the kind of look that could mean he was tired, or bored. Across the table from me, Rita kept him under close scrutiny herself.

"Did we go out again?" I asked Dad.

"No. You have four seventy-five." He laid the pencil across the score pad, and started to shuffle the cards. "You want to call it quits after this game?"

"No," George quickly said.

"Well, let's see how it goes," Dad said.

"I've about had it," Rita said.

"At least we had a close game in there," Muriel said. "It was a lot more fun at our table."

"You saying you got a better partner than you did last time?" Dad kidded her. He had been her partner the night before.

"I believe so," Muriel joked. "I believe that was the problem last night. I didn't have a good partner."

"Well, if that's the way this game works, Blake has the best partner in the history of the county," Dad said.

"Who's Blake's partner?" Stan asked.

"Well, look at the table, you big dummy," Muriel said.

Stan squeezed his eyes together and held his hand above his eyes, as if he was searching for something a long ways off. "Is that you, Rita? Are you Blake's partner?" he asked.

"Sure am," Rita replied.

"And a damn good one," I added.

"And not the first time she's been your partner, huh?"

The moment these bitter words left Jack's lips, the atmosphere of the whole room chilled. It became obvious to me that Jack was not drunk. His eyes were wide. His cheeks flushed. Even his neck had turned red. But his eyes were sky-blue clear, and his voice did not waver. He was completely sober, and for the second time that day, his presence commanded the attention of everyone in the room.

"Oh Jesus," Dad murmured.

"Yeah, we've been partners before," I said, hoping the question was this simple.

"That's what I thought," Jack said, his voice brittle, cold.

"What the hell is that supposed to mean?" I asked.

He snorted through his nose and looked around the room, at everyone, as if the answer was so clear he couldn't believe I didn't know.

Dad jumped in, his voice low and shaking. "Whatever it is you've got on your mind, Jack, you best keep it to yourself, especially in front of these boys."

"Why should I?" Jack asked, leaning forward from his sitting position. "Everyone in the county knows about it. Everyone but me knew about it until Steve Glasser let me in on the goddam secret."

"Get that son of a bitch out of here," Rita muttered, her teeth clenched.

Muriel started crying, quietly, holding a handkerchief to her eyes.

As Jack's accusation sunk in, and as I saw what it did to Rita, I lost my head. I didn't think, but acted completely on impulse. In one motion, I threw down my cards, tipped my chair to the floor and stood over Jack, my hands and knees trembling.

"If you're saying what I think you're saying, you better get the hell out of this house before I pound you right through that couch and into the floor."

I would have been on top of him if Stan hadn't jumped up and grabbed me, wrapping his arm across my chest. Dad also came up from behind, holding me around the waist.

"Easy, Blake. Step back and take it easy for a second," commanded Stan, who was suddenly sober.

Jack stared up at me with a stony, mistrustful gaze that turned my heart cold.

"After all you've put this family through, you accuse your wife of that!" I was yelling, in a voice that didn't sound or feel like my own. My legs felt like water, and the shouting echoed in my ears, as though I was in a metal building.

"You know where that rumor came from." Rita now stood next to me, her fists clenched at her sides, her voice shaking, her whole body quaking. "You know who started it, and you know why." She looked directly at Jack, but pointed off in the direction of Bob and Helen's house. "And if you're going to sit there and tell us you'd believe that . . . that witch before you'd believe me or your brother here, who took care of your children while you were off doing whatever is such a secret you can't even tell your own family . . ." She couldn't finish, and she wept, her eyes spilling onto her cheeks. "Ask your children," she screamed, pointing to Teddy, who was also crying. "Ask your children, Jack Arbuckle. They were there."

Jack's neck stiffened. His hands, which had been clenched, holding tightly to his thighs, loosened their grip and fell between his knees, hanging. But his face remained impassive, his eyes unbelieving. He looked as defiant and righteous as ever.

I wrenched loose from Stan's grip and bent down, pushing my chin up against Jack's. Stan tried to grab my arm, but I jerked it from his grip. Our chins touched. I pushed against him, feeling the soft breath from his nose.

"Do you realize how much you've put this woman through? Do you have any idea?"

Before Jack had a chance to respond, I felt someone shove me from behind, throwing me to one side. I fell, and looking up from the floor, I watched George dive into his father's torso. George's head landed against Jack's chest like a hammer, prompting a grunt from Jack, who lost his wind. Then George's right elbow flew up behind him, and his arm started a pistonlike pounding, thrusting his fist into his father's midsection. Stan and Dad both tried to restrain George, but besides being stronger than he looked, his rage was so intense that they couldn't contain him. Except for holding his arms up to his face, Jack made little effort to defend himself.

"She never did nothing to you," I heard George say through sobs. "She waited for you, and she never did nothing. And you left. You left us."

I scooted over between the forest of legs gathered around Jack, and wrapped my arms around George's knees. I pulled him to the ground. Then I crawled up his torso so that I could hold his arms.

"Calm down, George," I whispered in his ear.

"No." I was shocked by the force of George's reply. He struggled to break free of my grasp, but I held him firmly against the floor. The rest of the room was completely silent.

"Let me up, Uncle Blake," George muttered between his teeth.

I turned my head and looked up at Jack, whose face was bloody, although he didn't appear to be seriously hurt.

"Let him up," he said passively. Jack looked right at me. And it appeared from his expression that this attack from George had reached inside and struck something in my brother. It appeared that his son had touched a spot none of the rest of us had ever been able to approach. His eyes, for the first time that I could remember, looked to be free of their hooded suspicion. Instead, they showed an immense sorrow. A reflection of a pure emotion.

The look penetrated my own shield, and my arms suddenly went weak. George started to wriggle in my grasp again. I let him go, and he staggered to his feet, and backed up, staring at his father.

"How can you possibly even think you have any right to accuse me of that?" Rita asked Jack.

Jack turned his head and breathed deep, as if he was too tired to defend himself. He shook his head, a motion that slowly transformed into a nod, an acknowledgment.

And it was odd how dramatically the atmosphere shifted. This small crack in Jack's façade had split the tension in the room open like a needle breaking open a swollen blister. And the anger had been replaced by a somber, pervasive sadness.

"Why did you come back here?" George asked softly. "Why didn't you just stay away?"

Jack's eyes met George's, and they came as close to pleading as I've ever seen them. "This is my home," he said.

George just shook his head, then stalked out. I looked over at Teddy, and saw the face of a boy whose youthful idealism had just been shattered. He looked as if he could easily break into tears if he would allow himself to let go. But he dropped his head and squeezed his lips together.

Jack stood up slowly, deliberately, and left through the front door, wiping the blood from his face.

I went back to my chair, slumping into it with the kind of defeated feeling I always feel after a confrontation. I always seem to find myself wondering what I could have done to prevent these situations, or handle them differently somehow. There's no logic to this, of course. But I was sitting there, thinking that I should have seen that Jack's silence was foreboding, sitting there on the couch. The rest of the family also sat with sad, stunned expressions.

When we heard footsteps on the front porch, I thought to myself that we really couldn't handle any more, that it was too much for one day. The door swung open, and Jack entered, and I tensed, my muscles preparing for anything, even the possibility that Jack had retrieved a weapon and come back to use it. He walked right up to me, and I sat bolt-upright, and felt everyone around me do the same. But Jack stood right there in front of me, and held out his hand, inviting me to shake it. I looked at it, and thought for a moment, and I did. I shook it. I stood up and shook his hand.

That night I lay in bed, staring at the ceiling, my hands nestled into the pillow behind my head. My stomach was wound as tight as a ball of dried leather as I lay quietly thinking, and listening to the rustle of others in the house getting ready for bed. I couldn't remember coming any closer to wanting to kill somebody as I had been just a few hours before. I still felt a slight tremor in my arms.

Jack's accusation had led me to a nauseating realization. I now pieced it together that Helen's rumor had spread across the entire county. And I realized at last what spurred the reaction from Mom the night she kicked Bob and Helen out of the house. Helen must have suggested the possibility that Rita and I were having an affair. The depth and width of the lie, of the betrayal, seemed so immense that it filled me with a churning sickness. Not so much because of what people would think, although that did bother me some. But more because I couldn't imagine how Helen could be so heartless. It seemed that every time I convinced myself that I knew her limitations, she showed a color that was darker, more ominous.

That night, the mysteries of love seemed more mysterious than ever to me. How could a man who had shown no interest in his wife, in his family, for so many years, feel betrayed by a rumor, even if it was true? Would it really have surprised him if his wife sought comfort from someone else during the course of those ten years? It seemed even more surprising that she hadn't. And would it be that unusual if that person happened to be someone she saw every day, someone she was close to already? Who the hell was Jack to be jealous, especially after his display at the Roundup just months before? The more I thought about it, the more I wanted to go find Jack and pound on him. But I also felt an overwhelming urge to go to Rita, to provide some comfort from this latest stunt. I felt very protective of her that night. All these emotions eventually wore me out. Fortunately, before I acted on any of them, I fell asleep.

16

fall 1944

"Blake!" Rita's call from around the corner of the house echoed across the open space behind me.

"Yeah?"

"Do you have some paint to spare?"

"Oh, yeah. I have plenty. Come on over." I dipped my brush into the five-gallon can hanging by a hook from my extension ladder. We had nearly finished spreading the third coat of paint over the big house. With nearly everyone in the family taking up a brush in the evenings and on Sundays, the job had still taken over a month. The weathered, gray wood had been so dry that the first coat soaked in like water. The change in color was barely noticeable. Even now, the gray showed through in many spots. But we were running out of paint, patience, and most important, warm weather.

Rita rounded the corner, carrying a gallon bucket in her paint-spotted hand. She wore overalls with a men's undershirt, all covered with spatterings of white. She had her hair, nearly all gray now, tied up with a kerchief.

"How's it going over on your side?" I asked.

"Getting there," she answered.

"How about Jack?" Jack worked on the opposite side of the house.

"I don't know. Last time I looked, he was moving right along."

It was warm, early fall, when the days are almost as hot as summer but the chill of evening calls for at least a jacket. I also wore overalls and an undershirt, and I was too hot. If I hadn't been so worried about burning the top of my head, I would have taken my hat off. I climbed down and poured paint into Rita's can, then clambered back to my perch.

Life was good. Five years of better-than-average moisture. From the ladder, I could look in every direction and see meadows thick with grass grown back since our second cutting, in July. Although the color was fading, the green that shaded the yellowing fields was still brilliant for this late in this season. Each spring, we wondered if it would end. Was it going to be like the teens—so many good years followed by so much hell? We knew the shift could happen at any moment, and each wet year was greeted with a sigh of relief.

There was a soft, steady clicking in the air—the last of the locusts, which were now no more of a problem than the usual summer swarm of flies or mosquitoes. And the smells were strong, unlike the thirties, when the dust muted even the odors. I could smell the sagebrush, alfalfa, the livestock, even the air, and it all smelled clean and good, fresh.

I reached out as far to my right as I could and covered the dry wood, pulling the brush across each strip of siding, then back again to even out the paint. Inside the house, I heard the phone ring—two longs and a short.

"Is that Glassers'?" I yelled to Rita.

"I think so," she shouted back.

The county had installed our phone system that spring. It was a complicated setup—a party line, of course. We could make local calls by ringing the coded signals assigned to each neighbor. But if we wanted to call anyone outside of the direct area, anything more than fifteen miles away, we had to ring the switchboard operator in Capitol. A blind man by the name of Reeves ran the switchboard, and once he connected you with your party, you had to tell him what to say. He would pass on your message, then relay their reply. They hadn't been able to afford a system that connected you directly to the outside party, and because of Reeves's handicap, he couldn't write anything down. So it was important to keep your message short and simple. A phone call sometimes lasted an hour, with constant interruptions by neighbors trying to make their own calls.

The system provided a new form of entertainment, as many folks listened in on other calls. I have to admit I enjoyed picking up the line now and then myself. I wouldn't doubt that some calls had an audience of over twenty-five people. Some neighbors' calls were more entertaining than others, of course. Helen was always good for a few stories, and if you managed to catch Lonnie Roberts on the line, you always heard stifled laughter in the background.

A few days after the system was installed, our phone began ringing, time after time, one code then another, and another, and more, until I had to pick it up to see what the hell was happening, even though our code of three shorts hadn't rung yet. The line was filled with people: "Hello, hello"; "Who the hell is calling?"; "Is this some kind of joke?"

The phone continued ringing and ringing, until there were at least twenty people on the line trying to figure out what was going on. I assumed there must be an emergency—a fire or something—and that somebody was trying to alert the community. But finally a loud, confused voice came on the line.

"Hello? Oh, is this thing turned on?"

"Yes, it's turned on. Who the hell is this?"

"Oh, I didn't know. I was just practicing," the voice said, without identifying himself. Then he hung up. The whole county got a good laugh out of this incident, and for months after, there were several rumors about who would need to practice. There was some speculation that it was the ghost of Art Walters.

I climbed down from under the eave, lugging my paint with me, and moved the ladder over ten feet. About then, Teddy and George came up the path from their house. Pup followed behind, as did a bum lamb. Teddy still carried out the task of feeding the orphaned lambs, a job he did not enjoy but which he performed with his usual good-natured sense of responsibility. But as a sign of the good times, he only had one lamb to take care of that season. The lamb had become quite attached to Teddy, and because Pup also followed Teddy wherever he went, the lamb had decided that he too was a dog. When we herded sheep, he followed Pup into the fields, never making the connection that the flock we were herding was made up of his own kind. He stuck right with Pup while the dog nipped at the heels of the other sheep. George, in one of his more brilliant moments, had dubbed the lamb Mutt, short for mutton.

"Where are you guys headed?" I asked.

"We're going out to the north pasture to check on the cattle," George said.

"You need the pickup?"

"No, we're gonna ride," George answered. "Make a day of it."

"Today's the day to do that," I said.

"It's nice, all right," Teddy said, smiling.

Teddy was home from Belle Fourche for the weekend. He had started his sophomore year, and had been talking about college, if the war was over by the time he graduated. He roomed with the next generation of the same family in Belle Fourche that I had stayed with.

George had tried to enlist in January, but when they did the physical evaluation, they had discovered an irregular heartbeat. After so many months of agonizing about whether to take this step, his disappointment had been profound. For a couple of weeks, getting him to do anything was a waste of breath, and not just in the area of work. He hardly ate, or bothered to take a bath.

But once spring rolled around, and work had to be done, he snapped out of it, although any talk about the war sent him out of the room. He stopped reading the newspaper, and when the news came on the radio, if he didn't leave, he'd change the station or turn it off.

"You guys need something for lunch?" Rita asked.

"No, we're all set," George said, patting a paper bag in his hand.

The boys continued along the path toward the barn, George walking with determined strides, head bent, eyes focused on the path. Behind him, Teddy bounced along, loose and looking all around, with the dog and lamb trailing him. I rounded the corner to where Rita was, watching the strange little band of brothers and laughing to myself.

"That goddam lamb kills me," I said.

Rita turned from her painting. Pup padded along to one side of the boys, smiling, his nose pointed toward Teddy, as if being with him was the best thing he could possibly imagine. Mutt trotted close behind Pup, his ears flopping straight up and down.

The morning passed quickly despite the monotony of spreading paint, moving the ladder, spreading paint. My arms turned white from the elbow down, and my brush stuck to my hand.

"Are you guys going to be ready for some lunch pretty soon?" Rita's head appeared from inside the house.

"Oh, yeah," I said. "How long?"

"Ten minutes?"

"All right."

Jack and I soaped up and scrubbed as much of the paint from our hands as we could before settling into the dining room. The radio blared from the living room, and I knew Dad was in there, probably dozing. His hearing was going, his spirit diminished, and he now spent much of each afternoon napping. He was the only one in the family who hadn't done any painting.

"How's it going on your end?" I asked Jack.

"Pretty good." He nodded. "I think I might be able to finish up this afternoon."

"Me too," I said. "Rita?"

She reached for a carrot stick and nodded. "I'm going to finish for sure."

"Maybe we'll finally get this damn thing painted." I yelled into the living room, "Hey, Dad, how do you feel about having your house painted?"

There was no answer, and I knew he must be asleep.

Rita had made roast beef sandwiches and potato salad, and she had sweating glasses of lemonade waiting for us. We ate at a leisurely pace, in no hurry to get back out in the sun. Country music drifted from the living room, the voice of Bob Wills wailing away about trains. An electric fan beat with little effect against the heat.

"How's that dam coming?" I asked Jack, who was building a dam in a pasture on the far southern meadow, on Hay Creek.

"Pretty good," he said. "I don't know if I'll finish it before winter settles in. Depends how long this warm weather lasts."

Jack looked beat, and I wondered if he'd been getting enough sleep. The incident at Christmas had an interesting effect on Jack's relationship with the family. In most respects, he was still the same man. But he was doing some great things with the bulldozer. He didn't bother anyone. He didn't expect to be included in our family dinners. It had become apparent that he was never going to be concerned about what we thought about him. He was here to stay, unapologetic. But it seemed that having his suspicions about Rita and me out in the open had defused the tension.

Rita, Jack, and I sat eating our lunch, with little thought or residue from all the turmoil the three of us had endured, or caused. I was more comfortable around Jack than I could ever remember. I loved the fact that there were times such as this, when it felt as if we could live this way for a very long time without fear of revisiting all the unpleasant memories that seemed so important when they were happening. I seldom thought about George's death anymore, or Jack's role in it.

"Well, I think I'll get back to it," I said.

Rita and Jack also stood, stretching their muscles, ready to try and finish up. We moved stiffly, without enthusiasm, limping outside, back to our respective sides of the house. The sun sat mid-sky, like a light-bulb behind a brilliant blue bedsheet, and there was no wind. But a small bank of clouds had moved in along the eastern sky, providing a bit of hope for a break in the heat.

I grabbed my brush, which I'd left drying in the sun, and climbed back up on the ladder. And as I dipped my brush and moved my arm back and forth, back and forth, mindlessly, my thoughts drifted. I was thinking about water. I was thinking about how much our lives had changed since the rains came. And how things had gotten even better when Jack had figured out a way to take control of the water. His ability to reroute it and corral it provided options that had not been available to us in the early, homestead years, or during the Depression, although the technology would have been little use then anyway.

And I was thinking about how much it would help to have the dam that Jack was building now. How we wouldn't have to rotate our stock as much as we had. I was considering where we should winter the cattle and sheep when I saw a horse riding toward the house from the north.

"Who's that?" I asked, pointing.

"Looks like Teddy," Rita said.

"Hm." I squinted.

It was Teddy. The horse galloped closer, stopping long enough for

Teddy to hop off and open a gate. He didn't close the gate, which was unusual. There were cattle in the meadow beyond the gate, and he knew as well as anyone that a gate to a meadow containing cattle should always be shut. Instead, he swung back up into the saddle, and slammed his boots into the horse's ribs. He didn't stop kicking, even when the horse reached full gallop. This was also unusual, as Teddy was as gentle with horses as any kid I'd ever known. I started to climb down from the ladder, watching Teddy as I went. Pup and Mutt followed behind him, struggling to keep up with the horse's full gallop. Teddy was waving his hat, which he gripped in his left hand.

"Something's wrong," I heard myself saying.

I ran toward Teddy, who was already half off his horse when he reined in. He swung down onto the ground. All he wore were dunga-rees, which were soaked. His hair was also wet.

"George!" he shouted. "He's gone down!"

"He's what?"

"He's gone down, in the reservoir," he said, trying to catch his breath. "He went under."

Jack and Rita came running from opposite sides of the house.

"Oh my god," Rita said, seeing the fear in Teddy's face.

I ran toward the car, which we all piled into. I started it up, and took off toward the north meadow.

"Oh god," Rita said.

Teddy, through his breathless, choking tears, started explaining.

"We were swimming," he said, "and he swam out into the middle of the reservoir, and he started waving his arms around, and scream-ing, and he was holding his chest, and I swam out to him. . . ." Teddy ran out of breath, and when he tried to breathe, he started coughing. I thought of George's heart.

"Easy, Teddy," Rita said. "Take a deep breath." She put a hand on his shoulder.

Teddy stopped coughing, holding his chest, and took up where he'd left off. "I swam out to him, and I tried to get hold of him, but he was swinging his arms around, trying to swim . . . he kept hitting me when I tried to grab him . . . not on purpose, but he was just crazy, wild . . . and I couldn't . . ." Teddy stopped, shaking his head. "I couldn't . . ." He broke down, and started sobbing out of control, covering his eyes, burying his face into his knees.

I drove as fast as I dared on the dirt road, along the top of one of the dikes, across the river, and through three meadows. Jack jumped out to close the gates, and Teddy stopped crying after a while, sitting with his head in his hands, mumbling to himself.

I wasn't breathing, I realized. I was so intent on driving and not losing my head, I forgot to breathe. I inhaled deeply, and felt a blockage, like a balloon, in my chest. There was little hope, I knew, with the time that had passed. But no, I thought. Don't let yourself entertain that possibility.

At the reservoir, the water was still, smooth and silent. This frightened me, and again left little room for hope, but I again tried to push these negative thoughts out of my head. Jack and I both stripped to our underwear and dove in. The reservoir was only a hundred feet across, but in the middle, it was ten feet deep. Teddy said that George had gone down in the middle, so we swam toward that point. My arms tired before I was halfway there. My chest tightened.

I swam beneath the surface, trying to keep my eyes open. But the water was murky, and even when my eyes were open, I could only see a couple of feet in front of me. I floundered through the water, waving my arms around frantically, feeling my way for the touch of flesh. I bumped against earth. When I pushed away from it, I felt air against my back. I lifted my head, and realized that in my desperation, I had swum all the way across. I looked for Jack, saw no sign of him, and went back under, veering back toward the middle.

I felt my way along the bottom, thinking George might have sunk, and as the ground below me got lower and lower, I suddenly felt flesh against my leg. It responded, grabbing me, and I flung my leg out, trying to spin myself around. I kicked loose of the grip, and a moment later Jack and I came face-to-face, two white masks frightening each other in the depths of a fearful brown pool. We grabbed each other by the shoulders, as if assuring each other that we were not George. Then we turned away, in different directions. I felt his foot hit my own.

My lungs could not sustain me, and I had to come up for air. I gasped, and heard the sound of shouting. I looked over, and Rita and Teddy were pointing, shouting and pointing, but I saw that the foot they pointed at was Jack's, moving away from me. I dove, sinking again to the bottom and feeling my way toward the middle. And there he was, on his back, lying just a foot or two from the floor of the reservoir. His heels touched bottom, but the rest of his body floated, toes pointing up, his arms drifting at his sides. I couldn't see his face, nor did I want to, and I swam to his head and grabbed him around the chest with both arms. I started kicking as hard as my tired, burning legs would allow, pushing first off the bottom, then kicking like a frog, struggling to hang on to the limp, heavy torso.

I felt a touch from behind, and Jack was there. He swam under George and pushed, and a second later my head broke the surface, along with George's. I breathed, sucking huge gulps of air into my lungs, and started stroking with one arm toward shore. I felt Jack pushing from below, and once we got a rhythm, we reached shore in moments.

My knees scraped the ground and I stood, pulling George along until he was completely out of the water, where I laid him on his back and sunk to my knees at his head. Rita hit the ground next to his chest, and Jack fell, burying his face in his hands.

One look at George's face, and it was clear that he was dead. His mouth hung open, like the beginning of a yawn. His eyes stared, unfocused, and his skin was too white. Rita's head fell against his ribs, where she cried his name over and over, her body trembling. Teddy knelt beside his mother and rested his head sideways on her back, hanging his arms around her.

I started coughing, and water gushed from my lungs, into my mouth. I tasted the mud. Jack rolled over and sat up, looking over at his son. He breathed heavily, labored, with a pained look on his face. He lifted his knees, and rested his head against them.

Rita stopped sobbing and crawled to George's head, which she cradled in her lap. Her face was twisted, looking down at her son. She shook her head and stroked George's cheek, a squeak escaping her throat. Teddy still clung to his mother, kneeling behind her and resting his head in the crook of her neck. His mouth was turned down, and his eyes were squeezed so tight that the tears barely escaped.

I looked at George's face again, and the skin, which was usually such a dark, healthy brown, had faded to the color of dry earth—pale, dusty gray. His eyes were glazed. And even though it was obvious he was dead, I was taken back to the day I stared at the face of another dead man and saw something less than human. Unlike that day, when my brother looked like a different person, this was definitely George. I felt an urge to reach down and offer him a hand. I had to look away. But I wasn't willing to lose George yet. I didn't want this picture of him, lying naked on his back, his arms spread listlessly, his neck twisted slightly to one side.

For the first time in my life, I wanted to fight death. I wanted to prevent it somehow. I wanted to do something. So I threw myself on George. I fell on him and tried to pound life into his heart, to breathe air into him. I tasted the mud on his lips as I emptied my lungs into his. His ribs bruised my hands as I pounded his chest like a steak.

I didn't realize that I was out of control until my rhythm was interrupted by Rita's embrace. She wrapped herself around me and whispered softly to stop, that I was hurting him. And I did stop, and slumped exhausted, staring down at George, whose eyes stared dead and glassy at the sky. His chest did not move. His skin remained pale. I rolled off him, onto my hands and knees, and rested for a moment.

Teddy had come to a moment of silent repose, staring down at his brother with a look that reminded me of my fourteen-year-old self. He wasn't crying. He studied his brother and held his face steady. Jack had still not moved. His head rested on his knees. Rita left me and returned to her son. She stroked his face. She ran her fingers through his hair. The tears ran steadily down her cheeks.

A hundred yards from us, a small flock of sheep had gathered. They chewed the grass at their feet for a moment, then studied us. And then, as if one of them had sensed the death and signaled the rest, they took off, in unison, their woolly behinds bouncing, each at their own rhythm. And then the land around us was still, quiet—except for the barely audible click of the locusts. The cloud bank that had appeared around noon now lingered just above us. The air felt slightly cooler, as if there was a chance of rain.

Although I felt like lying down, I forced myself to stand, and began pulling my clothes on, starting with my undershirt, then my overalls. The movements felt strange, senseless. I had no notion of touch, or smell. I couldn't taste. My nerves were dead, and I realized that as much as I felt as if I needed to keep moving, to keep busy, to do something useful, I couldn't move. I fell to my hands and knees again, pummeled by the pain in my body. I stayed this way for a long time, my head hanging between my arms, the water dripping innocently, darkening the earth.

After long minutes of suspended silence, I looked up. Nobody had moved. Or spoken. Nobody appeared ready to move or speak. I noticed George's horse for the first time, standing patiently to the side, the reins hanging loose to the ground. He chewed on his bit.

"Someone's going to have to ride the horse back," I said, thinking out loud.

"I'll do it," Jack said.

"No, no. I can do it," I said.

"I want to do it," Jack insisted. "I'll do it."

"All right."

Jack stood slowly, as if it hurt his body to do so. He walked over, shoulders bent, and pulled his clothes on, in the unhurried way that one does early in the morning.

I stood near the car, and felt a sudden surge of nervous energy. I started pacing, and my mind searched with manic desperation for something to do, a task. I felt as though I would collapse if I stood still for another moment. Finally, I walked over and put my hand on Rita's shoulder. She sat motionless for a while longer, then stood up and started toward the car. I knelt at George's side and began to ease my hands under him, one beneath his knees, the other just below his neck.

"Open the trunk," I told Teddy.

"No!" Rita said, turning suddenly. "You're not putting him in the trunk."

I bristled slightly, then wondered what the hell I was thinking. Of course she wouldn't want her son, only minutes dead, in the trunk.

"I'm sorry," I said. "Of course not."

I lifted George and carried him to the car. His head flopped in the crook of my elbow, and I thought of how heavy a skull is. But other than his head, George was light. He was thin. He was too slight, too unfinished, to be dead.

I ducked inside the back door and settled George's feet onto the floor, then hefted his torso onto the seat, in a sitting position. His mother settled in beside him, first wrapping him up in his overalls, then putting her arms around him. And Teddy got in on the other side, also holding his brother.

As we drove away, I watched Jack in the rearview mirror, staring into the body of water he had created. It is a scene I have recalled many times since—a telling moment. For if there was anything that I believed Jack to be proud of, it was those reservoirs, his reservoirs. And now he pondered his creation, no doubt wondering how something he had worked so hard to build, perhaps the greatest accomplishment of his life, could have betrayed him so thoroughly. I believe it was the closest Jack came to realizing how much his son meant to him, and the closest he would ever come to expressing his sorrow.

Just before he was out of our sight, he stooped, picked up a large stone, raised it above his head and flung it with unbridled violence into the reservoir. The still surface exploded with water.

Back at the house, I still felt nervous, anxious to keep busy. My knees shook. I had to call the coroner. The call took a while, as Reeves had trouble understanding me. The connection wasn't good, and he couldn't make out the word "coroner." He thought I was saying "corner," which meant nothing to him. I lost my patience, yelling the word at him until he got it.

Then I made one more call, one I didn't look forward to.

"Helen?"

"Yes."

"Is Bob there?"

"Blake?"

"Yes."

Her voice went cold. "No. He's in town."

"Oh. Well, I'm afraid I have some bad news." My air passage closed up, and I had to clear my throat. I tried to speak, but it was still blocked. Finally, I blurted out in a burst of sound, "George is dead."

There were several small gasps on the line.

"You mean Dad?"

"No. Little George. He drowned . . . in the reservoir . . . just a half hour or so ago."

Another pause, with some sniffling sounds. "Oh Blake, that's awful."

For the first time that I could remember, I believed without a doubt that Helen was sincere, and that her grief was genuine. For that brief instant, I felt a kinship with her. And I was sorry that things couldn't be this way all the time.

"Yes, it is," I said. "It's a damn shame."

"Oh god," she said, in a helpless voice I'd never heard from her.

"Will you tell Bob when he gets back?"

"Yes. Yes, of course. Thank you for calling, Blake."

"Well, I thought you should know."

"Thank you. I mean it."

I turned from the phone, where Rita stood, staring at me with questioning, tearful eyes. I looked at her, then past her, my mind working, trying to think what needed to be done next. I couldn't think of anything. I couldn't think at all, and I looked behind me. The desperation to find something to do overwhelmed me. Then I broke.

Grief, it seems to me, grows much the same way a child does. To begin with, neither can speak, although both are adept at making their presence known—sometimes subtly, sometimes dramatically. The message may not be clear, but the depth of feeling, the passion, is never in doubt.

As it grows, and ages, grief develops a voice of its own, a voice that needs an attentive, patient ear to express its message clearly. And if it is ignored, the voice will eventually demand attention, until one day you turn around to find yourself looking it squarely in the face.

There is no choice in this progression. The progression happens whether you permit it to or not. The choice comes in how you respond. Some, like Jack, will always run from grief. Others bury it so deep that it makes them weak, and they need someone stronger to rely on.

I think before the day of George's drowning, I was running in my own way. His death brought me face-to-face with sorrow, and my grief grabbed me by the ears and shook me awake. It forced me to stand still for a moment and notice it, to take it seriously.

Because practicality can only explain death to a point. If a death puts an end to suffering, as with Katie, or with Art, or as the final chapter of a long, good life, as with Mom, it's easy to explain it practically and sensibly. But when there's nothing sensible about a death, such as George's, it leaves you with nothing to hide behind. The pain is right there. And that day, in a strange way, the pain felt good. It felt right. I didn't fight it. I didn't feel like crying. Unlike thirty years before, when my brother died, I wasn't rebelling against some latent desire to weep. I was sad as hell, but I knew it was right to feel that way. I knew I was supposed to be sad as hell.

And I think that was the one and only day I knew this absolutely. I took one look at Rita, and for the first time I understood why my people don't talk much. Because in that single look, I recognized that nothing we said to each other could match the feeling of shared experience. We knew, and we didn't need to speak. Instead, we fell together, holding each other.

And for as long as I stood in Rita's arms, I surrendered to my sorrow, and allowed my heart to twist into whatever shape it chose. And I knew as I hadn't thirty years earlier that George's death, my brother's death, was just as senseless and tragic as this one. And I knew for the first time that it felt damn good to miss people.

We had to wake up Dad to tell him. He sat forward, and braced himself with one hand on the arm of his chair, tilting his ear toward me as I told him what happened. He looked down, his eyes milky, as if they had been dipped in egg whites. His lips had long ago drawn into his mouth, as if all the words he hadn't said in his lifetime had pulled them inside. His mouth tightened into a finer, thin line. He said nothing, but his eyes closed, and he simply sank back into his chair.

And I began to miss him too.

17

summer 1945

The war is over. The county is crowded with fresh-faced young men with stubble for hair, eyes bright with the joy of being home, and being alive. But they are also weary, and wary. And I wonder, like I did with Jack when he returned, what they saw—what deep, unexplainable wounds they've suffered. Of course, we all read about the things that happened in this war, horrible things that make our own tragedies seem small, and I am sorry for any of these young men who have to keep such secrets.

There are also those who do not return. I see their families at social gatherings, eyeing the survivors with longing, and I feel for them too, because now I know about senseless loss, and what it feels like.

But outside, the fields are ablaze with the green flames of abundance. Everything is more lush than ever, the livestock so fat they seem to smile. As though the earth is celebrating peace in the best possible way—by creating.

A few weeks ago, I was alone in the barn, trying to doctor the hoof on an old cow, when Bob appeared. A man in a suit followed behind him. Not a western suit, either. He wore a city suit, with one of those hats they wear in cities, with a brim that doesn't curl up, but dips down in the front and is flat as a flapjack the rest of the way around.

"Blake, this fella came around asking about Jack. I thought you might be able to tell him more than I can."

I took the blade of my knife and lanced the infected spot, right in the split of the hoof. The wound opened, pouring blood onto the straw. The cow flinched and let out a short, surprised "moo," but her reaction was nothing like the stranger's. His face suddenly got longer, and a lighter shade. His mouth twisted, and he turned his head to one side. He was determined not to show that he was bothered by this operation, and he kept trying to look back at it. But each time he saw the blood and pus, he turned away, and he finally just walked a few feet toward the other side of the barn. Bob and I exchanged a discreet smile.

I poured some disinfectant over the wound and lowered her hoof back to the ground, then stood and wiped my hands on my dungarees.

"Well, I don't know if I can help you any more than my brother here," I said. "I don't know where Jack is. I'm Blake, by the way."

I held a hand out to the man. He shook it, trying not to hesitate or look down at what might be on it.

"Benson," he said. "Ben Benson."

"Really? Ben Benson?"

He looked puzzled, as if there was nothing unusual about that.

"Well, um . . . like I said, I don't know much." I paused. "You interested in some lunch? I'm just about to go in and eat."

He thought about it, glancing once more at my hand, then at his watch. "All right."

"I'm going to get back to what I was doin'," Bob said.

I nodded.

"Thank you, Bob," Benson said.

Ben Benson and I sat munching sandwiches and baked beans.

"When was the last time you saw Jack?" Benson asked.

I swallowed a bite and wiped the corner of my mouth. "Sorry to ask, Mr. Benson, but who is it that you work for?"

"Oh, I didn't mention that? Yes. I'm with the AIS," Benson answered. When he saw that I had no idea what this was, he spelled it out. "Army Investigative Services."

"Oh." I nodded, wondering what the army would want with Jack. "No uniform?"

"I'm not actually in the army," Benson said. "I just work for them."

"I see." I took another bite of my sandwich and chewed it up good before addressing his question. "Well, Mr. Benson, Jack disappeared the day his son George drowned in the reservoir out in the north pasture, in the fall of last year . . . September."

"And you haven't seen or heard anything from him since?"

"That's right," I said.

"That seems to be a pattern with him," he said.

I was surprised to find that I took offense to this statement, not because it wasn't true, but because of his condescending tone. "What do you mean?" I asked.

"Well, the reason I'm looking for him is because he deserted."

"Deserted?" I shook my head, thinking it was odd that they would be looking for him thirty years later, and wondering how it would possibly take them this long to find him. "When?"

"Back in '39, about the time the war started." Benson took a big swig of lemonade and wiped his mouth with a napkin. "The reason it took us so long to track him down is that he enlisted under a false name."

I took a minute to absorb this information. I must have looked shocked, because Benson sort of chuckled, shaking his head.

"You didn't know any of this?"

"Hell no," I said. "I didn't even know he'd reenlisted. He was in the army in the first war, but we didn't know where he was during the thirties." I looked down at my plate and shook my head. "I'll be damned."

"He was in from '34 until he deserted," Benson said, wiping his mouth again, very thoroughly.

"I'll be damned," I said again. "The goddam army."

"Bob's wife said that Jack was something of a scoundrel," Benson said.

The hair on my neck rose a little at the mention of Helen, but I tried not to show it. "Well . . . she's got her own way of seeing things," I said.

Benson studied me, thinking as he scooped a forkful of beans into his mouth. Then he took a small notepad and pencil from his jacket and set the notebook down on the table. He flipped it open and began writing. "Well, Blake, I might be out again soon, to do a more thorough investigation. But it may not be necessary. It doesn't appear that any of you know much. Bob took me out to the house where Jack lived, and we didn't find anything out there. And I talked to Rita, but she didn't seem to know much either. Your brother seems to have kept a lot of secrets from you folks." He tore the sheet from his pad and handed it to me. "But here's the number where I'll be for the next few days. That's my home address. If you think of anything that might help us, or if you hear from Jack, please let me know."

I took the paper and set it to the side. I sensed that he didn't trust me, and this offended me. Benson thanked me for lunch, then headed for the door. I got up to see him out.

"Good luck, Mr. Benson," I said.

"Pleasure to meet you. Don't hesitate to contact me."

He left and was halfway down the walk when a question occurred to me, and I called to him.

"Hey, Benson, what name did he use?"

He stopped and turned. "Westford. David Westford," he said. "Guy in St. Louis. When I first saw this guy, I knew it wasn't your brother. Nobody that fat could ever get into the army." He looked down, as if considering whether he should go on; then he walked back toward me, stopping a few feet away. "This Westford fella, when we first found him, claimed he didn't know any Jack Arbuckle, that the guy must have picked his name at random. We didn't have any reason to doubt him, but of course we followed up on it. It turns out the two of them had a little scam going. Your brother was a supply officer, in charge of distributing parts and supplies to different units. He was smuggling stuff—nothing big, but a lot of it—parts and small equipment, out to this Westford fella, who has a heavy equipment and parts business out there in St. Louis." Benson eyed me, gauging whether any of this information seemed to set anything off with me, probably looking for some sign of guilt.

"You never met this Westford character?" he asked.

I thought about telling him the truth, or telling him that I met Westford on the train to Omaha some twenty years back, but I finally decided I didn't want this guy snooping around any more than he had to. I shook my head.

He nodded, pushing his lips up toward his nose.

"Well, I'll be on my way." He waved.

"So long."

When he stepped out of the yard, Pup ran up to him, trying to get him to play. The dog raised up and kicked his front paws through the air, as if he was swimming. Benson danced backward, holding his hands out in front of him, holding Pup away, then moved toward his car.

Mutt was back out in a pasture somewhere, with her own kind. During feeding that previous winter, after we'd tried to get her to be a sheep, we'd find Mutt standing off to one side of the flock, as if she was guarding them. We tried to run her back into the flock, but she would charge them, just as Pup had taught her. It took a couple of months, but she must have gotten lonely enough to join them, probably thinking that she'd have to settle for their company, even though she was a dog.

Benson was almost to his car when he stopped one more time. "I'm sorry," he said. "I just have to ask one more thing, out of curiosity."

I walked into the yard, so he didn't have to shout. "Okay."

"Mrs. Arbuckle there . . . Rita . . ."

"Yeah? What about her?"

"I was very confused talking to her. I didn't want to ask, though, didn't want to offend her. Is she your wife, or Jack's?"

I smiled. "Neither," I said.

Epilogue

summer 1946

If I had sat down a few years ago and imagined how I wanted my life to look, it's hard to imagine that it could have worked out any better than it has. And yet I planned none of it. Jack's latest disappearance cemented what was already assumed—that I will take over the ranch. Jack's absence also opened the door, finally, for the first tentative steps toward a romance with the only woman I have ever fallen in love with. It started early one evening, when I swallowed the lump in my throat and stood on Rita's doorstep, asking her in a shaky voice whether she wanted to take a walk. She looked confused.

"Is something wrong?" she asked.

"No, no, nothing's wrong," I muttered. "Nothing's wrong."

Rita frowned, her eyes darting from side to side as she thought.

"It's just such a beautiful night out," I said, fully aware that there was little or nothing remarkable about it.

Rita studied me, then seemed to understand. A shy smile came to her face, and for the first time that I could ever remember, she blushed.

"Let me get my shawl," she said.

You would never have guessed that the two people strolling along the dusty path that evening had known each other for almost twenty years. We were both as tongue-tied as a couple of pimply teenagers. We were able to laugh about it later, after a few more walks, and a couple of candlelight dinners. It has been an odd courtship, with the two of us knowing each other so well. For one thing, neither of us had much experience with this type of thing to begin with. Rita and Jack had only dated for a few weeks before she agreed to marry him, and he was her first beau. So it was awkward by nature, but made even more so by our history.

The interesting thing about these developments was that I had absolutely none of the sense of triumph, or even satisfaction, that I might have imagined as a younger man. What I might have once seen as an arrival felt much more like a departure, a beginning. The sense that filled me was one of responsibility, thinking of the people who relied on the ranch, and in turn on me.

When I realized how much pressure I felt from this responsibility, with conditions being as good as they were, and with fewer mouths to feed, my respect and admiration for my parents compounded. It had always been hard for me to understand why my father seemed to have so little interest in anything that was happening outside of work. I had often wondered whether he cared about his family. But for the first time, it occurred to me that perhaps after six days a week in the fields, he didn't have energy to put into anything besides work. Perhaps he instinctively knew that the best thing he could do for all of us was to hold the ranch together. And seeing what that entailed now, I also saw how that put the responsibility for everything else on my mother. It was no wonder she was irritable, I decided. She had a lot to be irritated about.

These were not the only areas where my perspective had shifted. Oddly enough, it was Jack's last disappearance that convinced me that he didn't kill George. It's impossible to know for sure, of course. But the more I think about it, the more I believe that what drove Jack away from the ranch, and from us, was much more simple. It was the loneliness. It was the open space. It was the silent hours of grueling labor with nothing but your thoughts to keep you company. Your thoughts and memories. In Jack's case, difficult memories. Fishing his son from the reservoir he built. Finding George's body. And the consequences of that evening. His inability to respond, and Katie's death as a result. I'm sure that the talk behind his back didn't help, either. Despite his demeanor, Jack did care what people thought.

Seeing Jack fold at the site of his son's death helped convince me that he simply wasn't equipped somehow to handle situations like that. It was this that was perhaps hardest for him to come to terms with while he was here.

And I think in his own strange way, Jack knew this. I think that the reason he stayed away may have been because he was trying to protect us from the worst of him. Maybe I'm giving him too much credit, but I'd like to believe that he knew he wasn't good here.

All of which makes the other side of Jack's personality more compelling to me. The side that brought him back. The side that really did care about Rita, and the rest of us, enough that he tried one last time to adapt. There is something about this place that sets up its own little corner in your heart and lives there, I think. And it was strong in Jack.

And what this says in the end is a surprise to me. Because as much as I would like to believe otherwise, I think my brother and I are a lot more alike than we are different.

Just the other day, at the Pioneer Days in Albion, I let some of my old friends talk me into pitching again. I hadn't done it for a few years, for several reasons. For one thing, it hurt my arm if I threw for too long. It was also frustrating to go out there and try to do the same things I used to do and have my body not cooperate. But mainly I just wanted to give the young kids a chance. There were some pretty good pitchers around the county, and of course all of them wanted to pitch the whole game on the rare occasions that we had a chance to play.

But for some reason, people got nostalgic that day, and talked me into taking the mound for a couple of innings. I got up there and took a few warm-up tosses, and I actually felt pretty good for the first couple of batters. I started to feel at home again. It was fun.

We were playing against Capitol, and one young kid hit a nice two-out triple off me that first inning, but I struck out the last guy, breaking off one of my old curveballs on the third strike, and as I trotted off the field, I caught Sophie Roberts Melvin Andrews Carroll smiling at me. I was taken back to the first time I'd seen her look at me this way. And it was a good memory. I had come to realize that things had worked out better than they would have if she had married me. And I had been able to be perfectly civil to her the last few times I'd seen her. I still couldn't stand Albert, but that's another story.

The second inning, the first batter hit a grounder to short, which was fielded cleanly. The shortstop threw the guy out by a step, and a big Norwegian guy settled into the batter's box. His hair was whiter than the baseball, and his arms could have filled a good portion of my pant legs. He had that Norwegian manner, too, of appearing to be disinterested in what was happening. He didn't look fierce, aside from his size, or mean. Just huge.

But when he swung at my first pitch, a curve that didn't curve, he hit that thing a ton, and it came right back at me before I had a chance to finish my follow-through. I had been a pretty good fielder in my younger days. I was known for plucking a liner from the air just before it caught me flush in the mouth, or for reaching out and snagging a grounder that would have shot by most fellas. But this thing took me down, glancing off my forehead, just above my left eyebrow. Of course, I didn't know any of this at the time, as I was out cold for several minutes.

When I woke up, I tasted dirt. My face was pressed against the ground, and in my semiconscious state, I went through one of those frightening moments where I thought I had died. I thought I was dead, and that I'd been buried without a coffin, and that the dirt was directly on my face. But I heard a voice, then another, then a chorus of voices, surrounding me.

As I lay there, my face pressed against the earth, I thought what it must be like to be the land, and what you see every day when you are stuck there, lying immobilized, vulnerable to the winds and shifts in weather, and the inevitable comings and goings of clouds and hooves and wheels and teeth. And as people turned me over, then nursed and pampered and fussed over me, my mind wandered, thinking about how amazing it is that despite what the earth is subjected to, it still goes on. And how it responds to this abuse in remarkable, almost human ways.

I thought about how much we expect from it, and how it can be almost cruel in its stubborn insistence to withhold the things we ask from it. And how just about the time that we think we will never receive any of what we need from our beloved earth, she comes through, touching us with the smallest of gestures—a raindrop on the cheek, or a small sprout of alfalfa peeking through its hard surface. The land is loving, cruel, selfish, stubborn, and sometimes overly generous. It can be unbelievably kind. And incomprehensibly void of compassion.

I turned my face to the side, wanting to feel the earth against my cheek. And for as long as I was lying there, letting my head clear, and feeling the hands of my friends and family wiping the blood from my face, I held my head in that position, enjoying the rough, cool texture of the soil against my skin.

Acknowledgments

Aside from the birth of my son, Fletcher, writing this book was the most joyful experience of my life so far. Because it was loosely based on my grandparents, the research afforded me an opportunity to travel back into their time through the stories of so many wonderful people.

Fletcher was five when I finished this book. He is now seventeen. And there is a very simple reason that the past twelve years have been an incredible journey rather than a study in frustration. These people:

All love and gratitude to my wonderful family—Dad, Mom, Collette, Wade, Andrew, Mack, Flynn, and Ike. And to Fletcher, the only perfect story I've ever told.

Thanks to my editor, Yung Kim, who brought this book back to life. Howard Yoon, for his skills as an editor as well as agent. Michael Congdon. And the others at HarperCollins who lent their expertise— Laran Brindle, Elizabeth Pawlson, and Heather Burke.

To all Rowlands; Tanners; Lokens; Sloans; Andersons; Richardsons; Kirkhams; and, of course, Arbuckles, especially Lee Arbuckle for his wealth of information. And to the residents of Carter County for enduring with quiet dignity. To Michael Curtis for his continued encouragement. Lucie Prinz for the same. And Sue Miller for her inspiration and wisdom. James O'Keefe and Margaret Minister; Ted Smykal; Bob Christoph; Michael and Kira Yannetta; Kirk, Jeanette, and Derek Wayland; Sam Geffner; Phyllis Pinkham; Niall McKay; John Brennan; Andrew Lovett; and Tom Stefan for their support. All my friends at Foote, Cone, and Belding. Steve Klingman and Christine Palamedessi for their feedback. Lisa Queen. Doris Cooper. Liz Perle. And last, but definitely not least, friends of Bill W.